East of
Midnight

East of
Midnight

Karen S. Humeniuk

ARCHWAY
PUBLISHING

Archway Publishing books may be ordered through booksellers or by contacting:

Archway Publishing
1663 Liberty Drive
Bloomington, IN 47403
www.archwaypublishing.com
1 (888) 242-5904

Because of the dynamic nature of the Internet, any web addresses or links contained in this book may have changed since publication and may no longer be valid. The views expressed in this work are solely those of the author and do not necessarily reflect the views of the publisher, and the publisher hereby disclaims any responsibility for them.

Scripture quotations are from the ESV® Bible (The Holy Bible, English Standard Version®), copyright © 2001 by Crossway, a publishing ministry of Good News Publishers. Used by permission. All rights reserved.

ISBN: 978-1-4808-7534-0 (sc)
ISBN: 978-1-4808-7532-6 (hc)
ISBN: 978-1-4808-7533-3 (e)

Library of Congress Control Number: 2019903479

Print information available on the last page.

Archway Publishing rev. date: 10/17/2019

Endorsements

I just loved East of Midnight! One thing is for sure, it isn't a book to be quickly scanned, in my opinion; you really have to know the characters and see Ms. Humeniuk's wit exude from those words! That's a good thing for me because I want to get lost in the words and her imagery. There's so much going on in our lives right now that it was nice to "get away" and "get within." **Bonny Burbank Shuptrine**, gallery owner, Lookout Mountain, Tennessee.

East of Midnight, the story of two young people finding love amid the chaos of contemporary college life, is both heartwarming and soul searching. The theme of living with the consequences of our mistakes prompts the reader to reflect on his or her own salvation. Cameron and Lydia must learn to rely on God before they are able to love each other.

This uplifting story of two families connected by past tragedy and hope for a better future offers a potentially life-changing gift of faith. The author has a keen eye for detail and combined with well-developed characters makes for a book well worth reading. **Nancy Dykes**, Greenville, South Carolina

The story reminds me that Christians try to do what's right but become overbearing rather than letting the Spirit do the heavy lifting—which isn't good. Thankfully, God is patient, as the author's cast of characters discover. The story and the characters drew me in, leaving me wanting to know what comes next. **Debbie Nichols**, Clemson, South Carolina

Acknowledgments

Without the support and encouragement of many people, *East of Midnight* would be but a dream, passing through my head. To my husband, John Humeniuk, I extend an ocean of gratitude for his long-suffering patience, consistently tough critiques, and probing questions that forced me to plumb the depths of each unique character in the book you now hold.

Three longtime friends are due my deepest gratitude for their early support. The Reverend Robert H. Jones read an early, very rough draft and encouraged me to hone my skill. Roger Chastain, a prolific reader, brilliant intellect, and generous friend read a slightly better draft which his wife Bunny had set aside hoping to read. Since Roger was not a man who suffered fools lightly, his encouragement challenged me to create a story worth reading. Bunny, thank you for leaving that early, spiral-bound test copy in a place for Roger to find.

I am indebted to a league of friends, acquaintances, and several of my husband's patients who passed along compliments and encouragement in response to opinion letters—opuses in two hundred words or less as I called them—published in our local paper. Their encouraging words lingered long afterward, propping up my spirits when doubt weighed heavily. Thanks also to Eric Pedersen, PGA AI, Head Golf Professional at Chanticleer Course, Greenville Country Club, Greenville, South Carolina, for sharing his knowledge of men's golf and for many years of golf lessons. Professional thanks go to our neighbors in Wyoming: Gina and John Ed Anderson and Diana and Erik Saam who patiently shared their knowledge of ranching in Shell and the

Bighorn Mountains. I extend deep gratitude to Jon Lineback for his patience, wisdom, and humor, and to Gwen Ashe of Archway Publishers, who spent many hours patiently shepherding me through the various stages of the publishing process. Additional thanks go out to my editor Paul, and the talented artists and associates who worked with Gwen.

Finally, unending thanks are due to my late parents, Louie and Jerri Swanson, who lived Micah 6:8 –

> "He has told you, O man, what is good,
> and what the LORD REALLY WANTS FROM YOU:
> He wants you to promote justice,
> to be faithful, and to live obediently before your God." ESV

Dedicated to
My husband, John Humeniuk, M.D.

"For the secret of man's being is not only to live
but to have something to live for.
Without a stable conception of the object of life,
man would not consent to go on living,
and would rather destroy himself than remain on earth,
though he had bread in abundance."
The Grand Inquisitor, *The Brothers Karamazov*, Fyodor Dostoevsky

Primary Characters

(expanded list at the back of the book)

Cameron Asher

Family:

    Randy and Valerie Asher (parents)

    Judge Ben Asher, a.k.a. Grandpa (grandfather, deceased)

    Nathan and Becky Stedman (paternal aunt & uncle)

Friends:

    Paul Rizziellio, Aimee Duncan, & Justin Sloane (Chalmers, N.C.)

    Neil (roommate), Patrick, Trace, and Esther (UNC)

    Stan and Hannah Boehmer (Wyoming ranchers)

    Leo (full-time ranch hand); Drew, Todd, Sam & Mick (summer ranch hands)

Lydia Carpenter

Family:

    Anne and Marshall Carpenter (parents)

    Lois Carpenter, a.k.a. Nana (grandmother)

    Jake and Marrah Mapson (paternal aunt & uncle)

    Steve Carpenter (uncle, deceased)

Friends:

    Aimee Duncan, Marybeth (Chalmers, North Carolina)

    Ragini Ramasamy, Eydie You (roommate), Eliana Johansson (Duke University)

1

Cameron likened his talent for putting people at ease to the pleasure of making a long or difficult putt—for a birdie. If the ball dropped into the hole, cheers and loud applause rewarded even a poorly executed swing. When the ball stopped an inch short of the hole, the cheers turned to an audible sigh— *aw*. Everyone, including Cameron, enjoyed the almost-joyous moment with the expectation that a tap would drop the ball into the hole.

Lydia, who refused to pick up a club, disagreed. Using a play on the word *charm*, she had called his people-pleasing knack a kind of quark that patches theoretical holes, and thus, a patch job for quirks in his personality. In response, Cameron had teased her for attending his golf tournaments and later claiming to have been elsewhere. Despite her indignant protests, he often glimpsed her cheering from far behind the rope line, supposedly hidden from view. When he laughed, challenging her version of the truth, she stiffened her resolve and found other friendly taunts.

Similar friendly banter had been the hallmark of their friendship and evidence that behind her smile lurked a herculean heart, one that she kept from him with the ferocity of a mother grizzly protecting her cubs. Long ago, Grandpa had warned him not to make errant assumptions such as those he associated with Lydia. Instead, his blithe impressions and misconceptions now blistered his vanity and ripped holes in his heart. Indeed! And while Grandpa's warnings had proved to be true, his assurance that mistakes often light the paths that lead people home had not.

Cameron pushed against the back of the mesh office chair. The time had passed for pleading with Lydia, begging for forgiveness; the damage had been too great. Tipping the chair back, he stared up at the ceiling of the makeshift bar which masqueraded as Alex's bedroom when not called to its present higher use during his annual New Year's Eve party. For two hours since arriving at the party, Cameron had planted himself in the room, claiming to act as a bartender even though Alex had arranged the table for self-service. His strictly gratuitous offer hid the fact that, for him, the room served as a redoubt, preventing him from doing other stupid things and saying more stupid stuff.

Instead, as the minutes ticked away, the bastion of his conceit had crumbled. Pummeled by a maelstrom of denials and repudiations of how much Lydia meant to him, his idiocy had—stone by stone, dismantled the walls of his pride and revealed the ugly truth: Years earlier, he had conned himself into believing she was safe because she was only a friend.

But she wasn't safe. She was smart, fun, and dangerously beautiful. Sitting two rooms away, she wore a sweater the color of her hazel eyes, silver drop earrings that sparkled like her smile, and slim mahogany-colored pants—the same hue as the soft curls that hung about her shoulders. And worst of all—at the height of his folly, though she had arrived with him, he had left her to spend the evening talking to Paul, his best friend and Alex's younger brother. Meanwhile, he opened beers cans for Alex's guests who wandered down to the room at the end of the hall.

The sound of fluttering wings caught his attention as four sleek crows appeared among the ruins. One marked "Trust" perched atop one of several bottles of craft beer that he had set on the white molded-plastic top of the portable table behind which he sat. Another crow marked "Kindness" landed on one of two mismatched pillows that decorated the room's lone twin bed. Using its talons, it picked at the flattened cushions. "Patience" nested on the bed's serviceable duvet, while "Generosity" strutted across the top of an overpriced chest of draws. As they squawked and pecked at Cameron's ego, they repeated their insistent declaration: "Accept the fact that you will never be closer to Lydia or to becoming your better self than you are now."

A shadow crossing the floor drew his attention to the silhouette of a woman standing in the doorway, lit by the bright hall light. Her face hidden, she stood with one hand holding a bottle at her side and the other resting on the doorframe. For a moment, she lingered then sauntered over and placed one hip on the tabletop. Putting most of her weight on one leg, she draped the other luxuriant leg over the edge. Of the many women who had entered and asked for a beer, none had been as striking. The simplicity of her jewelry and the folds of the blouse she wore beneath a lavender pinstripe jacket and tucked neatly into the waist of her tight, knee-length business skirt gave notice that she was a woman who suffered no fools. Her gracious gray eyes lit the room with kindness even as her smile disarmed him.

Nothing, absolutely nothing passed before her unnoticed. This thought sent him to his feet. Behind him, the office chair spun ever so slightly, which she also noted.

"I didn't mean to startle you." The lilting accent of old Charleston adorned her voice.

"Not at all." If her elegance had interrupted his thoughts, the scent of her perfume now piqued his interest. "What is your pleasure?" His hand indicated the assortment of craft beers.

"I wonder," she mused, "where your thoughts wandered the moment before I disturbed you."

Her fingers played with the neck of the already-opened brown bottle, an unabashed statement that she had visited the other makeshift bar before walking farther down the hall to this room. *She wants to make a point. But what point?*

A faint smile pulled at one lipsticked corner of her mouth. "Do you play poker?"

"Sometimes." *And she likes games.* Cameron sat down in the office chair and rocked back. Stretching out his six-foot frame, he waited for her to play another card.

She, too, waited and then blinked. With a demure nod, she laid down a card. "I noticed that many of the young women, even some with companions, found their way to this room, choosing to pass the other room where they could easily grab a beer and go." Her brows danced above her smile. "Which raises the question: Why are *you* here? But don't answer just yet. Let me guess. You're in college, a junior, I assume, and like Paul, quite bright, seeing that you two are good friends." She leaned toward him and took a deep quaff of air. "And you're sober. How disgusting." She tilted her head to one side with another hint of a smile.

"Life's tough," Cameron said. He shrugged, offering no further explanation.

"Hmmm. Maybe." One eyebrow arched upward. "The attractive young woman who arrived with you has spent the evening talking to Paul, but then, what's in an impression? Oh, the possibilities. Clearly"—a decidedly sexy laugh joined her soft smile— "if you knew what a woman wants, you wouldn't be here." She pointed to the table. "I'm not talking about a giggling girl but what a *woman* wants. I don't think it's a stretch to assume that you're quite experienced with girls but perplexed by a woman. Am I right?" Crossing her arms, she propped her chin on a crooked finger, fixed her eyes on him, and then waited.

Cameron's smile faded. Previously, only Grandpa had the capacity to make him feel at once both worthy and clueless. She stood, stepped back from the table, and faced him. "When you discover the difference," she said, extending an elegant arm open-handed to indicate the drab room, "you'll find your way out of this"—she twirled her hand in a circle— "little hellhole. And perhaps you'll find your tongue." She arched the brow again and smiled. "Because you'll know what a woman wants."

She was disgustingly right. If Cameron's call to Lydia, inviting her to Alex's party, had taught him anything, it proved that he knew nothing about women. In particular, he knew nothing about Lydia.

The woman turned toward the door. "Have a nice evening. I'm sure one of the girls would be happy to make sure you do." When she reached the doorway, she again turned toward him. With her face hidden in shadow, she spoke kindly and sweetly. "You are adorable. And much too hard on yourself. Try these words: 'I'm sorry.' They may taste bitter, but they'll be honey on the ears of your audience. Not that I know what you have to be sorry for, other than for hiding in here."

Then with a shrug of her square shoulders, she was gone. In her wake, the air fluttered as a fifth crow furrowed its wings. It strutted to the middle of the table and stared at Cameron. This one wore a sign marked "Humility." It would not easily be assuaged.

A moment later, the silhouette of a younger woman appeared in the doorway and then walked to the table. Ever the gentleman, Cameron stood and asked with polite Southern hospitality, "What can I get? Coors? Bud Lite?"

"I'm not sure. What do you suggest?"

"Beer."

The woman, dressed in jeans, a loose gray jacket, and lemon-colored shirt, laughed heartily. "That's funny!" In many ways she seemed like the other girls, but she wasn't. Her curious smile reinforced his observation. She extended her hand. "I'm Sydney. We shared a public speaking class last year, spring semester. It was one of those electives designed to justify a department's existence by requiring people with serious degrees to vacate their subjective cloisters and convert to glorious objectivity. I just wanted a few tips that might help after I graduate."

"And did you find some? Tips that is."

"Yes. One in particular." Sarcasm dusted her slightly crooked smile as her hand pushed down on the edge of the mattress. It sagged noticeably, but not enough to keep her from leaning her slender frame against it. Cameron returned to the mesh chair as she continued, "The instructor, an in-your-face women's studies guru, thought nice is for suckers."

Cameron bit his lip to keep a grin from escaping.

After pausing to let him compose himself, she continued, "She seemed to believe that bullying works. Sadly, she was too incompetent to see it in herself, because she even bullied me."

Cameron bit off another grin, for Sydney was also a woman with whom no man should trifle.

"Well," she continued, "one day toward the end of the semester, she picked on a really cute guy who'd said almost nothing during the class. At her peril, having misjudged him, she treated him like prime sirloin because he wore 'I'm a UNC frat boy and damned proud of it' from the top of his curly blond head to the well-worn Sperrys on his feet. Fool that she was, she went after him with a verbal cleaver. But not so! He eviscerated her. Gone! He didn't attack her but rather shredded her argument with charm and an 'I've got your number' smile on his face. I was like, if this guy goes into law, I want him on my side." By then, Sydney could barely control her glee. "I bet you remember that day—not that I think being a frat boy is bad. I know plenty of bad boys who aren't in frats and good guys who are."

His brow twitched. "Thanks for the vote of confidence." Sadly, though, he didn't remember Sydney. He rocked the chair onto its rear wheels and smiled. "What was I to do? She sent out so many invitations; someone was bound to RSVP. So I did." And he had enjoyed doing so, immensely.

"What's a PhD good for if not to be lectured about the fine art of sarcasm?" Sydney's eyes twinkled.

He laughed, but his smile faded as he remembered several occasions when the instructor singled out smart pleasant women who didn't share her political views. Sydney must have been one of them. "I guess she thought bullying was cool. I don't like bullies, never have. It's my loss that I didn't remember you."

"That's okay." Sydney raised the bottle in a toast. "Here's to you from the rest of the class, many of whom silently cheered you on." A curious frown wrinkled her forehead. "Don't feel bad."

"What makes you say that?"

"Your eyes. They're sad as if something bittersweet whispered to you. I hope it wasn't something I said. The last thing I want is to make you sad." Her eyes studied him and then softened. She pointed the top of the brown bottle toward the noise beyond the room's walls. "You've been quite the talk out there. They're hoping you'll give away something other than beer." She wiggled her eyebrows. "Me? I thought you'd enjoy a little company."

And he did. For a while they talked, and he felt better, but he wasn't surprised when the conversation waned. Sydney rose to her feet. "I hope you feel a little better." Sydney smiled, waited, and then smiled again, but her eyes read his heart. "I'll see you around."

Cameron rose from the chair and extended his hand. "Yes, and when we do, Sydney, I promise I will remember you."

When the room was again empty, an old grinding ache gripped his chest. Since early middle school, his life had been, at times, covered with pluff mud—that dank silt lining the Carolina salt marshes that clung like tar to his legs and sucked the flip-flops from his feet. Millions of years in the future, he imagined, an archeologist would find strata of mudstone littered with petrified roots and flip-flops.

Sydney, though, had made him feel like marsh grass, swaying in the flood of new saltwater at high tide, washing away dreadful memories. In their place, he remembered Lydia walking across a dais, set on a football field, to accept her high school diploma. As she took the booklet, she had smiled at the gathered parents, friends, family, and unknowingly at Cameron. What he saw had stunned him. Not once before had he realized that she was as beautiful on the outside as he had known her to be on the inside.

Misery washed over him, carrying away the refreshing balm with the ebbing tide. He remembered Paul's retort after hearing that Cameron had invited Lydia to Alex's party. Knowing that Cameron had not spoken to her since he graduated, two and a half years earlier, he called Cameron's decision "masterfully shortsighted," but his exact words had sounded more like "What were you thinking?" Cameron's invitation, though, had not been impulsive. It grew from roots planted every Monday night from his sophomore year of high school through graduation, when Lydia had been his as they worked side by side at a soup kitchen, sharing an uncomplicated, undemanding, and deeply satisfying friendship. Like Grandpa, Lydia had read his soul. A month or so after Grandpa died, Lydia had joined her mother, volunteering at the Café, and then quietly slipped into his heart, filling the void that Grandpa once filled.

Grandpa had been a wise man. He had warned Cameron not to think too much about himself lest he, like Tantalus of Greek mythology, finds himself standing, bound shoulder to toe, surrounded by water but unable to quench his thirst or attain the very basis of happiness, both bodily and spiritual. The warning had been for naught. For now he stood bound chest deep in water, with happiness forever beyond his reach. And with no hope of ever escaping.

A woman dressed in a light blue sweater and jeans—and with a face as lovely as Botticelli's *Venus*, came through the doorway. Without hesitation, she dropped onto the bed, stretching out across it to face him. She propped her head on the heel of her hand and watched him through chocolate-brown eyes. Cameron leaned back in the mesh chair, hooking his thumbs in his belt loops, and rocked forward and back as the staring contest lingered.

In the end, Tindal blinked. She pursed her lips in a pout that melted into a light smile. "Mom asked about you. She's Scottish and wanted to know if you are, too, or if 'Cameron' is merely a name."

Cameron laughed heartily. "Wow. I'm honored. Maybe. I'm named after my grandfather—Benjamin *Cameron* Asher. He was Ben. I got his middle name. And yes; he was Clan Cameron," he said with a grin. "They've been around central North Carolina since the mid-eighteenth century. Or so I've been told."

"Oh-h-h-h. Can I ever imagine you in a kilt." She stifled a smirk. "If you'd worn one tonight ... just imagine what all those girls out there would have done," her eyes gleamed. "We'd say over your grave, 'If only for a pair of pants, he'd be with us today.'"

Cameron laughed as a ray of sunshine pierced his miserable pit.

Tindal sat up and snuggled against a pillow. Her fingers stretched a red curl into a soft wave. "Don't tell Seth, but this is also Italian. He thinks I'm an Irish rose. I'd like to leave him to his fine fantasy." Her laughter ceased. "Which reminds me of the reason I'm here." She fluffed the less mangy of the two pillows and then leaned against it. "Seth sent me—so count yourself lucky." A sardonic smile skipped across her face. "He can't believe you're here and your date is out there, talking to Paul. He was ready to come down and yank your ... well, he used a different word, but you get my point?"

"I do. Thank you." He smiled as he rocked the mesh chair.

"I cleaned up his actual words."

"I can imagine what he said."

"If I remember correctly, and I do, you volunteered to bartend at a party earlier this month." If she expected him to flinch or look away, she was sadly mistaken. Still, she leaned close enough to smell his breath. "You're sober!"

"And that's a problem?"

"I'm not sure, but that night a most remarkable girl wanted your attention in the worst way, but you ignored her." Tindal's eyes narrowed. "And you also broke the cardinal rule of bartending—don't imbibe!" She settled back onto the bed, legs crossed under her. "Big-time."

A tall, burly guy and an Asian girl entered the room and asked for three craft beers from brewers that, they claimed, were no longer available in the other room. Tindal watched Cameron fill the request. As they left, she turned to him. "How do you do it?"

"Do what?"

"Flirt like that?"

"I didn't flirt. I'd never flirt with a girl who's with a guy that size!"

"Well, her eyes said otherwise."

Cameron threw his arms out and gaped in self-defense. "I didn't do any-thing!" He clamped his mouth shut. "I swear!" His hands dropped into his lap. "Okay." *No more excuses.* "You're right." The time for honesty had come. "Yes, I had too much to drink." Even if Tindal didn't need to hear the full truth, then at least, he'd be truthful with himself. "But it led me to do something I've needed to do for three years"—yes, he had called Lydia, hoping to get her out of his head— "but it didn't work out the way I thought it would."

"And that's why you're here, and not out there?" She pointed toward the main room.

A mirthless laugh escaped his lips. "Yes." *Yes,* he'd slithered into this hole, and it was time to walk out of it. He stood, bent his elbow, and offered it to her. "May I escort you back to Seth's care?"

"This was too easy."

"Not really." Taking her hand, he guided her off the bed and wrapped her hand around his elbow. With a faint nod, he escorted her to the hall, where he released her arm, letting her walk before him. Since most of the guests had merrily congregated on the open-air pass-through landing of the three-story walk-up unit, only a few sat talking on the main room's sofa and chairs.

Paul and Lydia sat at the dining table, talking. And laughing. And happy. But then Lydia looked up. Seeing Cameron, her smile faded, and his stomach sank. She didn't even glare when another—no, when every other girl would have thrown knives at him.

"Hey, stranger," Paul said, injecting levity into the dreadful silence, "have a seat."

Cameron pulled out the chair next to his friend and across from Lydia as Paul continued, "We were talking about her engineering classes. I'd forgotten that you two used to compete for math awards."

"Yeah, we did." Cameron smiled, and Lydia blushed. Gone, though, was the happy smile that had greeted him earlier in the evening, the smile that crumpled his knees. Gone, too, was everything that once watered his dry, parched heart.

Paul stood. "We were talking about basketball—a nonstarter for me at Princeton. But Lydia's at Duke, and you're at UNC. You should be able to find *something* to talk about." With a bow, he excused himself, leaving Cameron and Lydia staring at each other.

Cameron offered a few feeble comments. She responded, but her clasped hands and stiff back spoke volumes. He checked the time. Ten. A momentary thought of sharing a kiss at midnight tingled his lips, but reality sank in. "I guess you'd like to go home."

She shrugged. "I guess so." Her stiff lips sent shame coursing through every vein and artery, scalding the lining of his heart. During the drive to her parents' house, a few banal comments broke the suffocating silence even as inextinguishable joy tingled his chest. The delight of sitting so close to her rained down on him but failed to wet his tongue enough to put words in his mouth. Instead, they walked to the front door beneath a soot-blackened sky that earlier had been awash in stars.

Lydia put the key in the lock. Then she turned with a faint "Thank you. It was good to see you again."

"I ...." Nothing, not the refreshing sound of her voice, the comfort of her bright eyes, or the luscious curls that crowned her head, could draw words from his mouth. Still, a few leaked out. "I *am* glad you came." Cold regret washed over him. "I'm sorry."

For a second her brow knit and her head tipped sideways as if startled upon seeing a shadow lost in a fog. The frown vanished just as quickly. She opened the door, repeating, "Thank you," went inside and pushed it shut.

As the bolt clicked home, Cameron's knees went limp beneath him. He braced one hand on the door frame and buried his face in the other.

Cameron opened the door to his silver Ford Escape and gave one last glance at the darkened windows of Lydia's parents' house. She was gone. He put the SUV in gear and drove to the next block, where he stopped. With the engine running, he considered returning to Alex's party, but that meant facing Paul, Seth, and Tindal, the first being the hardest. Instead, he drove to the Montebello section of Chalmers and stopped in front of a stately Georgian house. On New Year's Eve, only Justin would open the Sloane family's ornate beveled-glass door.

"Well, look who the cat dragged in." Justin's predictable sneer sat easily on his oval face with its thick brow and deep-set eyes. "Looking for a party? I heard you were at Alex's. And that Paul stole your date. Is that why you left early?" The furrow between his eyes deepened.

"I had my reasons."

"Yeah. I'm sure you did." Justin shrugged and stepped back. "Come on in." He turned and walked down the hall, speaking to the polished antiques and ancient paintings rather than to Cameron. "When'd you hook up with Lydia?"

"She's not a hookup."

"Are you so sure? No, wait!" A smile slithered across his face. "You're right." A cruel furrow joined the others in his thick brow. "We're talking about the Arctic Princess. Wouldn't you like to board that cruise line? So-o-o warm."

Cameron glared at him, ready to smack him. But he didn't. Instead, he followed him down the carpeted steps to the basement recreation room. The mahogany paneled room, overlooking the home's terraced lawn, gardens, pool, and tennis court, had been their playground when he and Justin, who was nearly a year older, were children and young teens. During middle school, they had parted ways. Cameron had thrown himself into golf and schoolwork while Justin did whatever suited him at any given moment. As children, Justin had seemed imposing and charismatic, but no longer.

After graduating, Cameron had hoped to distance himself from Justin, but a year later Justin pledged the same fraternity. How? Cameron didn't know or care. But it threw them together again, if only for a year. Now, Mr. Sloane's well-appointed game room and the well-supplied bar that he never locked had been reason enough to keep the friendship going, particularly since Justin's parents never bothered him when friends stopped by—and were unlikely to develop a new habit.

"So what about Lydia?" Justin pulled a beer from the refrigerator. "I thought you dropped her years ago. Cold turkey!"

Cameron's hand clinched momentarily. But why argue with a bigger fool than himself? In the basement, he found a former classmate and a stranger standing next to an ornate pool table. Each held a cue stick. He nodded to them then turned his attention to the liquor cabinet. After scanning the labels, he pulled a bottle of Glenmorangie single-malt Scotch from the shelf behind the bar. The label drew a smile: "Aged in bourbon casks." The good stuff but not too expensive. He filled an old-fashioned glass about half full. With the glass in hand, he dropped into an overstuffed armchair. He rolled the glass, watching the amber liquid coat its sides as he envisioned Lydia—the lilt in her step, her crisp Midwestern accent. A smile twitched his cheek, but other images pushed and shoved their way into his thoughts, demanding his attention.

He gulped half the remaining Scotch, wincing as it seared his mouth and throat. The sound of her key locking the front door of her parents' house rang in his ears. He drained the glass and half-filled it again. He contemplated disputing Justin's despicable assessment of Lydia's reputation. Rather than drawing Justin's attention, he tapped his fingertips together, checking to see whether the scotch had worked its magic. It had not. He returned to the bar and refilled his glass with Maker's Mark. He downed the liquid, paying scant attention to the burning sensation and even less to the taste.

He watched the others, none of whom played well, though some played better, aided by several beers. Beyond their shouts and taunts, a trophy fish caught his eye. Posed as if forever leaping from some forgotten stream, it hooked Cameron's sympathy. He too was gasping for air while frozen in time. He scanned the other trophies and stuffed animal heads that lined the walls. Again, he tapped his forefinger against his thumb. Neither was numb. He returned to the bar, grabbed the bourbon, and refilled his glass. He dropped into the overstuffed chair and studied Justin and the others who stumbled around the pool table. Sometime later, a smile crept across his face as the light touch of oblivion settled over him.

Someone jostled his shoulder. He vaguely recognized Justin's voice talking to Paul and Alex.

"It's not my fault. He poured every drink all on his own. And no, I wasn't in the mood to stop him."

Good. For once Justin's apathy had worked in Cameron's favor.

"His mom called," Paul answered. "I told her I'd bring him home."

"Aren't you the saint?"

Yeah, he is. Cameron's head spun too wildly for his mouth to form words. Since the ninth grade, he and Paul had shared the best of times. Several hands reached under his armpits.

"Come on, Cam." Paul lifted Cameron's shoulder. "Help me out. Stand up."

Cameron relaxed, hoping to appear heavy. "I don't want to go home."

"Why not?" Alex asked.

"That's okay." Paul lifted Cameron to his feet. "Cam, would you rather go to your uncle's house?"

"Yeah." Uncle Nathan would lecture him but little more. Cameron tried to stand but pitched sideways. A hand grabbed him and kept him from falling. He closed his eyes as Paul led him outside. Once settled in the car, Cameron leaned his head against the side window.

The next thing he recognized was his uncle's kind but strong voice. "Cameron, give me your hand." Uncle Nathan, tall and lanky, leaned toward him with his hand extended. The respected architect had long reminded Cameron of an I-beam wrapped in foam. Though seemingly rigid, Uncle

Nathan was dependably comforting, which was the reason Cameron ran to him after making truly stupid decisions.

Cameron wrapped his arm around his uncle's neck and stood. Though teetering, he stepped forward. As the driveway's gravel crunched beneath his shoes, he remembered Lydia's eyes as she closed the door. If starting over was possible, he would. "Hi. I'm Cameron," he'd say. "I'm not the jerk you think I am."

He stumbled, almost missing a step, and then heard the comforting thud of shoes crossing the wooden porch of the hundred-plus-year-old farmhouse. Inside, his aunt waited. He pushed his cheeks into a smile. "Hi, Aunt Becky."

"Is he okay?" she asked. "Hi, Paul. Thank you for picking him up."

Paul heaved Cameron into the house. "I'll do it again if need be."

Cameron glanced in his aunt's direction, uncertain that he saw her.

"He'll be fine in the morning." Uncle Nathan's voice rose above the echo of Cameron's leaden feet. The walls sounded close. Oh, a hall. "Here you go." Uncle Nathan loosened his grip, and Cameron dropped onto a bed, his head fell onto a pillow, and everything vanished.

He awoke to sunlight streaming through white cotton shades. He covered his eyes against the brilliant light as memories from the previous evening raced through his head. *Ugh.* He pulled the pillow over his head. What a jerk he'd been.

Some time later he awoke. His mouth tasted worse than soggy cereal, but the smell of coffee had roused his stomach. He sat up and dropped his legs over the side of the bed. Next to the bed, sat a pair of slippers and a robe that Aunt Becky had set out for him, but he wasn't a guest. He'd imposed himself on her and wasn't worthy of her kind gesture. Instead, he ran his fingers through his mussed hair and wandered down to the kitchen wearing the shirt and jeans he had worn the night before.

"Good morning, Cameron." The pleasant but set expression on Aunt Becky's long, handsome face was no match for the elegant smile that normally greeted him. He owed her an apology because lying had never cut it with her. "Would you like some grits and coffee?"

"Yes, please." Cameron sat down at the small breakfast table. His aunt set a steaming cup of coffee and a plate of hot grits and scrambled eggs in front of him. He salted the grits and stirred in a butter pat, but after a few swirls, he put the fork down. Not even his favorite breakfast looked appealing. Uncle Nathan sat across the table from him, reading the morning paper. A cup of coffee sat next to him.

"You do know," his uncle said without looking up, "that what you did last night was neither smart nor legal."

Cameron studied the grits and melted butter. Well, at least he hadn't tried to drive.

His uncle picked up his cup and met Cameron's gaze. "I don't mind that you asked Paul to bring you out here, but you should think twice before getting wasted." He took a sip without looking away from Cameron, a sure sign that he was ticked. "Paul brought your car over this morning, and your mother is waiting for you at home. Anytime you're ready I suggest you head back so she'll stop worrying." With that, he returned to his breakfast.

Obviously, Uncle Nathan was unaware that Cameron's universe had blown apart, taking every possibility of happiness with it. Thankfully, his uncle wasn't in the habit of prying.

Shortly after eleven, Cameron returned home. A rich aroma filled the kitchen where he found his mother pulling a pan of cornbread from the oven. She smiled for him. "Hi, sweetie." Her cheerful greeting didn't hide her disappointment.

He pushed his hangover and aches aside and smiled just for her. He draped an arm over her shoulder and kissed her cheek, a flagrantly manipulative effort to ingratiate himself that had worked for years. In his most contrite voice, he whispered, "I'm sorry I didn't call." With his free hand, he lifted the lid of a large pot, releasing delicate tendrils of steam laced with the scent of olive oil, garlic, ham, and mushrooms. "Who is this for?"

"I'm taking dinner to Sally Ritter. Her husband passed away last week, and I volunteered for New Year's Day. She's originally from Iowa, so I'm making everything but black-eyed peas"—she wiggled her eyebrows— "and collards."

"No black-eyed peas?"

"No black-eyed peas or collards. I substituted split-pea soup and a wilted spinach salad. Remember, it's for her. There're enough things for good luck: ham, cornbread, greens, and peas—of a sort," she added with a smile.

If his mother was anything, she was resourceful. Unfortunately, she was also curious and thus brimming with questions he did not want to answer.

Hence, overstaying his welcome was not an option. "I am sorry about last night. I should have called." He kissed her cheek and excused himself. "I need a shower."

"How is Lydia?" his mother asked as he turned to leave.

"Fine. She had a good time," Cameron said over his shoulder. Yes, Lydia had enjoyed talking to Paul, which was truthful. And Cameron's fault!

"What's her major?" his mother asked.

Lydia's major? He hadn't asked, but Paul had said something before he excused himself. "Engineering."

"Is she enjoying Duke?"

"I suppose." He should never have told his mother that he had asked Lydia out. "I'm going upstairs." He strode through the breakfast room where his father sat, reading the morning paper. He hoped his mother understood that going to Uncle Nathan's rather than coming home had nothing to do with her and everything to do with avoiding his father. Doing so, though, had wounded his mother, which made Cameron hate his father all the more.

As Cameron showered and dressed, memories from the previous night lingered, taunting him even as his mind wandered back to a happier time: to a random late afternoon on a Monday during high school. Once again, he stood next to Lydia, serving food and doing chores as needed at the Park Street Diner, a soup kitchen that served Chalmers's homeless population. He fell back on the bed and closed his eyes as the weight of disappointment lifted from his chest. Again, he and Lydia filled glasses with ice, sweet tea, unsweetened tea, and sometimes water. He listened to her laughter as she chatted with people who came through the line seeking a hearty meal and whatever kindness they and the other volunteers offered. "Mrs. Dempsey," he imagined hearing Lydia speak to a hunched, toothless young woman with dirty hair, "I love the way you fixed your hair today. It brightens your eyes."

Like Grandpa, Lydia liked gnarly people with drooping lids, crooked gap-toothed smiles, and strange odors. With each passing week, he'd come to appreciate her intelligent and pleasant conversations. Only after Justin Sloane embarrassed Lydia at a party on the Friday night before he graduated from high school did Cameron realize how much he'd come to enjoy her reliably uncomplicated and undemanding friendship. He had planned to apologize to her the following Monday, but in the early hours of Sunday morning, Justin had taken Cameron's truck on a fatal joyride, without either his permission or his knowledge. In doing so, he destroyed Lydia's trust in Cameron and their friendship.

Moments earlier, Officer Hammett had cleared him of any connection to the accident that filled the intersection of Cornwall Street and NC-340 in Chalmers even though his truck was one of the two vehicles involved in the accident. An hour earlier, Officer Hammett and her partner had banged on the door of Cameron's parents' house, awakening him. The second officer had snarled at him, nearly accusing him of complicity in the auto wreck that now surrounded him. His answers, though, had satisfied Officer Hammett who then drove him to the scene to claim his truck.

When they arrived, the sights and smells had glued him to his seat in the officer's patrol car as he watched Officer Hammett and others who continued to survey the street. Finally, he swallowed hard then climbed out and into the eerie predawn light. A sickeningly sweet stench assaulted his nose. Antifreeze. Overhead, the traffic signal changed, but nothing moved. No car awaited its permission to continue. His truck stood to one side with its hood up and front smashed in.

Officer Hammett approached him, "You can get what you need from your vehicle, sir."

"Thank you," he answered without taking his eyes off the second auto that stood several yards away. Its mangled driver's door hung on a single hinge, its seat empty and bloody. Both vehicles looked totaled.

The sweet smell grew stronger. Nausea rose into Cameron's throat as a woman from his father's insurance company approached. With her attention monopolized by her cell phone and emails, she seemed rude and indifferent even as she handed him a piece of paper. "This is for your father. I have everything. We'll file for you." No hint of compassion or empathy softened her clipped voice or lit her vacant eyes. "I've called a tow truck, so you're good to go."

Just leave? How? Cameron's head spun, and his stomach convulsed. He turned away and grabbed his knees to heave its contents. As he steadied himself, someone handed him a paper towel and then a water bottle. It was Officer Hammett. Behind her, flashes of brilliant blue light lit the wet pavement, pieces of metal, and the car belonging to Mrs. Duncan, his father's cousin. Cameron had seen her daughter Aimee, his childhood friend and distant cousin, when he arrived. For a second their eyes had met as the paramedics lifted her mother into the ambulance. He'd never seen such pain and fear. He wanted to comfort her, but how?

The blue light flashed on and off, on and off. If Cameron had hidden his keys, this wouldn't have happened.

As distant cousins but close in age, he and Aimee had played together as toddlers and were later tossed together during family outings with the expectation that they'd entertain each other and not bother the adults—which turned out well as they became close friends. After Mrs. Duncan's funeral, Aimee had assured him that he was not to blame. She also pushed him to call Lydia to tell her his version of events on Friday night. That she supported both him and Lydia, with whom she had become instant best friends shortly after Lydia moved to town during middle school, had not surprised him since the two girls shared many similarities. But what did Aimee expect him to say to Lydia? "Oh, yeah, Justin arranged everything and failed to tell me that you would be my date." Cameron knew exactly how well that excuse would go over.

Now, after mulling over his dilemma for three years, he still couldn't find the right words. Instead, earlier in the evening, when she opened the door at her parents' house and smiled at him, every synapse in his brain had frozen. Every excuse had evaporated along with every possibility that an apology could resurrect her impression of him. Permanently.

Cameron stared at the empty room. Roadkill muck lined his parched mouth, but his mother, calling to him from the bottom of the stairs, caught his attention.

"Your dad and I are going out to your aunt and uncle's house for dinner tonight. Do you want to come with us?"

Of course not. "No, thank you."

"I left half a quiche in the fridge. You can heat it up for dinner. Call if you need something."

"Thanks."

As the sound of her footsteps retreated toward the kitchen, Cameron's mind retraced the path along which time and distance had spun the desultory consequences of his arrogance into a spider's web of stupidity. Lydia had been more than a quiet haven from girls who talked incessantly about nothing. She had been interesting. Even though she was a year younger and a grade behind him, they had challenged each other in calculus and physics. She also raved about Conrad's *Heart of Darkness*. In detail. Why? —He couldn't imagine. He shook head, remembering how Justin had taunted him about her looks, but other guys said she was the hottest girl at school—probably because she ignored them. A year after he graduated, she too had crossed the dais to receive her diploma. But then she smiled at the assembled family and friends—and reversed the polarity of his world.

He momentarily considered Uncle Nathan's lecture about the joys associated with temperance, but remorse squeezed his head like a vise, blocking out everything except the unrelenting throb caused by his undaunted stupidity. He had but one source of relief: Mr. Sloane's bar. He drove to Justin's house where he played pool and drank until one the following morning. As sobriety began to return, he drove to Uncle Nathan's house.

"I'm sorry, Uncle Nathan," he said with as contrite a voice as he could conjure, "I couldn't go home."

His uncle stepped back, impassive as ever. "Come on in." He didn't ask for an explanation, nor did Cameron give one.

Cameron stumbled down the hall to the spare bedroom, where he fell into the bed and the pillow's embrace. In the morning, he slid his feet into the slippers he'd ignored the previous morning then wandered down the hall. He found his uncle sitting at the breakfast room table, alone—and dressed in a suit. Oops; it was Sunday. "Y'all going to church?"

"No," his uncle answered without looking up from the paper. "We just got back. Your aunt's upstairs. Matt went to lunch with some friends." Uncle Nathan wasn't smiling. If yesterday he'd been ticked, today he was a dark thundercloud and Cameron was sitting in the shadow of its anvil.

"I *am* sorry." Cameron eyed his uncle, but the gray-haired man didn't flinch. "I'll apologize to Matt. I didn't set a good example for him." He sighed, happy to have listed the appropriate talking points.

Uncle Nathan looked up, still without smiling. "That's true." He returned to the newspaper.

Yeah. Cameron could explain New Year's Eve as too much celebrating, but how could he tell his younger cousin—Wait! No! He hadn't! His throat choked shut. His body twitched. Perhaps he had not been as sober as he had imagined himself to be when he arrived here. Cameron dropped into the chair opposite his uncle, braced his elbows on the table, and buried his face in his palms.

He had broken the promise he made to Grandpa days before he died, a promise never to drink and drive. With pancreatic cancer ravaging his grandfather's body, Cameron would have promised the moon to keep him alive even a day longer. But Grandpa understood his mortality when he asked Uncle Nathan to watch over Cameron, a responsibility he gave to Uncle Nathen, his son-in-law, and not his son, Cameron's father. Since Cameron had just turned sixteen and had no experience with alcohol, the promise had been easy ... until the Friday night when Justin arranged a blind date, two days before Mrs. Duncan died.

Later that night, long after Lydia climbed into Justin's car and sat down next to him, Cameron took his first drink—gallons it seemed at the time—and broke his promise. Fortunately, Paul had taken Lydia home before returning and taking him home. Ashamed and chagrined by his behavior, he'd been scared enough by the incident to avoid alcohol during his freshman year, but his promise vaporized the following summer.

Cameron plopped his forehead on the top of his aunt's English pine table, but the rustle of the newspaper drew his attention. He lifted his head and met his uncle's cold gaze. A chill pushed him deep into his seat, though sinking between the floorboards would have been preferable.

Uncle Nathan set the paper aside. "This morning, I talked with Stan Boehmer, a friend of mine from college. Every summer he hires guys your age to help on his ranch in Shell, Wyoming. He says he has room for you. It'll be a good experience."

"Spend the summer? Why?"

"It'll be fun."

Those words had never preceded anything that Cameron considered fun.

"I thought," his uncle said with no hint of frivolity. Then he smiled. "Hey, I promised your grandfather, and I'm going to keep that promise. Okay?" His grin eased, and his gaze softened. "Besides, it's a great place to get away and sort things out." He paused and studied Cameron, who wanted no part of the suggestion.

"But Uncle Nathan—"

"Don't get your pants in a knot. Your father hasn't agreed yet. I'm hoping he will. I mentioned it so you could get used to the idea."

"But what if I have other plans?"

"Like what?" Uncle Nathan chuckled. "Like using a research job to pad your med school application?"

"Sounds good to me."

"Do you know what a doctor's life is like?"

What could an architect know? Besides, with a ninety-fifth percentile MCAT score and a GPA that was the stuff of dreams for most applicants, the question wasn't whether he would be accepted but where. His confidence grew. "They make lots of money."

"Really? Then get a job at your father's insurance agency. The hours are great, and the money's better."

No way! Cameron stood and poured himself a cup of coffee. "I like the lifestyle."

"And what is that?"

"Lots of time to play golf." Cameron grinned and sat back down. "Sounds good." Time on a golf course increased the appeal of any career.

Uncle Nathan's smile vanished. "Medicine is about more than acing tests, and plenty of doctors aren't rich. Besides, you'll need a far better reason than golf when a patient tanks." Ice crystals dusted the silence, catching Cameron's attention. "Also, a DUI can get you expelled." The crystals turned to sleet and crackled as they bounced off the tabletop and floor. "You have to master your drinking, or it will master you."

Cameron lifted the coffee cup to his lips. "I was essentially sober when I drove last night."

"You think so? Regardless, it wasn't smart—not in the least."

Cameron glared at his uncle, scanned his limited knowledge of

Wyoming—it's a long way from anywhere, and narrowed his gaze. "Professor Krasotkin offered me a research job for the summer. And the frat house is within walking distance of my apartment, so I don't have to drive."

"I certainly hope you're right."

"Then there's no reason for me to go to Wyoming." He rolled his eyes. "Wyoming!"

"You always did have your grandpa Ben's spunk. Let's see what your father says."

Uncle Nathan picked up his coffee cup and turned back to the paper. He knew Cameron wasn't an alcoholic. Nah. It wasn't going to happen. Uncle Nathan was bluffing.

Since arriving as a freshman at Duke, Eliana Johansson had yet to tire of riding the bus that shuttled students between East and West Campus. Whether it was packed with students or nearly empty, she had only to glimpse outside to be transported away from the madding crowd of school and the pressure cooker of class. Each season changed the colors scattered through the woods, but the undulating boundary line that separated swaths of neatly mowed grass from rumpled woods infested with vines and weeds that stood beyond it, had remained. Whether she sat or stood, held a strap or a pole, and no matter the direction of travel, the margin and the gently bobbing motion of the bus had sung to her in whispers that soothed her soul. This day, upon boarding, Eliana had happily wrapped an arm around a chrome-plated pole, content as her ambling ship of state rambled over the knotty pavement. She even chanced to imagine that no one, not a single person on the bus, knew her name.

"Hey, Ellie." The voice pressed its course beard against Eliana's ear; his lips touched her cheek. She pushed him away but not before his arm reached around her and the pole, pinning her to it as his other hand found its mark, which was not the pole but her hip. "Will I see you at the party tonight?"

The voice belonged to one of several classmates she never enjoyed seeing but into whose company she had been thrown far too often. "In your dreams!" She jammed her elbow into his side and pushed herself away. She lunged toward the front of the bus and found another pole. A few students turned to look, not voyeurs but simply startled from their thoughts, much as she had been startled from hers. Like the eyes that glanced up as she bumped her way forward then looked away just as quickly, she refused to give the man even a fraction of her attention, not even a glowering glance. Instead, Eliana fixed her eyes on the nodding pavement. When the bus stopped at Swift Avenue, she gladly watched him exit through the rear doors. With his head held high, he strode up the hill, giving neither the bus nor its occupants a moment's notice.

A woman pushed against her, shoulder to shoulder. "He's a creep." Eliana spun her head, surprised to see her close friend Allison, who must have boarded the bus at the last stop. She leaned her head close. "I saw who just got off," she whispered. "He didn't bother you, did he?"

"No." Eliana watched the man until the bus rounded the bend and continued toward West Campus.

"I keep telling you; it's not too late to report him."

The rude man had not been the student who gave her a ride back from an off-campus party, raped her, and then unceremoniously left her passed out and half-naked under the elevated pedestrian plaza connecting the dorms to the Bryan Student Center. But he might have been. Of course, like all the others, he would have said it was consensual. Who could say that he was wrong? Which was largely the reason she had refused to give his name. Another male student, while taking a shortcut on that cold January night, found her. He called a friend, and the two had wrapped her up and literally carried her to the emergency room.

The incident had created a momentary blip on the public psyche of the student body. Though school officials continued to press, seeking the man's name, overt interest had quickly faded, but not from the eyes and lips of those who knew her. A few impertinent professional voyeurs in the liberal arts department—who didn't know her—militantly claimed to be her ardent defenders. *Yeah, right!* If, as she believed, the persistent counselors still held her best interests at heart, she was equally certain that others had not. If some of her classmates in the economic department imagined that the night had resembled Annibale Carracci's fresco, *The Triumph of Bacchus and Ariadne*, or other scenes from *The Loves of the Gods*, they were wrong. The truth was far more sordid and common. Though Allison was a true friend, Eliana had long since made up her mind. She wasn't going to report him.

When the bus stopped in front of the chapel, Allison repeated herself. "I'll keep reminding you. You should report him."

"I'm hungry ...." Before she could finish, a student walking across the quadrangle headed from the dorms (probably) toward the library, caught Eliana's attention. "I'll call you." Seeing Allison's startled face, she grimaced. "I'm sorry," she said as she hopped from the bus and took off in long, rapid strides in the direction of the library's entrance. She reached it just in time to see the petite brunette disappear into the library. Once inside, Eliana first trotted and then slowed as the gap narrowed. She crossed the main lobby and arrived only a few yards behind the woman as she opened the door to the stacks.

She dodged a student who stepped between them but remained close enough to follow the woman up the stairs—not too close, though, so as to attract attention. As Eliana hoped, the woman climbed to the fourth floor of Perkins and took a quiet seat at the rear of the building where a bank of windows overlooked a service road and woods. Eliana's brain spun around a question that had plagued her for more than a month, a question that only the woman could answer. Ignoring the throbbing noise of her rapidly beating heart, she sat down next to the woman, who turned to her, smiled, and continued to set up her workstation. The moment had come!

"Hi, Lydia," Eliana whispered, glancing around to assure herself that, as expected, no other students were nearby. "My name is Eliana—"

"Hi. My roommate, Eydie You, is an econ major with you. You impressed her, and Eydie isn't easily impressed."

"Oh ... uh ... I won't bother you. I'm sorry." Eliana started to rise.

"Please. Don't leave." Lydia reached out but hesitated, having come neither so close as to be disquieting nor so quickly as to seem insincere. "You're not bothering me."

"You're sure?"

"Yeah. Absolutely."

Eliana sat down. For a second, cowardice gripped her heart, but she'd come too far to retreat. "Thank you for the compliment, but I know that my ... incident ... my failure"—her breath caught and held, but then she sighed— "was your first thought when you saw me."

"Not really. Well, maybe, but ...." This time Lydia rested her hand on

Eliana's forearm. "Yes, because I know more than you think. The two guys who took you to the emergency room are friends of mine. We were all worried because they said that your body was so cold when they found you."

Eliana shrank back, not from Lydia's kindness but from the memory of that miserable night. Lydia's candor, though, had banished everything she had planned to say as she raced across the quadrangle. Everything—that is, except the purpose that jettisoned her out of the shuttle bus. So she might as well begin with the most pressing point, which was not the attack in January.

"I know you're a Christian and that you attend InterVarsity," she began softly. "I'm not. And obviously, I don't." Her throat tightened, "And if I thought you'd preach to me, I would have avoided you from now to eternity." Her chest heaved in another half-sob. "But ... and I'm sort of ashamed of this, but a week before that incident, I overheard you talking to Eydie and another friend. I couldn't help but eavesdrop because of what you said."

Until that moment, Lydia had been sympathy personified, but it vanished, replaced by a light laugh and deep puzzlement. "What did I say?"

"It was right after classes resumed after the winter break—"

"Christmas?" Lydia inserted.

"Whatever. What caught my attention was that you were spitting mad at some guy you saw on New Year's."

Lydia's brows leaped in surprise. A faint frown followed as she pulled away. "Oh?"

Eliana had run the memory through her head a dozen times, each time focusing on one point. "You described going on a date with him, this guy from high school. You two had been friends, but clearly, you liked him, a lot ... and he hurt you deeply, which was reason enough to be angry. But from what I could gather, you two never had sex." Lydia leaned farther away as her eyes opened wide and her mouth clamped shut. So Eliana continued. "That's not my world. I've never known someone to be that kind of angry at a guy she hasn't had sex with."

Her chest heaved, but this time she held it, thinking hard about what to say, for Lydia's eyes telegraphed her thoughts: She was more stunned by this last statement than anything else Eliana had said. "I mean," she pressed on, "everyone has sex. It's just what people do. They check each other out. Though probably you and Eydie don't. So hearing you guys talking was ... I mean, you're attractive, smart and nice—things that attract guys—but you don't have sex with them."

Lydia, having regained her composure, shrugged a bit sheepishly. "Uh, no. We don't."

A strange feeling of relief came over Eliana. Having said the hard part, she allowed her shoulders to sag. Though certain that no one had wandered into the rows of stacks, she lowered her voice. "After ... my incident, Duke assigned a counselor to me. She wanted—wants, to know who left me that night and what had happened. I told them it was off campus, but they wanted a name. I won't give it to them because I couldn't sleep if I did." Lydia frowned, looking puzzled. "Why? Because the only difference between that night and those other times was that I ended up under the plaza. It wasn't the first time a guy forced himself on me"—she swallowed hard and finished the equation— "nor the first time I gave in."

As Eliana unreeled her story, Lydia had neither picked up a book nor opened her laptop. Now, though, she reached out and gave Eliana's hand a comforting squeeze. "I'm so sorry."

"What for? Because it was a cold night?"

"No. Well, I mean, yes. I'm sorry that so many men have taken advantage of you."

"Advantage of me? Yeah, he was pushy but also—I gave in."

"No, he assaulted you. That's rape."

"Well—what is rape anymore? It's just an accusation. I've seen it go both ways. I've seen it destroy innocent guys. Remember, I gave in." Eliana held her breath, cringing as the next thought refused to be withheld. "I was almost fifteen when I first had sex. It was at a basement party where everyone was drinking and having sex. This guy wanted it, and the parents were upstairs. Mom had already put me on the pill. She assumed I was already 'sexually active,' as she put it, though I wasn't. She wasn't protecting me. She didn't want another baby around after my older sister decided not to have an abortion. Of course, the baby daddy disappeared."

She ran her thumb along a textbook's binding. "I gave in because I assumed there was something wrong with me and that having sex would fix it. It didn't." She sighed. "Mom wasn't the best example. She divorced my father while she was pregnant with me—said he was running around. Supposedly.

Someone else said she left because she could, —she's a Trust Baby. I suppose."
Whatever. "I never met my father, but that didn't stop her from believing in
marriage. Dad, as I call this stepfather—he's her third husband—treats me like
I'm invisible. He gave me lingerie for my sixteenth birthday." Eliana shook her
head. "Can you believe it? And with the tags still on, so I could take it back if
I didn't like it. What was he thinking? But at least he remembered."

For the first time in forever, Eliana's eyes burned, but she looked toward
the window and the serene blankness of the trees and faceless buildings.
Finally she turned to Lydia, whose quiet attention hadn't flagged. A part of
her wanted to take back every agonizing word. Another part was glad that
she could not. Having emptied her heart, she whispered, "I've used enough
of your time. I know you came here expecting to be left alone."

"No." Lydia tapped her computer. "This can wait." She pinched her lips
together and glanced out the windows. Then she turned to Eliana. "I can't say
that I understand what you've been through and what you're going through,
except to say that you're an amazing survivor."

"Survivor?"

"Yes. You're beautiful and smart. You've got spirit and strength, but you're
carrying a lot of ... pain. Please call the counselors. Tell them what you told
me. They're trained to listen and help you navigate these issues. You have so
much going for you."

Really? Something ferocious lit Lydia's calm eyes, rocking Eliana back on
her heels with a new feeling. *Wow!* "I'll think about it, but," she added, "I'll
never give them his name. Never."

"Fine. They can help you without knowing who hurt you."

"Maybe, but you didn't answer my question," which now seemed irrelevant and ... shameful. Or at best a miserable reminder that she had given in
to the guy. She'd caved.

"Someone once asked Eydie," Lydia said softly, breaking into Eliana's con-
fusion, "if she and I are saving ourselves by not having sex. That doesn't hold
water. What your mother did was cruel because she stole something precious
from you. With that said, though, try to forgive her—not for her sake, but for
your sake. Forgiveness heals the giver whether or not it helps the recipient.

"Some people, in and out of Christianity, say God only loves Christians,
but that's not true. He made this world; he made you. Therefore, he loves

you. John Calvin gets a bad rap for being harsh, academic, and thin-lipped, but he made the point that God gave us the ability to think and talk so that we can talk to him. He wants us to talk to him. He gave cats and dogs an abundance of affection and personality, but they can't count or describe love. But we can. Obviously. In a similar, mystical cosmic balance, God loves every human because he is good and loving. He shares his great love whether-or-not the person loves or believes in him. You and I both feel his love. Furthermore, he carries our—*our*—fears and burdens when we feel beaten down. His nature is to lift us up when we think we can't go on.

"Most importantly, his righteous nature infuses everyone with a sense of justice. Regardless of their faith, your counselors have that gift. They may not be able to remedy an injustice, but they want to try. That's the core of their ability to help others. None of us can love beyond ourselves without God's love. Anywhere there is goodness; there also is God's love. It isn't something to be grasped, but as a broken bone heals, hidden from sight by skin and muscles, so also God's love heals our broken hearts. Even when no one else, not even our closest friends see the damage and pain, his love brings relief."

Until now, Lydia's face had been kind and soft, but a calm ferocity and serene confidence now smiled back at Eliana. "You don't have to love God for him to love you. These people—who feel so much ill-will toward others—stole all kinds of things from you, which was terribly wrong, but they didn't turn God against you. And they didn't steal your dignity or your will to survive."

"What did they steal?"

"That's not for me to say. That's a question you should ask the counselors, so they can help you gain back some of what was stolen from you."

So, what is love? She had no idea, but regardless, Lydia was wrong about something having been stolen: A thief can't steal what Eliana never had—*that something you call love.* "It's not that simple."

"No doubt, but think of it as two options. You can let the accumulation of these assaults destroy you, or you can take charge. Despite the complication, believe that you are worthy of being loved. And I will heartily, and absolutely, say that you are worthy."

Lydia tilted her head as if a tentative thought had crossed her mind. "Two hours ago—before you sat down next to me here in Perkins, I believed you are worthy." Lydia's steady smile sagged. "You're right; it is complicated.

Please, look back. I know there was once someone, several people who loved you. Someone smiled at you and said, 'You are loved.'" Lydia's smile returned. "Please ... talk to the counselor."

Humph. Well, why not? "Okay. I'll call her." Eliana paused and then smiled. "So what about this guy in your life."

"In my life!" Lydia laughed. "Certainly you jest!"

"Oh, come now." Eliana leaned toward her and with an impish grin, whispered, "Of all people, I think you know I tell no secrets."

"That appears to be true. But you want to know about someone I buried in my deep, dark past."

"Of course!" Eliana chuckled. "What else would I want?"

Lydia heaved a sigh. "His name is Cameron Asher. And he's a junior at UNC."

"UNC? . . . Girl!"

"Yes. I had such a crush on him, and he never knew it. He was the dream of every girl in school because he wasn't just cute—tall, curly blond hair, blue eyes—he was also nice. Every Monday for three years from five to six thirty, he was mine while our mothers worked at a charity kitchen."

"He served food at a soup kitchen? No!" She thumped her chest. "I think I'm in love with him."

Lydia grinned and wiggled a brow. "We knew each other so well, we were so comfortable with each other, that ... it was frightening—almost siblings, but definitely not siblings. Then it all went wrong."

And? Eliana tipped her head and motioned for Lydia to continue.

"It started several years ago, when a friend of his, Justin, rigged a date between us. Except while Justin told me one story, he told Cameron a different story. You can imagine how that went over."

"Not well."

"Not in the least. But the worst was yet to come. The next night, Justin got drunk, stole Cameron's truck, and then ran a red light and killed my best friend's mother, who was also Cameron's aunt once removed. I knew Cameron too well to believe that the date was his idea or that, as Justin claimed, he had given him the keys.

"With a lot of counseling and cajoling from Mom and Nana, I forgave Cameron—but it didn't matter. Everything between us had changed. He closed up. All I wanted was a phone call ... to talk like we used to. But he didn't—until two days after this past Christmas. Out of nowhere he called and invited me to dinner and a New Year's Eve party, given partly by the older brother—Alex— of his truly good friend Paul. I was so excited; I was beside myself. But during dinner, he was ... a dork! I can't describe it in any other way. Everything went wrong. Once we got to the party, he disappeared to one of the makeshift bars and became its volunteer bartender. No, he didn't do a double-up— 'one for you and one for me' act. But that thoughtful move left me talking with Paul until around ten when Cameron took me home." Sarcasm laced her voice. "All he could say was 'I'm sorry.' By then, I was disgusted." Her eyes scanned the ceiling. When she turned back to Eliana, her anger balloon appeared to have burst, and something between exasperation and sorrow had replaced it. "I don't know if I even care anymore."

"I don't suppose you've heard from him. Or disemboweled him?"

Lydia laughed. "That idea has a nice ring to it. I'll keep it in mind."

"It's hard for me to imagine being so close and stopping .... All the guys I know want bennies with their friendship. So what did you do? How did you get there—friendship and no bennies?"

"When I first met Cameron, my grandmother gave me a piece of advice. She said that a woman is at her best when she learns to fly fish, which means being neither flirtatious nor submissive. According to Nana, we are the stronger sex. We choose to bring out the best in men by waiting for the fish—a good man—to come to the fly. It's not a tease but a question for the fish and for us. Who am I? And who do I want to be with? According to Nana, men like to do three things: compete, fix things, and have sex."

"Ow-w." Eliana's grin spread across her face.

"When we indiscriminately toss bait around, they take it, enjoy it—and more, then leave us holding the empty hook." She arched a brow then half laughed. "When we become the aggressors, they step back and take the easy road. Competing and fixing things require work, so they lapse into number three. You get the point. And when that happens, all of us become our lesser selves. A good man wants to know that you like him while believing that he has found you. Like fly fishing, it's a twosome dance that requires patience, but the scenery can be awesome, or so the magazines claim. As for

Cameron—we had a lot of fun. But no. The fires of Hell will have turned to ash and ice long before I toss another fly in his direction."

"And I thought you were a good church girl."

"I am, but I love Dante."

"That sounds like an interesting discussion for another day." For the first time in ages, even more than when riding the shuttle between campuses, Eliana's heart felt light.

Outside the windows of the Blue Feather Café in Chapel Hill, the chartreuse leaves of spring had ripened to Kelly green. A few late azalea blossoms sparkled among shrubs carpeted with tender leaves while pine pollen coated every surface with gummy yellow dust.

Inside the café, Professor Krasotkin, a small, slender man, leaned solemnly toward Cameron on crossed arms atop a graffiti-scarred tabletop. "You seem to think that good and evil will always coexist like feuding siblings, but you're wrong." A stiff but kind smile familiar to several decades of chemistry students caught the corners of his mouth. "Good does not need evil to exist but stands on its attributes. Instead, evil makes us appreciate goodness. But we must listen—and learn."

Cameron turned to Esther, his perennial chem lab partner, and Trace, a fellow chemistry major and fraternity brother, but neither budged. "Come on, guys," he pleaded. "Help me out."

His friends remained mute. Still, Cameron deserved a break. The spring semester had been long and grueling enough. He didn't need word games, at least not an hour before his thermodynamics final, the last exam of his junior year. But why had Professor Krasotkin turned a birthday celebration—his fiftieth—into something else—something depressing?

The professor continued, "Your father may be annoying, but he isn't evil, nor does he hate you. He probably thinks he's being helpful. Relax. A summer in Wyoming isn't the end of the world."

Maybe not, but it was way too close. "Professor, you know my dad." Cameron glanced at Trace, who instantly looked away. "You know what a pain he can be."

Sure he did. In scattered incidents during the three years of Cameron's tenure at UNC, both Esther and Trace had seen Cameron's father's trove of bad behavior that veered between meddling and apathy while ignoring Cameron's achievements. "Get yourself right with God," his father had commanded, "or you'll rot in Hell." Maybe he said "burn," but one was within a short putt of the other.

The professor handed Cameron a folded slip of paper. "Here. Put this away, and then give me a call sometime during the fall semester."

Cameron started to open it, but seeing the instantaneous arching of his mentor's eyebrow, he stopped and tucked the paper in his pocket.

Professor Krasotkin's manner belied the return of his genial smile. "It isn't your father who concerns me, Cameron. Hate destroys the person who carries it, not the person whose behavior generates it. This summer think about what you want from life, and while you're at it, try to find something admirable about your father."

"But, that's just it—"

The professor's smile widened, cutting him off. "I believe you all have a final exam to take, and I have one to give." Professor Krasotkin stood and nodded to the other two. "Esther. Trace. Thanks for the coffee. I'll see you all back on campus in a few minutes."

After the professor left, Trace and Esther talked, but Cameron heard little of what they said. Grumbling to himself, he studied the closed door of the café through which his mentor had left. Only Professor Krasotkin was allowed to be so blunt.

A few minutes later, Esther stood, splayed her fingers, and rolled her hands outward, mimicking a magician prepared to reveal a great mystery. "It's showtime."

Trace groaned. Then he stretched, more giraffe than man, and followed Cameron and Esther out to the wide porch that faced Rosemary Street. Once outside, he air-punched Cameron. "You're going to bust the curve, aren't you?"

"Nah. Are you on your way to the exam?"

"No, I've got just enough time to find a corner and pray, really hard. Note that I didn't say study hard. It's too late for that." A mirthless grin etched his face. "See y'all in a while."

As Trace strode toward Franklin Street, Esther grabbed Cameron's arm and held him back. Her dark brown eyes weren't laughing as they often did. A brown curl clung to her eyebrow, adding severity to her glare. "Krasotkin is right. Yeah, your dad can be a massive pain, but you've got to make the best of it."

"Gee, thanks." Her father was down-to-earth and friendly, so "making the best of it" was an easy suggestion. "Are you going to the exam?"

"Not yet. I've got to hang up my swimsuit." She lifted a Carolina blue gym bag. "I practiced my freestyle to loosen up for the exam. Don't look at me like that. We each have our chosen form of punishment. Mine's perfecting my stroke." She smiled and nudged him. "I'll see you in the exam. I guess I *should* say goodbye now. I'm sure you'll finish ahead of me."

"Maybe not."

"Yeah, you will. And you'll ace it." Her exaggerated scowl was predictable, even though her grade would be similar. "You'll *also* have fun this summer." She popped his arm with her gym bag—an impressive punch coming from such a slender girl.

"Yeah, sure!" He rubbed the bruise. "So I'll see you in the fall?"

"I certainly hope so."

When the traffic light at Franklin Street changed, allowing them to cross, he flashed a grin. "Besides, how would you get through senior year without my irresistible smile?"

"It'd be tough." Esther laughed as she stepped onto the sidewalk and turned right.

"See ya." As she crossed South Columbia Street, he watched and wondered why he wasn't attracted to her. In many ways, she was everything he wanted: athletic, fun, honest, and attractive in a wholesome, unvarnished sort of way, but there was the problem. She not only believed in God and Jesus, but they intruded into her life. He watched the gentle sway of her stride. Delightful, but not enough—and she wasn't Lydia.

Turning back toward campus, he eased into an agile gait and jammed his hand into the front pocket of his jeans. As he did, he felt the tip of the folded paper Professor Krasotkin had handed to him. He pulled it out and read without missing a step.

"'Twas brillig, and the slithy toves'"—his smile widened— "Did gyre and gimble in the wabe; / All mimsy were the borogoves, / And the mome raths outgrabe.'"

Cameron liked to use the quotation from Lewis Carroll's *Through the Looking-Glass* when friends or sometimes even he stumbled over words and tried to make sense of some matter, important or not. Why, though, had the professor picked that verse? Lacking an answer, Cameron slid the note into the front pocket of his backpack. As he lengthened his stride, he wished as he had a hundred times before that his father was more like Dr. Krasotkin.

To the west, beyond the trees, a peal of thunder undercut the sound of cars whooshing past. A sudden moist breeze gained strength, ruffling the tails of the blue oxford shirt that he wore unbuttoned over a gray T-shirt emblazoned with UNC.

"Yo, Cam. Wait up!"

Cameron spun around and smiled at his roommate but did not change the clip of his pace or direction. Though stocky and several inches shorter, Neil usually kept up with him. Thunder rumbled louder. The sky darkened enough to turn the streetlights on. "Where've you been?" he asked.

"I went back to the house to pick up a notebook. Sometimes I wonder why it was so important to move out of the frat house." Neil nodded toward the white Colonial building set well back and sheltered by spreading oak trees on the opposite side of the street. "It was a lot more convenient than Mr. Cobb's rental."

At the beginning of the year, Cameron and Neil, along with four others, had rented a well-worn brick house three blocks north of Franklin Street. Each year, the owner, Mr. Cobb, rented the house to guys in Cameron's fraternity, the same frat he had joined decades earlier. "Why any landlord would willingly rent to a bunch of frat brothers beats me," Cameron said, "but it's quieter, and I like that."

"So where were you?" Neil asked.

"I was at the Blue Feather. Today is Professor Krasotkin's fiftieth birthday. Trace, Esther, and I treated him to coffee and dessert. We're cheap company. Ha! He invited us to a party after the exam. It's down in the dining area."

"Hey, you and Trace can't miss our celebration."

"Certainly not!"

"Nor Rita?" Neil grinned and wiggled his brow.

"What a lousy day to have a big birthday." Laughing, Cameron turned his face away from the wind as lightning flashed, followed by a rumble of thunder. "Come on; this mess is turning to rain."

"Why are you in such a hurry?"

"I like to be early."

"You're too compulsive." Neil laughed. "Ah, yes. Your buddy Esther!" He lifted his free arm and flexed it.

"Hey! She's on a swimming scholarship. Besides, she's cute."

"Yeah. So says the guy who collects incredible babes like Rita as easily as a dog collects ticks. There you are, tongue hanging out, chasing a Frisbee, and ticks jump on." Neil laughed. "Then again, people who make friends with their professors are weird."

"Krasotkin's cool. I can't believe nobody else took advantage of the time he made for them. I'd go by for help—"

"Help? You?"

Cameron picked up his pace as a gust stirred the leafy canopy above the sidewalk. "Why not? I like talking to him. He's really funny."

"Did Trace tell you that Krasotkin talked at the Campus Crusade meeting last week?"

By now Neil was panting, but hearing rain hitting the leaves high over-head, Cameron kept up his pace. "That's your thing. Krasotkin and I don't talk about religion. Besides"—he pulled one cheek into a half-grin— "he's too quirky to be a Bible toter. You've seen his ties." Cameron lifted his chin while his free hand reached up and straightened an imaginary tie. "Esther says they're awesome."

Suddenly, the noise of an engine behind him caught his attention. Turning only his head, Cameron froze. A momentary flash of lightning sil-houetted the hulking mass of an auto, only fifty yards away, careening toward them. In a heartbeat, he grabbed Neil and bounded for shelter behind the broad trunk of an ancient oak. The car veered toward them, jumped the low curb, and rumbled across the brick-paved sidewalk before swinging in a frantic arc back onto the wide street, cutting in front of an oncoming transfer truck.

"Turn your lights on!" Neil shouted. Cameron watched and dug his fingers into the thick, moist bark of the tree. Neil turned to him, mouth agape, rain matting his hair to his head. "Doesn't he know the road turns into a one-way at the light?"

Darkness followed the truck, swallowing Cameron as he stood, his eyes riveted on the truck that raced onward. "Not ... not again," he said through his clenched throat. *There's a car in every lane.*

"Turn right, you idiot!" Neil screamed.

"They don't have a chance." Cameron's jaw locked, barely allowing the words to escape. "He's going too fast." Images flashed across his inner eye and then vanished. Squinting, he leaned forward, his fingers digging deeper into the wet bark. The vehicle raced toward the doomed drivers.

"Stop!" Neil screamed. The car, now distant, looked no larger than a toy.

Lightning lit the air, but instead of thunder, the sickening sound of metal crunching against metal startled Cameron. A shudder rattled him, but only the sound of rain blowing across the sidewalk filled his ears. Stiff and pale, he stared into the darkness, keeping his knees from buckling by sheer force of will.

Suddenly, Neil started to run toward the wreck, but Cameron's feet refused to move. Neil stopped partway down the street and turned to Cameron. "Aren't you coming?"

Of course not! Cameron stepped back from the tree. He knew what Neil would see—crumpled cars and shards of glass—and what he'd smell: antifreeze. Cameron didn't need to see or smell it again, but Neil knew nothing about Mrs. Duncan, the wreck, or any of the events that followed, descriptions that Cameron had not shared and would forever keep to himself. The rain sent a runnel of water over his forehead. "No, I've got to get to the exam."

"Aren't you curious?"

"No." Cameron's stomach churned.

"You've got time." Neil's brown eyes, shadowed by the storm, narrowed into cold, black nuggets of coal. "Give it a break, Cam."

"No!"

"Fine!" Neil turned and ran down the road.

In the distance, steam, backlit by a streetlight, rose in curls from the battered automobiles. Figures moved about the wreckage, some ducking their heads close. Another shudder rose from within and convulsed Cameron's body as he watched Neil disappear into the darkness, a silhouette trotting toward the light. *The chemistry building.* He gripped the strap of his backpack and jolted forward but veered to the left, away from the direction Neil had run. He ducked behind the Kenan Music Center and strode toward the main campus, a route that placed Abernathy and Swain halls between him and the accident.

Cameron quickened his pace, all the while keeping other buildings between himself and the accident. Sirens wailed in the distance. *Review! To determine molar enthalpy* $H_m = H/n$. Staring only a yard ahead of each long stride, he jammed his feet into gear, but the memory of the accident that had taken Mrs. Duncan's life pummeled his head. The police had not charged him, nor had the Duncan family blamed him. Only his father had blamed him. But then, after Grandpa died, blaming Cameron without reason had become expected. Two months after Grandpa's funeral, Cameron's father and older brother Trent had argued, both screaming, using words that never should have been said. Afterward, Trent had moved away. From childhood, his father had adored Trent more, much more, than he had ever liked Cameron. What kind of father would drive his son away? But then, what kind of father refused to attend his son's high school graduation?

"If you weren't so selfish and immature," Cameron's father blurted, "you'd have better friends than the likes of Justin Sloane. And none of this would've happened." The deepening furrows in his brow cleaved his forehead. "Give me one reason why I should attend your graduation."

Cameron lowered his voice and stuffed disappointment behind a rigid facade. "Because I want you there."

"Well, you should have thought about that before you gave Justin the keys to your truck."

Cameron hadn't given Justin the keys. Justin had stolen them while Cameron slept. "Dad. At least come to the awards ceremony."

"Why? So that they can call you up and hand you some worthless sheet of paper?"

"I'll be getting two chemistry awards. They're not worthless."

"You think that just because you're the only valedictorian this year, there are no consequences for that accident? You can't just brush it away." His frown disappeared, replaced by pure evil. "Enjoy the spotlight while you have it. These accolades may be the last you'll ever see."

Two and a half years earlier, his father had kept his word. He had not attended any part of Cameron's graduation. Afterward, every discussion between Cameron and his father had turned into an argument—not the explosive ones but the seething writhing kind that slowly blister the relationship, leaving festering sores after each confrontation. Such had been the argument about Wyoming. Though Uncle Nathan's offer likely had been well intended, it gave Cameron's father a veiled excuse to send Cameron to the farthest end of the world—a dubious blessing.

Cameron quickened his pace as he crossed in front of Carroll Hall, but a sudden vision slowed his feet to a stop. No one stood before him, yet every muscle slumped as for an instant he recalled Grandpa's smile, but the apparition flickered and vanished. The rain battering his skin stung, but the memory singed his soul. Grandpa was gone.

Cameron stared into the empty air a moment longer, then forced one foot forward and then the other, pulling him toward the chemistry building. Grandpa had guided him, even gently chastised him, but in everything, Grandpa had loved him. He had talked about the things Cameron would face, about love and faith, but mostly about the future—Cameron's future without Grandpa: an unimaginable future that had become the present.

He lengthened his stride as the rain beat harder against his head. Soon it ran down his back and soaked through against his skin. He tried to think of something, anything else. To his horror, Lydia and New Year's Eve came to mind. He remembered her gaze, cold and distant, as she closed the door. Though as beautiful as Rita, Lydia was like Esther. She had seen right through him.

Concentrate! He began to run. Uncle Nathan was wrong. A summer spent in the Wyoming boonies wouldn't change anything. It certainly wouldn't turn his father into a paternal paragon. Instead, his uncle had deprived him of the one bright spot in his life: a summer in Chapel Hill.

What was the next step in the formula? He raced down a set of steps. At the back entrance to the building, he slid his card through the security pad and flung the door open, letting it bang against the block wall. Another student ducked in behind him and dashed down the corridor. Cameron did not follow her but instead fell against the wall, his chest heaving, his eyes staring at the ceiling. Relief at last.

A minute later the door opened, and another student disappeared down the hall. When his breathing slowed, Cameron pushed himself away from the wall and walked to the large lecture auditorium. He dropped into a desk a third of the way up the tiered rows of seats. Slouching, he stared into blank space. Fifteen minutes later, Professor Krasotkin entered, gave instructions, and then handed out the exam—old school all the way.

A rustling of paper briefly filled the room as Cameron opened the exam and plunged headlong into the comforting world of numbers and formulas. The subject, thermodynamics, one of his favorites, tested his knowledge of the mathematical laws governing how fluids move in patterns of ever-changing symmetry. Answers followed in lines, stacked one below the other down the page. Time slipped by on the fringe of his awareness. Finally, he checked the time. Eight-fifty. Though he had finished the last question ten minutes earlier, a personal rule required that he not leave any exam until more than a third of his fellow students had handed in their tests and departed. He counted heads, but few had left.

Having worked too hard to let an unintended mathematical error deprive him of an A+, he carefully rechecked his answers. While he typed numbers into his calculator, the specter of the car dashing toward the headlights returned and washed a chill over him. Had the driver of the other car survived? He certainly hoped so. Regardless, it wasn't likely that the drunk driver who had careened past Cameron would have the kind of political connections that kept Justin out of prison. His father, the great Alan McDermit Sloane, attorney at law, had purged Justin's record, or so Justin had bragged. Cameron couldn't decide who was the bigger thug, father or son.

Long ago he had wondered whether Mr. Sloane's efforts had been directed against Justin, not in his favor, as if the father had worked to destroy the son who had embarrassed him. Cameron's father would never have that opportunity. Cameron had no plans to self-destruct. He tapped his pencil eraser against the desk and glanced at Dr. Krasotkin, seated at the front of the auditorium. When Cameron's father heard that the professor had encouraged Cameron to become a doctor, he had dismissed the professor's opinion. Other fathers bragged when their sons earned grades far below Cameron's GPA, but no accolade or award had been enough to earn his father's respect. After Trent moved out, nothing had been good enough.

Cameron drummed the pencil's eraser against the test, chiding himself. Esther and Professor Krasotkin were right. He needed to get over it. He turned back to his exam as the click of the calculator keys faded into the low drone of the ventilation unit. He checked another answer then glanced at the professor seated at the table. What kind of chemist filled his office with Russian and African art, diagrams, photographs, and other pieces of eclectic clutter? Accessible, inconspicuous, and prone to fits of dry wit, Dr. Krasotkin was a man whose skin fit him well, which was reason enough for Cameron to conceal his weekend partying.

Cameron read the next answer and flinched. He gasped and his heart pounded faster. *What a stupid mistake!* His stomach knotted as he erased three lines of numbers and letters. He replaced the valuation in the formula and wrote in the correct answer. After he'd verified his results, his pulse slowed. He relaxed into a comfortable slouch—with his right hand supporting his cheek, his left hand once again tapped his pencil against the test.

The sound of footsteps behind him pricked his attention. A student appeared, descended the steps along the wall, and dropped his test on the table. With a nod, Professor Krasotkin acknowledged the delivery; then he turned back to a magazine spread open before him. Cameron returned to his answers. Ten minutes later, he counted his classmates, heads lowered and pencils scribbling. Still too many remained. Two girls stood and descended the steps, dropped their papers on the desk, and left. Again the professor nodded and continued to read the magazine.

One by one, more students handed in their papers. Cameron took a final head count. Enough had left. He gathered his papers and descended the steps. When he dropped his test on the table, the professor picked it up and, without looking up, scanned his answers. Cameron's skin tingled. Should he wait or leave? The professor held up one hand, motioning for Cameron to wait. A long, uneasy silence passed before the professor looked up. "Why don't you take another minute?" He handed the test back.

Cameron's pulse pounded in his throat as he returned to his seat, but when he examined his calculations, his pulse plummeted. He had used the wrong chart. He flipped through the charts at the back of the exam, repeated the calculations, and wrote the correct answer. Again, he checked the numbers, stood, and descended the steps. When he placed the exam on the table, Professor Krasotkin looked up, nodded, and—as he had with all the other students—returned to the magazine.

Once out of the room, Cameron nearly danced along with the racing pulse of his heart. Grandpa! Professor Krasotkin was a great deal like Grandpa.

Happy to have the exam and semester finished, Cameron strode up South
Columbia Street. He smiled at the thought of the fraternity party that awaited
him. Interestingly, the very fraternity that had meant so much to his father
decades earlier had become Cameron's resort, a delightful reprieve from work
and worry. As long as he could remember, his father had pointed to fraternity
membership as the keystone of success, the nectar of life itself, the course of
prestige, confidences, and collateral. The bitter irony, by Cameron's estimation, was that—for him, it had been the exact opposite: an entertaining source
of liberation and libation.

While his father had warned him about the difficulty associated with
joining a fraternity, membership had fallen into Cameron's lap as easily as
manna from heaven. So easily that, when Trace, who had been a friend since
middle school science camp, chose to rush the fraternity, Cameron had joined
him—while ignoring the fact that it was the same fraternity his father joined.
And why not? Charity and fellowship were the basis of friendship. Thus, while
he watched out for his friends, they—Esther, Trace, Neil, and of course, Paul
watched out for him. His father had also foretold the difficulty of making
top grades at UNC—no partying! Again, Cameron had experienced quite the
opposite, though he vehemently disagreed with the derisive Duke student
chant that called UNC a "safety school." If such was true, then why bother to
become a Robinson Scholar? Besides, his fraternity brothers had been known
to throw parties in his honor after his grades brought up the frat's overall

GPA. But if he disliked his father's obsessive social networking, Cameron despised his gratuitous devotion to Bible studies and church. Having lost two of the most important people in his life, Grandpa and Lydia, Cameron had no time for his father's God—the one who'd left Cameron out to dry.

Halfway up the hill, a flashing blue light pierced the darkness, startling him. The accident! Almost three hours after the collision, floodlights set on poles still lit the scene. A small crowd looked on, though most had lost interest in the mangled cars. Shards of glass, puddles of radiator fluid, and fragments of metal littered the wet asphalt. Nearby, one car stood with its roof peeled back. A tow truck driver tied chains through the wheels of another battered car, the same car that earlier had careened past Cameron, securing it to the bed of his truck. Two police investigators still worked the scene.

As he approached a group of bystanders, a girl who wore her dark hair pulled up in a clip spoke above the general noise, "It could have been my mom in the car that was hit. I'm so glad it wasn't."

"I heard she was in town to help her daughter move home for the summer," noted another girl.

"The police took the other driver," a guy added. "He was so drunk; he didn't get hurt."

Cameron shivered and stepped back. Where was the EMS truck? Of course, it had left, but what about the woman? Was she ...? The nauseating smell of radiator fluid and burnt rubber flooded his head, wrenching his stomach. He turned and edged to the rear of the crowd where the lingering wind sent shadows, cast by the floodlights, dancing like demons. Looking straight ahead, he raced northward in long strides while his fertile imagination ran with abandon. The accident ... Justin ... and his cousin Aimee.

When he reached the tree that had earlier shielded him from the maniac, he stopped and turned back toward the brightly lit intersection. Darkness collapsed the air around him. *Run*, he thought. But where? The labs and his usual haunts weren't open. Cameron spun around and looked toward the white clapboard antebellum fraternity house with its wide porch and fluted two-story columns. The rusted muffler of a passing car momentarily blocked the cheerful noise that blared from inside. Again, he spun around toward the steaming wreckage as the memory of Uncle Nathan's voice rose above the din: "If you don't master your drinking habit, it will master you."

Sure, he'd partied almost as hard as he studied, but that didn't make him an alcoholic. He wasn't like the crazed driver. But who was his master—his anger or his ambition? More than ever he wanted to flee, someplace quiet and far away. The damp breeze, a visceral reminder of the earlier thunderstorms, wrapped around his legs and swirled upward until it ruffled his hair. His imagination revived memories of the dark, unforgiving hours after midnight on the weekend before he graduated from high school.

"Thanks for the ride." Paul opened the passenger's side door and climbed down from Cameron's late-model Ford F150.

"I owe you, man." Cameron nodded to one of the best friends a guy could have. "Thanks for listening ... and for taking Lydia home."

"What are friends for? Besides, you can thank me after you apologize to her. You'll do it Monday. Right?"

"Yeah. I owe it to her."

"Yes, you do. Oh, and if Justin offers you another blind date, ask for her name. Or say no."

"Yeah, well, it won't happen again. Anyway, I owe you one."

"Yes, you do," Paul laughed, a single, sharp but jovial retort, "but don't imagine that I will be so kind the next time you get drunk and ignore her."

"Lydia? She's a great kid." He shook his head. "Why didn't you or someone warn me about hangovers? I never want another one."

"Lydia's anything but a kid. Call her!"

"I will." Paul was right. Cameron hadn't intended to ignore or hurt her, but when someone handed him a beer, he didn't think. Instead, he took it while obsessing over the stupidity of having let Justin con him into taking a blind date without asking the obvious question, *What is her name?* He downed the second beer to quell his anger at Justin for telling Lydia that Cameron would be her date, while lying to Cameron, telling him that his date was "new in town." He took the third beer while trying to figure out how Justin knew that Cameron and Lydia were friends, a fact that Cameron had assiduously guarded.

None of his closest friends knew about his friendship with the petite brunette whose bright smile and quick wit had been a pleasant refuge precisely because she was keenly intelligent, discreet, and uncomplicated. In other words, she wasn't interested in dating him. For three years, they had been Monday evening friends, working together at the Park Street Diner, and he wanted to keep it that way. So he had taken the fourth beer while trying to find a way to explain his dilemma to her.

Thus, while he spent the day contemplating the unimaginable, several important facts had coalesced. First, he had broken a promise he had made to his grandfather, vowing not to drink, much less get drunk, before he graduated from high school. For three years, he'd kept his promise with little thought and no incidents. A week short of graduation, he demolished it. Second, he'd thrown his friendship with Lydia out the window by allowing his lack of alcohol tolerance to defeat his better instincts. Finally, a degree of sobriety had shamed him into the realization that she knew no one at the party except himself and Paul—and of course Justin. As a result, he had begged Paul to keep her company and to take her home. Paul had returned to the party and had driven Cameron home.

All in all, the night had been a snake pit of stupidity, but it had not been beyond redemption if, as Paul insisted, he found Lydia on Monday and apologized—which he planned to do. Afterward, he would move to Chapel Hill, she would go in her direction, and their friendship would die an unremarkable death. Cameron sighed. "She deserves better all the way around."

"Yes, she does."

"I'll talk to her first thing Monday. I promise."

Paul shut the door then leaned into the open window. "Are your folks back from Charlotte?"

"No. Dad stayed for church. Wahoo!"

"Don't be so cynical." Paul stepped back. "Tell your mom I said hi, and thanks again for the ride."

As he drove home, Cameron rehearsed various apologies that he might use when he saw Lydia on Monday, though none sounded like they'd work. Rather than grabbing a snack from the kitchen, he let his wretched stomach send him upstairs where he climbed into bed, clothes and all. Since his mother wasn't home, she wouldn't chide him about changing.

Sometime later, in the dark hours of the night, the door chime rang.

Cameron groaned and then shuffled down the wide, curving foyer stairway and opened the front door. "Justin. What do you want?"

"Dad kicked me out, and Julia's on a rant." He teetered sideways. "She toked something weird. So here I am."

And drunk! "That's unusual?" One eyebrow jerked upward.

"What?"

"Never mind." Seeing Justin list sideways, Cameron opened the door wider. "You can sleep on the sofa upstairs, in the TV room. You know the way. I'm going back to bed." Too tired to make sure Justin did as he was told, Cameron returned to his room, changed clothes, and dropped into sleep.

The doorbell chimed, awakening him. He looked at the clock. Two-thirty A.M. *What now?* The chime rang again.

"I'm coming." Cameron opened the door and blinked. Two police officers stood before him. "Yes, sir?" He ran one hand through his hair, studying their stern faces.

"Do you own a silver Ford F150?" One officer asked.

"Uh, yeah. My uncle gave it to me."

"Then this is for you." The officer pulled an official paper from a small, thick black notebook. It was a warrant to inspect Cameron's house.

Surprised, curious, and a bit offended, but too tired to argue, Cameron let them in. They asked to see the liquor cabinet but found it locked. "I don't have a key," Cameron volunteered. "Why are you interested in my truck?"

"Did Justin Sloane have your permission to drive it?"

"No, sir."

"Do you know where he is?"

"He's upstairs, at least I think he is. Hey! Justin!"

The officers exchanged glances, leaving Cameron to imagine that something was very wrong.

"We'll give you a ride to your truck, but you'll need to find another means of getting home."

Neither officer had hinted about the sight that awaited Cameron or the reason he would need an alternate ride home. Instead, they took him to a scene too horribly similar to the one that now littered South Columbia Street in Chapel Hill. That night, almost three years earlier, Cameron had arrived in time to see Aimee Duncan as EMS workers lifted her mother into the emergency aid truck. Mrs. Duncan had survived for a day but died the following morning. Later, Aimee had called to tell Cameron that she didn't blame him. She blamed Justin and only Justin. And while Cameron had been grateful for Aimee's forgiveness, he also wanted her best friend Lydia Carpenter to forgive him, but Justin had turned difficult into impossible.

On Monday, two days later, Cameron had seen Lydia at school but had avoided her. Summer had followed, along with a thousand excuses that strangled his voice whenever Paul suggested that he call her. Cameron's memory of his father's face and his anger—hot as asphalt on an August afternoon—never faded. "When Justin came here bombed-out drunk"—his father's voice had sizzled like rain falling on that same sun-parched pavement— "you shouldn't have left him alone. You knew better. You ignored your responsibility and as good as murdered my cousin."

His father was wrong. Cameron had not ignored his responsibility. Justin—and Justin alone—was responsible for what he did. Cameron's artless retreat from Lydia, however, had shielded him from culpability for a year and a week, but not a day longer.

A burst of laughter from the fraternity house drew him back to the present —the party. A sigh leaked into the night air—Lydia was in the past. History. End of story. More laughter erupted from the house. Well, at least Neil and Trace were there. They'd watch out for him. Rita would also be there, waiting from him. What about Rita? Cameron closed his eyes and imagined the Park Street Diner, its motley denizens, and Lydia. For a moment, the massive oak tree blocked his view of the house where Rita waited for him, looking for his return from his exam. The tree's spreading canopy wrapped him in peaceful memories of Lydia's cheerful banter.

"Hey, Cameron." A hearty voice spoke from the direction of Hill Hall. "What are you watching?"

Cameron turned as an underclassman from a neighboring fraternity stepped into the street's ambient light. His convivial smile returned. "Nothing."

"I'd invite you to join our party," the young man nodded knowingly, "but it sounds like your house has a better one."

"Not true! Y'all throw a great party."

Cameron bundled up his aborted attempt to find happiness and joined the sophomore as the two walked toward the frat houses. While the younger man talked, Cameron nodded but paid more attention to the wet lumps of matted oak leaves that lined the street's gutter and littered the gnarly roots of the ancient trees that separated the sidewalk from the street. Through the preceding summer—now long past—the leaves had been a sheltering canopy. Autumn had turned them brown and scattered them. Winter's harsh winds then blew them into the gutter where the snow and ice turned them black. Now, as spring invited new leaf buds to swell and burst, the half-rotted leaves were nothing more than debris. Like the leaves, Cameron had been cast off, and worse yet, sent to Wyoming without thought—debris with no means of redemption.

"See ya next fall," the young man called, as they parted ways.

Cameron reached the frat house and crossed its wide porch but hesitated short of the door, recalling how Professor Krasotkin and Uncle Nathan had conspired against him. His fingers knotted into a fist and just as quickly relaxed. *Why bother?* He stared at the screened door. Why couldn't his father leave him alone? *Who knows?* But at the moment, he at least had a choice: Party time!

He opened the screened door. Music blaring from multiple speakers greeted him through a smoky haze. A few of the brothers, having finished exams, had returned home. Others sequestered themselves in their rooms, cramming for their last final. Most, along with their girlfriends, relaxed in the main room, resigned to the finality of their grades and the unlikely expectation that a perfect exam score would bring up their GPA.

Cameron dropped his backpack next to Patrick, Trace's roommate. He eyed Patrick, eyed his beer, grinned at Patrick, and then helped himself to a taste. "It's warm! Ugh. And to think that I thought this," he tousled Patrick's thick stand of curly red hair, "meant you were Irish and knew better."

"Yeah, well, I am, but I've been celebrating since five."

"Hasn't being one of my best buddies taught you anything?" Cameron laughed and then drained Patrick's beer.

"Yeah, I've got to stay sober enough to keep you out of trouble."

"Not tonight." Cameron grinned at his freckle-faced friend and then poured a glass of rum and fruit drink, but mostly rum. He turned and flopped into one of the abused but well-padded side chairs.

"You aced the exam, didn't you?" Patrick half smiled, half snarled. "What I want to know is why I have to beat my brains out while you skid through chemistry half drunk."

"I'm blessed!" Cameron laughed, as a slender yet shapely young woman sat down on his lap and crossed her long legs over one arm of the chair.

"Are you finished?" Rita asked.

"With exams, yes. With Bacardi, no."

Rita ran the tip of one finger around his lips while her other hand slid through his hair. "You take this so seriously."

"Of course."

"Why?"

"Tradition. It's the bane of the Asher family." Behind his half grin, half-formed memories of his uncle's talk merged with vague pictures of Wyoming. He took another long drink and then lifted his glass. "To tradition."

"You're winning, of course." Indifference leached through Rita's words, despite her upbeat tone.

"Of course." Cameron tipped the glass back, emptying it.

Rita leaned closer until he saw only her dark brown eyes. "I was just wondering," she said, brushing his ear with her lips, "if somewhere in all that genius, you'd noticed what time it is?"

"Yeah. It's almost ten."

Patrick stepped closer. "Hey, Rita, what are you going to do without Cam all summer?"

Momentarily interrupting her focus on Cameron, Rita glared at Patrick long enough to gain his attention then whisked her attention back to Cameron, dismissing Patrick altogether. She smiled sweetly at Cameron, pouting her lips, puffy and deliciously wet. "After all the fun we've had, you're not *really* going to leave me here, are you?"

Well. He told her where he would spend the summer. What did she expect? Cameron nudged her to stand, retrieved his glass from her long fingers, and filled it with rum. "You're right. We do have fun."

Neil reached for Cameron's glass.

"Not so fast." Cameron held the glass beyond his roommate's reach.

Neil relented, and Cameron took a long slow drink. Then he grinned. "I just finished my last exam. I've earned this." He tipped a slightly loopy smile at Neil as he wrapped an arm around Rita. With the glass in one hand, he lifted a long lock of her brown hair and sniffed. The scent of her soft perfume coaxed a smile. He brushed her cheek. "We have a good time together. What else matters?"

The rum worked its magic. With one arm around Rita and a glass of Bacardi in the other hand, he danced her across the floor to a slow rumba, the rhythm of which only he heard. Every few steps, he took a sip until the glass was again empty. Despite the rum and his best efforts, the emptiness inside his chest grew, pushing everything else aside. "One minute," he whispered into her ear. As he half-filled his glass, he saw and ignored the glances that Patrick and Neil exchanged. He returned to the chair and pulled Rita back to his lap.

Neil walked over and again reached for his glass. "Why don't you wait a while before finishing this one off?"

"No need." Cameron glared at his roommate, took a long drink, and then nuzzled Rita's neck. "Ignore him." He kissed her cheek. "Ever since Christmas break he thinks it's his duty to police me. I'm not driving anywhere tonight, and you're content with having a good time. Right?"

"Yeah." Rita smiled as her fingers brushed his cheek. She scowled at Neil. "That's right."

To emphasize her choice, she kissed Cameron, who responded by wrapping his arms around her. Her shoulders swayed as the kiss lingered, slow and warm. Neil retreated. Finally Rita sat up and smiled. *How nice*, but rather than kissing her he stood before brushing his lips against hers. Satisfied that she craved more, he embraced and kissed her again—a long, slow, moist kiss.

When he finished, Rita pulled him close, pressing her chest against him. With some senses blissfully excited and others delightfully dulled, a sly grin crept across Cameron's face. He winked at Neil and Patrick as he led Rita to the door. With his arm draped over her shoulder, they wandered toward the small brick rental house north of Rosemary Street. Once in his room, he pulled Rita down onto his bed; then he closed his eyes and dreamed. With each kiss and caress, the emptiness within his heart retreated, replaced by a passion that Rita was welcome to assume, at least for now, was meant only for her.

6

When Cameron awoke shortly after nine the next morning, Rita was absent, but she would return. He threw some clothes on and wandered out to the front porch, as such a structure might be called. The porch included a stoop with access to the front door and a short staircase down to a larger porch that wrapped a corner of the brick veneered house. Triangular-shaped chips of terra cotta tile decorated the porch and stoop; both lacked a cover or roof. A low wrought-iron handrail flanked the stoop and surrounded the larger porch. A rustic, notably weedy garden, barely a foot wide, followed the footing of the lower porch. At six feet wide, the porch served as an excellent place to relax.

Cameron pulled a cheap, plastic lawn chair close enough to the iron railing to brace one foot on it. Thus settled in, he pulled a baseball cap down over his forehead and tipped the chair back. Donning a pair of sunglasses to shield his eyes from the bright sun that filtered through the yard's dense canopy of pines and hickory, he rested his other foot on the chipped-tile porch and rocked, striking a delightfully nonchalant pose. Trace joined him for a while as the two watched one of their roommates pack his car. At noon, Neil pulled up a chair. "Ah-h. Finally finished! So, when are you leaving?"

"In a while." Cameron tipped back on the chair's rear legs.

Neil also leaned back. "Was that your dad on the phone first thing this morning?"

"Yeah."

"What did he want?"

"He wanted to make sure I'd called his friend at the business school."

"And did you?"

"Yeah."

"You're not caving, are you?"

Cameron rocked the chair and thought about the gray-haired business professor who had invited Cameron to dinner two months earlier. He had seen his grades and expressed his desire for Cameron to apply for grad school, but he had only accepted the dinner invitation to get his father off his back. He had no plans to apply.

Neil grinned. "Okay, I assume from the silence that you stood up to your dad."

"No. I called. Last week."

"Where's Rita?"

"I don't know."

"What's she doing for the summer?" Neil's smile faded. "No, the right question is what are you two doing when you get back in August?"

Cameron took off his glasses and rubbed his eyes. Would he and the brown-eyed beauty even be together in the fall? He could do far worse than Rita, the darling of the fraternity and his constant weekend companion since late January. But.

"I take it that you still don't know."

Obviously Neil was not impressed by Cameron's indecision, but he didn't understand Cameron's dilemma. "Rita isn't easy to ignore ... or dump." Indeed not. "And I don't ghost."

"But you'll lead her on."

"No."

"Then what's wrong with her? But hey, I thought Addie was nice. Do you even know what you want?"

Cameron studied him and then looked away. "Sure I do."

When two housemates joined them, the conversation turned to other topics. Cameron listened, nodded, and shrugged appropriately but thought about Rita and that amorphous blob known as the future. What would a future with her be like? Would she love him if he was poor? Would she adore him when he was old and gray? Unfortunately, he was certain that if Lydia ever forgave him, if she ever loved him, she would never leave him, but Rita wasn't Lydia. When the others left, Cameron turned to Neil. "The truth is, I don't want to lose Rita, but I'm not ready to encourage her."

"I suggest you make up your mind."

"Why? Rita's not like Addie. It might work."

Six months earlier, Addie, a tall and attractive pre-med student, had asked about her future with Cameron. She too had been with him every weekend, night and day, but the pleasure had been fleeting. When Addie was nearby, Cameron had thought about her, but as soon as she left, memories of his once-upon-a-time friend Lydia had slowly returned.

Neil rocked in his chair. "Cam, I know this isn't the coolest suggestion, but have you ever considered just dating a girl and not jumping in bed with her? Don't glare at me like that. It's not a religious thing. It makes sense. Did you ever *really* get to know Addie?"

"I didn't just sleep with her. I thought she was the one."

"It looked that way to everyone else. What happened?"

"I don't know. One day I woke up and ... man, I thought she was it ... then nothing! That's when it hit me. If I couldn't love Addie, then okay, what *do* I want? Maybe that perfect girl doesn't exist." Of course, that brilliant thought had led Cameron to invite Lydia to Paul's New Year's Eve party four months earlier.

"I'm glad to hear your heart isn't a total wasteland." Neil closed his eyes and turned his face toward the sun. "So what about Rita?"

"She's cool." *Yeah, well.* "But ..." He twirled his cap. *But ...* He set the cap on his head, pulled the brim down over his eyes, and leaned back. "I want someone who's exciting, even when she's mad at me. I used to know someone like that."

"What happened?"

"We went different ways."

Speak of an understatement! Cameron leaned his head back and watched a squirrel leap from the spindly branches of one tree to another as both branches swung wildly beneath its weight. Should he tell Neil about Lydia? Maybe. Then again, Neil would never believe him: he hadn't joined Cameron and Paul, after finishing their freshman year in college, when they attended the graduation ceremony for Chalmers High School.

From the upper bleachers of the high school's football stadium, Cameron and Paul had a clear view of the ceremony's dais which stood at the fifty-yard line and set fifteen yards in from the sideline of the grassy field. Between the dais and the sideline, rows of black-robed graduates waited in folding chairs to hear their name called. A capuchin-capped school board member announced the next name. "Madeline Cantrell."

Paul leaned close. "Can you believe that was us last year?"

Ms. Cantrell crossed the stage and nodded as she took her diploma and shook the principal's hand. The speaker called the next name. "Lydia Carpenter."

Cameron put his fingers to his mouth, ready to let loose with a loud whistle and applause as his former friend stepped onto the dais, but a breeze caught her hair, lifting it. Her below-the-knee length robe billowed, high-lighting her slender legs, accentuated by thin spike-heeled shoes. Then she did something that nearly knocked him from his seat. She turned to the audience and smiled. It was a simple act—soft, kind, and feminine. His fingers stopped before reaching his lips as he stared, undone by the sight of her. His cheerful companion at the soup kitchen was no longer a kid. She was more than beautiful. She was stunning.

Cameron watched the branches rebound as the squirrel scampered away. "I wondered if she'd changed, the girl, that is."

"Have you talked to her?"

Cameron hunched deeper into his chair, not an easy feat considering the chair's flimsy construction. "Yeah. Over Christmas break, I took her to a New Year's Eve party at Paul's brother's place. I guess I was expecting something different."

"Like what?"

· "I thought maybe she might have changed ... or something. I don't know." *Wow*, he thought, *being both truthful and willfully deceptive is way too easy*. If Neil so wished, he was welcome to assume that she was neither fascinating nor wonderful. So much for telling him the truth, but big deal! Lydia was gone, and Rita was here. She liked him, and he wasn't ready to let her go, at least not completely.

Cameron stood and looked down at his roommate, who probably wanted a more detailed answer. He wasn't going to get one. "I've got a few things left to pack. When Rita comes back, tell her ... tell her whatever you want."

An hour later, Rita returned. She found Neil, still sitting on the porch. "Where's Cameron?"

"I'm right here." Having finished packing, he had come to the front door, expecting to join Neil.

As he opened the screen door, Rita sauntered to him with a Styrofoam cup in hand. "I know how much you like coffee. It's the Ocracoke blend from Southern Seasons. I thought it would help keep you awake on the drive home."

Cameron took the cup and kissed her cheek. "Thanks."

She obviously expected more from him, but he had nothing to offer. Nothing. She followed him to the parking area at the rear of the house. She leaned against his Ford Escape's rear passenger door. Beneath a Carolina blue sky dotted with puffy clouds, he piled the last two boxes of books and a pillow into the back of the SUV.

She coiled her finger around the collar of his shirt. "Why *are* you spending the whole summer out in Wyoming?"

"Sounded like a good idea."

"But why won't you write?"

He stepped back, pulled down the rear door, and pushed until the latch caught. Straightening his back, he turned and faced her, a safe yard's distance separating them. "Maybe I will." He pinched his lips lest something inappropriate should slip out—something close to the truth. "Well, see ya."

"Is that all you're going to say?" She took a step closer, her eyes flirtatious but sad. "When we make love, it's like there's no one else in the world. Doesn't that mean anything?"

Cameron jammed his hands into his hip pockets and stared at the ground. He kicked a loose stone. What could he say? He wanted to love her, but— Maybe if the summer helped him forget Lydia, then he and Rita could start over in the fall. Maybe.

He lifted his eyes, but when he met her gaze, the truth escaped. "You deserve better than me."

Turning away, he opened the driver's door and climbed in. As he drove west toward Chalmers along Interstate 85, he turned the music up until it drowned out the noise in his head. Far down the interstate, his mother awaited him. She had called three times while he packed and twice more as he drove home. At least someone would be glad to see him. All too soon, though, he would kiss her goodbye and board a plane for the distant, lonely rangeland of Wyoming.

7

The dull rattle of two wooden cogs turning, grinding, but not quite connecting filled one of Lydia's ears while the other remained blissfully buried in her pillow. Not yet ready to awaken, she heaved a sleepy sigh and reached up to pet Beatrice, the cat that lay curled next to her pillow. She stretched one leg, sliding it between the sheets until her foot nudged a warm, immovable object. Another cat—Mia. Ah yes, she was home, and all was right with the world.

Beatrice nuzzled Lydia and licked her cheek, but the touch of her scratchy tongue sent alarm bells clanging right down to her toes. Lydia sat bolt upright, at which Beatrice scrambled off the bed. *I forgot!* She threw back the covers, pulled on shorts and a pullover, grabbed a pair of deck shoes, and then dashed down the hall, skipping breakfast. She drove to the marina on the western shore of Glenlaurel Lake. There she found Aimee setting the rigging on her father's Flying Scot. "Good morning, and I'm sorry," she called as she raced toward the sailboat. "I forgot to set my alarm."

"No problem. Hop in." Aimee finished tightening the main halyard. "I'll be the mate today."

A gentle breeze sent smooth ripples into the marina that stood behind a sheltering point of land that jutted out into the lake. Lydia hopped into the stern and checked the centerboard, tiller, rudder, sail, and various lines as Aimee pushed off. Though the reservoir was not large, its north-south orientation often, as today, channeled the prevailing wind into an even draw. It was a good day to sail.

When the sailboat passed the point, the breeze cupped the sail and pulled them out into the lake. Lydia set the boom and rudder while Aimee fixed the centerboard and set the jib to match.

"Wahoo!" Aimee exclaimed as the wind tipped the boat, sending it skipping across the water. With the wind whipping tendrils of her ponytail across her face, both girls leaned back, shifting their weight to balance the pull of the wind. Lydia wedged the mainsheet into a cam cleat. With the mainsheet in hand—and the tiller extended, she joined Aimee. Up and down the lake they raced, running northward and tacking southward.

"Here comes a gust!" Aimee pointed at a patch of waves, burnished with windblown ripples. Lydia watched two lengths of yarn that Mr. Duncan had tied to the shrouds to show wind direction and matched the angle of the boom. The boat dipped slightly as both girls cheered it on, all the while holding on and smiling from ear to ear. As the sun rose into the sky, motorboats and their wakes appeared in increasing numbers. Content with having had the lake to themselves for almost two whole hours, they eased the sail and set a leisurely pace.

"So," Lydia asked with one eye on the waves and the other on Aimee, "how was it at Clemson? And how's Mason?"

"He's fine. I loved my design classes, but sophomore slump nearly killed me. I'd been warned, but not nearly enough." Aimee brushed aside a few windblown tendrils of hair. "Dad had to come down and hold my hand. I'm such a baby!" She twirled the loose end of the jib sheet, making loops like a jump-rope. "How about you?"

Lydia laughed. "I discovered that in the land of Type AAs, a simple Type A like me has to ramp it up a notch. I picked mechanical engineering because I like the job prospects but also the program. My classmates are competitive, but not the in-your-face competitors of biomedical engineering. Still, in February, I was sure they'd thrown me into Jordan Lake without a life jacket and expected me to swim fast enough to catch the lifesaver they'd thrown to me. It, though, was of the mind to float farther and farther away. The concept of 'sink or swim' took on a whole new meaning, but I earned the respect of a professor who put me in touch with a research project. So plugging ahead while gasping for air paid off."

"Better you than me." For a while, the conversation continued much as it had in texts throughout the spring until Aimee's face took on a look that often preceded a comment that hewed a little too close to some unmentionable truth. "Are you still seeing Tanner?"

"Seeing each other? That's a stretch. We study together, some times. He makes a point of meeting me for dinner—a lot. We hang with the same people—a lot with Intervarsity, though he has saved a seat—squeezed me in, at several basketball games. But he never asks me out." She shook her head. "Couples at least hold hands. We don't. We're friends, but it works. That said, he isn't holding someone else's hand." Lydia laughed, but Aimee didn't join in. "We write and text. The end. —Wake coming."

Aimee let out the jib as the boat waddled over the waves, but her body language clarified the situation: the distraction was momentary. She had another purpose in mind. "Well," she began, spinning honey into her voice, sweet but not cloying, "what about Cameron? I think you two are cute together."

"Ready to starboard." Lydia lifted the mainsheet from its cleat and turned the vessel's nose into the wind. The sail luffed as she and Aimee slipped to the opposite side of the boat and settled into the seat. "When did you ever see us together?"

"A couple doesn't have to be seen together for others to know that they like each other." A distinctly contrary smile crossed Aimee's face. "I heard he's on his way home today."

"A couple?" *Tsk!* Lydia tightened the sail. "And your point?"

"Have you talked to him since New Year's?"

"Surely you jest." Lydia scrolled through a list of topics to turn the discussion away from Cameron. The wind, though, had other plans as it grabbed the sail and yanked the boat forward. Caught off guard, she released the mainsheet from its cleat and let several inches of the cord run through her hand, slowing the craft and erasing her imagined list. Determined not to let the moment get away, she blurted her last disjointed thought—something about gyroscopes and how they continue to revolutionize technology.

Aimee, though, couldn't have looked less interested. "Nope. You're not getting off that easily." She shook her head. "I know how you feel. Your heart says one thing and your head another."

"No, not really."

"Well, listen anyway."

Lydia smiled at her dear friend, leaned back, and acceded to her fate.

"I know Cameron let you down, but he called ... and it wasn't a half-hearted call. Aren't you curious to know why he called and why he blew it?"

"No."

Aimee waved away any possible offense Lydia might mount, "I won't excuse what he did, but it sounded more klutzy than cruel. I don't think the evening went the way he expected. I say that because, when his grandfather died, something happened that he can't get out of his head."

Lydia frowned. "Those two thoughts are wildly disconnected."

"Not really. I believe you're both central and incidental to whatever it is."

"No, I'm not."

"Silence! I've had plenty of time to think about what happened three years ago, a few months ago, and six years ago. For me, it boils down to some very mixed-up messages about what is and isn't fair.

"Cameron isn't the type who tests the limits. He's loyal and doesn't turn truth into whatever he thinks he can get away with. If anything, he's acting as if 'truth' has him by the nape of the neck. But he isn't stupid. Say what you want, but he's one of the good guys. They're the ones who race in to help, even at their peril.

"But they also know that any of them, even Tanner, could be victims of false accusations. Of course, there are those where a woman makes a claim and is believed—without inspection. The guy is guilty, and the accuser is innocent. The unintended consequences, however, erode the guy's existence—just as the wake of a motorboat batters the shore long after the boat has passed from sight."

"Where are you going with this?"

"I feel sorry for the good guys. Dad's one of them, and I've seen what he goes through now that he's starting to date. It's just as tough for them as it is for us, but we ... women seem to have forgotten, or misplaced, the fact that guys need us—and I'm not the 'us' that Dad needs. When hyperbole is thrown around like peanut shells at a barn dance, the truth gets lost. Tanner, Mason, and even Cameron can try to scratch the bull's-eye off their chest, but no one cares. It's a mixed-up world with misplaced assumptions about what's right. Reflection and nuance require too much time, so baseless claims go unchallenged."

Aimee arched a brow and made sure Lydia saw it. "No, your claims against Cameron aren't baseless, but we're not silent weaklings. We're strong. Unfortunately, we use it to get our backs up when some guy doesn't do what we think he should. As Christian women, we're called to use our heads, examine the evidence, and defend good men." She shifted her shoulders and turned a blithe smile into the wind. "Think about this. We can look at an issue from ten different directions and then file our conclusions because God built that into us, probably because he thought of it as an asset. We abuse that ability when, long afterward, we pull out those filed conclusions and misuse them. Guys don't do that. They go from A to B to C to D." As she listed each letter, she wagged her finger at the sail. "Unlike us, they'd rather fix something than revisit A. When they get to F, A is ancient history. But not for us." She again arched a brow at Lydia. "This isn't to say that they forgive and forget ... They definitely remember. Still, to them, rehashing stuff is a waste of time.

"That isn't to say they can't obsess. Dad obsesses. When he does, he spins his wheels, sometimes burning right through to the axle. My uncle recently divorced after thirty-plus years of marriage because his ex-wife kept dredging things up—sometimes in front of me. Nothing was too little. My uncle just wanted to move on. That's Cameron, but he can't. Something's eating at him, keeping him stuck."

Lydia rolled her eyes but also half-smiled, knowing Aimee was just getting started. "Ready to come about."

Aimee switched to the opposite side and continued, "Here's my point: has he lied to you?"

"Well, that depends. When is saying nothing a lie?"

"True, both lying and saying nothing have consequences. But while lying hurts others, saying nothing often hurts the person who fails to speak. For example, when Christ showers us with mercy but we do nothing, we hurt ourselves by being our natural selves, not our redeemed selves. Right? Cameron and I got together when he was home for Thanksgiving. We had fun, but afterward, I was more convinced than ever that he's one of the good guys and that he's not happy."

"I feel cheerfully peripheral to his issues. Thank you ever so much."

"Humph! My point is about strength and where we get it. When you get knocked down, you get back up. I couldn't have gone through losing Mom without you. And I'm just as certain that Cameron also needs you."

Lydia frowned. "He has a strange way of showing it."

Aimee raised her index finger, signaling for a pause, which Lydia granted with a nod. "When life isn't fair," she continued, "you and I go on. Cameron can't. When his grandfather, Judge Asher, died, a delightful glint in Cameron's eyes flickered and went out. Before that, he went to church and took on life with a smile. Afterward, he wouldn't talk about God or countenance hearing others talk about faith. He wouldn't stop the conversation or get angry. He'd simply walk away—no big deal. Now, imagine how this boat would behave if you let go of the tiller in a strong wind. All kinds of thing would happen, none of them good. Well, that's what he did. Cameron let go of the tiller and, instead, took a strong dose of society's quick-fix antidote for misery."

"I heard about Addie, his most recent 'fix.'"

"He broke up with her." Aimee pointed her finger at Lydia, "Before he called you. Which is the reason I want you to cut him some slack."

Lydia sighed. "Wake coming." She let out the mainsheet. "You haven't convinced me that I have any part in this. Cameron is ... *was* one of the happiest people I knew." As the boat regained its level, Lydia joined Aimee and set the boat into a comfortable broad reach. "His parents are happily married. His father happily owns a successful insurance company. He was the happy star of the golf team and one of the happiest, best-liked guys in school. Girls drooled over him. What doesn't he have?"

Aimee's eyebrow flickered upward as a mirthless laugh escaped her lips. "Misery can masquerade as happiness, and accolades can mask misery. Cameron may have given up on God, but I don't believe that God gave up on him, which doesn't mean he'll prevent Cameron from making some really stupid decisions. Cameron knows he's partly to blame for those issues, but that truthful self-awareness means that a big mountain is standing on his foot. He's going to have to climb that mountain to get it off his foot. Look at it another way. Justin Sloane is miserable because his family makes dysfunctional TV families look cotton-candy wholesome. Knowing this, I've learned to feel sorry for him—deeply sorrowful, enough to stop hating him because hate can destroy me. I won't have that. So, instead, I pray for him. It might take something bad to change Justin, but something good could change Cameron. Please, be patient with him. And kind."

Skepticism got the best of Lydia, painting a wrinkled frown and narrowing her eyes. "You know something about Cameron that you're not telling me. What is it?"

"Mom said that something pernicious began to grow inside his family during the summer of Judge Asher's illness, right after you moved to Chalmers. Everyone knew and loved the judge, but when he died, Mom said a cloud settled over the house. That perfect family fell apart. Yeah, they have a great veneer. Mr. Asher was a godsend for my family after Mom died. His agents walked us through each step and went far beyond necessity." Aimee paused to catch Lydia's attention. "Mrs. Asher and mom were good friends. She is one of the reasons I will always come to Cameron's defense." Aimee turned her face into the wind. "After Mom died, I learned that tragedy forces us into making decisions we never thought we'd make ... not all of which are good. So we must pray.

"Your grandmother didn't punch a card, asking for a child with Downs, but she loved your Uncle Steve and surrounded him with love. Who knew I'd lose Mom while I was in high school, but out of the void, I learned to burrow into the depths of God's love for me. Now I pray for Dad, one of the good guys. Modern society can frown all it wants on marriage, but God doesn't." Aimee paused as a windblown tear trickled across her temple. "Sometimes, I wake up from a dream sobbing because, moments earlier, Mom was alive, and we were doing something together. I don't blame God or Cameron." She turned to Lydia, who recoiled from the intensity of her gaze, a look that read her soul.

"Ready to come about." Even as Lydia made the turn, a pall fell over her, enveloping her, raining shame down on her. "I'm sorry. I'm being childish." Aimee had fought a tough battle and won. "I'm glad you love Cameron. And clearly, I don't know him as well as I thought I did." She waited for Aimee, hoping she'd say something while praying for words of absolution. None came. Aimee wasn't in the mood to let Lydia off lightly. "If he calls, I'll be civil—for you. I promise." *However, he isn't going to call.* "And yes, life is unfair. And for some, it's terribly cruel. A few weeks ago, I made a new friend whose life would have destroyed me. The cruelest cut came when her mother put her on the pill rather than guiding her. She was fourteen. That was brutal on so many levels because it said, 'I don't want your mess.' I could say she treated her daughter like trash to spare her from picking up the pieces, but she dehumanized her daughter. That's beyond heartless."

"What did you say? Is she a Christian?"

"We talked, and no, she's not even a marginal Christian, but I like her. She has a biting humor—which I love!"

"You would!" Aimee laughed and pulled the jib sheet from its cleat. "We'd better get back."

Lydia turned the boat toward the marina. Aimee was right. People don't request misery. They asked for happiness. Nana loved Uncle Steve and drew her family together. "When I was little, I dreaded our annual visits to Chalmers because I was afraid of Uncle Steve. I couldn't see his tender heart, but Ben, Nana's longtime companion, taught me to love Uncle Steve. Ben was like a father to Uncle Steve. After all, Grandpa Thomas died when Uncle Steve was around four or five. So when Ben died, Uncle Steve was more upset than anyone. I wanted to go to Ben's funeral, but Mom and Aunt Deborah, on impulse, flew to Venice, Italy—and took me with them. Ben was like the centerboard of our family. He kept us upright, no matter how the wind blew. Sometimes I think Ben and Nana married but didn't tell anyone." For the first time all morning, sorrow joined the breeze, blowing across her face. "I miss Ben. I miss my uncle, but I won't even try to imagine how much you miss your mom."

Aimee seemed to drift but then returned, "While life hasn't been fair, it is good." As she spoke, the boat approached the middle of the lake. Without another apparent thought, a smile whisked away the glint of sadness. "Let's go for it!"

Lydia pulled the mainsheet from its cleat and caught the wind. The boat skidded across two wakes as the marina drew closer. When it was a short distance away, Lydia let out the sail and Aimee lowered the jib. Moments later the boat slid behind the protective point and into the harbor. Lydia loosened the lanyard that held the mainsail, encouraging it to spill wind.

As Aimee gathered the jib, a thought crept out from behind a forgotten curtain. "Of all my memories of Ben, the best are threaded together by the way he looked at Nana. I can't imagine why they tried to hide their love. It was too obvious. Regardless, I want a man who loves me the way Ben loved Nana."

Lydia hopped onto the dock and grabbed a bumper, placing it between the boat and the dock. "Let's get this put away. Mom and Nana are expecting me for lunch at Aunt Marrah's house."

"Of course I'll invite Nana," Marrah muttered aloud to the empty kitchen. *Sigh. But only for you, Lydia.* She tore off a piece of plastic wrap and covered the bowl of freshly made chicken salad. Under any other circumstance, Marrah was loath to invite her mother, but Lydia had insisted. Marrah gently lifted the heavy bowl, using her right hand and her left forearm, then slid it into the refrigerator. "Most people would gladly invite their mother to lunch," Marrah grumbled, "but Lois Carpenter isn't their mother."

Marrah placed the dirty spoon in the dishwasher and wiped off the counter. With the chicken salad, rolls, shortbread cookies, and sweet tea ready, she walked out onto the deck that stretched across the back of her house. Thirty feet below the wide deck and eighty feet (perhaps) out from the house, waves lapped against the shoreline of Glenlaurel Lake. Sets of stairs, set along a concrete path, marched down the slope to a small deck attached to the rocky shoreline. From it, a narrow ramp stretched thirty feet to a floating dock that housed Jake's twenty-six-foot Cobalt cuddy cabin motorboat. Two kayaks, hanging from the dock's roof supports, and the Lightening Class sailboat bobbing between two red buoys completed his flotilla.

Jake bought the Cobalt after selling his Master Craft ski-boat, having acquiesced to Marrah's insistence that he'd outgrown slalom skiing—which he insisted was the only way to ski. Jake, who loved just about anything related to water, purchased the house overlooking the lake on the condition that his close friend Nate Stedman would design a terrace for Marrah—who hated everything related to the water, to unite their disparate interests. Nate had succeeded masterfully.

His design included a slate-encrusted terrace that Marrah called her *Xanadu*. Located midway between the house and lake—adjacent to the stairs and walkway, the terrace half nestled into the rocky hillside and half projected from it—supported by an eight feet tall stone-faced retaining wall. A steel-and-wire handrail capped the retaining wall and served as a backdrop for a dozen clay pots from which a host of colorful flowers and vines spilled. A dining table with chairs for six stood near the center of the terrace and in front of a stone fireplace that faced the path and stairs.

Marrah surveyed the table where a vase of cut flowers, plates, napkins, and cutlery awaited Lydia and Lydia's mother Anne—and of course, Lois. Satisfied, she turned, ready to return the kitchen, when a hawk perched atop a tall, nearby oak tree caught her eye. As she watched, the raptor spread its wings, lifted into the sky, and then spiraled upward. In an instant, it tipped its wings and flew directly overhead. As it passed, she spun, pinning her hand against the railing. "Ow-ah!" Excruciating pain shot from her wrist, up through her elbow and into her shoulder. The Norco she had taken earlier in the morning had worn off. Holding her wrist to her chest, she returned to her bathroom for another pill. *Lois thinks I take too many of these. She'd think otherwise if it had been her wrist.*

Marrah returned downstairs just as the doorbell rang. She opened the door and beamed. "Lydia! I'm so glad to see you. Anne, your little girl is all grown up, and so beautiful."

Marrah nodded to Lois, then stepped back, inviting them to enter. Once in the kitchen, Marrah turned to Anne. "If you'll take the chicken," she said, pointing to the bowl, "Lydia can carry the coleslaw—" Where was it? Had she made it? She blanched, remembering that she had, but ...?

"Here it is." Anne's voice echoed patience and kindness, which Marrah desperately needed.

As the ensuing hush grew awkward, Lois broke the silence. "I'll take the basket of rolls and shortbread cookies."

Anne handed the coleslaw to Lydia as Marrah, with two hands, lifted the pitcher of sweet tea. She followed the others down the stairs to the terrace. *Let's see if Mother can keep her promise: no talking about religion. If Lydia or Anne brings it up, that's okay. And that sanguine smile of hers has half of Chalmers snake-charmed into thinking she's Mrs. Wonderful; ugh! Of course, half isn't all. The rest don't know what I know, but if they do, if they ever meet her dark side, then they'll agree with me.* When she reached the table, Marrah set the pitcher down next to a bud vase filled with daisies, fern, and dangling nasturtiums. *Lovely.*

Lydia set the slaw beside the pitcher. "This is beautiful. Thank you."

For a while, the conversation floated along as carefree as ripples on the lake. It helped that Lois's words were few, none of them about Jesus.

"On gorgeous, blue-sky days like this," Lois said, her smile widening, "I'm reminded of how much I miss Wisconsin—though I don't miss the mosquitoes or winter."

Quiet, woman!

"Nor do I!" Anne laughed. "When Marshall asked me to marry him, I wondered about moving north. My parents moved south in the late forties. Dad missed the snow, but Mom never looked back. She hated winter. But Marshall was worth it—and it didn't hurt that I kept my Southern accent. It's like peanut butter—once it gets stuck on the roof of my mouth, nothing short of scratching it off could make it go away. So Lydia, did you and Aimee have fun sailing this morning?"

"We did."

Marrah relaxed into her chair as Lydia described her morning—until she mentioned Aimee's mother. The thought revived memories of the night, a decade earlier, when her younger brother Steve suffered his first heart attack. He recovered, but others followed, leading his doctors to warn that his heart, already weakened by a congenital anomaly related to his Down's Syndrome, had entered a period of slow unrelenting decline. Despite the warning, Marrah had been wholly unprepared when the final attack came. *Breathe*, Marrah told herself. *Breathe*. Thank goodness she had taken the extra Norco.

"I'm amazed," Lydia added, "that Aimee doesn't blame God. I don't think I'd be so forgiving."

Marrah held her breath, hoping Lois did not seize on Lydia's comments as an opportunity to pontificate. Every hair on her neck stood at attention. She watched Lois, checking her response, but Lois said nothing. *Good.*

Lydia turned to her grandmother, "Or understanding."

"Jesus strengthens Aimee, and if you need it, he will strengthen you."

Marrah watched a detestable smile slither across Lois's face. *Breach of contract*, she wanted to scream. *You promised!* For Lydia's sake, though, she clenched her fists in her lap and held her tongue. Since Lois had paid Lydia's tuition at Duke, she would also pay Marrah's son David's tuition. Making a scene could be costly—not that Jake couldn't afford tuition at whatever school

David chose. Lois had earned a lot of money through shrewd real estate deals during the years since Marrah's father died—during her senior year in high school. Supposedly. Still, it seemed odd to Marrah that her mother had accumulated so many rental properties, including several retail properties in downtown Chalmers, when her husband had not been a wealthy man. While Lois had not threatened to use her money to control David, she had long enjoyed using any excuse to meddle where she did not belong.

Marrah lifted the teapot with her left hand. Instantaneous heat ran up her arm. Anne grabbed the pot as it dropped from Marrah's useless and embarrassing hand.

"I'm sorry." Marrah grasped her wrist. "I just can't—"

Lydia took Marrah's arm and gently rubbed her taut muscles. "Does that feel better?"

Of course it did. The Norco had not protected her.

While Anne filled Marrah's glass, Lydia continued to massage her wrist. "I could never be as strong as you've been."

Marrah caught Anne and Lois exchanging glances but ignored them. Such hypocrisy. She turned to Lydia. "I'm not brave."

"That's so like Uncle Steve. You're kind the way he was."

Lydia's innocent comment pierced the unprotected soft tissue behind Marrah's collarbone. Steve had gone through so much. Lois was a terrible mother. How else could she leave her younger son alone on the day he died? *People who think Lois is a saint don't know her.* Marrah glanced at Anne as silence fell over the women, a silence so heavy that she imagined she could hear the fish breathing. *Look at Lois, feigning sorrow. Regret! That's what she should feel.* Once again, Lois's sins had burned someone other than herself.

From that moment until they left, Marrah neither spoke to nor looked at her mother.

8

Two days after returning to Chalmers and two days before Cameron's scheduled flight to Cody, Wyoming, Paul had called him, inviting himself for a round of golf at the Montebello Country Club. Cameron had agreed despite the skill gap between Cameron's buddies and Paul, who rarely walked onto a course. Everett played well, and Josh, a talented, lifelong golfer, had—after graduating from Davidson several weeks earlier—begun to prep for that hoped-for day when he would turn pro. Cameron had no such desire. Thus, unlike Everett and Josh, who complained about the soggy course after they sliced or hooked their shots, he was just happy to be on it.

Neither they nor Paul needed to know that for Cameron, focusing on his swing cleared away thoughts about his immediate future. Now, three and a half hours after teeing off, he and Josh approached then teed off the Champion tees of the seventeenth hole. They joined Everett and Paul who teed off at the white tees. Paul, being the last of the four, watched his ball hook toward a stand of oak trees. He turned to Cameron. "Did you see where my ball landed?"

"It's in the leaves over on the left." Cameron slung his bag over his shoulder and followed the other two, who had already set out. Then he stopped. Paul had played well enough and with enough aplomb to avoid sparking Josh's impatience and thus didn't need to ask twice for help finding his ball. Nor had Cameron forgotten the probable reason Paul, whose friendship was both a blessing and a curse, had invited himself. The curse came in several forms—intellect, memory, and curiosity—all of which had access to way too many free gigabytes. Since New Year's, Cameron had artfully denied Paul any chance to use those gigabytes by asking annoying questions. And today would be no different.

Cameron studied the lay of his ball on the narrow, risk-reward, five-hundred-yard par five fairway. As he had hoped, the far slope of the low ridge running from right to left across the fairway halfway to the pin had added length to his drive. His fade had also worked, mostly, since his ball sat just left of center in the fairway's very narrow neck with minimal impact from the slope's leftward radiating curve.

Josh had also executed the fade, sending his ball over the low, crossover ridge and into the middle of the narrow sward beyond it—an impressive three-hundred-plus-yard drive, stopping eight yards farther than Cameron's. Something under two hundred yards remained to the green. He and Josh could pull off the necessary approach shot to score an eagle if they were careful. Everett's ball had landed on the ridge, stopping about fifteen yards past the crest. With a lay-up and a precise fourth shot landing on the green, he should make par—assuming his approach stayed on the green and didn't roll into the water. Paul, however, had hit left into a patch of hard packed dirt with trees blocking any forward pitch. He'd need to chip nearly sideways onto the fairway and then lay up before the water. That opinion, however, Cameron would leave unspoken.

Throughout the spring semester, Paul had exchanged numerous emails and texts with him without wandering into Cameron's no-man's-land of unwise inquiries. That said, Cameron's respite from scrutiny had lasted longer than expected. If Paul had invited himself to play golf to sate his curiosity, as Cameron suspected, then his questions about Lydia would be answered on Cameron's terms, not his. Now, with Paul's ball lying nearly out of bounds, Cameron accepted that his luck had run out. He couldn't leave Paul to scrounge for his ball alone.

Paul heaved his golf bag onto his shoulder. "I don't suppose you bothered to call Lydia to explain what happened on New Year's."

Did I hear somebody say something? Cameron scanned the fairway. *Nope. It must have been the wind.*

"If Lydia ever accepted a date with me, I'd do everything in my power to make sure I had another, and another."

"And you'd succeed."

"Don't I wish. But no. A certain somebody got there first."

Cameron scanned the sky. "I thought it'd be hot today, but this isn't bad."

"I wonder who 'he' could be?" Paul suggested—loudly. "And he isn't at Duke. No, he's at UNC. What fun! But I didn't invite myself to play golf to talk about what's obvious. I wanted to talk face to face when you couldn't run away—about Justin."

As if I have anything good to say about him. Cameron reached the spot where he expected to find Paul's ball. Pointing to it, he frowned. "Justin?"

"Yeah." Paul caught up and looked down at the leaves. "Wow. You're good. I never would've found it." He plucked leaves and a long stick from around the ball and prepared to swing. As unflappable as always, he examined his grip and added, "Don't look so perturbed. You knew there'd be a price to pay when I picked you up at his house on New Year's." He glanced at Cameron, arched a brow, and then peered at the fairway as he prepared to swing. "It was very nice of you not to take all night to get wasted. What did you do? IV it?" He swung his club. The ball caught air and landed twenty yards away, perched on the upslope to the ridge.

"Nice save."

"Thank you. Anyway"—Paul picked up his clubs and joined Cameron, who was already several strides ahead of him— "when Dad decided to join the staff at Chalmers Memorial, it was good for him, but it stank for me. I'd grown up in northern New Jersey with images of Southerners burnished by videos of tornados, trailer parks, and toothless, barely intelligible descriptions that began with 'It sounded like a freight train.' That proved not to be true, but the blond-haired, blue-eyed golf course rats that we called WASPs were just as snobby. Then I met you. I'd already met Justin. He doesn't look like a WASP, but he has snobbery down cold."

They reached Paul's ball. He studied the uphill lie but turned to Cameron, not his ball. "The contrast between you two couldn't be more stark. So I wondered, how are you friends with him and an Italian Catholic like me?"

"And you reached what conclusion? But first, take your shot."

Paul tilted his head to one side, studying the ball. "It's a long way, isn't it?" He laughed, more at himself than anyone else. "I'll need my seven and my rosary just to lay up."

Cameron flicked his eyebrows and grinned. "If you say so."

"I do." Again, Paul studied his ball's lie, gazed down the fairway, and took a casual practice swing. Finally, he took his stance over the ball and, after a few waggles, swung away. The ball caught air nicely, bounced crisply, and rolled to within ten yards of the creek.

As Cameron strode across the ridge toward his ball, Paul continued. "So tell me about Justin?"

Justin? Cameron added length to his loping strides and calculated his shot carefully. It needed to be precise if he hoped to make an eagle. And his point. Yes, he planned to make the eagle. No one, not Paul or Justin, had the right to dictate Cameron's choices—not whom he dated, what he did on his dates, or how he partied.

He approached his ball and studied the green. Its close-cut grass on the left rolled gently down, for two yards, to the edge of a pond that followed part of the fairway and the length of the green. On the right side, a creek, approaching from the rear, also hugged the length of the green and a grassy slope that dropped precipitously into the creek's boulder-strewn belly. After passing the green, the creek followed the fairway for another sixty yards before turning and slicing across it. Like Paul's ball, Everett's second shot lay a few yards short of the creek as it crossed the fairway.

Ahead of Paul and Cameron, Josh readied his second shot then sent his ball high and long. It dropped onto the green. Though it sagged to the left, it sat on the green. He needed a good putt to eagle, which was likely, given his experience playing the hole. As Cameron approached his ball, Paul announced his plans, "I'll pick up."

"You're only lying three. Go for it."

"I appreciate the vote of confidence, but I don't need to lose my pride and the ball in the water."

Cameron grinned. "Your choice." Then he stepped back, taking in every detail of the fairway and green. He selected an iron and followed his usual routine, pausing to breathe. Then he swung, hurling the ball long, high, and straight. It dropped onto the green with backspin, leaving a divot before rolling toward the pin then stopping within two yards of it. Not bad.

"Were you showing off?" Paul asked without looking at Cameron. He turned to his friend. "Or making a point? Or both?"

"Whichever you wish." Cameron picked up his bag. "Yeah, Justin's a snob." He strode toward the green. "My point should be obvious. Nothing has affected my handicap." He turned to Paul and telegraphed his thought: *And it won't.*

"See? You made my point. Justin needs you far more than you need him. Why do you hang with him?"

"Maybe for the same reason you hang with me."

Paul stopped. His smile vanished. "No, Cam. You've always been a good friend. Justin uses you."

Cameron shook his head. "I thought I used him on New Year's—or at least his father's vodka and single malt Scotch." The conversation had reached a loop with nowhere else to go. Paul thankfully seemed to realize the same, for he said no more about Justin.

At the end of the round, Paul gave the advice Cameron had expected all along. "Call Lydia."

No harm came from his advice about either Lydia or Justin. And nothing changed. The two made plans to meet in August after Cameron returned from Wyoming and before Paul returned to Princeton. If Paul's challenging intellect and reliable character had been essential elements in their friendship, Justin had lacked even a shadow of those fine qualities. The friendship that began when he and Justin were in pre-school and had endured many changes but continued largely because their mothers kept putting them in close proximity—first in a playgroup and later in several sports, including golf. All of that was now over, and Paul had correctly assessed the mangled remnants of Cameron's friendship with Justin.

The vast difference between the Sloanes and Ashers left Cameron wondering why his mother had tolerated Justin's mom, year after year. Cameron's mom was kind, thoughtful, and generous. Justin's mom was a flake. Regardless, that cesspool of history prevented him from simply walking. Sadly, Paul was far too nice to understand why some friendships couldn't or wouldn't just die.

The following morning, Cameron awoke to his mother's bright smile. "Your dad and I are going to Aunt Becky's and Uncle Nate's for dinner. Do you want to join us?"

What? Spend his last night at home being lectured by his father while the uncle who exploded his summer plans looked on? "Thanks, but I need to pack."

At six, the tall grandfather clock in the dining room struck the hour with a light chime that echoed through the silent house, reviving unwanted reminders of New Year's and the horrific summer that lay ahead. Having finished packing, he found Justin's standing offer to play pool and have a few beers was no longer boring. He drove to the Sloane house.

"Hello, Mrs. Sloane." He smiled at the slender woman who opened the door.

"Hi, Cameron." Her blithe smile masked a heart ruined by a husband who knew no bounds when exercising his male prowess. "It's nice to see you. Justin's downstairs."

Cameron nodded and descended to the basement, where he found Justin and two friends playing pool and drinking. He joined them for a while before walking out onto the brick terrace that overlooked the expansive lawn, pool, and tennis court, beer in hand. To his left, the fading sun cast shadowy patterns across the immaculate grass where he and Justin had once tumbled. On more innocent days, the two played tennis on the court that lay partially hidden behind a hedge at the end of the terrace. Beyond the clay court lay the creek where he and Justin spent long hours looking for tadpoles and crayfish. Afterward, they would dive into the swimming pool, only to shiver later as they sat in soft chairs, eating ice cream under the shade of broad umbrellas. Closing his eyes, Cameron remembered the scent of honeysuckle in bloom. Still, by the time they entered high school, Justin's ill-conceived decisions had eroded their friendship until little more than habit remained. Cameron watched the sunset then returned to the pool table and the ever-watchful glass eyes set into the grotesque heads that stared down at him from every wall.

"Here, Cam," Justin said, handing him a cue stick. "You're the only one sober enough to break the rack."

Wow! Cameron mused as he took the stick. *So Justin isn't totally allergic to "truth."* He aimed, recalling the miserable circumstance that initiated the slow demise of their friendship. He recalled the exact day and hour when it ceased to exist—the day Justin arranged a date between Cameron and Lydia.

"Justin, you bastard!" Cameron shouted. "You said my date was a stranger, that I could dump once we got to the party. You lied! What'd you tell Lydia?"

"That you wanted to ask her out, but you were too shy."

"*What?*"

"You should thank me." An ugly smile curled across Justin's face. "I did you a favor."

"Favor? She's just a kid."

"A kid? Obviously, you haven't looked at her lately. Everyone else has, and you know it."

"She's not that kind of girl."

"No kidding. But if she fixed herself up and showed a little skin, she'd be hot. Really hot."

"You don't know when to quit, do you?"

"Quit? That's royal. I'm not the one who got drunk and left her talking to Paul all night. I didn't hurt her. You did that one all on your own."

Justin was right, but Cameron wasn't going to admit it. "Then why'd you give me the beer?"

"Hey. It was a party," Justin laughed. "You could have said no."

Afterward, Justin continued to invite his old friend to his house, and Cameron continued to visit again and again. And again.

Cameron studied Mr. Sloane's macabre collection of stuffed trophies. Strangely, Justin seemed to be just another trophy, a notch on his father's belt, an empty shell. Cameron's father was merely annoying by comparison with Mr. Sloane, which was perhaps, the real reason Cameron returned to Justin's basement.

Cameron wobbled the beer can. Yep, he'd emptied it and several others, but he wasn't drunk. "Control your drinking," Uncle Nathan had said.

Cackles and the sound of slapping hands and cue sticks knocking to-gether filled the room, drawing Cameron away from his musing. Someone had scored. A ball had finally found a pocket. Passion! There was the reason he returned to the morbid basement with its hideous glass-eyed beasts. Though capable of great cruelty, Justin had never been indifferent.

Cameron lifted his empty can and spoke above the noise. "Hey, every-body. Here's to Justin."

"To Justin!" His friends shouted, too stupid to interpret Cameron's acer-bic intent. When they turned away, a cold smile escaped as, under his breath, he added, "And here's to you, Dad."

Early the next morning, Cameron descended the wide, curving stairs in the foyer of his parents' house, then followed the hall that led beneath the staircase. After spending nine months among beaten-up furniture, he found the home—with its ten-foot ceiling, antique furniture, and Persian carpets—oddly comforting. He wandered back to the kitchen and poured a cup of coffee. Beyond the tall windows, early dawn lit the brick terrace and manicured backyard.

"I'll be out in a minute," his mother called from her bedroom just beyond the family room.

An hour earlier, Cameron had heard the garage door open and a car in the driveway. He knew without being told that his father had left without saying goodbye. Why should he be concerned? He'd be away for less time than a semester. Perhaps his father had trotted off to help a policyholder in the emergency room—an unlikely excuse since he assigned that pleasure to subordinates. No, his father had simply left to avoid saying goodbye to his son.

Cameron took his cup and returned upstairs. He checked his bags and slung the backpack over his shoulder. He towed the duffle bag into the hall. At the first room, he stopped. The door stood ajar; he pushed it open but did not enter. Finally, he flipped the wall switch and washed the room with low incandescent light. A bunk bed with neatly tucked covers hugged one wall. Chairs, lamps, books, and sundry decorations sat as they had for six years, undisturbed. On another wall, gold and marble trophies spread across shelf after shelf, sparkling in the light. Photographs of football and soccer players filled the remaining walls. Most focused on a tall, handsome young man who often appeared in a dirty uniform, holding a gleaming trophy aloft.

Cameron leaned close to a photograph of the dark-haired youth with the broad smile who had earned the trophies, soccer balls covered with signatures, engraved glassware, and other souvenirs. He found a photograph of the same young face standing next to Cameron's father, who draped his arm over the young man's shoulder. His father's broad smile pierced Cameron's heart.

Though Cameron had won numerous golf trophies and awards, his father had rarely attended his tournaments.

Anger, envy, and dismay clamored in his heart, but the commotion was pointless. His father was not going to change, nor would Cameron appear in a picture with his father's arm around his shoulder. No. Never. Once again, envy scraped a tender nerve, but he set it aside. His father should have stopped having children after the birth of Cameron's sister Andrea, while he was still interested in fatherhood.

Shaking off the pain, Cameron moved to a frame with a mat board cut in a pattern of window panes. It held eight photographs, each with the same four faces. Beneath the pictures was the inscription: "To Trent, Andrea, and Cameron, the best grandchildren any man could have. Love, Grandpa."

In the first picture, Trent, about age ten, and Andrea, about age eight, stood beside Grandpa, gray-haired but youthful-looking for a man in his early sixties. He held on his knee a two-year-old boy with ivory-colored, curly hair. The older two children wore soccer uniforms, and in every picture, all wore smiles. In successive photographs, time passed, and the children grew taller while Grandpa grew older. In some photographs, Trent wore a clean football uniform, in others a soccer uniform. In the early pictures, Andrea wore soccer clothes but held a golf club in the later photos. As the youngest child grew, both he and Grandpa held golf clubs. In the next to last photograph, Trent, tall and handsome, wore a graduation robe. In the last, Andrea, a petite blond, wore a similar robe. Grandpa, though, had aged greatly. Cameron raised his hand to the last photograph and rested his index finger on Grandpa's warm smile. Tears stung his eyes. *I miss you.*

"Cameron, are you ready?" His mother's high voice called from down the hall.

Jerking his hands to his cheeks, Cameron wiped the tears. He turned to face his mother in the doorway. She would not have condemned his tears, but he did not like feeling exposed and vulnerable, even to her.

"Honey, why are you in here?" Her lilting Southern accent assuaged his pain. Time had been kind to her, a fact that Grandpa attributed to the generosity of her spirit. Gentle thoughts and words, he had said, always put lines in the right places.

Cameron shrugged his shoulders. "I was just looking around."

She leaned close to the picture of Cameron and his grandfather. "Have you heard from Trent lately?" Her cheer faded momentarily, but quickly returned, perhaps recharged by the photographs. "I love that set of pictures."

She wound her arm around Cameron's upper arm. "Grandpa loved each of you so much." She leaned closer as if whispering a secret. "You, though ... you were his favorite. You were his spirit, and he was your heart. In some ways, you were very different, but in others exactly alike. Relationships like that are gifts from God."

Cameron's jaw clenched, but he forced a smile, one that was for her alone. Surrounded by Trent's photographs and memories, she seemed small and frail though she stood only a few inches shorter than he. The dustless air of the room—empty since the blistering argument that erupted between father and elder son a few months after Grandpa's funeral—had sapped her vitality.

The incomprehensible out-of-the-blue argument began when Trent announced his engagement to Emily Wilson, which should have been a happy event. Its finality had surprised Cameron, but its intensity had not. As the years passed, Cameron had often heard his mother beg his father to reconcile with Trent, but his father had refused. Once Andrea commented on the heavy toll the festering enmity between their father and brother took on her mother.

"Trent called before I went out last night," he finally answered. "He asked about my grades."

"Have you heard anything?"

"I got an A in biochem and microbiology, but an A-minus in my history elective."

"Wonderful!" She smiled and led him out of the bleak room. "I'm so impressed. I'm glad you inherited your father's intelligence. My side isn't nearly that smart. What about thermodynamics?"

His smile broadened as he bounced his eyebrows. "A-plus. Trent was impressed."

She laughed. "Trent thinks you'll be a great doctor. You kids amaze me. Trent wasn't the student that you are, but he seems to have a knack for understanding business. Maybe moving to Richmond was good for him."

"What about you? What do you think I should do?"

"You can do anything you want."

Had the sentiment come from someone else, a foolish soul might have called it disingenuous, but such feelings were beyond his mother's comprehension. She truly loved all her children well.

"So why's Dad sending me to Wyoming?"

"Honey. He loves you. He loves both of his sons just the same, and he's not sending you away. Aunt Becky says that Stan is wonderful. He's been friends with your uncle for years. I'd take that to mean you can trust him." Her smile widened into one that Cameron recognized as being a period at the end of her thought. "Besides, your experience with Uncle Nathan's horses will help. You'll probably be an old hand." When he shook his head in disbelief, she laughed. "Okay, so what else is new?" She patted his arm. "Uncle Nathan will be here any minute."

"I heard Dad leave. Where'd he go?"

"He needed to finish some work before going to the Bible conference later today."

"I saw his schedule. The conference is in Charlotte, and I'm flying out of Charlotte." Anger clawed at his throat. "He could have taken me. What's so important about some Bible conference?" Even Cameron recoiled from his angry tone, but the bitter flood continued. "My flight leaves an hour before the first meeting." When she didn't answer, Cameron sliced apart her tacit defense of his father. "Mom, he doesn't care!" He pointed at Trent's room. "If it were Trent and not me who was leaving for the summer, Dad would've found the time." Bitterness saturated his breath as he grabbed his duffle bag and brushed past her. Suddenly, he turned. "Oh, yeah." Sarcasm sizzled the dry, cool air. "That's why he hasn't spoken to Trent in six years. Dad *really* loves his sons."

"Cameron, please." Strain marred her smile. "He loves you."

"Mom, don't defend him. He doesn't care what happens to me." With his caustic retort still echoing in his ears, Cameron charged down the hall. At the head of the stairs, he stopped. His shoulders slumped, and he turned back to face her. "I'm sorry. I shouldn't say that. I promised Grandpa I wouldn't." Anger, though, still creased his brow.

"But —"

Instantly, resentment snapped its long whip. "Dad doesn't care," he barked. "It's Uncle Nathan. He's trying to be helpful."

"Honey, please."

Although she knew he was right, Cameron knew his anger at his father's rejection had once again lashed her without touching his father. He coiled his whip. "I'm sorry."

"It's okay." She wrapped her arms around his neck.

For a moment, he absorbed the warmth of her embrace and inhaled the scent of her skin. Much as he might wish, he could not run from his father forever. It would only kill his mother. He lifted his head and smiled, but not because he was happy. At least she loved him. He turned and descended the stairs from the second floor with one bag hanging from his shoulder and the other bumping the carpeted edge at each tread. Before he reached the last step, the doorbell rang.

"Ready?" Uncle Nathan's smile was a comforting and yet distressing reminder of what lay ahead.

For the next thirty minutes, he and his mother rode in near silence while Uncle Nathan drove southeast toward Charlotte. A 1979 Porsche 930—replete with a whale-tail—passed in the opposite direction, drawing *oohs* and *aahs* from Cameron and Uncle Nathan and a patient sigh from his mother. Uncle Nathan provided a brief defense of American muscle cars, but other than an occasional comment from his mother, only the bump-bump of tar strips and gritty asphalt under the tires broke the silence.

As the airport drew ever closer and home slipped farther away, Cameron was confronted with the argument between his father and brother five and a half years earlier, two months after Grandpa died. He had returned home from Paul's house and walked into the middle of the terrible fight. As the yelling intensified, Cameron had begged his mother to take him out to Uncle Nathan's and Aunt Becky's farm. And she had. For several hours he had hidden in the stable, grooming his uncle's quarter horses, while his mother returned home hoping to ameliorate any damage. Later that night, when Uncle Nathan drove him home, Cameron found the house eerily silent. In his absence, Trent had packed his clothes and left. A week later, he moved to Richmond and never returned.

Frequent arguments between Cameron and his father had followed. After each, Cameron had found solace with friends like Paul and by playing golf and working at his uncle's farm. Lydia had also proved to be a haven. None, though, had filled the holes left behind by Trent and Grandpa. As he watched the woods and fields slip by, Cameron wished once again that he was returning to Chapel Hill rather than boarding a flight to Wyoming.

"You think I'm an alcoholic," he blurted.

"No, I don't." Uncle Nathan turned the car onto the ramp leading to the eastbound lanes of Interstate 85.

"Sweetheart." His mother turned around and smiled. "You'll have fun."

"Sure." Cameron flipped through a mental file of pictures Uncle Nathan had shown him of the ranch.

He glanced at the rearview mirror and saw Uncle Nathen's eye, momentarily focused on him and not the surrounding traffic. "Your mother's right. You'll see life a little differently." He turned his attention to the highway. "You're still thinking about medical school, right?"

"Yeah, but I won't drink when I'm a doctor."

"Are you sure you want to be a physician?"

"Yes! And working in Dr. Krasotkin's lab would have scored a knockout on my applications."

"Maybe, but the range will, too. It unmasks your demons and polishes your strengths. It's not like visiting Trent's in-laws."

Cameron laughed. "No kidding. They own show horses, but I could learn the same thing on your farm."

"Nope."

Cameron caught the reflection of his uncle's eyes in the rearview mirror. Uncle Nathan was strong yet kind, good-humored, and unflinching. His patient gaze was everything Cameron hated and needed. Though Uncle Nathan had become both haven and mentor in the vacuum after Grandpa's passing, Cameron doubted that the Wyoming boonies would make a difference.

Uncle Nathan turned onto Little Rock Road and followed it past acre upon acre of parked cars belonging to people who had boarded a plane at Charlotte's Douglas International Airport. At the Delta drop-off, he navigated the car into a slot behind a Ford van. High school students poured out of it, each one wearing a T-shirt with the words, "Son Summer," emblazoned in flaming waves of orange and yellow across the back.

After climbing out of the car, Cameron pulled his uncle out of his mother's hearing. "How many of those 'good Christians' do you think got drunk or laid last weekend? Fifty percent? Seventy percent?"

Unperturbed, Uncle Nathan glanced at the teens, who bubbled and laughed as they gathered up their bags. "Some may have, but that reflects on them, not God's power or holiness."

Perhaps. Perhaps not. As Cameron stepped onto the curb, two of the teens leaned against the front of Uncle Nathan's car. The guy grinned at Cameron; then he draped his arm over the shoulder of his attractive blond companion and kissed her. The girl glanced at Cameron and blushed. He smiled back and then walked to the rear of his uncle's car.

The foolish kid had flaunted his masculine prowess in front of the wrong man, and Cameron was not impressed. After putting his backpack on the sidewalk, Cameron noticed that the girl continued to watch him rather than her friend, so he smiled, easy and nonchalant. She instantly smiled back. Cameron smiled again. Had all things been equal, he would have won the trophy. She would have followed him and left the pompous jerk behind. Game over! Luckily for the guy, things weren't equal.

A moment later, the group filed through the terminal's wide electronic doors. The girl glanced a final time at Cameron. He smiled back. *Hypocrite.* When he turned to pick up his bag, he met Uncle Nathan's stare. Instantly, Cameron laughed. "That was *way* too easy."

He turned to his mother. When she hugged him, seemingly oblivious to the flirtatious interlude, every other thought vanished. Instead, he recorded her scent, certain that he would retrieve the memory.

Uncle Nathan extended his hand and laughed. "You're a trip."

Cameron grinned and grasped his uncle's hand. He let his mother kiss him one last time. One step short of the electronic doors, he heard Uncle Nathan call, "Give Stan a chance. He might surprise you."

9

After waiting a seeming eternity at the Delta Airlines gate, Cameron watched his fellow passengers line up, hand their tickets to the attendant, and disappear down the ramp. When his section was called, he picked up his backpack and forged ahead. From his seat, he watched the ground crew scurrying about among hoses and baggage carts and envied them. Later that night, they would climb into their beds, kiss their loved ones good night, and wake up to the musty scent of a North Carolina spring morning. He, however, would wake up in a strange bed in a distant land.

Ten minutes later the plane turned onto the runway and then rumbled and rattled into its takeoff. Cameron watched the ground fall away and scanned the cars inching along Interstate 85, wondering if one belonged to Uncle Nathan. The road, though, disappeared behind him, gone from view as the plane turned south toward Atlanta. Soon the black-green forests, russet-colored dirt, buildings, and farmland of North Carolina faded into the blue haze. Cameron leaned his head back and tried to think of something, anything, other than home.

Marrah reached behind a set of neatly folded scarves until her fingers found the small Norco bottle. As she pressed on the lid, a painful twinge surged from her mangled wrist up to her elbow, but she was undeterred. She opened the bottle. Without this pill, the pain would become unbearable.

When only one pill fell into her hand, her heart rate quickened. Knowing the prescription had run out, she reached into the back of the drawer and felt between the scarves until her fingertips touched and then withdrew another bottle, one from a different doctor, one she could have refilled. She counted the pills; they would hold her beyond her next scheduled appointment, which was two weeks away.

Marrah swallowed a pill and replaced both vials. She straightened her shoulders and descended to the kitchen.

Late in the afternoon, Cameron boarded a small jet out of Salt Lake City bound for Cody, Wyoming. After eight hours of flying, running, and waiting in airports, the small interior surprised him. Though it looked like most planes, it was half as large as most and twice as cramped as the buses he had ridden to golf tournaments during high school.

Outside his window, a vast expanse of concrete spread in every direction. Beneath him, the concrete seemed close enough to touch the belly of the plane, though of course, that was not possible. Everything beyond the airport looked dreary—gray buildings, tan dirt, and brown mountains sporting snowy white caps. Only the mountains looked inviting—sort of.

The pilot taxied toward the runway then turned onto it. Without a second's pause, the plane lurched forward, rattling and shaking as it picked up speed. Moments later the wheels left the ground even as the accompanying vibration shook the entire cabin. As the plane rose higher, the rattle became disconcerting. Just when the plane seemed to level out, it dipped and the vibration ceased. Was he about to crash? He glanced at the ground and was surprised to see that the plane had risen quite high. Below, thin ribbons of pavement sporting tiny vehicles gave way to a patchwork of odd squares. They, in turn, yielded to splotches of yellow and blue-gray mudflats along the shore of the Great Salt Lake. As the roar and vibration settled into a vaguely normal uproar, he relaxed—only to have the plane dip and the rattle return. He gripped the armrest as the plane leaped higher, surmounting the peaks along the eastern shore of the lake. With each dip, Cameron's stomach knotted again. If the engines stopped, would it matter? He glanced around at his fellow passengers, most of whom seemed indifferent to the incessant noise and bouncing. He leaned back and tried to relax as the plane bobbed ever higher above the empty expanse of brown plains that spread to the eastern horizon. With the first dip, Cameron had said a prayer, but now he mused about being splattered across a Utah mountain. What a way to start the summer.

Soon, the droning harmonic of the engines settled down but added no comfort. Nor did the endless empty brown landscape that stretched east and faded into a brown haze. A few rugged peaks, piebald with snow and ringed with puffy clouds passed beneath his feet and piqued his interest, but flat brown dirt did not. Everywhere he looked, he saw brown—brown, brown, brown.

When the man next to him ordered a gin and tonic from the attendant, Cameron envied him. After bouncing like a human basketball, Cameron needed something stronger than water or cola, but having inherited his mother's youthful face, he could only wish for August and his twenty-first birthday. Slowly, the distinctly uninviting landscape soured regret into a bitter taste not unlike Mr. Sloane's twelve-year-old scotch—minus the benefits, of course. Instead, the barren land slipped by at the speed of one of the sermons he had heard while growing up, or worse, riding home after church while his father drove five miles per hour under the limit, probably just to irritate Cameron. He heaved a sigh and wondered again about New Year's. What if he hadn't gotten drunk, or if he hadn't avoided Lydia? If she hadn't changed ... would his life be better? Soon, disappointment trumped loneliness; frustration trumped disappointment, and exhaustion trumped frustration. He did not notice when sleep overtook him.

When he woke, he checked his watch. If the flight was on schedule, he should be able to see Cody. Outside his window, however, he saw only dry ground, craggy mountains, a few patches of brown trees, and snow. He pressed his forehead against the glass, looking ahead of the plane. In the distance, a verdant postage stamp dotted with houses appeared. Cody? What else could it be? But where was Yellowstone National Park? Didn't Cody sit just east of the renowned park filled with lush meadows, deep green forests, and wildlife—as pictured in the brochures? Instead, the plane landed and rolled to a stop in front of a squat tan government building that was as bland as the landscape surrounding it. So where was Yellowstone? Nowhere in sight.

Disappointed and in no great hurry, Cameron waited until the other passengers disembarked and then grabbed his backpack. As he stepped out of the plane and descended to the tarmac, a hot, dry wind blasted his face. Surprised, he paused to scan the horizon. Other than a few puny, wind-tossed trees, ill-mannered junipers, and miles of chain link fencing, he saw only brown mountains and brown landscape. Until that moment, Cameron had not realized how much he had hoped that the rest of Wyoming looked like Yellowstone, but it didn't. Worse yet, while the road to the park traveled west, he was headed east to the town of Shell, a profoundly bizarre name for anything lying anywhere in Wyoming, or close to Cody.

Lacking another choice, he dismissed the lush images and walked toward the terminal. Once inside, he saw a slender man of medium height, dressed in a patterned blue cotton shirt, leather vest, and jeans, who nodded to him and stepped forward. Every detail of his rugged appearance was forgettable, every detail except one. Framed by deep wrinkles and leathery skin, the kindest and calmest face that Cameron had ever seen smiled at him. Serenity hung from his square shoulders like a long-favored jacket, warm, weathered, and comfortable. Cameron liked his style, but style amounted to almost nothing.

The man extended one hand while the other held a dusty ball cap. "Hi, I'm Stan Boehmer. You must be Cameron."

"Yes, sir." Cameron accepted his firm clasp, which was at once cheerful and confident. "Pleased to meet you, sir. Thank you for picking me up."

Grandpa had taught Cameron that a firm handshake should always mark his introduction, especially if he felt intimidated or hesitant, which he did. Cameron grabbed his duffle bag from the conveyer belt that sat only a few yards inside the small terminal.

Stan picked up Cameron's other bag. "How was your flight?"

"It was fine, sir." Cameron smiled and continued to inspect Stan's appearance. Each detail attested to a candid and unassuming character. Stan, though, was part of the reason that Cameron was in Wyoming and not Chapel Hill, which was reason enough to distrust him.

"Fine weather we're having today."

Cameron glanced across the treeless landscape and blue sky, dotted with insignificant clouds. "Yes, sir." Without question, Stan had a different definition of fine weather from the one Cameron held. Once in the parking lot, Stan tossed Cameron's bags into the back of a dusty late-model Dodge Ram 2500 diesel. A thick layer of ochre-colored dust covered the body of the truck, obscuring all but the cab's deep, burnt-red colored roof.

"Climb in." Stan slid onto the seat without excusing the clutter and dust. "You might want something to drink before we get to the ranch. There's a cooler behind your seat. Help yourself."

"Thank you, sir."

Cameron lifted the lid but saw only ice, a gallon jug of water, and Solo cups.

"It's from our RO, so it's drinkable." Stan turned on the engine.

Drinkable? And other water is not? "Thank you, Sir." Cameron, though, wanted something stronger than water, but he was thirsty and did not want to insult his host. He poured a cupful. "Would you like one, sir?"

Stan chuckled. "Sure, why not."

Cameron handed Stan the cup and poured another for himself. With a set smile and his elbow resting on the sill of the open window, Stan turned eastward onto the highway, a two-lane road that seemed to go nowhere, at least no place inhabited. Civilization, it seemed, remained in Cody as Stan sped across the flat arid landscape surrounding the empty highway that scratched a thin black line, stretching from horizon to horizon.

Cameron asked a few innocuous questions: where Stan had grown up; how long he had owned the ranch; what Cameron should know about cattle. He was glad that Stan was quick to offer long answers. Stan had grown up in Worland. He had purchased the small ranch about twenty years earlier from his uncle after his cousin decided to move to Denver. Stan's wife was named Hannah, and they had two grown children: Their daughter and son-in-law lived in Billings, Montana, and their son lived in Greybull, a town several miles west of the ranch, where he worked at the bank. Stan's main income came from an internet consulting business. Less came from the cattle business, which took lots of time and required summer help.

"I'm proud of our kids." Stan smiled, but his unabashed pride sent Cameron sliding an inch closer to the passenger door. "In spring, they come to help during branding. In the fall they'll come back and help prep for winter,"

Stan continued. "My son is saving his money to buy the ranch someday. You'll never starve out here, but additional income helps when it gets cold, and you want heat."

As the miles passed, Stan talked about the cattle business, fencing, annual cycles, the market, and even a little about the political environment, though that was the one subject Stan seemed least willing to discuss. In his opinion, the state was okay, but the federal government—he said he'd keep those opinions to himself.

For a while, they rode in silence. With no town or end to the road in sight, Cameron asked the single most important question about Stan's personal life. "Mr. Boehmer, how do you know my uncle?"

Stan laughed. "Everybody calls me Stan. But you asked about your uncle." He glanced sidelong at Cameron while his smile widened. "When I first met Nate, he was the most polite person I'd ever met. Until just now, I'd forgotten what he sounded like." His grin widened. "Don't misunderstand. Nate is quite the gentleman. Anyway. We went to college together in New Jersey. If the school hadn't put us on the same hall as freshmen, I wonder whether we would've met or, if we did meet, whether we would've seen past our differences. A lot more than manners and accents separated us."

As Stan talked, fresh dry air swirled through the cab, ruffling the dust, sundry papers, and tools that cluttered the seat and dashboard. "Back then I was an atheist, and Nate thought horses were something that little girls rode in shows. But then again, the world was different. Most of our classmates were into either drugs or politics, neither of which appealed to us. Every weekend, the dorm would clear out. The rest were into either some sort of sit-in or pot parties. So with nothing to do and nobody around, we kept running into each other in the hall or the common room. With Nate being the friendly sort that he is, we started talking."

"Are you still an atheist?"

"No. I like to say that Nate made sure that changed." He flashed a grin at Cameron. "As if my decision was up to either of us. The timing may have been mine, but not the decision. Still, without Nate's friendship, I might have spent more time in the wilderness, and he would've stayed away from horses. Instead, God found me, and Nate discovered the western saddle." Again Stan laughed, but Cameron only smiled, stiff and polite.

So Stan and Uncle Nathan were Christian friends. Furthermore, Stan considered Uncle Nathan to have been an important element in his coming to faith. *Odd.* Though Cameron had lumped his aunt and uncle into "regular church people," he had never considered Uncle Nathan to be an ardent Christian or associated him with Bible studies or prayer groups. Still, the basis of the enduring friendship created yet another reason to treat Stan with great caution. If Uncle Nathan had expected Stan to make Cameron "religious," then he would be sadly mistaken.

For what seemed like an eternity, the radio played country music, and Cameron stared out the window. As they passed through Greybull—a veritable forest of trees, but only compared to the surrounding wasteland—Stan noted the levees designed to keep the Bighorn River in its banks and other points of interest. East of town, the road returned to the dry highlands. On the eastern horizon, Cameron noticed an indistinct line of hills, capped with clouds, rising only slightly higher than ridges closer to him.

"We're almost home." Stan pointed to his left. "It's just behind that low ridge."

Home?

The truck continued up a long, gentle incline. When it crested the slope, the sight before Cameron erased his polite but jaded smile. Before him stood a long mountain range, rising high above dry bench lands. A vibrant valley, blanketed with fields and dotted with black cattle, spread across the toe of the massive wall. Snow, not clouds, laced the ridges and peaks, which ran from north to south, blocking his view of everything to the east. Huge ribbons of creamy taupe, salmon, and soft pink stone zigzagged across the steep face of the impenetrable wall. Lit by golden rays from the afternoon sun, the mountains melted Cameron's cultivated veneer.

Stan glanced at him. "They're beautiful, aren't they?"

"Yes, sir." Cameron had read pamphlets and websites referencing the state, but nothing had prepared him for the mountain range that stood before him.

"That's the Bighorns," Stan noted as the road descended into a wide valley.

For a moment, a low rise, dusted with a lacy, olive green mantel, blocked Cameron's view, but as the road again crested, the mountains reappeared, closer and more magnificent than before. "Unassuming, yet undaunted; fore-boding, yet patient; complex, yet breathtakingly simple" aptly described the range that jutted above the flat valley that lay at its feet. Suddenly, he felt very much alone. His mother and everything green, comforting, and familiar lay beyond the mountains, prairies, rivers, and cities of the continent. And yet, something mysterious within the mountains beckoned to him.

Meanwhile, Stan turned off the main highway onto a paved side road that ran north across the green valley, parallel to the mountain range. Opposite the mountains, a low dry ridge covered with short grass marked the western edge of the lush fields. As the road reentered the valley, the mountains disap-peared, only to reappear a mile farther along as the road returned to the dry bench lands. Now even closer, Cameron saw tiny black dots spattered across the stony ribbons. Similar dots marched along the ridge.

Stan broke the silence. "Those black dots you see along the ridge; they're full-grown trees."

"Oh." The mountains were even higher than he had guessed.

Several miles north of the highway, Stan turned left off the road onto a dirt driveway that led down into a valley covered with green fields, a winding creek, trees, a barn, and various outbuildings. "That's Beaver Creek," Stan noted, pronouncing it *crick*. He crossed a small bridge spanning the creek and stopped next to an unassuming, metal-roofed ranch-style house set at the base of a dry hill and shaded by two tall gnarly trees. One porch extended along the front. A second, larger enclosed porch enjoyed a panoramic view of the mountains. A barn, corrals, a chicken coop, and other outbuildings lay a short distance from the house. Long lines of fencing, mostly pole and barbed wire, encompassed and divided the fields. A profusion of weeds and wildflowers marked each.

Stan finally smiled, broad and relaxed. "Welcome to the G-Double-T ranch."

"Where's Shell?" Cameron asked.

"It's on the main highway, but we didn't go that far." Stan grabbed Cameron's duffle bag and walked toward the house. "It's a nice little commu-nity. It's got a restaurant, Celia's Kitchen, and several ranches along the creek. And a campground. That's about it, besides quite a few ranches that aren't in town. Greybull has most of everything else."

The door of the house opened, and a dark-haired woman of about fifty appeared. A smile almost as wide as the mountains filled her face. "Hi."

Stan turned toward Cameron. "This is my wife, Hannah."

Hannah extended her hand. "Welcome." Her firm grip erased Cameron's exhaustion and melted his defenses. "We're glad to have you. Won't ya come in."

The eclectic decor of the simple but comfortable interior reminded Cameron of Aunt Becky's decorating style where each family heirloom held a story, and none were boring.

"We eat here." Stan pointed to a long table that stood close to the window and faced the mountains. "There's a pool table in the barn. We have a cabin in the back where you and the others will sleep."

Cameron followed Stan to a recently built T-shaped log cabin behind the house. The interior included two small bedrooms, one on each side of a wide central hall. A bath with two showers, three sinks, and two toilets extended from the rear of the building. Each bedroom contained a set of bunk beds and a twin bed, lockers, and a chest of drawers. The central hall held two benches, coat pegs, and a wood stove. Prints of the Grand Tetons—one with snow, the other without—hung on the wall in each bedroom. Two windows with screens in each room provided cross-ventilation, which was good since the building lacked air conditioning.

"There'll be five of you in here this summer," Stan added as Cameron examined the bunks. Each included a mattress laid atop a piece of plywood. Atop each mattress lay a stack of sheets and towels, an army blanket, and a pillow.

"Drew, one of the guys, is out in the barn," Stan continued. "He picked the single in this room. The other three will arrive later tonight."

"Then it's okay if I use this one?" he asked, nodding toward a bunk in the room Drew had chosen. When Stan nodded, Cameron threw a duffle bag onto the lower bunk and hoped that, when the others arrived, they picked beds in the other room.

Stan leaned his shoulder against the doorframe. "In the morning, I'll give you a tour of the ranch and introduce you to the horses. Oh, and did you bring a hat?"

"No, sir."

"No one ever does," Stan laughed. "That's all right. We have extras, but if you like, we'll go back to Greybull and buy ya one. Well, when you're ready, come on up." Stan turned to leave as Cameron opened his duffle bag. "Hannah has dinner waiting." At the door, he stopped and turned back to Cameron. He seemed to wink, but only his brow moved. "Oh, and we get up early."

After he left, Cameron stared at the rough-hewn door. He had eaten little during the day and had arrived before five by Stan's time—seven by Chalmers time—but he wasn't hungry. He drank a glass of water, but it merely washed away the grime that lined his throat. It didn't touch the unquenchable emptiness. His hunger for something other than food collapsed the walls of his stomach, causing them to rattle against each other.

Wishing, hoping to see something familiar, he walked to the window between the two beds and leaned his elbows onto the rough-hewn sill. Fifty yards or so away, an unkempt post-and-wire fence ran—ambled—following the rim of a hill that separated the flat valley from the highlands. As daylight faded into looming shadows, a silence weightier than his darkest dream settled across the valley. Overhead, a sky white with stars descended toward the eastern horizon but stopped abruptly at the jagged edge of an impenetrable black expanse extending from north to south—the immovable mountain range. The resolute, indifferent wall that absorbed both light and life was, however, comforting.

Cameron sat down on the edge of the bed and paused a moment before flopping onto his back. He slung his forearms over his face. For a while, he listened to the wind, soft and rhythmic. Laughter drifted in from the main house, but nothing lifted his spirits. His eyes stared into the darkness while his heart crept back to his childhood when he curled up next to his mother. In all his life, he had never felt so unloved, so far away from home. Later, he fell asleep, barely noticing that for the first time in forever, silence engulfed his soul.

10

Someone should have told the engineers who designed and built Glenlaurel Lake to pick a site on the eastern side of Chalmers, not the western side. Had they done so, then each evening Marrah and Jake's house would be bathed in the warm rays of the setting sun. Instead, shade cloaked Marrah's garden at four in the afternoon, the exact time when moisture, rising from the lake, became ambrosia for powdery mildew. Calling the thick white scum that coated Marrah's zinnias and roses "powdery" defied logic, since the fungus also loosened varnish from furniture, peeled paint off buildings, and floated small boats. She may have exaggerated, but the nasty slime's ability to sap the life from otherwise healthy plants, leaving them pale and impotent, was no exaggeration. Only Lois had similar power.

Marrah tamped the ground around a freshly planted zinnia, but an all-too-familiar buzz started in her fingers and spread to her hands. The irritating tremor spiraled upward, vibrating every muscle. Nobody else could see it, but it was there. It reached her head and ricocheted against her skull. Her wrist ached. Trying to think the pain away, she remembered her brother Steve and the fun they had. If Lois had taken better care of Steve, he wouldn't have died.

Seven months and two days earlier, her brother's heart had failed. One year, one week and two days had passed since Marrah fell from the ladder, landing on her left hand and shattering the end of her ulna bone. Nine weeks had passed since her last surgery, but her left shoulder still twitched in pain, and her hand still trembled. It had been too much to manage.

Suddenly, the muscles in her hand cramped, causing her to drop the plant. She raced to her closet and the drawer filled with neatly folded scarves. Gasping for air, she found the pill vial and popped one in her mouth. As she did, she saw her reflection in the mirror. Who was the red-faced ghost that stared back at her? Though only forty-eight, she looked sixty. *A little help from Lois rather than constant criticism would help.*

Disheartened, Marrah trudged back to the garden and the flat of zinnias. She was about to sit down when she saw Jake on the dock, washing his kayak. He must have taken it out and didn't see her run up to the house. Thank goodness. She sat down and watched him, wondering again when he would leave. *And he will. Everyone does.* Lois! Her mother had invaded everything, even Marrah's marriage. It was obvious when Jake and Lois talked. *Oops, he's coming up.* She tried to smile, but her heart sank. *A smile won't change his mind.*

Jake picked up a small begonia. "These will look good."

He leaned down and kissed her cheek, but only afterward did she glance at him as he returned to the dock. Though his brown hair had long since turned gray, age had not reduced his energy or slumped his masculine shoulders. *Why would a man like Jake want to stay with someone like me? He's only staying for David. Next year, after David graduates from high school, he'll leave.* Marrah sighed. Mildew, that sticky white gunk, had claimed more than her roses and zinnias.

"Aunt Marrah!"

Startled, Marrah jerked around and saw Lydia bouncing down the steps. *What a relief!* "Hi!"

Lydia stooped next to her aunt. "These are beautiful."

"I forgot you were going sailing with Jake."

"Yep. Won't you come with us?"

"No. You know I hate sailboats."

"I don't believe it! Come on. You'll have a good time." Lydia dropped to her knees and picked up a set of zinnia seedlings. "Besides, I can't leave you here alone."

"Alone?"

"Yeah. Didn't David go camping with his friends?"

Yes, he did. Marrah leaned away from her niece's bright smile, the one that appeared whenever the cracks in Marrah's veneer had grown too large. She pushed another plant into the ground.

Lydia sat cross-legged on the flagstone path. "Why are you sad?"

"Do I look sad?"

"Sometimes." Lydia popped a plant out and handed it to her aunt.

Marrah made a hole and pushed the plant into it. She didn't need to look at Lydia to know she was waiting for an answer. "I suppose I've been pretty cranky lately." She pushed another plant into the ground.

"I know Uncle Steve loved to help you in the garden. This is the first summer without him. I know you miss him."

Looking down, Marrah sighed. The child was simply too young to have seen into Marrah's heart. "It is."

"I miss him too .... Aunt Marrah, you were very special to him."

In a dark corner of Marrah's mind, a distant memory cast off its dusty shroud. Her hand fell to her lap. "*Steve* was special." She relaxed, sitting back on her heels. In the distance, she saw Jake preparing the sailboat to be taken out. A breeze ruffled its luffing sail and a moment later brushed Marrah's cheek, sending strands of hair across her eyes. The soft touch awakened a long-forgotten secret that she had shared with no one, not even Jake.

"I used to love to sail. After we moved here, we spent several summers driving up to New Hampshire. One of Dad's friends owned a cabin on a small lake that we leased. It was old, charming and had an outhouse that—I was told—reached to China. Well, I had taken a few lessons on this lake and decided to try my skill with their small sailboat." Memories of the post-and-plank dock and cold, clear water returned. "I had talked up my skills so much that Steve begged to go with me. In fact, he insisted. No one could be so cheerfully persistent." Her eyes drifted to the open lake. Staring out across the water, she continued. "The lake wasn't very big, and at thirteen, I should have known better than to take Steve with me.

"So off we went—by ourselves, in a boat with only one sail. What could go wrong? Lots—because I forgot that he couldn't swim. Thank goodness I remembered to put a life jacket on him, but not on me." Marrah shook her head. "Everything was fine until a motorboat went by—a spectacular antique

Chris-Craft. The varnished wood shone like the sun. I was so enthralled that I didn't see its wake until it hit us broadside and knocked Steve off."

Lydia's mouth fell dropped open. "What happened?"

"Steve panicked. Without thinking, I jumped in after him. I'd had life-saving courses but overestimated my skill level. Of course, he surfaced, but he was flailing and too strong for me to help him. He was also gulping water. I couldn't get close enough to grab him without being drowned." In the distance, a large boat streaked past, a white rooster tail of water flying behind it. "He started to choke. I can still see his face. He was blind with fear." She turned to Lydia.

"I didn't know it, but Dad had watched us go out and was waiting in the motorboat, ready to help. I didn't hear him approach." She shook her head, "I can't describe how I felt when his strong hands grabbed Steve. He grabbed me, too. Afterward, Steve coughed up a lot of water, but other than that, he was fine. But I almost killed him." Marrah sighed as another, quieter boat passed in the distance. "This was before his first heart surgery, but the doctors expected that he'd need them, sometime. I was lucky ... and I haven't been out in a boat since." She grimaced. "I'm sorry." She turned to Jake. "Look. He's ready. Go have fun."

"I don't think that was the reason Uncle Steve didn't like this lake. He talked about everything, but he never mentioned being in a boat with you. Please, come with us."

"Maybe someday, but not today."

"Okay, when you're ready, let me know." Lydia stood and smiled at Marrah. "I'll take you."

Marrah watched her turn and bounce down the steps. With a light hop, she was on the boat, following Jake's instructions. As he cast off from the dock, the wind tossed Lydia's long curls, scattering them. She waved to Marrah. "Just say the word, and I'll be there."

The child was much too old for her age. Jake also waved, but her heart sank. If he knew her true self, he'd leave today and take David with him. The boat passed Kelly's Point, caught the wind, and scudded across the waves. In twelve months, David would graduate. One year. Then Jake, David, and the sailboat would be gone.

11

Soft snoring rustled the dry air, reminding Cameron that the summer he had long dreaded had begun. He checked his watch. Five A.M. He jammed his head under the pillow, but sleep did not return. Beyond the window, morning lit the hillside behind the cabin. Cows mooed, and a creek gurgled, but they weren't the sounds he wanted to hear.

Turning onto his back, he remembered the day in March that set his fate in stone. He had returned home for spring break. While he prepped to join friends for a hike along the Appalachian Trail, his father had come to Cameron's room—an extremely rare event. When he left, Cameron's summer job in Chapel Hill was history.

Cameron tightened the laces on his boot, then looked up, surprised to see his father standing in the doorway of his bedroom.

"Nathan has a job for you in Wyoming." His father's thin lips disappeared into a slit. "I believe you've discussed this with him."

"He mentioned it during Christmas break, but I have a research job with Professor Krasotkin."

"Well, it's all worked out. You're going to Wyoming."

"No."

"Yes, you are." His father turned and left.

"You're not getting off that easily," Cameron yelled at the empty doorway. As with every other time his father came to Cameron's bedroom, he had announced an edict and left. To Cameron's disbelief, he returned.

"I'm getting off light?" His father's eyes narrowed, and his lip twisted. "No, son. You're the one who's getting off easy. Not me."

He turned to leave, but Cameron shouted, "If you were even a remotely decent father, I wouldn't have a problem."

His father stopped. Then he half turned and glared. "So I'm the reason you get drunk all the time?"

"Yeah."

"Get real, Cameron. You get drunk because you won't grow up. I had to grow up way too early to stand here listening to you complain that *I* ruined *your* life."

"Don't throw that at me again." Cameron had heard the story a thousand times. "It's not my fault that Grandma died when you were ten."

"Twelve."

"Whatever. Grandpa told me all about her, so I know he missed her. What about you? Do you miss her, or do you hate Grandpa because he loved her?"

From the day Trent moved away, the same argument, with almost the same words, had erupted repeatedly between father and son. Each time, it had ended with his father turning his back on Cameron. This argument was about to end the same way, but the object, Cameron's summer, changed everything. "You're not walking out," Cameron yelled down the hall at his father, who had reached the top of the stairs. "I'm not afraid of you anymore. If you're going to ruin my future, you're going to tell me why."

His father stopped in the doorway and smiled, a cold, cynical smile. "I'll pray for you, son." Then as always, he turned away and descended the stairs.

Cameron rushed to the top step and called after him, "Save your breath. If I ever walk back into a church again, it won't be because of you, and you'd better believe that it'll be a cold day in Hell before I do. You can pray all you want, but you're the number one reason I'll never go back."

The air in the cabin grew cold, and the silence deepened as Cameron remembered the bright spring day, a week later. Professor Krasotkin had asked him to meet him for coffee after class. As he approached the chemistry building, the scent of freshly cut grass had blended into the rich aroma of wild onions hinting that summer and the end of the semester were close.

"Cameron, close the door," Professor Krasotkin nodded to the door. "How are you?"

"Fine, sir."

"I want to talk about the summer." With those few words, Cameron knew that something was terribly wrong. The normally jovial professor continued in a quiet tone, sounding as if he were miles away. "I spoke to your father yesterday."

Cameron turned pale. "About what?"

"He said that he had made plans for you."

"He can't do that!"

"Take it easy. This isn't the end of the world."

Cameron choked. "You agreed?"

"No, no." The professor's voice barely disturbed the air. "Here, I picked up a coffee for you." Cameron took the cup and then sank into the chair he had so often lounged in, but his appetite had vanished. Instead, acid gnawed holes in his stomach. Professor Krasotkin continued, "I've arranged an alternative for you. Dr. Edelmann has a project, funded to start in the fall. I think you'll like it."

"Why?"

"You mean the job?"

"No. Why are you giving in to Dad?" Cameron searched the dark brown eyes of his mentor. "My father doesn't deserve ...." Unable to meet the professor's kind gaze, he looked away. His jaw clenched, stifling tears.

"He's your father. I'd be irresponsible if I did otherwise."

No! He couldn't! Cameron's throat tightened. He shifted his weight, feigning cool indifference. Had his father also told the professor about his drinking, a secret that Cameron had carefully hidden from the professor? Certainly not! "Did he tell you why he wants me to go to Wyoming?"

"No, and I didn't ask."

"Why not?" Didn't the professor care?

"He started to tell me, but I told him that I didn't need to know. It was important to him, and that was enough. Cameron, I know you well enough to know that you've been running from something for a long time. I don't know what it is, but this detour may be in your best interest."

"But why? I mean. What makes you think I'm—?"

"Running? That's not hard to see. You have a big heart, but you share it very sparingly. I'm not sure that I deserve the honor that you've granted me this year, but for some reason you trust me. I don't want to betray that trust, so though it may sound counterintuitive, I think this time you need to do as your father wishes. When you're on your own, you can decide how your relationship with him will continue.

"Two important reasons led me, shall I say, to direct you in this way. First, you're one of the brightest students that I've had the honor of teaching. You absorb the information as easily as you breathe, plus you're committed to your work. It's a great combination, and it's the reason that Dr. Edelmann wants you to work with him. He was very impressed when he met you. Secondly, I understand better than you may imagine the quandary that you face."

"Didn't you get along with your father?"

"Though my father wasn't the problem, I, too, faced a detour. Someday"— his mouth twitched— "but not this semester. Next fall or later, come back, and I'll explain it. Now, take a deep breath and relax. This is going to work out."

It's going to work out. Yeah, right! Cameron turned over in the bed and stared up at the unvarnished plywood board that supported the upper bunk. In the dim light, he recited to himself. *"'Twas brillig, and the slithy toves / Did gyre and gimble in the wabe.*

Again he closed his eyes, but sleep remained elusive. The sound of someone in the other room snoring reminded Cameron that three other men had arrived during the night. He leaned his head over the edge to see if one had claimed the upper bunk. Seeing the blanket still neatly tucked, assured him that it was empty. Good. Only Drew, the cabinmate that Stan mentioned, shared his room.

Cameron pulled his head back and lay still. While he stared into the darkness, his mind replayed the events of the previous day, right down to the details of the plane gasping and bouncing on the air currents above the Great Salt Lake. He supposed he should be glad that he had not ended up splattered across a Utah mountain, but also, he remembered his mother's advice to think about something positive. When he failed, which usually happened, she had smiled and told him to try harder.

How, he wondered, had his parents, such opposites, lived under the same roof for so long? He was glad that his mother loved her husband and hoped that his father also loved her, though he doubted that his father loved anyone. Someone less resolute than his mother might have given up, but Cameron was glad that she had not. For that, his father should be extremely grateful but probably wasn't.

After a while, he heard Stan talking to another man. He climbed out of bed and looked out the window. Seeing no one, he returned to bed and listened to the echo of their voices and then silence. Fully awake, he thought about having a beer, but drinking before dawn didn't sound appealing. Still, the thought lingered a moment before turning stale. Getting drunk alone had never appealed to him. He needed a party more than a beer. Yes, that was what he wanted. Maybe one of these guys liked to party. Maybe. Hmm. Finally, a positive thought. He smiled and turned over then pulled the covers over his shoulders and nestled into the hard-pack that passed for a pillow.

A little later, he heard boots clumping across the wooden porch; then the door swung open. Behind Stan's trim frame the blue-gray light of dawn lit the sky and filtered into the cabin. His rich baritone voice echoed off the walls: "Time to get moving."

Shielding his eyes, Cameron sat up on his elbows as moans arose from the other bunks. Someone turned over, but only Drew jumped out of bed. With a shy grin that smiled at the morning rather than Cameron, he disappeared into the bath.

"You guys may think we have all day." Stan cracked a smile. "Time's a-wasting. Breakfast is ready."

Oh, wow. The last thing his stomach wanted at six in the morning was breakfast—a party maybe, but not eggs and bacon. Coffee was different. Stan turned and, with heels clunking against the thick floorboards, disappeared. *Yeah, coffee will do.*

Cameron threw back the covers and climbed out. At the door to the bath, he met a tall dark-haired youth the same age as himself. Noting the stranger's scowl, Cameron decided not to vie with him for the other shower. Having ceded the bath, Cameron glanced at the other two men, one in each bunk. One was chunky and the other slender. Both looked to be several years younger than he, too young for anything worth doing. Within minutes, brilliant light flooded the room as Drew exited the bath with a towel in hand. He had shaved but not showered. Cameron recoiled from the thought but then assured himself that, though he hadn't witnessed the event, Drew must have showered the night before.

A tall, strapping man with a round, pocked-scarred face, Drew threw on his clothes, cast a furtive glance at Cameron, and dashed out the door. He bounded off the porch without using the steps. When he reached the corral, he waved at someone Cameron could not see, probably the man Cameron had heard talking to Stan. The man soon came into view just past the barbed wire fence, leading a chestnut quarter horse. His spry gait and agile body movements matched those of someone in their forties, but his rugged skin belonged to a man far older. He laughed as he spoke to Drew and turned the horse out into the corral. Stan also appeared. His genial and casual familiarity with Drew quickened Cameron's curiosity but did not improve his impression of him. In fact, he felt quite the opposite.

Within a few minutes, Cameron had observed three distinct personalities in his new cabinmate. Drew, who—he guessed—was a few years older than Cameron, had first appeared frumpy and shy, then assertive and rude, and finally relaxed and confident. The first two of this mixture of traits had piqued something less than Cameron's admiration, but the sight of his casual familiarity with Stan and the unnamed ranch hand instantly whetted his competitive spirit. For Cameron, the whiff of a contest and rivalry was a far more intoxicating pleasure than a six-pack of beer. He jumped in the empty shower, dressed, and dashed out the door.

During breakfast, he continued to log his impressions of Drew's behavior.

Guarded, dull, and defensive came to mind as Cameron watched him devour the fresh pancakes and coffee in total silence. When Cameron asked Hannah innocuous but friendly questions about the ranch, she answered by gently prodding Drew to join the conversation, which he did not. Curious. If Drew knew and seemed to like Stan and the ranch hand, why didn't he respond to Hannah's kindness? He even avoided eye contact with her. *Hmmm.* Once finished, Drew abruptly left, letting the screen door bang behind him. Ah, yes. The second personality had returned. Drew's refusal to show Hannah even a hint of gratitude or civility seemed strange, which both repulsed and intrigued Cameron. Why did Stan tolerate Drew's abrupt and ill-mannered behavior, for evidently, Drew possessed his approval?

Cameron finished his coffee, washed the cup and then thanked Hannah. As he opened the door, determined to catch up with Drew, he was met by his other cabinmates staggering up to the house. Hannah welcomed them with an offering of fresh pancakes while Cameron—steeped in Southern manners—smiled and introduced himself. The man who had challenged him for the shower was named Todd, and the younger two were Sam and Mick. Only Todd appeared to be old enough to purchase beer and share a six-pack, which was good since Drew's essential strangeness had disqualified him as a candidate for either.

"It's nice to meet you," Cameron nodded politely. "I think I'll head on out. See y'all outside."

As he said, "Y'all," Todd frowned, probably a knee-jerk response to Cameron's Southern colloquialism. He then spoke to Hannah in a distinctly Northeastern accent. *Ah, yes.* Cameron nodded to Hannah, smiled at Todd, and left. He'd encountered similar responses from Northerners before and knew that a genial attitude usually improved uninformed opinions, at least about him. In time, the same would be true of Todd.

Cameron approached the barn where he saw the ranch hand grooming a paint horse. "Hello, my name's Cameron," he said and extended his hand.

"Howdy, I'm Leo." Cameron liked the firmness of his handshake. "Glad to meet you. Come this way, and I'll introduce you to your horse."

Cameron followed him to the corral adjoining the barn where several horses awaited riders. Inside the barn, Cameron followed Leo's instructions, grabbing pieces of tack from the barn, taking mental notes, and generally doing as instructed. He followed Leo outside, where they joined Stan, who motioned to Todd and Cameron. "You two come with me. Leo will help Mick and Sam."

Stan untied a chestnut gelding and handed the rope halter to Cameron. "His name is Azariah."

"Hello, Azariah." Cameron let the horse smell his hand and then ran his hand down its long nose. "Will he be mine for the summer?"

"If you two fit."

Cameron smoothed the horse's mane along his neck. "So it's you and me against the world, is it? What do you like?" The horse eyed Cameron but gave no sign whether they would "fit." Stan instructed Cameron to mount Azariah and adjusted his stirrups. He added a few comments about holding the reins and then turned to Todd. Left alone, Cameron leaned down, patted Azariah, and whispered.

Twenty minutes later, Stan gathered the newcomers together. "Have any of you ridden horses before?"

None, including Drew, raised their hand. So Cameron also held back. He added "shrewdly dishonest" to the list of details that described Drew.

"Well, you'll learn fast." Stan and Leo mounted their horses. Stan offered about ten words of instruction regarding the cattle and turned his horse toward the road, and everyone followed. A hundred yards up the road, he stopped and pulled open an orange steel gate. Leaning forward on the saddle horn, he smiled. "We're moving these cattle up the road today. It isn't far." He turned his horse toward the road. "Let's get going."

Hannah joined Leo and entered the pasture while Stan waited on the road outside the gate. Without hesitation, Drew also entered the pasture, but Cameron and the other newcomers waited, neither following Leo nor joining Stan. Cameron waited a moment longer, watching Stan, and then saw Drew's slim figure in the distance. He seemed clad in confidence like a gladiator suited in boiled-leather and coarse linen. Focused determination waved in the wind like the red plume on a gladiator's helmet. Experience was his shield, protecting him from danger, and a sheathed sword was ready to beat back misfortune. With every stride of his horse, Drew defined differences between himself and the other summer hands, including Cameron, who wavered, needing to be prodded. With so little instruction, particularly to a bunch of greenhorns—except of course Drew—Stan had created an every-man-for-himself situation, thus proving Uncle Nathan's note that the rancher would surprise him.

Undoubtedly, Cameron needed to take care of himself. He nudged Azariah toward the open gate. In the distance, Drew, Hannah, and Leo had scattered across the pasture and placed themselves between the herd and outer fences, thus turning the moseying black cows toward the open gate. Cameron glanced back at Todd and the others, but none had moved. To his surprise, he remembered an obscure piece of advice from Uncle Nathan: cows want to see the horse and rider, yet they move forward when the rider is behind them. Thus inspired, Cameron spurred Azariah toward an unattended section of the field. When he reached a group of cattle, he rode around, placing them between himself and the gate. To his amazement, the lumbering beasts turned and wandered toward the road. Fifteen or more minutes later, Drew, Cameron, and the last cow exited the pasture. He nodded and smiled at Todd, Mick, and Sam who waited. None had moved since he left them.

Plodding along behind the dumbly obedient and mildly irascible cattle, which, as Leo noted, constantly complained about being bothered, was—to his surprise—oddly pleasant. At noon, Stan assigned work to his new helpers. He sent Todd, Mick, and Sam to help Hannah. "Drew, Cameron, you'll come with Leo and me."

With the newcomers thus divided, Stan led the meandering herd toward a deep cleft in the range. As Cameron approached the mesmerizing mountains, a voice from someplace far behind the first ridge called to him. Stalwart and timeless, generous and alive, the range demanded his attention. High above his head, the stony wall drew an undulating line, separating itself from the endless pale sky that stretched westward. In Chapel Hill, buildings and a high canopy of leaves obscured any definition of a line drawn between sky and land, wrapping a green blanket around everything, holding it in place. In Chalmers, the Blue Ridge Mountains scribed a low, humble line above the western horizon. Here, the sky engulfed Cameron while the mountains and the treeless land challenged his sense of scale, reducing miles to feet.

By afternoon, the men had pushed the small group of lumbering animals up the narrow cleft and into a pasture set among rolling peaks. Only then did Cameron turn Azariah around to look behind him. To his surprise, they had climbed high above the valley that now lay like a dun blanket, stretching to the horizon. With gleeful condescension and absolutely no sympathy, he remembered Todd and the younger men who had been left behind. Their chores—whatever Stan had assigned to them—paled in comparison to the sights that now surrounded him.

Even so, throughout the ride, Cameron had watched Drew. His many personas, including the rude young man who'd ignored Hannah hours earlier, remained an obstacle to friendship. His deficiencies, however, did not prevent Cameron from noting Drew's adroit skills that presented Cameron with an ever more savory challenge, one he planned to match. Catching up with Drew's abilities, however, would require practice and patience, but determination had always been Cameron's strength.

As the cattle spread across the pasture, their complaints petered out, overshadowed by the wind that swept across the grass and brushed Cameron's cheeks, sending his heart soaring. Home no longer seemed quite so far away, but he freely credited Azariah for his enjoyment. After all, it was Azariah who knew the land, the cattle, and the ways of both. Leaning close to Azariah's ear, he stroked the horse's neck. "I think you and I are going to do just fine."

Perhaps the summer would not be a complete disaster.

12

For the next three weeks, Cameron bumped and bungled his way up a steep learning curve in ranching. He credited much of his success to Azariah, but Leo had also rescued him from the consequences of ignorance, specifically, a potentially expensive mistake on the first day. After unloading the horses from the trailer—Stan had trailered them back to the ranch from the high meadow—Cameron had led Azariah to the corral and was about to release him when Leo, hollering at the top of his lungs, stopped him.

"What's wrong?" Cameron asked, flushed and retreating until his back pressed against Azariah's shoulder.

"Never let him into the corral with his saddle on." Leo took the rope halter. "Son, you must not have been raised around cats and dogs."

"No, sir. Dad's allergic to them."

"Well, I'll overlook it this time." Leo loosened the cinch. "Azariah is just a really big dog. He's had that saddle on all day, and his mind is set on doing certain things, among them a good roll on the ground."

Putting his face close to Azariah's eye, Cameron grinned. "Not you!" To which the horse snorted.

"Yeah, he'd love that." Leo removed the saddle. "But it's a sure way to break this."

A few days later, Leo joined Cameron in the tack shed. "So you never had pets." Leo's eyes twinkled as he hung up two bridles. "That's amazing 'cause you and Azariah seem like a matched set."

"He's pretty much in charge."

"That's why I can't give him to just anybody. He'd have made hash out of those other guys." Puzzled, Cameron studied Leo. "I'm not kidding," Leo continued. "I was surprised when Stan said that you'd be riding him. It seems you won Azariah's heart. He trusts you."

Open, uncomplicated, and talkative, Leo seemed a polar complement to Stan. So Cameron followed on Leo's heels, while still watching and trying to copy Drew's superb skill with animals. Studying Drew, though, had not changed Cameron's opinion of him. While confident ease continued to mark Drew's behavior around anything on four legs, the gladiator remained essentially strange and even offensive around the two-legged variety.

By the end of the third week, Cameron had moved from Ranching 101 to Ranching 102. He had watched the community event known as branding, where neighboring ranchers helped out. He'd mended wire, groomed horses, and set gated irrigation pipes. He had even helped remove fallen tree limbs, brought downstream by high water, that blocked Beaver Creek. He'd learned that the deep double notch in the mountains, through which they earlier led the cattle to high pasture, was known as the W. Whether related to horses, cattle, irrigation, or the range, he had learned that something always needed to be tended, mended, adjusted, or corralled.

At night, though, a heavy silence blanketed the ranch, particularly after Leo returned to his home in Shell. Each night, beginning with the night after he arrived, Stan and Hannah had extended open invitations for Cameron and the others to join them for after-dinner conversations on the front porch, but only Drew accepted. Since the discussions almost always reverted to Bible studies, Cameron had stayed away. Drew's participation, however, had added yet another persona to the squad inside his head, one that further distanced Cameron from him.

Rather than joining the porch gang, Cameron often played pool with Todd, despite losing. Being humiliated was far superior to the alternative: Stan's evening obsession with Bible study meant that it wasn't a question of if he'd drop a homily on Cameron, but when. Whether hearing about Cameron's drinking habits or his relationship with his father, someone was sure to have provided plenty of fuel for a sermon, which was the last thing he needed.

Around mid-afternoon on Saturday, the second weekend of June, it dawned on him that while Stan had deftly allowed him the freedom of the range, he had also limited his access to the conveniences in Greybull. As a result, nothing stronger than Hannah's iced tea had touched Cameron's lips—a fact that needed to change, but Cameron had a problem. Todd, disgustingly self-absorbed and lazy, was the most likely ... no, the only candidate to help Cameron find both a party and something strong to drink.

He found Todd on his bunk, plugged into earbuds and staring at a magazine.

"Want to hitch a ride into Greybull?" Cameron asked. "I heard that the Horseshoe Saloon isn't particular about checking IDs at the drive-through. What do you say? Want a beer?"

"No!" Todd snorted, "I want something *way* stronger than beer."

That wasn't going to happen, but maybe he could change Todd's mind. Cameron walked to the other side of the cabin then turned and stared at Todd who seemed oblivious to everything in the universe beyond the reach of his earbuds. Disgusted, Cameron left, flinging the cabin door open. So much for Todd and beer. Without a beer, a party, or anything else to look forward to, he strode out to the corral, where he saddled and mounted Azariah. He turned the horse toward the road, crossed it, and followed a path up the hill to Bureau of Land Management land at the base of the mountains. Surrounded by grass, sage, and mountains, he let the sky envelop him as a delightful dream returned, one that had visited him with increasing frequency when he was alone with Azariah. He imagined Lydia riding with him, talking and laughing, all in slight variations of long-ago conversations. In waking dreams, she rode along as comfortable as Hannah and as much in love with the range, the endless peace, and freedom, as he. Yes, she too would love Wyoming.

Several hours later he returned recharged, invigorated, and ready to take on any challenge and interlopers, even the Centurion—Drew. He found everyone eating dinner. "Wow. It smells great in here." He grinned and sat down next to Todd.

"Welcome back." Hannah handed him a bowl of chili.

"Thank you." Cameron smiled and turned to Todd. "So how was your day?"

"What do you care?"

Ugh. Some things hadn't improved. He turned to Tweedle Dee and Tweedle Dum, names Cameron had assigned to Sam and Mick. One grunted with his face just above the plate.

"Well, I had a great day." Cameron glanced around the table. "Just a little while ago, I saw a couple of pronghorns. Azariah and I must have been quiet enough because they came very close." Only Hannah and Stan appeared interested, but Cameron didn't care. He'd had a good afternoon, and he was ready to take on all comers, whether in a foul or fair mood. "Mrs. Boehmer, this is wonderful," he continued with a hearty laugh meant to shame Drew, Todd, and the twins.

"I'm glad you like it," she answered.

"Hey, Drew, can you teach me how to use the whip? Todd, you should get him to show you, too. He snaps that thing and barely catches a cow's heel, then off they go."

Neither Todd nor Drew looked up from their plates. *Typical. What jerks! Oh well.* Cameron swallowed a spoonful of chili. "Drew, seriously, I want you to show me how it's done."

"Yes, Drew," Hannah said to the diffident young man stuffing chili into his face. "You're very good at it."

Drew didn't look up. *Really!* Since somebody needed to be civil, Cameron persevered. "I thought cows only mooed when they were happy. Those guys moo like crazy when they aren't the least bit happy."

"You're thinking of lowing," Stan added with a restrained chuckle and glanced at Cameron.

Nice. So he wasn't totally dull. "Isn't lowing what the cattle did when Jesus was in the manger? Wasn't that the way the song went? 'The cattle are lowing, the poor baby' ..."

Stan's grin widened. "You've given it a whole new meaning."

"Yes, sir, and thanks for the compliment about my singing." Cameron laughed, glad to see that *someone* had a sense of humor.

"I like your voice," Hannah intoned, "and don't worry about the noise the cattle make. They don't like being bothered." She turned to Drew. "How were they today?"

"Same as always."

"Cameron." Hannah smiled, friendly and easy, "did Drew mention that he's an assistant chef at a restaurant in Erie, Pennsylvania? Maybe you can get him to share some of the recipes."

Cameron grinned at Hannah then turned to Drew. "Wow. You're a chef. What kind of restaurant is it?"

"Italian."

"I like Italian." He tipped his chair back onto the rear two legs and noted Stan's quick smile. Ah, yes, he had Stan's attention. "Back home, Italian usually comes with pizza. I'll bet your food's good."

"It's okay."

Ah yes, the gladiator at the trough. All work and no play made the dude rude, dull, and annoying.

Even before dinner ended, Cameron's cheer began to fade. After helping Hannah with the dishes, he joined Todd and the Tweedles, who came to life around the pool table. Cameron again hinted to Todd that they should drive into Greybull.

"If I get into town," Todd growled, "it won't be to buy beer. I'm sure that even here, a hundred miles from nowhere, there's someone who's got what I want. I just gotta find him ... or her."

Wow. A man with a heart like Justin's. A man to be avoided. But Cameron still wanted a beer. Thus, after the pool game broke up, he followed tedious, vain, and obnoxious Todd back to the cabin. Never in Cameron's life had he expended such a Herculean effort to get drunk. Beer and willing friends had always been readily available. Inside the cabin, Cameron found Todd already lying on his bunk, shoes still on, reading the same magazine he had read every night since arriving. Perhaps, Drew was not the strangest character on the ranch.

"Yo!" Cameron smiled, then walked to his side of the cabin and busied himself. Todd said nothing, nor did he move. Cameron washed his hands and then carried the towel over to Todd's side. "So what did y'all do today?"

"Nothing."

"I heard you cleaned up the corral. You should have come with us, or don't you like following behind a walking fertilizer factory?"

"Are you kidding?"

"No, it's fascinating." Cameron laughed then snapped his towel at a moth that flitted near the end of Todd's bunk. "Got 'im!"

"Stupid animals."

"Yeah, well, they can't be that stupid. They found every drop of water within a mile, even if it was only a mudhole." Cameron laughed. "I think I'll be saying, 'Go, cow,' in my sleep."

"Sounds like you're just as stupid as them."

Was a beer worth this much aggravation? Maybe. Cameron smiled. "What are you listening to?"

"None of your business." Todd glared at Cameron and then at the magazine.

What rock did this slug crawl out from under? Cameron stuffed his enmity behind a grin. "So do you play golf?"

"What are you trying to do?" Todd twisted his face into a knot.

"I don't know. Waste time." Cameron returned to his side of the cabin and considered his options. He had none. Party choices—or anything else that offered an escape—didn't exist. Todd was it. He again walked back to Todd's side of the cabin as more than half of his head suggested he quit. "You know, we could make the best of this."

"You've got to be kidding. This is a prison. Can't you tell?"

"I noticed the barbed wire, but it's for the stupid cattle. So what do you say we work together?"

"There are enough rednecks around here. I don't need to be bothered by one more."

Redneck? No one had ever referred to Cameron as a redneck, and he was well aware of the usual qualifications for the title. *Jerk!* Cameron returned to his side of the cabin.

"Quit bugging me," Todd hollered. "Man, don't you even know why you're out here?"

Ready to snap back, Cameron instead picked up a Cussler novel that he had brought with him.

"You're here because you're an alcoholic," Todd hollered.

Really? Okay. In slow, even steps, each heel knocking against the dry floorboards, Cameron walked to Todd's room. He stopped in the doorway, his lips taut to contain his temper. "I turned down a job in cancer research to come out here. Maybe alcohol is your problem, but it's not mine."

"I'm not an alcoholic. I killed somebody."

"Okay. Fine." Cameron smiled, but he wasn't laughing. He didn't need Todd's venom.

Without hesitating, he returned to his bunk and climbed in. He opened the book; then he slammed it shut. He'd forgotten that he'd finished it the previous night. Thumping his knuckles against the cover, he sorted through a revised list of options. None included staying in the cabin with Todd, so he left, letting the screen door slam behind him. In the distance, he heard Stan, Drew, and Hannah talking on the front porch. Todd's disposition had been vile, but not enough to send Cameron running to a Bible study.

Instead, he sat down on the darkened steps that led into the washroom where Hannah kept a large freezer. Assured of privacy, he leaned forward, interlocked his fingers while supporting his elbows on his knees, and forcibly calmed his temper. For a second, he imagined how Todd might have killed someone but laughed at the prospect. Murder required too much energy, and Todd was not into "effort." At least the twins, Sam and Mick, worked hard. So what could he do? He could find something to read. Hmm. Not a bad option. He remembered the tall bookcase that sat against the back wall opposite the television. Books! Lots of them. Maybe one was worth reading. Maybe.

Not wanting to attract attention, Cameron removed his boots and slipped through the door. He crept up to the bookcase and read the titles: *The Divine Comedy, Moby Dick, War and Peace, The Brothers Karamazov*, among others. Whoa, whose books were these? The next shelf held a neat row of paperback books with identical, color-coded bindings. Each carried the name of a book in the Bible: *Galatians, Ephesians*. Some included multiple books while a few individual books appeared in two volumes—all were written by men named Barclay and Boice. None of the volumes matched those in his father's collection, but several matched books he had seen at Uncle Nathan's house.

Cameron picked several books from the top shelf and scanned them: *A New Eusebius, The Cost of Discipleship*, books by Frances Schaeffer and others by R. C. Sproul. All appeared to be "dissertations designed to inculcate" or rather indoctrinate the reader, as an English professor had once described similarly obscure books. Cameron laughed. Stan was even weirder than he had imagined. How could Stan, a man with a prodigious knowledge of the Bible, keep from hammering Cameron for his lack of faith—or tolerate Todd, and the twins for that matter? Stan may have been different from Cameron's sanctimonious father and his stiff-lipped Christian cronies who trekked off to Bible studies ad nauseam, but that didn't change Cameron's opinion about Christians in general.

So about Stan: What kind of man ran a ranch, herded grumpy cattle, and advised small accounting firms, all while holding a private faith and reading classic literature in his free time? Stan was indeed surprising. Finally, Cameron picked *The Count of Monte Cristo* and retreated to the cabin where he climbed into bed. Around ten, Drew returned, showered, and climbed into bed without saying a word.

Darkness shrouded the mountains, seeming to erase their existence, as loneliness settled around Cameron. Gone were the warmth of the sun, Hannah's ready encouragement, and Leo's watchful eye. Instead, Cameron's roommates felt as comforting as corpses. He pulled his blanket over his shoulder and tried to imagine Lydia's smile, but he could not. Instead, he remembered her eyes staring straight ahead as he drove her home on New Year's. In the dark hour before midnight, his protective levees crumbled, flooding him with a river of memories. Among his many mistakes—including having let Justin ruin his life—the most painful had been underestimating Lydia, and how much he loved her. The truth poured over him. He could dream about her, but she would never join him on the open range or anywhere else.

Ever since Grandpa's death, Cameron had lived two lives: smiling and happy by day, but at night, smothered by emptiness. As time crept by, everything Cameron loved seemed farther and farther away. A sigh heaved his chest as he remembered his mother. Like an angel, she comforted him, saying she loved him regardless. He nuzzled into his pillow, remembering her scent and wishing she was near.

Dr. Vanderholf's examination room had become altogether too familiar in Marrah's opinion. Too often during the previous year, she had waited in the same metal chair, in the same small room, washed with cold fluorescent light. She checked her watch, sighed, drummed her fingers on the tabletop, and picked up a pamphlet, the same one she had read during four earlier visits.

Finally, the door opened, and Dr. Vanderholf entered carrying a tablet. He extended a hand to her. "So how is your summer going?" he asked.

"Fine, but I think I overdid it while gardening."

"What's the problem?"

"My wrist swells up and makes it hard to sleep. If I turn over wrong, it wakes me up."

"Let's take a look."

The young doctor sat down and took her hand. He drew it toward him, extending her arm. He twisted her hand one direction, then the other, watching the movement of the tendons and bones. "Does this hurt?"

"Some."

He checked his notes, then leaned back in his chair and studied her. She smiled to ease the skepticism she read in his calm gaze. He gave a few instructions, added a few pleasantries, and then shook her hand again.

Seeing him turn to leave, she blurted, "I'm out of my prescription."

Again, he studied her. "I'll write another one, but I want you to try to use fewer of them. I also want you to go more frequently to the physical therapist. The receptionist will make you another appointment. If you're still not improving, I want to consider a different treatment."

Reflexive fear knitted Marrah's brow. "More surgery?"

"No, not necessarily. But I want to see you in September after you've worked with a PT."

She agreed. He wrote the prescription, then left. When she arrived home, she read the sheet and counted the pills—too few to last until her next appointment. A vein in her left temple throbbed. Reducing the number of pills she took was not an option, but what could she do? She went to the drawer with the neatly folded scarves and withdrew a vial. She counted the pills and stared at them. Her original count had been correct. Both prescriptions would run out before Labor Day. In the past, when she stopped taking the pills, she'd fallen to pieces, screamed at Jake, or cried all night, alone in the darkened guest room. She missed her brother and wondered how long Jake would stay. How much more could she—or he, take?

She touched the pills with her fingertip, lining them up. It was wrong to take so many, but she had no choice. The Norco helped her wrist, but it also helped her believe that Jake might stay. And it shielded her from memories no sixteen-year-old should have. No daughter should see her father die. As a starving man craves food, she longed for a different past, to no longer see him crumpled at her feet, unable to save him when no one answered her cries for help. Afterward, Steve had become her shelter, protecting her from the memory of that day. When he died, the memories had flooded back, drowning her. Jake had only stayed for Steve. Soon, he would leave. Then she'd only have the pills. She'd try to cut back, but not now.

So to get more pills she needed another prescription, and that meant seeing another doctor. Her ob-gyn doctor had written the second Norco prescription. She needed someone else. She scanned the internet, checking each location on a map. She needed to stay off the prescription grid, but with a legitimate source. She found one who wouldn't know she'd faked Lois's ID. Then she'd only have to deal with Lois—and only if she found out. She dialed the number. What doctor wouldn't want to help a patient with an injury such as hers? After speaking to the receptionist and working out insurance details, Marrah made an appointment for early August.

13

If Cameron had inherited anything from Grandpa, it had been his resourcefulness, a useful talent that had served him well. Never in his life, though, had his choices been so few. Since spring break, life had pushed him until he stood with his back pressed hard between two adjoining walls with gallons of wet paint surrounding his feet, but he had not painted himself into that corner. Instead, Uncle Nathan had gleefully grabbed a brush and paint, gallons of it, when he suggested that Cameron spend the summer with Stan. To survive, Cameron had pumped air into his enthusiasm each morning, only to have it deflate by midafternoon. But for his friendship with Leo, the routine would have been unbearable. June ended with no real improvement, leaving Cameron exhausted from failed attempts to make the best of a really bad situation.

After lunch on the last Monday in June, he found Leo working alone in the tack shed. "Afternoon," he said, casually leaning his shoulder against the doorframe. "You know, in the South, people like to ask where someone is from. You don't seem to be from around here. So pardon me for asking, Where *are* you from?"

"LA, mostly." Leo grabbed a drill and toolbox and carried them outside, "but we've been here fifteen years. Sandy gave me a choice: move or get a divorce. I was in a low-paying, dead-end job, and our two young boys were getting older, so I didn't fight her. She said she'd heard about a rancher in Wyoming who needed help." The rancher was Stan, and the rest was history, a very long history, but Cameron enjoyed hearing the details. When he reached the end of his story, Leo paused and turned to face the mountains. "It's hard to believe that I get paid to enjoy that million-dollar view. I guess that makes me a king." Leo picked up a box of wire staples while Cameron wondered if his life could be that simple. "Last night, a neighbor's stray cow wrangled with the fence along the BLM. And won. Drew's out there, mending it. I need to take these to him. Come on along."

Cameron hopped in Stan's Polaris Ranger with Leo who drove to the north end of the fields. Leo entered the wet draw then climbed the dry slope and found Drew in a sagebrush littered corner. From atop the bench, the mountains looked shorter but longer as they rose above the spectacular swath of green fields that marked Stan's land. Above the fields, a grey-green bench sloped upward to the base of the mountain. From Cameron's perch, it seemed as if majesty and humility had fused, becoming king and pawn entwined and inseparable.

Later that night, in the dark hours before dawn, Cameron awoke to the sound of rustling sheets and muffled sobs. Several times since arriving, he had awoken to similar noises. They had come from Drew, flailing about in the dark. Earlier, Cameron had buried his head under his pillow, perturbed by the nocturnal whimpering, but this night, sympathy, perhaps piqued by curiosity, kept sleep away. Rather than asking Drew directly, though, Cameron decided to ask Leo in private.

The following day, he found the perfect opportunity when Stan sent Cameron, Leo, and Drew to the base of the mountains where a dozen heads of cattle, having broken through a fence, now munched in a thick stand of tall junipers and greasewood. After flushing most of them out, Drew, astride his horse Obed, reentered the brush for the last few heads. Seeing Leo alone, Cameron rode up next to him, leaned on the saddle horn and asked, "What's with Drew?"

"Him?" He nodded toward Drew. "Why?"

Rather than asking a direct question, Cameron entered through the back door. "How does he know this ranch so well?"

"That's easy. This is his third summer."

No wonder, but, "Why? Can't he get his problems worked out?"

"Problems? Is that why you think you're here?"

Cameron flushed but persisted. "Yeah—well, maybe. We're all misfits, not you, of course."

Leo tipped his head back and laughed heartily, which sent blood rushing to Cameron's cheeks. "That's not why you're here. Particularly not the two of you. We need the help. Why, even Mick and Sam are getting used to the place." At that moment, a cow scrambled up the embankment and out of the bramble, then immediately turned back toward the scrub. Leo spurred his horse, cutting in front of the wayward cow. For a moment it stared at him but then trotted toward the open grassland while Leo rejoined Cameron. "Ya know, some people are born with the worldly equivalent of a full tank. Others come in sitting on empty. Depending on how you see things, wealth and poverty aren't opposites. Either one can make or break us. If you think you're the master of your success, this place will break you." He nodded. "Survival depends upon where you find your strength." In the distance, Drew whistled, catching Cameron's ear as he coaxed the cows that still hid in the dark green and mustard yellow bramble. "If you want to know about Drew," Leo nodded toward him, "ask him. You might be surprised."

You might be surprised. It seemed to be a popular adage, but Cameron had yet to be surprised by much. Still, he considered Leo's suggestion. Through the following two days, he watched Drew but remained content to keep his distance. On the third day, Stan sent him with Drew to the upper pasture with a packhorse loaded with salt-lick blocks, each a cubic foot in size. They rode in silence, except when the silence became more disconcerting than talking, at least for Cameron who remembered Drew's nocturnal struggles. Since "weird and out of sorts" still described Drew, Cameron endured the silence. Finally, it became unbearable. "Hey, Drew. I was watching you with the lasso the other day."

"It's called a rope."

"Oh." So much for a conversation.

To Cameron's surprise, Drew continued with a guarded smile. "Here, I'll show you." He reached back and loosened the straps that held the stiff coil of twisted nylon to his saddle. "See? This one has a nylon honda." Drew pointed to a three-inch long, oval loop formed by a piece of hard nylon with a deep, outward-facing channel that held the rope in place. A knot secured the rope to the loop. The rest of the rope, having been threaded through the honda, formed another loop that Drew held in his right hand. "First, you slip enough rope through the honda to form the loop you want; then you catch the rope, like this." His right hand, holding two strands of the rope, slid to a point about eighteen inches from the honda. "That's the spoke," he pointed to the two strands of rope. "Now, you hold the coil with your left hand while you swing your right hand, making a loop." He lifted his right hand, shoulder-high, and began to swing the rope over his head. "Success depends on where you keep your elbow." With a flick of his right hand, Drew released the loop and lassoed a rangy sagebush, all while astride Obed. He jerked his hand, cinching the rope; then he smiled at Cameron. "That's all it is."

No longer the Roman gladiator in full regalia, Drew had bared his head; the helmet with its plume was missing. He still wore the warrior's boiled-leather breastplate—his essential weirdness. He carried the shield of experience, but what kind of gladiator sobs in his sleep? Perhaps beneath Drew's intimidating armor, a vulnerable heart pulsed. Maybe a soul hid within, one more scarred than Cameron's.

"Here." Drew held the rope so that it formed a large circle. "Hold it like this." He handed the wobbling loop to Cameron. "Spinning it both directions keeps the rope from twisting."

Though he held it as Drew instructed and gave it a spin as directed, the honda slipped, and the rope dropped to the ground. After several tries, Cameron handed it back.

"You'll get used to it. Just give it time."

Perhaps Drew was not as weird as Cameron had imagined. Had the gladiator also loosened the straps on his protective breastplate?

Late that afternoon, Cameron found Leo leading a horse to the corral. "Did you speak to Drew?" Leo asked.

"No." Though he should have.

"Give it a try. We're not different from him. We're just better at hiding our fears." Leo removed the halter. "Sometimes, the wind around here can get going, channeled between the mountains and hills." His thumb rubbed the thick rope. "It's scary."

"You? Scared?"

"Sure." Leo released the horse and closed the gate as a chicken scurried by. "Why not? Do you think I'm that strong?" Cameron dared not answer. If the wind could spook Leo, then what would Cameron do?

Leo leaned against the gate. "When I first started working here, I was in the habit of feeling sorry for myself. Then one weekend in May, smack in the middle of high water, the sky opened up. Rain poured for two days, sending mud down Trapper, Horse and other creeks to join icy water coming down from the mountains. Incredible! While this was going on, Stan takes me down to the big bridge next to the highway as it crosses Shell Creek. On a day like today, it's a nice trout stream, and the bridge looks like it could last through the ages, but not that day. The water was flying, churning in thick muddy waves, climbing over themselves to escape. Just like that, Stan walks out on the bridge and turns to me, waving for me to join him. I was *not* going out there but Stan knew better. He knew how well it'd been built and the foundation beneath it. That flood couldn't harm it. I'll never forget the sight. There he stood, in the center of the bridge with his arms spread out and his poncho flapping wildly about him, his eyes like beacons. He had some kind of a wild and rebellious smile across his face. He shouted, sorta to me, but loud enough for anyone willing to listen. 'On what rock do you stand?' He wanted me to trust God as thoroughly as he did. He didn't care if he got washed away. He knew he was safe. He extended his hand and just smiled, speaking sorta quietly, 'Come, stand in the living water.'"

"What'd you do?"

"I stood right where I was and watched him out there. Then Stan threw his head back and laughed. 'Why are you afraid?' He asked, but I didn't move. You see, I misunderstood his question; or rather, I wasn't ready. I wanted muddy dirt right under my feet. I didn't trust anything I couldn't grab ahold of. Stan isn't like that. He was out there, but he wasn't alone. God was with him. He wasn't afraid of the storm or the earthbound water. It could wash him away, but God wouldn't fail him." Leo's kind smile lingered as his eyes brightened.

Finally, he laughed, startling Cameron. "Feel that wind, Cameron. Reach your hand out!" Leo held up his hand with its palm turned into the wind. "It's the hand of God." With a shrug, he pushed away from the gate and turned toward the barn. "I've got two quick pieces of advice," he said with a wink. "Enjoy Drew's friendship, and give Stan a break."

Cameron's eyes followed Leo, but not a muscle moved. Cameron had held Stan at a distance, and for a good cause. If not for Stan, he wouldn't be in Wyoming. A gust of wind buffeted his hat. In the distance, Drew let out a whoop and an even louder whistle and then appeared at the head of the dry wash. In front of him were two cows, a mother and her calf that had strayed too far into the sagebrush. Seeing Drew's unassuming smile, Cameron remembered Leo's advice to speak to him. But while he realized he might have misjudged Drew, he still didn't trust Stan.

After dinner, Cameron walked outside and studied the long face of the Bighorn Mountains. The sun, low on the western horizon, washed the ridge in rich salmon and orange and awoke the mysterious voice in Cameron's heart. "They are magnificent, aren't they?" someone behind him said. Turning, Cameron saw Drew with an easy smile that didn't fit any character so far on Cameron's list of personas. "I like the way you handle Azariah," Drew went on. "He's a fine horse."

"Thanks." Cameron smiled and turned back to face the mountains.

"You should try learning to rope the calves," Drew continued. "I took Azariah out yesterday while you were helping Leo. He already knows what to do. He won't lean in."

"What do you mean?"

"To rope a calf, the horse has to work with you. They have to be trained, and Azariah's a quick study. Stan's son Mark trained him. So tomorrow, if you want, I'll show you the basics. It's all about reading Azariah. You can do it, 'cause you listen to him." Drew, the gladiator, had not only removed his helmet but had also unlatched his protective breastplate with a smile that was at once candid and wise. "Let me know when you're ready."

With a shy smile, he turned and walked away. Later that night, Cameron heard him on the porch with Stan. The calm rhythm of their voices lacked the rabid compulsion so characteristic of the discussions Cameron's father led. But regardless, Cameron wasn't ready to join them. Instead, he walked out into the open yard between the main house and his cabin. Overhead, a profusion of stars dusted the night sky. Only on cold winter nights had he seen half as many stars. Finally, he retreated to his bunk, where he reread emails from his mother and then picked up his book. Later, as he lulled between waking and sleeping, he relived New Year's Eve. In his dream, unlike that night, he and Lydia found a quiet corner where they laughed, talked, and even kissed. The thought of holding her in his arms soothed his aching heart.

14

Lydia watched the beaming bride and groom as the minister spread his arms before the assembled friends and family at Chalmers First Baptist Church. "I present to you, Mr. and Mrs. Daniel Gunn McCall."

As the happy couple, arm in arm ascended the aisle between pews bedecked with flowers, Lydia leaned close to her grandmother. "Please tell me that someone my age didn't just get married."

After the couple passed and the sound of rustling silk faded, Nana chuckled. "Does it bother you?"

Lydia painted a gracious smile on her face and waited to answer until the parents and grandmothers of the newlyweds, each lady on the arm of a tuxedo-clad usher, had departed. She leaned closer. "Yes," she whispered, stifling her sarcastic glee.

All around, smiling but subdued men and women nodded and whispered greetings as they moved toward the rear of the century-old church. A lady or two waved to Nana, who smiled and nodded, but after most had passed, Lydia defended herself. "Chloe's too young."

"My dear," Nana smiled, overtly demure, "I'm qualified to be the old woman, not you. What you mean to say is that *you're* too young, and that's fine."

"I'm going to be like Mom and take my time, spend a few years on my own."

"That sounds reasonable."

Lydia adored Nana's polished elegance but also the sarcasm that sometimes lurked behind her polite decorum. "Nana, I mean it."

"I'm sure you do, and I'm proud that you have such wonderful plans for the future."

Lydia accepted defeat and wrapped her arm around her grandmother's. "I never knew Grandfather, but if he knew to marry you, then I want to marry someone like him. I wish I had known him."

"He was a very fine man."

"Is that why you never remarried?"

Nana brushed a stray hair away from Lydia's eyes. "He was close to perfect."

Fifteen minutes later, Lydia found a parking space in the crowded lot of the Montebello Country Club, Chalmers's prestigious golf and tennis association. Even though Nana had kept a ladies' membership for decades after her husband died, Lydia had deemed the club to be the favored haunt of the popular people in her high school, including Cameron Asher. Thus, while she sometimes joined Nana for dinner, her visits had been rare. She made an exception, though, for Chloe.

Inside the ballroom, urns overflowing with hydrangeas and roses—and set atop tables festooned with lace and tulle, scented the air with the sweetness of a summer garden. Cream-on-white Toile de Jouy lay draped across serving tables covered with trays offering cold shrimp, assorted cheeses, fruit, various canapés, crab cakes, and petit fours, all in keeping with the bride's style, and genteel expectations. Despite being the oldest daughter in a socially notable family, Chloe Morton was as likable and down to earth as Aimee, her distant cousin and close friend. Though Chalmers's convoluted, multigenerational family connections sometimes seemed snobbish, Lydia had come to accept that Nana, through time and friendships, was now a part of that world. So when Lydia asked, Nana answered with typical nonchalance. "Her grandmother is an old friend of mine. Also, Ben's late wife Sylvia was Chloe's great-aunt, though I didn't have the pleasure of meeting Sylvia."

"Oh." So Aimee really was related to half the town. Lydia thought about asking the age-old question, "Why didn't you marry Ben?" but the answer would have been the same: "Sometimes we choose to accept things as they are, not as we might like them to be."

Nana nodded toward a group of young women. "Aren't those your friends, Aimee and Marybeth?"

Lydia brightened. "Yes."

"Go ahead. I'll find you later."

Lydia kissed her grandmother's cheek, smiled, and went to join her friends, even though they were talking to two of Lydia's least favorite people: Taylor Wyatt and Rachel Cumberland. Lydia straightened her shoulders, confident she knew exactly how to extract Aimee and Marybeth from the conversation.

"Oh-o-o!" Taylor cooed, "Can you believe that Chloe got married?" She eyed and simultaneously snubbed Lydia. "She was so quiet. I thought she'd never get married."

Never marry? She's only twenty-one, and lovely.

"Well, you know," Rachel shot a glance at Lydia. "She went to Converse for an MRS degree."

An MRS, at Converse? I don't think so. She majored in music therapy.

Taylor, Rachel's sidekick, added, "I wouldn't call Daniel 'cute.' Or is he called Danny?'"

Evil tickled Lydia's imagination as she pondered whether Rachel, a diminutive and plump marshmallow, or Taylor, who appeared to have a lifetime membership at a tanning salon, could find someone a tenth as nice as Dan. Fortunately, two former classmates joined the group. Lydia grabbed the opportunity, nodded to Aimee and Marybeth, and rolled her eyes, inviting them to join her somewhere else, anywhere.

Aimee tapped Marybeth's elbow, but as they stepped away, Rachel spoke. "Lydia, how's Duke?" Her dark brown eyes gave Lydia a once-over while a sneer wrinkled her round cheeks.

During high school, Rachel and Taylor had been a power duo with dubious popularity. Everything about Rachel irritated Lydia, from the rhinestone-encrusted clip that held back her thin brunette hair down to the Prada on her feet. Most of all, she disliked Rachel's dangerously manipulative tongue. Hence, her answer: "Fine." Her smile telegraphed what she didn't say: *So how goes it at Elon?*

"Found any rich guys yet?" A wicked glint in Rachel's eye shared company with her calculating question.

"They aren't rich today."

Aimee pulled Lydia's elbow, ready to exit. "Rachel, it was so good to see you."

"Hey, Lydia, I hear you played around over New Year's," Taylor gushed, with the unkindest leer Lydia could imagine. "With Cameron Asher."

Since Rachel rarely walked away when Taylor dropped morsels of gossip that were sure to feed a hungry crowd, the worst was yet to come. Luckily, the crowd was small. Rachel flashed a cold smile at Marybeth and Aimee, daring them to defend Lydia, on whom she fixed her eyes. "What'd y'all do?"

Behind a stiff smile, Lydia scrolled through a list of Nana's social graces. She distilled the strongest—a raging fire soon burns up its fuel, so be patient—into a cold gaze, a tactic that required mating disinterest and decorum while saying nothing.

"Uh-uh, girl." Rachel turned to Taylor and almost meowed. "I heard he got drunk and went off with another girl."

"That's not true," Marybeth snapped.

"Whatever." Rachel lifted her chin as her eyelids dropped, leaving only slits. "Guys like Cameron have lots of rebound chicks."

The remark was vintage Rachel, but it stung. Lydia squeezed Marybeth's hand and whispered, "It's all right."

"No, it isn't." Marybeth flushed. "My cousin was at that party. She said he was stone sober!"

Where did that come from?

Marybeth had long been one of the mildest, sweetest people Lydia knew, yet now she spoke up. "Cameron was a real jerk, not at all cool, but Lydia behaved like a lady."

"Oh," Rachel seized the opening. "He was missing Addie. She broke up with him right before Christmas." A weasely smile contorted her face.

"I heard he was devastated," Taylor added with the flick of an eyebrow.

Lydia ignored the bait, but the raging fire had plenty of fuel and an audience of snakes at its command. Lydia stepped back, inviting Aimee and Marybeth to follow.

Rachel, though, wasn't finished. "Cameron and Addie lived together for almost a year, but he's got Rita now. She lives at the house on weekends—all weekend. We've met. I like her style."

Was Lydia supposed to be surprised by Cameron's nocturnal behavior? Still, Rachel's revelation only increased her dismay that she had ever imagined that he might be thoughtful and intelligent—or that they had anything in common. But enough! It was past time to leave, but how? Religion! It would irritate Rachel and send Taylor running.

Before she could speak, Rachel caught Aimee's arm. "You should see Cameron and Rita together. Both tall, blond, gorgeous. Perfect for each other."

Lydia steeled her determination to leave. "Rachel, did you see Marybeth's article in the *Chalmers Chronicle*? She wrote about a group of retired Christian businesswomen who use their experience and faith to empower young, at-risk girls. Isn't that great?"

"No." Taylor lifted her nose high enough to drown if it rained. "Nursing homes stink." She turned to scan the crowded room, probably looking for unattached men.

As Lydia again stepped back, Aimee threw a terse smile squarely at Rachel. "You're lying about Cameron."

No! Please, let's just leave, but Rachel's eyes flashed at the scent of fresh blood. Lydia tugged at Aimee's sleeve, but Aimee ignored her.

"Oh, it's the truth," Rachel jeered. "Everybody knows about Rita."

But who cares?

"I know," Rachel gloated, "because I date a guy in the fraternity next to his, and I've seen them together." She leveled her eyes, thin and harsh, on Lydia. "He's *nuts* about her."

A breeze lifted the sheers covering the tall French doors and washed Lydia with the fabulous scent of gardenias and providential inspiration: build a backfire! She managed a smile, one that would have made Rembrandt's Saskia proud. "I heard great things about your new guy." Whether it was true or not, she didn't care.

"Yeah, and he's really cute." Rachel turned to another girl who had just joined them. "He's a lacrosse player."

Finally! One by one, Lydia, Aimee, and Marybeth slipped away from the clutch as Rachel regaled her chicks.

After escaping to the opposite side of the ballroom, Aimee shot a caustic glare at Rachel and then turned to Lydia. "She's just jealous."

"No, it's just her way." Lydia found a table and sat down. "Aimee, I've thought a lot about what you said when we were sailing last month—about Cameron, that is." She heaved her chest into an audible sigh. "I'm glad for his sake that you love him." She hadn't asked to be his cousin. Nor had she lorded it over Lydia. "No, I should have known better than to accept his invitation to Paul's New Year's party. It's not your fault that I read more into the relationship than he did. We were friends at the diner. Nothing else. Just buddies."

"That's where you're wrong," Marybeth declared, catching Lydia by surprise. "You were two people who allowed each other to be yourselves. I saw the way he used to look at you." Without blinking, she turned to Aimee, who stared into the crowd but saw no one. "Aimee, what are you thinking?"

Melancholy had enveloped Aimee, hiding her smile. "Seeing the usher escort Chloe's mom to her seat was sad, but seeing Daniel dancing with her just now ... well." She turned tearful but fiery eyes to Lydia. "Cameron didn't deprive me of someday seeing the love of my life dancing with my mother. Justin did that. Please, ignore Rachel and everything she said. She wants you to be as miserable as she is."

Lydia played with a paper napkin. "It was a stupid crush. Cameron isn't my type, and I'm not his." Lydia shrugged. "And now, even the friendship is gone, and that makes me sad."

She packed away her bruised pride, filed it under lessons learned, and then approached a truth that she had long avoided. Pride and shame had energized the pity party she had staged at Aimee's house the night after the date that Justin had set up between her and Cameron. Had she not indulged her childish whim, she would not have been at Aimee's house. She would have been at home in her bed when Nana called shortly after midnight, saying Uncle Steve had been admitted to the ER.

"Sweetheart, your father and I are meeting Nana at the hospital. It's Uncle Steve."

Lydia's heart leaped into her throat. "What's wrong with him?"

"Nana took him in earlier. The doctors said he had a heart attack."

"I want to go."

"No. I don't want you on the road this late. I'll call you."

For the next hour, Lydia tossed, sleeping briefly and checking the clock. One thirty. She jostled Aimee's shoulder and told her about Uncle Steve. "Tell your mom I'm going to the hospital." Lydia dressed and packed, but when she reached the kitchen, Mrs. Duncan met her. Lydia pressed her point. "I can't sleep. I need to know if he's all right."

"Okay, but I'll drive."

After Mrs. Duncan dropped Lydia off at the emergency room and drove away, Justin Sloane ran a light, hitting her broadside. Whether or not Aimee forgave Cameron, Lydia couldn't erase her memories of the sad events that followed, vivid images that whispered to her above the music and noise of the wedding.

The sound of sirens again pushed sleep aside. Another ambulance had arrived at the emergency room where Lydia waited. Leaning her head on her father's shoulder, waiting for news about Uncle Steve, she'd grown used to the constant noise of the waiting room. This time, when the ambulance entry doors swung open, Lydia stared in stunned disbelief as Aimee, sobbing and clinging to her father, appeared. *What happened?*

Seeing Lydia, Aimee rushed to her, shaking from head to toe. "Lydia, I'm so scared."

Lydia hugged Aimee to her chest, hoping not to shake as well. "It's going to be all right." But Lydia had no point of reference; then she realized that the patient surrounded by nurses, EMS technicians, and equipment was Aimee's mother, Mrs. Duncan. Panic engulfed Lydia, and then an arm wrapped around her shoulder. It was her mother; she guided the girls to a seat, putting Aimee on one side and Lydia on the other. While Aimee sobbed uncontrollably, Lydia clung to her mother, who held them both and rocked and rocked, and rocked. Through the light of dawn and into the morning Aimee and Lydia huddled, surrounded by her mother's protective wings. At ten, Aimee's father approached, his shoulders slumped by a burden that no father wanted to carry. Dark bags hung beneath his eyes that seemed devoid of life.

"Aimee, honey, you need to come and say goodbye to your mother." He turned to Lydia's mother. "Anne ...." For a moment, he fell silent. "With God's grace, she can still help someone ... at least her organs can. She wanted it that way."

He extended his hand to Aimee, who collapsed into his arms, sobbing. Lydia stood, shaking, watching father and daughter turn to leave, arms wound around each other. Then Aimee spun around, facing Lydia. Lines etched her cheeks and tears rimmed her eyes that were wide with fear. "Come with me." Lydia recoiled. "Please," Aimee asked, stifling a sob.

Lydia's chest collapsed, crushing her heart. Tears burned her eyes. She couldn't. She turned to her mother, red-eyed and hoping for some excuse, but she said nothing. Lydia looked back at Aimee. In that instant, God alone, it seemed, filled her with courage, preventing her from self-preserving flight. She heard her mother whisper, "I'll come with you and wait outside."

Helpless to do otherwise, Lydia stepped into the chasm that had swallowed Aimee. Sobbing and shaking, she followed her friend, then stood next to her in the dim fluorescent light of the ICU room. Aimee stroked her mother's hair as the ventilator's slow rhythm heaved Mrs. Duncan's chest upward, then stopped to let it fall. Aimee's father and older brother came and went from the darkened room, making plans for when the machines were turned off, but Aimee stayed by her mother's side. Through the day and night, Aimee stayed, holding her mother's lifeless hand, and Lydia stayed by Aimee's side. The following morning, Mrs. Duncan died.

Grace had prevented Lydia from hating God, but she prayed for the day when she might understand his reasons for letting Satan wrench a hole in Aimee's life. Though God had claimed Mrs. Duncan for eternity, it still seemed terribly unfair.

In the background, the emcee announced, "Mr. and Mrs. Daniel McCall will now take the first dance."

Lydia turned to Aimee. "I believe you forgave Cameron, but I'm not so generous. The guy Rachel described seems too real to me."

"Rachel was lying."

"No, but when Cameron didn't talk to me about Justin, ever, it was like lying. I don't like people who lie to me."

"Y'all," Marybeth interrupted, nudging Lydia's shoulder, "his parents are here."

She nodded her head toward a group of people who stood several yards away. Lydia blushed as she recognized his mother, tall, slim, blond, and attired in a simple but exquisite aqua suit. Next to her stood a man an inch taller, with striking features and dark hair speckled with gray. Though Cameron favored his mother in many ways, his ice-blue eyes came from his father. She had seen those eyes when she entered the ballroom and wondered why they looked so familiar. Now she knew.

"Don't worry." Aimee glanced at his parents. "He's not here."

"Yeah. He's in Wyoming for the summer," Marybeth added.

"Wyoming?" Lydia laughed, mocking them. "Y'all. Enough! Marybeth, I read your article. It was great."

"Yes, do tell." Aimee brightened but also squeezed Lydia's hand and looked her straight in the eyes. "Please remember ...." Lydia grimaced and waited. "You didn't know Cameron before Judge Asher died. He was this happy kid and then afterward terribly sad—that is, until he met you. I, too, saw the way he looked at you. It wasn't silly puppy-eyed love but contentment, that happy glint I used to see. Please, be kind to him."

"Yes, ma'am. I can do that." But Aimee was wrong. She had to be. Then a strange feeling in Lydia's gut laughed. Gleefully! Regardless, Aimee and Marybeth were much too serious. "In the meantime, I'll practice my beauty queen wave." Lydia swiveled her hand. "Did you know this wave thing also works as a decongestant?"

"No!" Marybeth snickered.

"Yes, it does," Aimee interjected. "I saw it used ...."

Lydia laughed but looked past them to the dance floor where Chloe and Dan waltzed in a close embrace, their eyes seeing only each other. Once, in quiet moments long ago, Lydia had dreamed of being in Cameron's arms, dancing as Chloe now danced. Someday she and Cameron would dance and share a loving gaze, a gentle touch, but with someone else.

15

A s Drew once noted, routine Saturdays were no different from Monday or any other day of the week. The horses and everything else still needed attention, though not as much. Sunday was different. Typically, Todd and the Tweedles slept until nine or later while everyone else was up by six thirty, which was long after sunrise. Since arriving, Cameron had split the difference, typically being up no later than seven thirty.

After breakfast on the second Saturday in July, he emailed his mother and then wandered out to the corral to groom Azariah. "Good morning, sir." He stroked the horse's nose. "Look what I brought. Carrots. Yeah, you like them." The previous night, Drew had again tossed noisily, tormented by nightmares; one had caused him to cry out shortly after midnight. What cataclysm had he endured that now slipped out in violent dreams? Afterward, Cameron stared at the ceiling and considered waking Drew. By comparison, his painful memories paled when held against those that haunted Drew.

Cameron brushed Azariah's neck and fed him another carrot. "If you think I give you trouble, you should see my sister-in-law! Oh, man. She's a tough cookie. You're such a softy, she wouldn't need to tame you; you'd follow behind her, nudging her with this big nose and pleading, 'Pet me, please.' And she would." The horse grabbed another carrot as Cameron brushed then smoothed its back. "Yeah, but she rides English style. You have no idea what that means." When Azariah finished the last carrot, Cameron put the rope halter on him and strolled him around the corral. "It means that she'd expect you to obey her." He leaned close to Azariah. "You don't fool me. I know who's the boss around here and it isn't me!"

"Cameron!"

He turned to see Stan approaching. Despite his usual easy stride, something about him seemed different, more open.

"I'm going into town. Drew's going too. Want to join us?"

Of course! After two months on the ranch, Cameron would jump at any chance to go into town. A week earlier, he'd ridden with Leo into Shell to meet a trio of fly fishers who had rented Stan's mountain campsite for a week. He never imagined that the dimmest vestiges of civilization could look so good.

"First," Stan continued, "I thought we'd take a ride partway up Highway 14."

Cameron grinned at Azariah, "Sorry to leave you, bud." He removed the halter. "We'll bug the cattle this afternoon."

Finally! A ride beyond the ridge and into the stalwart mountains. *Come*, the mountains whispered. Ten minutes later, Stan, Drew, and Cameron climbed into the pickup. When he reached Highway 14, Stan turned east. Red hills—reminiscent of Carolina clay—lined the approach to Shell Canyon. A sign recorded the age of the surrounding rocks: Jurassic Period, 160 million years. A short distance farther, the road entered a narrow gorge cut by the creek as it exited the mountain. Inside the gorge, a sign read: Permian Period, 260 million years. A short distance farther, the road rose higher; a sign read: Mississippian Period, 350 million years. A series of switchbacks lifted the road as it entered and then climbed the southern face of a massive canyon hemmed in by vertical cliffs that rose another thousand feet above it. A thin black line topped the encircling rock wall; Leo said that was pine trees. Below the roadbed, dry grasses and sage blanketed the slope until it dropped from sight, hidden by the vertical, weathered-granite walls of the gorge.

Halfway up the canyon, Stan stopped at a turnout nestled into a boulder-filled ravine that cut sharply into the pine-shrouded slope. Paying little heed to Stan or Drew, Cameron crossed the road and jumped the guardrail. From there, protected from passing cars, he surveyed the canyon's wide, north side. He inhaled deeply, filling his chest with cool, clean air. To the west, the sides of the canyon formed a V-shaped window that looked west across the haze-shrouded tan benches and verdant farmland of the Bighorn Basin. From the height of his vantage point—perhaps three thousand feet above the basin, ridges that stood a thousand feet above the valley floor appeared to be no larger than vague ripples blown by a breeze across the surface of Glenlaural Lake. Across from his perch, on the canyon's south-facing slope, boulders, some larger than pickup trucks, lay strewn across the tawny grass and sagebrush-covered ground. If the sky and rolling splendor of the rangeland had awed Cameron, the vast canyon and the wind, whistling up from the basin humbled him.

Cameron heaved a sigh and absorbed the majesty of the canyon for he dared not look behind him. Drew had mentioned that Stan planned to stop at a spot where he liked to pray. Cameron was welcome to join them—because that's what Christians do: they welcome the wayward. *No thanks.* A car whisked by behind him as his foot brushed a clump of nodding grass. The parched plants were more likely to "choose Jesus" than was he. In fact, if he were able to leap across the canyon and stand atop the distant cliffs that guarded the highway and Shell Creek, he would feel no farther away from Stan than he did, sitting on the guardrail—mere yards away from them. Were he able to stuff the Andromeda galaxy into the space between himself and Stan, he could calculate that distance, but it would be irrelevant because he already felt that infinity stood between them. In a sense, the vast expanse of space would continue to feel smaller—more intimate and confined—than the immeasurable canyon created by the incomprehensible choice that separated him from Stan and Drew—and Lydia.

A few more cars whisked past behind him. The breeze rustled the sunflowers, sending them dancing, as time crept by. The defiant voice of the mountains caught his ear. Rather than peace, though, it spoke with the sound of battle, raging in a dark corner of his heart. Two armies appeared and faced off on the distant, grassy northern slope. The general leading one army commanded Cameron to stand up for himself: "Reject your father's God!" The opposing general summoned Cameron's curiosity: "What do Stan and Uncle Nathan believe?" Without warning, the first general hollered, "Prepare for battle!" The soldiers formed regimented lines and began to march, followed by a fleet of catapults and trebuchets. Each army, now ready for battle, flung boulders at each other across a forbidding cleft that ran north, cleaving the canyon's northern face. One general stated his cause: It was God's fault that Cameron's father wished Cameron had never been born. Charge! Wave after wave of soldiers raced forward beneath a cloud of dust, hurling their stones right at Cameron's heart, but his mind drifted. What about Drew? Something had ripped apart his heart, but he trusted God. Why? The second general shouted: Attack! Soldiers moved forward then, as suddenly as the battle began, it ceased. Silence filled the canyon.

"Are you ready to go?" Stan's deep voice jolted Cameron, but not a muscle twitched.

"Yes, sir."

During the thirty-minute drive to Greybull, Drew talked nonstop about cattle and horses while Cameron slumped into a corner of the rear seat. He stretched his legs out and watched the dreary landscape pass beyond his window. Meanwhile, the armies reassembled their ranks. *Rat-a-tat-tat* came the cadence of the drums. What did Stan care? Not much. *Rat-a-tat-tat.*

When they reached Greybull, Stan parked in front of the co-op. Drew turned to Cameron, "Aren't you coming?"

"No." Cameron rolled the windows down and watched a bentonite truck roll past. *Rat-a-tat-tat.* Two pickups passed, drawing his eye to the Horseshoe Saloon, which stood a block farther south, reviving his plan to buy a six-pack. *Rat-a-tat-tat.* Uncle Nathan only thought he understood. *Rat-a-tat-a-tat.* Having cut Todd and the Tweedles as plausible drinking buddies, Drew became Cameron's last resort. *Rat-a-tat-tat.* A good party was overdue. *Rat-a-tat-tat.* And Drew was old enough to buy beer. "Hurrah!" the ranks of the first army shouted. "Hurrah!"

A fierce quiet settled around Cameron as the generals of the second army huddled, preparing a defense. Fifteen minutes passed, and neither Stan nor Drew returned. *Rat-a-tat-tat.* Both sides rattled swords. Stan and Drew should have invited Cameron to join them in prayer. He would have turned them down, but that's a Christian's job, save the fallen. And Cameron was definitely fallen. *Rat-a-tat-tat.*

"Hey, Cameron." Drew sounded unusually excited.

Startled, Cameron looked up as Drew opened the passenger's door, his eyes dancing. "Look what I got." Drew held out a nylon rope twined around itself into a large loop. "It's yours. Stan said you needed your own."

"Oh." Cameron took the stiff cream-colored rope and examined it.

"Now you can make it respond to you."

Cameron slouched deeper into his seat, studying the loop formed at one end. He shrugged and set it on the seat next to him as Stan drove toward Blair's grocery. Perhaps his chance to get a beer had arrived. He followed Drew, who wore his cheerful, distinctly annoying persona. Once inside, Stan turned left toward the vegetables and disappeared. Cameron pulled Drew in the opposite direction, toward the neighboring store that held a license to sell alcohol. He lowered his voice. "What do you say we buy some beer? I'll pay, but you buy since you're legal, then we'll split it."

"I don't like beer." Drew's face dropped, becoming the flat, dull face that formed Cameron's first impression.

"You just need the right company."

"I don't want a beer. What do you think of the rope?"

"It's nice." Undaunted, Cameron followed Drew to the chips and dip section and made two more unsuccessful attempts.

Drew frowned. "I don't want a beer." He walked away and then turned and smiled, innocent as a doe-eyed calf. "You could join Stan and me after dinner."

"Tell you what," Cameron lied. "Maybe I will after a game of pool with Mick and Sam. I just thought a six-pack would help me sleep better."

"It keeps me awake."

Again Drew turned to leave, but Cameron grabbed his upper arm. "So you do drink."

The remnants of Drew's simpleton smile vanished. "Not anymore." His shoulders slumped as he freed himself from Cameron's grasp. He seemed ready to speak but was either unable or unwilling to do so. He stepped aside and disappeared around a wall of chips and snacks. Cameron turned around and saw Stan, watching from the end of the long aisle. Stan waited a moment longer as the lines around his eyes deepened into a stern glare. Finally, he walked toward Cameron and passed without smiling. Cameron watched him turn right toward the checkout counters but didn't follow. The drums in his head were silent. No generals called to their armies. The battlefield was empty. He was alone with only his conceit for company.

During the ride back, Cameron set his jaw while sending a few furtive glances in Stan's direct, but mostly stared out the window. Was this what rock bottom looked like? Back at the ranch, he helped Drew empty the truck but wished Stan would speak his mind. Several times, later in the day, he passed Stan who nodded but said nothing. Why didn't he chastise Cameron, mete out punishment, or do something to put the inevitable behind him? Instead, Stan came and went, talked, and was in every way his normal self. Midweek, he remained cool but accommodating, that is, related to getting work done. At night, the memory of Stan's eyes watching Cameron refused to fade. Beer had lost its allure, but Cameron's aversion to Drew returned, causing him to choose his seat at the table with care, leaving an empty seat between himself and Drew.

At the end of the week, he caught Stan glancing sidelong at him. The wrinkle in his brow, the faint downward turn of his mouth, and even the slight tilt of his head seemed oddly familiar. Cameron had seen the same mannerism before. *Grandpa—he always scolded with his eyes. Never with words.* Waves of homesickness rolled over him, tumbling ego over pride in a sandy churn before pounding him against the unforgiving seafloor. For a reprieve, he found Azariah and led him to the barn. As he brushed the horse's back and sides, his heart poured out the truth.

"I blew it this time. Come on, boy. Let's take a walk." As Azariah nuzzled Cameron's cheek, Cameron slid a rope halter over his ears and then led the horse through the gate and along the rutted road that followed the alfalfa fields. "I shouldn't have bothered Drew about buying beer. He and Stan act like nothing happened. —I mean, Drew talks to me, but *I* can't talk to him." Cameron glanced at the mountains, hoping for guidance and longing for absolution. "I was wrong. I know I disappointed him." He kicked several stones and watched them skitter ahead of him. "Drew's not that bad .... Todd's a jerk, and Sam and Mick are—well, what can I say? They don't want to be around me either, but Drew did. Yeah, he's a bit weird, but he's okay."

Cameron's foot found a perfect stone. First he kicked it ahead along the drive; then he kicked it harder and sent it into the drainage ditch that lined the field. "He's almost too nice, but ...." Cameron's smile returned. "He's got a decent sense of humor—as long as I watch my language, that is. Man, does he blush easily." The next thought erased his smile. "Azariah, the worst part is that I disappointed Leo. He hasn't said anything, but he doesn't have to. He's so easy to read." He reached the end of the field and turned around.

"Why doesn't Stan *say* something? You know, get fiery mad, like Dad does. Get it over with."

He walked most of the way back in silence. As he drew closer to the corral, he saw Drew kneeling next to Seth, Hannah's Appaloosa. What might he be doing? Having no idea, he wiped Azariah's cheek and then leaned his forehead against the horse's dense hair. "To think I thought I could be as good with y'all as he is." Drawing closer, Cameron watched Drew smooth his hands over the horse's bandaged leg. The gladiator had laid aside his crested helmet, shield, and sword. His linen shirt and boiled-leather breastplate lay nearby, revealing ropy scars that crossed his soul—but only scars, not open wounds.

Drew looked up and smiled, open and unafraid. "Yo, Cameron. Come look at Seth's leg. His foot caught a hole in the creek bed yesterday. It's a mild sprain. The vet showed me how to wrap it." Drew took the rope halter and led the horse slowly into the center of the corral. "See. He doesn't mind." Seth took several slow steps, following Drew's gentle pace. He even nuzzled Drew's shoulder. "Here." Drew held out the rope. "Take him for a walk. He likes you."

"He likes me?"

"Yeah. Didn't you notice? He's Azariah's buddy. They're always rolling around and chasing each other. So since Azariah likes you, Seth does, too."

Cameron took the rope as both horses followed him, Azariah on his left and Seth on his right. Throughout his life, Southern charm had pulled Cameron out of many tough places and turned many an enemy into friends. Now, though, it was time to give respect where it was due—to Drew. He owed him more than an apology for having spread between them, like mortar be-tween bricks, the cultured mantel of Southern hospitality designed to keep Drew at bay. The reliable shield against strangers—that said "Y'all stop by," as a polite gesture—not an actual invitation, had failed him. He glanced at Drew whose guileless eyes watched and smiled—a feature that Cameron had come to like. His thoughtlessness, though, had hobbled their friendship. Without smiling, he returned Seth to Drew and thanked him. He released Azariah and headed back to the cabin. Perhaps tomorrow or the next day he would know what to say.

16

Shortly after two in the morning on the following Sunday, Cameron awoke again to the sound of sniffles. Drew was again wrangling with his monsters. He soon slipped back into a quiet sleep, but Cameron remained awake, listening to the breeze rustling the leaves of the cottonwood trees and wondering if Stan knew about Drew's nocturnal struggles. If he didn't, then someone needed to tell him, and Cameron seemed to be that someone. But he wanted to speak to Stan alone.

Steeling his determination, he set aside his distrust of Stan and went to breakfast. When the first opportunity to pull him aside arose, Cameron hemmed, hedged, and said nothing. When Stan, Hannah, and Drew left for church, Cameron chided himself for bailing. Drew deserved better.

Finally, late that afternoon, he found Stan working next to the irrigation pivot. Ignoring his sweaty hands, he forged ahead—and then reversed course. *Hannah!* He'd talk to her instead. He found her in the kitchen putting dishes away. "Mrs. Boehmer, um, eh ...." Throughout the summer, she had reminded him to call her 'Hannah.' His mother's voice in his head, however, echoed strongly: *Please address adults as Mr. or Ms.*—which a Southern accent graciously encompassed as both Mrs. and Ms. Now, though, he needed to mollify her. "Hannah ... I thought y'all might want to know about what happens when Drew's asleep."

"He had another rough night?" Sadness flickered through her smile, increasing the gentility of her face.

"Yes, ma'am. I didn't think anyone had noticed."

"No, the others haven't. Drew told me."

What a relief. Cameron wanted to leave, but his feet refused to move. Instead, his thought voiced itself. "What's bothering him?"

"Here, sit down." She pulled out one of the chairs at the large table where he had eaten every day since May. "Seeing that you've become friends, Stan and I agreed to tell you about Drew's family. Maybe you can help him."

"Me?" Cameron lowered himself into the chair.

"Sure." She put a large pot in the sink and turned on the water. "Before coming here a few years ago, Drew had been on drugs, off them, back on again, and in and out of trouble, but his father Pete refused to give up on him. Pete did the best he could after Drew's mom abandoned him and their four boys when Drew was only two. Sadly, she reappeared twice. The second time Drew was ten, and she brought two young daughters with her."

Hannah finished scrubbing the pot, rinsed it, and set it aside. Then she sat down across from Cameron. She clasped her hands and rested them on the table. "Pete agreed to take her back, but on the condition that she would get clean. Four months later, she was back on drugs and took off, leaving the little girls behind—and ripped Drew's heart to pieces." She propped her elbows on the table and buried her face in her hands.

When she dropped them and looked up, sorrow and kindness merged in her soft gaze. "Thanks to Pete, the older boys survived, but Drew was devastated. Sadly, he later got into drugs himself. Pete tried so hard, but he couldn't prevent it—the drugs having become a substitute for her love. When she died of an overdose four years later, Drew went into a tailspin. He made friends with guys and girls who experimented all kinds of ways. For a while, he dangled over the abyss of drugs, some of them supposedly benign, until he was eighteen. After several near misses, a series of unfortunate and illegal decisions dropped him in front of a judge who just happened to be an old friend of Stan's." A small smile appeared. "Just happened. I don't believe things simply happen. Fate is another word for chance. The judge listened to Pete's impassioned pleas, put Drew on probation, and sent him here. Don't get me wrong. We're not counselors. We run a ranch."

Cameron stared down at his hands, folded together on the table, his fingers locked and impotent. "I thought he was much older than me." Oh, how he had misjudged Drew.

Hannah reached across the table and patted his forearm. "It's not us. It's the place." She again patted his arm. "Cameron, it changed the way you see him. Didn't it?"

"Yes, ma'am."

"He trusts you, but you need to go easier on yourself." When she smiled, he wanted to run for the door, but his feet felt nailed to the floor. "You didn't know about Drew's past."

No, but he could have asked or at least listened when Drew opened up to him. Instead, Cameron had ignored him. Drew deserved better—a better friend than Cameron. He stood and looked at the floor, said, "Thank you, ma'am," and turned away.

"Cameron." Hannah's voice halted his feet. "Stop running from Jesus."

His mouth twitched. "Yes, ma'am." Without turning to look at her, he nodded but felt her eyes following him. *She doesn't understand. She can't.* Once outside, he jammed his hat down over his brow and strode toward the corral. Drew and Stan had gone to cut hay on Stan's fields that lay closer to Greybull. They would not be back for several hours, which gave Cameron time to be alone on the open range.

"Here boy," he called to Azariah, but the horse had seen him coming and greeted him at the gate. After saddling the horse, Cameron mounted and spurred him toward the BLM. At the base of the W, he entered the cleft, following a cow path. No longer did he fear the boundless land of jackrabbits, sage, and rattlesnakes. It was, instead, the perfect place to be alone. He followed a meandering creek and trail as both rose higher until he found a spot where the creek bed opened and the flow slowed, providing water for Azariah, and shade, a grassy spot, and a view across the basin for him.

He dismounted and exchanged Azariah's bridle for a rope halter which he hitched to a small cottonwood tree, leaving enough slack for the horse to reach the water. Within seconds, Azariah smacked the water with his front hoof and nodded his head up and down. Water splashed everywhere, soaking Cameron.

"Attaboy," Cameron laughed and turned his face away from the water. In another season, the horse might have dropped to his knees and rolled in the stream, but summer had reduced it to a meandering rivulet. Instead, Azariah made himself at home, munching the grass and drinking the water. Cameron sat down on the saddle pad and used the saddle as a backrest.

The cool breeze, flowing down from the mountain, washed over him. He closed his eyes as a dozen visions flickered and vanished. He remembered the night of his last exam, the maniac's car, and the accident that shattered the night. A woman, the mother of a fellow student, might have died, but Cameron had not cared enough to ask Neil, who ran toward the wreck, about what he'd seen. Instead, he'd nursed a hangover and worried about himself. The memory was followed by older, happier times, filled with raucous laughter shared with his father and Trent, long before the ferocious argument that shattered their family. Perhaps if his father apologized, Trent would come home. After all, Trent had married Jacqueline and not Emily. Maybe then his family could be whole again. But the vision faded. How could two people—his father and brother—who had been so close, now hate each other so deeply? Why was forgiveness so difficult?

Another memory welled up. Shortly before Cameron's fourteenth birthday, he and Grandpa had stopped at a small waterfall, shaded by a thick canopy of branches, next to the Blue Ridge Parkway. Cameron had listened from his seat atop a lichen plastered boulder around which a swift-moving mountain stream flowed. Nearby, Grandpa had read aloud from his Bible, his mellow voice blending with the sound of the gurgling water. "There I will make a horn to sprout for David; I have prepared a lamp for my anointed." As Grandpa read aloud, a ray of sunlight had broken through the leaves, scattering glitter across the wet stones. Fascinated by the sparkling light, Cameron had reached out his hand, trying to catch it in his palm. "It's like I can feel it." Grandpa had answered, saying that it wasn't a paradox—whatever that was. Then with a smile and twinkling eyes, he left Cameron with a mystery: "Here's a riddle: Find the water that breaks and heals at the same moment and you'll understand. 'Lift up your heads, O gates! And be lifted up, O ancient doors, that the King of glory may come in.'"

Cameron never had and still couldn't solve the riddle. It made no sense, but he couldn't forget it. The next summer, Cameron and Grandpa returned to the waterfall, but not to solve the riddle. Instead, Grandpa had talked about the future, about things that Cameron would face. He told Cameron not to squander his heart, but to protect it. Later that week, Cameron learned the reason that Grandpa had spoken about things Cameron didn't understand or yet know—that Grandpa's doctors had delivered a dreadful diagnosis: pancreatic cancer. Two months later, he was gone. Two months after his death, Trent had moved out, and Cameron's family disintegrated. A week after Trent moved away, Lydia walked into the Park Street soup kitchen and into Cameron's life.

Cameron closed his eyes and felt the cool breeze and smelled the fresh air. Then as his breathing slowed, sunlight, shining through the poplar leaves, shimmered and quaked in a delicate dance on his eyelids, evoking a vision of Lydia. She walked toward him with a calm smile gracing her face. As she leaned over him, the wind caught her hair, tossing it about her head, creating a halo of fire and coal. The silhouette of her slender frame sent his heart racing. As she leaned closer, the corners of her mouth lifted, and her rounded lips formed the same delicious curve that had stopped his heart as she walked across the dais during her graduation ceremony. Her eyes sparkled, but the light faded, replaced by the solemn sadness that had enveloped her the day of Mrs. Duncan's funeral and again when he drove her home on New Year's Eve seven months ago.

"I'm so sorry." He reached to touch her cheek. "I wanted to explain, but I didn't know how. It was like something protected you—from me."

A deep sigh emptied his chest; then Lydia's smile returned, small and soft. She knelt and laid her hand upon his chest. Beneath her gentle touch, his heart pounded. She paused, winced, and then lifted her hand and lay down beside him. The fresh breeze ruffled the grass. Nearby, the creek gurgled over its stony bed; their eyes looked toward heaven. She entwined her fingers between his. He closed his hand around hers. It was almost ....

Something warm, wet, and velvety brushed his cheek, interrupting his dream. Cameron sputtered and opened his eyes, only to see Azariah's muzzle an inch from his face. He sat bolt upright and looked around, hoping to see Lydia, but the dream had vanished. Only Azariah, the creek, the cottonwoods and junipers, and his pounding heart remained. Again, Azariah nudged him. Cameron stood and pulled the horse close to his face. "You'd better not tell," he snorted. He smacked his dusty jeans in a useless effort to shake off the dirt. As he stepped into the bright sunlight beyond the dappled shade, a strange emptiness echoed through a wide hole in his heart. He missed Lydia more than ever, but the silent mountain had lifted his burden. He didn't feel good, but he felt better. The memory of Grandpa and the sparkling waterfall along the Blue Ridge Parkway returned. What kind of water could break and heal at the same time?

He saddled and mounted Azariah. They followed the path beside the creek, the horse munching at will—well, sort of—while he wandered back toward the ranch and wondered about Grandpa's riddle. Still stymied, but having exited the narrow gorge, he pulled up on the reins. "Well, buddy, I guess it's time to go back." When the path widened into a roadbed, he spurred Azariah into a gallop and then stopped at a high point on the dry benchlands. There he turned Azariah around to face the impenetrable range that towered above him, reaching toward the sky.

Again the voice in the mountains called to him. A yearning to race back up the W seized him. But he wouldn't stop at Stan's meadows. The voice called from someplace deeper and higher within the imposing range, where a special spring, stream, or waterfall held the answer he needed. "We'll go there, Azariah. We'll go there." He patted the horse's neck. Yes. Before he returned home, he and Azariah would flee to the mountains. He spoke aloud to the stony range: "I promise."

He turned Azariah toward the ranch. With the breeze in his face, the scent of sage surrounding him, and the intoxicating mountains behind him, peace enveloped him. Frustration, fear, and doubt had driven him into the wilds, but the deep cleft had set his heart free.

At the top of the bench above the ranch, he stopped one last time and turned to face the Bighorns. He thought about Drew and his father, Pete. As much as he admired Pete, a nagging truth deep in Cameron's soul refused to be ignored: a force greater than Pete had changed the path of Drew's life. Who, though, had gone into that pit and raised Drew out? He moseyed down the sloping road and mulled the dilemma of Drew's father, but a sad truth dominated his thoughts: nothing between him and Lydia had changed. She could not be his. He scanned the green valley, the ranch buildings, the dry hills beyond the pasture—things he had come to love—and sighed. He needed to forget her, to forget her for good.

Groping for a better memory, he recalled a fishing trip with Trent years earlier. After leaving at daybreak, they had stopped the boat in a small cove but ignored the fog as it slowly engulfed their boat. The sound of a passing boat, unhindered by the fog, led to the realization that the fog only clung to the shoreline. However, they could not reference their position and were out of both gas and cell phone service. Rather than degenerating into an argument, they had burst into laughter, which caught the attention of two fishermen who spared them from their stupidity.

"That was funny." Cameron dismounted and led Azariah to the corral. He removed the saddle and turned the horse into the nearby field. "I'll check on you later." After closing the gate, he returned to the house while reconsidering Hannah's comment: "Drew trusts you." Was she right? Once inside, he poured a cup of coffee and then found Drew and Todd in the main room, watching a baseball game.

"What's up?" Cameron nudged Todd to move farther down the sofa so that he could sit next to Drew. He grinned as he sat down, nodded to each of them, but said nothing. Instead, he leaned back into the thick padding. He crossed his legs, resting one ankle on the opposite knee, and smiled at Drew. Drew's eyes narrowed, but he smiled back. "Who's playing?" Cameron asked.

"The Braves and the Brewers."

"The Braves? They're my team! Well, one of them," Cameron grinned. "Who's winning?"

"The Brewers."

"Oh. Okay. So which team are you for?"

Drew scooted slightly farther away. He watched the screen, glanced again at Cameron from the corner of his eye, then back at the screen. Finally, the hint of a smile appeared. "The Braves."

"Put it there!" Cameron raised his hand for Drew to smack.

For an instant, Drew hesitated, then looked past Cameron to Todd. Apparently satisfied, his smile burst into a single hearty laugh. "Ha!" He smacked Cameron's palm. "Go, Braves!"

Cameron checked Todd's reaction. *Ah, yes–* Todd's predictable glare was at once restrained and cocky. Throughout the next two innings, cheers erupted along with jovial comments. "Throw it to second, Ramón ... yes!" Cameron yelled.

"He's out!" Drew called, pumping one fist.

Cameron smiled. The world and its rules had changed, and that was good. When the game ended, Drew took orders for iced tea. Cameron raised his hand, but Todd refused to acknowledge the offer. After Drew disappeared into the kitchen, Todd puckered his upper lip and snarled, "Why are you bothering with him?"

"Why not?" Some things had not changed.

"'Cause he's an idiot," Todd barked, then stood and glared at the kitchen door. "Of course, if you want to make a fool of yourself, don't let me stop you."

Cameron? Make a fool of himself? No. Not when Todd was doing a stellar job of being a first-rate ass. Instead, he laughed. "Lighten up, man! The day's already hot enough."

"What are you up to?"

"Nothing."

"Are you still looking to get a beer? If you are, I'll help."

Cameron's grin froze and then returned with cold confidence. "No, actually I'm not. My birthday is in two weeks, and I can wait. Besides, all I wanted was a good time, and since no one around here drinks, I had to make do. And I did."

"You're a dork."

"I'll take that as a compliment." Cameron pulled a corner of his mouth into a half smile. When Drew returned from the kitchen, Cameron took one of the glasses and thanked him. "What else is on?"

Drew plopped down next to Cameron. "There's a golf tournament that's about half over."

"You don't play golf, do you?"

"Yeah, I used to caddy for Dad when I was a kid. He taught himself to play by watching the pros on TV." Drew grinned, wide and confident. "He's good. He only played the public courses, but he's sort of a local celebrity."

"No—" Cameron swallowed the next word and then grinned as he looked up at Todd, who still stood staring down at him. "That's my game! If you want to know the one thing this summer ruined, totally; it was my swing. My style with horses has gone way up, but I don't even want to think about what's happened to my swing."

"All right," Todd snorted. "Spend your day with that nutcase. What do I care? You're both rednecks."

"Whoa." Cameron grinned and popped his eyebrows upward. He nudged Drew as Todd stormed away. "You know what? I think he's right. You're a little red. Hey, check mine. Is it red?" Cameron leaned forward and pulled back his collar.

"Yeah, you're a little sunburned."

"Tough summer! Gained a red neck and lost my swing."

"Stan has a set of clubs." Drew offered the gem with quiet innocence.

"No-o-o-o-o." Cameron pushed himself into the pillow, staring at Drew with wide, playful eyes. "Say it isn't true! How'd I miss them? I thought I'd sniffed out everything of value around here. I would've found a set of clubs."

"I haven't seen them, either." Drew's matter-of-fact answer hinted that he, too, had stifled a smile. "Stan doesn't play very well, but I'm surprised he hasn't gone down to the course at least once this summer."

"*Course?* There's a course around here?" Cameron could barely contain his excitement.

"Yeah." Drew's smile crept out of hiding. "Down in Basin."

"No way!"

"Yeah. There's a sign for it near the co-op in Greybull, but I guess it got lost among all the advertisements for the high life in Basin." Drew laughed with no hint of caution. "It's just nine holes, but it's decent. The fairways are narrow, which is a sort of hazard, but the grass is well watered and main-tained–as are the mosquitos and cutter bees."

"Cutter bees?" Cameron grinned, gleefully playing the role of a desperate golfer. "Then load up with Off!" Earlier he had played a cool hand when he tried to con Drew into buying beer, but now he let loose with hole-in-one craziness. "That's it! Why are we still here?" Cameron cocked his brow. "You know, I once read that there's a rule against concealing knowledge about golf courses."

"No way!"

"Yeah, they punish you by making you caddy for a first-time golfer."

Finally, Drew's defenses collapsed, revealing the person that Cameron had heard in the distance talking and laughing with Stan and Hannah on the porch late into the night. "Wyoming golf may be off the PGA radar," Drew said, chuckling as he slouched deep into the sofa, "but it's not bad. I guess it's too late to go today."

Cameron jumped to his feet and charged toward the kitchen, a devilish sparkle in his smile. "It's never too late if the course is open. Nine holes shouldn't take long. Let's find Stan."

"You haven't played with him," Drew called as he hopped up and followed. "He's slow!"

Cameron soon cajoled Stan into driving to Basin for a round of golf. Even if Stan was the world's worst player and the course was as featureless as a table, Cameron was hot to go because there was nothing worse than having a course nearby and not giving it a try. Thirty minutes later, Cameron stood on the first tee of the Midway Golf Course and surveyed the mostly flat but lush, and somewhat short fairway. As Drew noted, it was narrow enough to challenge Cameron's rusty swing. For the next two hours, Drew played well, Stan played terribly, and Cameron never stopped smiling—even using Stan's rusted clubs, which should have been ditched a decade ago.

After dinner, Cameron watched Stan walk out onto the porch for his evening with the Bible and debated joining him. Like every previous night, however, his feet walked away. He returned to his nightly routine of billiards and reading *The Count of Monte Cristo*. Afterward, he fell asleep, but nothing woke him before dawn and the new day.

17

For weeks, Marrah had dashed from activity to activity, from pill to pill, but found no relief. She needed a sanctuary, and only one sufficed: the front porch of her best friend, Melanie Powell. Nestled into a long, flat valley hedged in by the foothills of the Blue Ridge Mountains, the late-nineteenth-century farmhouse, surrounded by two hundred acres of woods and farmland, had long been Marrah's haven. With a view dominated by a magnificent hundred-foot granite outcrop, flecked with scrub and streaked by water, Melanie's front porch was as close to heaven as Marrah could imagine. She sipped Melanie's fabulous sweet tea and pushed her foot against the wooden floorboards, sending her chair rocking in long arcs. "I could sit here forever."

"It is pleasant," Melanie said with a laugh, "and I don't take it for granted."

A breeze drifted around the southern corner of the house and swayed the bouquet of late-season flowers that filled pots and beds in front of the wide porch. Half listening as Melanie discussed her vegetable garden, Marrah watched a hawk soar in wide circles just above the trees that capped the massive granite wall. The graceful raptor tilted its wings and caught another thermal.

"I agreed to do the Hope Springs Christmas program again," Marrah's voice faded as she watched the bird of prey.

"I thought you decided against running it this year."

"I said something to that effect, but Priscilla ignored me." Marrah doled out each word, wishing they weren't true.

"It's still July. Let someone else do it. Just say you changed your mind."

"It's not that easy." Marrah took a long sip of tea but glanced at the glass, wondering. *What was I about to say?*

"Of course it is," Melanie insisted.

What is? Oh, the Christmas gift collection program at church. Saying "no" was easy for Melanie. Marrah watched as the hawk drifted higher. "I have to do it. If I don't ... Umm." Melanie didn't—*couldn't* understand. Fiercely independent people like her faced adversity as easily as Marrah ran from it. Marrah tipped the glass of tea sideways. Beads of condensation collected and ran down the glass, just the way dreams coalesced and rambled through her head. In the distance, the hawk swooped close to the towering outcrop. *Freedom personified.* She lowered the glass and again tipped it sideways, sending more drops of condensation down the side. She watched them ring the bottom and puddle on the coaster. "Jake isn't happy ... with ... me." Several more drops slid down the glass. "He's planning to leave."

"Are you okay?" Melanie leaned close; a frown knitted her brow.

"I suppose." Marrah took a sip, set the glass back on the table, and then rocked slowly. "I just keep wondering ...." She let the chair slow to a stop and ran her finger around the rim of the glass. When she turned, Melanie's stern expression startled her. *What was wrong?* A spasm twisted the muscles in Marrah's cheek, distorting her face. She pushed hard against the floor and sent the chair rocking in long arcs. "Jake *is* going to leave."

"No, he isn't."

"If you heard something about Jake," the breath barely passed Marrah's lips, "about his plans, you'd tell me. Wouldn't you?" Melanie glared at her. Tennis balls would have bounced off her furled brows. She didn't understand Marrah's dilemma; if she did, she wouldn't be so harsh. Marrah stopped the chair and then pushed hard against the floor, sending it in long arcs again. "Maybe I should leave him. I think about it, but ...." Her fingers drummed the arm of the chair. "Not yet."

Her hand trembled like a leaf trapped under a windshield wiper. For a month, the tremor had returned whenever the dosage of Norco wore off. When she clasped her hands, and the embarrassing tremor failed to abate, she had increased the dosage from six to seven tablets per day. Taking fewer pills brought the tremors back with a vengeance.

She lifted the half-filled glass of tea to her lips, but its weight didn't stop her hand from shaking. She needed another pill. When her lips formed a wormy, squirming line, she became desperate. "I'll be right back." A while later, she returned to the rocking chair. Melanie leaned close, sterner than ever. Marrah's eyes darted, searching every inch of Melanie's face. *What was wrong?*

"Jake loves you."

I don't need to be patronized. She rocked the chair harder. She wasn't some wayward child, and Jake *would* leave. She looked away and searched the sky for the hawk. Where was it? She rubbed her forearms and was pleased to discover that the tremor had ceased.

Glancing back at Melanie, she again recoiled. Melanie's stare could have frozen hell twice over. Hoping to distract her, she changed the subject. "Weren't you saying something about your tomatoes?"

She picked up her glass of iced tea then stifled a gasp. The tea was warm and the glass dry. She checked her watch. Was it correct? If so, more than an hour had elapsed. How was that possible when she had only been away for a second? Would Melanie call Lois? "Please, don't!"

"What?" Melanie leaned closer. "You're mumbling. Are you all right?"

A furrow marked Melanie's brow. *Oh, no.* She saw something. She would tell Lois. The furrow in Melanie's brow deepened. Where was the hawk? Marrah's fingernails dug into the chair's underarms as she scanned the granite rock. *There it is!* She locked her eyes on the raptor. "It's beautiful, isn't it?" Marrah nodded toward the predator. "Effortless grace." Her chair slowed to a stop. "I wish I could ride a thermal."

After discovering the golf course in Basin, Cameron found that time on the ranch had picked up speed as he trekked off each Sunday afternoon, and sometimes on Saturday, with Drew in tow, for a round of golf. He routinely extended an invitation to Stan, who declined just as often. In addition to joining Cameron for golf, Drew taught him how to drive Stan's windrow cutter and baler for the alfalfa fields, with help from Stan's GPS app. Cameron even discovered that the twins, Sam and Mick, were mildly interesting; their uninhibited sort of craziness reminded him of Patrick. Todd ... well, what did he expect? Miracles?

For several weeks, the terrible dreams that had shattered Drew's sleep abated, but they returned in the cool darkness on the first Friday in August. Cameron thought about calling out to him, asking if he could help, but instead said nothing. The following morning, Cameron searched for Stan, hoping to find him alone. Just after lunch, he drove Stan's Ranger out to an irrigation pivot where he found Stan using the lowered tailgate of his pickup as a workstation. With distinct nonchalance, he sauntered up to Stan. "What are ya doing?"

"Cleaning these heads."

Cameron examined the inside of a sprinkler head. "Calcite." He shrugged his shoulders when Stan glanced up. "Where's your vinegar?"

Stan looked at him, arching his brow, then examined the white powder that covered the metal head. Not wanting to appear disrespectful, Cameron tightened his jaw to restrain a laugh. Stan's face said he knew about vinegar and calcite.

"Hand me that screwdriver." Stan pointed to his toolbox. "By the way, I see you finished Dumas."

Cameron picked up the tool and handed it to Stan. "*Monte Cristo*? Yeah." He shuffled the ground around his feet, sending puffs of dust into the dry air.

Meanwhile, Stan unscrewed the metal cap of the head that dangled from the arching, twelve-foot-high trussed boom. When linked to additional identical booms, each supported at one end by a set of massive mud-jack wheels, it formed a reticulated hundred-yard-long bridge that, when anchored to a pivot, slowly scribed concentric circles around the field. "Did you like it?"

"Yeah, it was good." Cameron leaned against the tailgate and watched Stan.

"I see you picked up Dostoevsky's *Crime and Punishment*. How much have you read?"

"About half."

"What do you think?"

"I like it." Cameron picked up a spare diverter. He balanced the corrugated metal disc on the tip of his finger and gave it a spin. Glittering light sparkled from its ruffled edge. "Raskolnikov talks to himself too much and obsesses all the time."

"True, but why?"

"He justified killing the pawnbroker, calling her a wart on society, but felt guilty for killing her sister, whom he liked." Cameron set the diverter on the tailgate. "Guilt turned into an obsession that caused him to hurt the people he loved." Cameron crossed his ankles, sending puffs of dust into the air. "That's all I've read so far. At times he's more obsessed with the consequences of his action. That breed guilt which imprisons him—without walls. Guilt and anger"—he set the diverter back in its place— "aren't a good mix."

"So what about Sonya?"

Cameron picked up a rubber washer and rolled it like a small wheel across the tailgate. "She wants him to confess, saying it'll erase his guilt." However, Cameron hadn't tracked Stan down for a literature lesson. He'd come for Drew whose tortured soul was the opposite of Raskolnikov's self-righteous egotism. "Sir, something's wrong with Drew."

Stan held the sprinkler head up to one eye while pinching the other shut. "It's been a down week for him." Apparently satisfied with what he saw, Stan slipped the head onto the end of the hose and secured it.

"But why?" Cameron stammered. "At least, he seemed happy when we played golf."

"Yeah, he was. He loves to play."

"Can't he get things worked out?"

"If only problems like his were so simple. I've got to check on a headgate up the road. It stopped flowing." Stan lifted his ball cap and scratched the bare spot just above his right temple before pulling the cap down and covering his head. "Follow me back to the barn, and we'll use the Ranger."

"So will he ever be right?"

Stan glanced sidelong at Cameron. Then he grinned, neither startled nor condescending. "Right? What is right? You know his background." Stan parked the truck and climbed into the passenger's seat.

"Yes, sir. Sort of." Cameron turned the mud-spattered off-roader toward the road.

"I guess. It depends upon what you mean by being 'right.' None of us is 'right,' if you think about it. We've all got flaws. If you mean he'll return to Erie, go to work, pay his bills, and along the way find something to smile about, then yes, he'll be just fine. He's been fine for two years, but the battle isn't over."

"What about his nightmares?"

Stan shrugged. "I'm a rancher and an accountant. I can't predict what lies ahead, but he knows where to find peace and someone who will never leave him."

"You mean his father?"

Stan pointed to the headgate surrounded by a large mat of mud and weeds, lying beneath a large cottonwood limb. "Must have been the wind last night."

Clearing the debris would be a muddy job, which, according to Leo, was all in a day's work. Stan pulled a chainsaw from the back of the ATV. "Drew will be all right. He knows who can fail him and who won't." While Stan cut through the larger branches, Cameron pulled other branches and debris out into the brush, leaving a tangle of sunflowers that had sprung up in the moist ground next to the gate. Stan straightened his back and turned to Cameron. "I think you know where he turns when the past overtakes the present."

Cameron bent over, ready to grab the last branch that blocked the water, but he stopped and stood, glowering at Stan. Yes, Drew would claim that Jesus had kept him out of trouble, but Cameron didn't share Drew's conviction.

"Nathan says you want to be a doctor."

Relieved that Stan had changed the subject, Cameron smiled. "Yes, sir. More than ever."

"Did something change?"

"Yeah. I've watched Drew with the horses, not just Obed, but all of them. He has a way with animals; it's as if the horses smell trust, and they calm down. I want to be that kind of doctor."

"A touch. A voice. Kindness is an art."

"Yes, sir. It is." Cameron pulled the last branch out of the waterway and then rinsed his thick leather gloves and hands in the water that flooded the newly opened ditch.

"By the way, you handle Azariah very well. He can be strong-willed."

"Thank you, sir. And yes, he can."

"Nathan said that you'd be good with the horses." Stan examined the headgate and stood, satisfied with what he saw. "That's it." Again, he let Cameron drive back toward the house. "If you listen to your patients as well as you listen to Azariah, you'll be a good doctor." He shook his head and continued, speaking over the noise of the engine, "When I see kids come here, looking good on the outside but beaten up on the inside, it's hard to think of humanity as fundamentally decent. It's an excuse that we use when we know that we're not as smart as we wish we were. Drew has no such illusions, but if you take a lesson from him about choices, you'll be a better doctor." Stan smiled, "Here's the key to any lesson from Drew: learn to hear what he isn't saying, and you'll discover the reason for why he does anything. As a wise man once wrote, our choices tell others who we are and influence who we become, because rarely do we want something that isn't in our best interest. The question then becomes, if we want to be independent individuals, can our wants arise from something outside ourselves? And if so, from whom?" He pointed to the dry, sage-covered range. "Now, I might want to grow corn on bone-dry land, but it isn't in my best interest to waste time and money getting water to it. However, self-interest and common sense don't always align because we're social creatures. Instead, self-interest may contradict common sense when emotions are at stake. So listen to what Drew isn't saying."

"You're kidding, right?" But Cameron knew better. Since arriving at the G-Double-T ranch, Cameron had walked a path around Stan, but now he followed him, asking questions all along the way. That evening, Cameron joined Drew at the corral and listened with pleasure to anecdotes that had earlier gone in one ear and out the other, but he still wasn't ready to follow him to the porch for Stan's evening discussions.

18

Marrah stared into the mirror. For months she had avoided it, but today, which would have been Steve's forty-second birthday, she had nowhere else to run. Her only other option was simply not to wake up. But she had, and the reflection in the mirror made her wish all the more that she had not. Lines etched her sallow cheeks and crinkled her lips. The Ambien hadn't done its job, but that wasn't her fault. She, not Lois, had remembered Steve's birthday. She had talked to Lois an hour earlier, but Lois didn't mention the date or Steve. Hateful woman. A shudder rattled Marrah's insides. She needed another pill, an extra one, just for today. Maybe if she took fewer ... no, that only drained her courage, making her more vulnerable. She needed all the courage she could muster.

She found the pill vial beneath her scarves, poured a glass of water, and popped a pill in her mouth. She went to the handrail in her bedroom, leaned over it, and called to Jake who was somewhere downstairs. "I'm ready. I need to put my shoes on."

Marrah opened her closet and looked through it. Pushing skirts aside and lifting the hems of pants, she still couldn't find her hiking shoes. Jake wanted to hike along the Blue Ridge Parkway, so she needed them, but where were they? She returned to the bedroom and looked under her bed; seeing nothing, she returned to the closet. To her surprise, she saw one hiking shoe, lying on its side in the middle of the floor. That's odd. She picked it up, glanced around for the other. Frustrated, she sat down on the floor, but as she did, her head swirled. She steadied herself, leaned back, and let her eyes close. Wispy visions appeared and brightened. *I wonder what Steve would like to do today?* Somewhere far away, a shoe thudded against a carpet. *Steve. There you are.*

"Do you have the baseball and bat?" Martha picked up the picnic basket her mother had prepared. "Look." She opened it for her brother to see inside. "Mom fixed your favorite. PBJs!"

A smile lit Steve's round face as his hooded eyes opened wide with glee. "Mom's great!"

"Yes, she is."

"Dad said we'd play baseball. He promised." Steve danced. "You're coming, aren't you, Martha?"

"Yes."

"Is Marshall coming?"

"No. Remember? He's away at college, a long way away." Martha smiled. "But guess what I have?" She held out a package wrapped with a bow.

"He remembered my birthday," Steve exclaimed. "Martha, are you going away to college?"

"Not yet, but when I do, I'll always come home for your birthday."

Two arms wrapped themselves around Martha's shoulders. Her mother's voice whispered, "Steve loves you so much, and so do I." She kissed Martha's temple. "I don't know what I'd do without you."

A hand shook Marrah's shoulder. "Honey ... wake up."

Startled, Marrah sat up but saw only the pants and skirts in her closet. Then she turned, looked up, and saw Jake.

"Are you okay?" he asked. "Melanie called. They're waiting for us."

Melanie? Oh. He's right. Melanie and Wesley were expecting them. *Why? What for?* Marrah checked her watch. *What? It can't be that late.* Her eyes darted to the row of pants that hung just beyond her feet, but the delightful moment had been but a dream. *A memory?* "I'm sorry," she mumbled. "I was looking for my other shoe."

"Isn't that it?"

Marrah looked and then flinched. The missing shoe lay only inches away. Once again, the line between reality and dreams had grown gray and pale.

On Sunday afternoon, Stan drove Drew and Cameron into Cody to play eighteen different holes of golf rather than two sets of the same nine holes. Cleaning Stan's golf clubs had improved Cameron's game almost as much as playing among the course's resident pronghorn antelope, which lounged in the shade of various diminutive trees.

For a week, the days and chores had passed quickly, even as the cattle did what cattle do best—graze, sit, stand, moo, graze some more, and fertilize the land. He reconsidered Stan's comments about choices, wants, and desires, but since wants and possibilities no longer coincided, he stopped thinking about them. After breakfast on Friday, he found Drew near the shed setting up the windrow cutter.

"Hey, Cameron. I'm heading out to the fields; want to join me?"

"Sure." Cameron had ridden with Drew the last two days and enjoyed the mindless respite as the tractor rambled across the field, tracing straight lines back and forth. Back and forth. Cameron picked up the tail end of an earlier conversation. "I'm going to eagle those par fives. I can feel it. It's in the wrists. My game is coming back."

Drew laughed. "I'll believe it when I see it!"

When the field was two-thirds complete, Stan drove up in the ATV. Cameron called to him, "Do you need something?"

"We're ahead of schedule, so I checked the weekend weather, and it looks good. Want to take Obed and Azariah up to the high peaks? It's two days in and out of the Cloud Peak area. Sam and Mick can help Leo and Hannah down here. What do you think?"

No answer was needed. Cameron's smile spoke loudly enough. The next morning, Cameron and Drew loaded the horses plus a packhorse into the long trailer, while Hannah explained wilderness etiquette, including "leave no trace" and bear deterrence. Ten minutes later they were off. Unlike the first trip into the mountains, Cameron happily stretched his legs across the backseat and enjoyed the spectacular view as the truck and trailer wound slowly up the long grade of Highway 14. Stan occasionally pulled to the side to let the faster traffic pass but plodded along, moving deeper into the Bighorn Mountains. After picking up a permit at the ranger station, they crossed Shell Creek and then climbed to a small, mostly abandoned ranch.

"This is as high as we can go with the trailer until the BLM improves the road." Without raising a sweat, they unloaded the horses and prepared them for passengers and supplies. Two hours after leaving the ranch, Stan led them, one by one, onto the dirt road and followed its rutted path through a thick pine forest. Each bend in the road carried them higher until it emerged from the wood on the side of a steep slope overlooking a wide alpine meadow that draped across the valley far below them. In every direction, similar meadows, mottled with patches of sagebrush and salted with wildflowers, painted a panorama of piebald mountains, aspen copses, limestone outcrops, and endless sky. The rugged peaks that Cameron longed to see, though, remained hidden from sight.

"Which way are we going?" he asked.

"Over that ridge." Drew pointed southeast.

Stan pointed west, across the vast basin, to a pale blue line etched across the sky above the western horizon. "Yellowstone is beyond those mountains." He turned to his left and pointed to several ridges draped with meadows and forests. "Our upper pastures are in that direction." He turned again, facing south, "and that's where we're going." He pointed to a distant hazy-blue ridge. "Cloud Peak Wilderness."

Yes! The trio descended into an alpine valley and climbed out of it into a wood, set about with limestone outcrops that towered above the trees. The mountains seemed at once both older than time and as fresh as the breeze. In the distance, other jagged peaks, stony gray, spattered with snow and dusted with blue haze, jutted above neighboring peaks whose height ranged between nine and ten thousand feet above sea level. The valley below his feet, the meadow that rolled into the distance, and others like it stood between eight and nine thousand feet high.

"We'll have lunch here." Stan dismounted and tied Obed to a sapling that would not hinder the horse if he chose to leave, but he didn't. Drew followed Stan, but Cameron heard the voice within the mountains again. Somewhere beyond the ridges, splotched with sage-dotted meadows, meager aspens, and spruce, ran a spring that held the answer to Grandpa's riddle: water that would break and heal him.

As Saturday afternoon drifted toward evening, the trio crossed meadows and wandered between lichen-covered rocks and woody scrub that clawed at the horses' ankles; they plodded through thickly grown dry forests. At night, they settled into a sheltered campsite to sleep and repeated the same leisurely pace the following day. An occasional conversation ruffled the pervasive peace, while Cameron measured time by the seesawing of Azariah's easy gait. Every detail amazed him, from the spent seedpods of lupine to the song of meadowlarks blending into the hush of the wind. The slow movement of time matched the rhythmic wind and the pattern of rocks, grass, fir groves, and songbirds as they rode farther into the backbone of the Bighorn Mountains.

On the morning of the third day, Drew awoke early. "We don't have far to go now. It's just over that ridge."

Though he had yet to solve Grandpa's riddle, Cameron smiled—even after fording streams and passing waterfalls, none of which solved the riddle. An hour after breaking camp, the group emerged from the confines of a spruce forest into a lush tundra covered with short grass, tiny flowers, and football-sized rocks. From there, the path angled steeply upward to a rocky saddle where Stan stopped. "Look behind you."

Cameron turned to face north. Far below, wide meadows carpeted the sloping ridges. Scattered outcrops, many collared with black-green forest, spread below their feet. Despite passing the timberline, Cameron only now realized how high they had climbed, having reached twelve thousand feet above mean sea level according to Stan who glanced at Cameron. "But the best is yet to come."

They passed a small lake and continued slightly higher, passing two more lakes surrounded by a landscape riddled with rocks and layered with variously colored stone. Small plants huddled among the rocks as Azariah nimbly stepped around them.

When they crested another saddle, Cameron sat, transfixed with wonder and disbelief. Before him lay a crystal lake, cradled in a monumental amphitheater filled with boulders that stacked, teetering but immovable, one atop the other. Miniature flowers poked their heads from beneath every rock. Piles of stony rubble descended to the water, with smaller pieces slipping between the boulders, forming gravelly cones that tumbled to the water's edge. Below Azariah's hooves, a shallow, brilliant green bog spread until it reached a beach covered with glossy granite pearls. Icy waves, egged-on by the wind, lapped in gentle ripples across the pearls and against the shore.

A knowing grin twinkled in Stan's eyes. From childhood, Cameron had lived near and hiked among the lush green mountains of the Blue Ridge, but he had never seen mountains such as these. He had scrambled up ancient granite boulders, their gray surfaces mottled by countless varieties of moss and lichen. He had crossed fast-moving streams strewn with glittering rocks. Climbing through those verdant slopes had been like climbing into Mother Nature's womb, steamy, close as skin, and overflowing with the sounds and smells of life—and death.

The sight before him was at once strange yet familiar, immortal yet vibrantly alive, frightening yet graceful in its magnificence and perfection. Closing his eyes, Cameron felt the silence and heard again the voice that had called to him since he first saw the mountains. Now though, it flowed from his heart, creeping into every capillary, quickening every cell with joy as he remembered hearing Grandpa read from his Bible beside the Blue Ridge Parkway. Now as then, peace and excitement swept like the cool mountain air deep into his chest where it fused with the core of his being.

Drew walked up to the water's edge, knelt, and scooped a handful of water then splashed it across his face—no, thanks. Meanwhile, Cameron helped Stan secure the horses well back from the water. "That felt good," Drew gasped then panted as he rejoined Stan and Cameron. "I've been waiting to do that since yesterday. That was fabulous." Clearly Drew was familiar with the stunning view and only slightly impressed or at least not surprised by it.

With the horses settled and pulling at stands of alpine grass, Stan and Drew climbed up onto separate sun-drenched boulders and relaxed. Stan laid back, stretched his legs, and covered his face with his hat. Drew pulled his legs up and leaned back, bracing his elbows on the rock. Cameron remained at the water's edge.

"Impressive," Stan said from beneath his hat.

"Yeah." Cameron studied the spectacular amphitheater a while longer and then climbed up next to Drew.

A sheepish but silly grin inched Drew's cheek upward. "It's the silence, you know. I take it home with me, thanking God for this place." Drew took his hat off and twirled it. "Cameron, he does care about you. I know you don't like to talk about Jesus, so forgive me, but you see, faith is like being here. It's okay to feel utterly insignificant—and safe."

Cameron turned away. In a few days, he would board a flight back to North Carolina. The end had come too soon. He closed his eyes, hoping to memorize the gray cliffs, the blue water, and the breeze. "I don't want to leave."

"Neither do I."

Cameron turned and studied Drew before turning back to the mountains and the lake. For a long time, he simply stared. Finally, he asked, "What will you do when you go back?"

"Work at the restaurant." He shrugged, "I think of it as a blessing. When you get home, it's not going to be easy. It wasn't for me." He rolled the brim of his hat. "After the first summer here, I went back and hung with the same guys, did the same junk. I don't want you to go back to the same old mistakes." Cameron turned to Stan, who lifted his hat, shrugged, and then settled it back over his face. "What about your dad?"

"I was told," Cameron said with a grin, "that there are just ranch hands out here."

"I'm no shrink. Still, what about him?"

"Who knows?"

"I know." Drew's bold candor caught him off guard. "You've got to take him as he is, and that's not easy." Drew hesitated. His cheek twitched. "Parents aren't perfect. Someone told me that it's not an accident that in the Ten Commandments, the one that tells us to honor our parents is the first one that applies to the way we deal with each other. I wasted a lot of time loving and hating Mom at the same time. I may never love her, but I'm learning to honor her."

Cameron clenched his jaw and stared across the water to the stony amphitheater. Love his father? That was his problem! If the range had taught him anything, he had discovered that he loved his father, deeply, a fact that made "getting over it" much more difficult.

"It's better to let it go." Drew had never sounded so calm and confident.

Cameron studied his new friend and oddly felt his anger abate. Meanwhile, Stan neither spoke nor moved, which didn't mean he was not interested. Cameron did not doubt that he had listened avidly.

He grinned at Drew. "I'll consider it. You know you're going to be in my head, scolding me. And who knows, you may be right." Unfortunately, Cameron had yet to understand why his father behaved as he did, especially toward Trent. If he were lucky, his father would leave him alone. Entirely. Cameron sighed and leaned back.

Then just before his head touched the rock, and as his hand held his hat an inch above his face, Drew spoke. "So do I ever get to hear about the girl in the picture?"

Cameron reversed direction and sat up, glaring at Drew. He opened his mouth, ready to demand an explanation, but with a hearty laugh, Drew cut him off. "Relax! I wasn't snooping. I found it on the floor a few weeks ago. It must have fallen out of your book. I stuck it back in before the others saw it. She's pretty. Who is she?"

Cameron turned to Stan, who had lifted the brim of his hat enough to grin at Cameron. *Traitor!* Cameron slid off the rock and strode to the water's edge. For a second, he stared at the distant shore and then spun around to Stan. "What do you know?"

"Not much," Stan said from beneath his hat. "Nathan did ask me to keep an ear out for anything that you might say about someone named Lydia."

So it was true. All summer, Stan had known about Lydia, but what else did he know?

"Lydia!" Drew exclaimed. "Woo-hoo! See? I'm telling the truth. I never told Leo or Stan that you had a girlfriend. Wait! What am I talking about? *Of course* a guy like you has a girlfriend. But why hide her?"

Cameron glowered at both, but he was mad at himself. He wanted to rave about her, to shout his passion across the water to the mountain and to hear it echo back.

Stan spoke into his hat, his fingers locked together on his stomach. "He'll tell us when he's ready."

Drew scooted up the rock to a place that formed a backrest and grinned at Cameron, who immediately turned his back on both. Drew, though, deserved an explanation. "You're not missing anything." Cameron kept his back to them. "I *could* wish it was that exciting." For a long time, Cameron watched the pattern of ripples as the breeze brushed the surface of the crystal water then faded, but a deep ache and massive regret glued his mouth shut.

"You're lucky." Drew's voice was almost inaudible. "Girls like her don't even notice me."

Cameron turned to Drew, whose innocent vulnerability had long ago vanquished Cameron's image of the once-gladiator. "That's where you're wrong. She'd notice you, and it wouldn't take all summer for her to figure out that you're a cool guy—a bit strange, but cool." Cameron turned back to the crystal lake. His chest ached. Withholding the truth from Drew at this point was an insult to him and their friendship. Cameron followed the line etched between the rocky peaks and the azure sky as the full truth, not the one he argued to himself, found breath for the first time in his life. "I first met Lydia when our mothers worked together in a soup kitchen. The Park Street Diner."

"I'm impressed. It's not easy to serve people who often need a dentist and a bath even more than they need food." Stan sat up, clasping one knee and looking as candid as the day they'd met in the Cody airport. He hadn't changed since that day, but Cameron had.

"It wasn't my idea. Grandpa—" The name caught in Cameron's throat. "Grandpa died when I was fifteen, right before school started." He pinched his eyes, but the burning only abated. "I can't believe how much I miss him .... He knew Mom volunteered at the kitchen and asked me to help her. He said that when I got lonely, I should smile at the people we were serving. At first, I thought I'd puke." He blinked to ease the tension. "You're right. Working at the kitchen wasn't cool, but I'd do anything just to imagine I could make him happy.

"The second week I was there, Lydia came with her mom. She wasn't silly or prissy like other girls. She liked those people. Seriously! There was this one regular, Mrs. Dempsey. Every week, she'd come in with these outrageous things in her hair. She must have been the original hippie and never ceased to be one. I thought she looked like a long-haired hag from a horror movie, but Lydia saw something else. Before long, I did, too."

Cameron returned to the rock and sat next to Drew, pulling his legs up and crossing his arms on his knees. "We'd meet every Monday night. Before long, it was like I'd known her all my life, so the last thing I thought of was romance. Besides, she was a kid." He glanced at Drew's incredulous face and laughed. "You don't understand. She has gorgeous hair, but I never saw it. She wore it in this thick braid, something old-fashioned that started at the top of her head. It made her look even younger.

"Over the summer, I caddied at the golf course and didn't see her. When school started, the guys were talking about a gorgeous new girl. They weren't drooling over a newcomer. They were talking about Lydia, minus the braid. Most girls think that the only thing guys notice—" He decided not to embarrass Drew. "You've been there, but girls can be attractive in many ways. Stan, her hazel eyes are stunning. I'm not kidding. And her skin. It's like cream." Cameron threw a stray pebble at Stan to catch his attention. When he looked up, Cameron grinned. "She's skinny, but I don't care; it's her hair; when the sun shines on it—oh, man! It's got all these shades of copper. And her smile ... I can't take my eyes off her."

"So what was your problem?" Drew slid from the rock and walked out to the water.

"I didn't want a girlfriend. I didn't want to get serious. You know what guys think about in high school. But 'thinking' and 'doing' are two separate things." He watched Drew search the beach, picking pebbles up and examining each one. "For the next two years, it was great. Yeah, I took girls out, but we didn't do anything, and I didn't lead them on. Then every Monday, I had Lydia all to myself, right up until graduation—'cause we were buddies. We could talk without all the complicated stuff, so I never realized that I was in over my head." Drew turned around and rolled his eyes. "Hey! Give me a break. I liked what we had and didn't think it needed to change."

Drew grinned as he wrapped his finger around a pebble, drew back his arm, and sent the stone skidding across the waves. "Ten! A record!" Concentric circles spread in a line along the stone's path. "Cameron, you're crazy. Did you at least take her to the prom?"

"No, I took someone else. That would have complicated things. Besides, she didn't go out much, so I let things ride."

Drew had drawn his arm back ready to let loose with another stone but stopped and turned to Cameron. "Excuse me? Let me get this straight. This stunning girl wasn't being asked out? Are you sure?"

"Yeah. I listened to the talk around school. She didn't market herself."

From Stan's direction, a loud laugh filled the air. "So that's what it's called today?"

"Well, it's what girls do. You don't have to guess what they think. Some post it. Lydia isn't like that, and since one of her best friends is my cousin—distant, I had inside info. Also, Lydia's grades were a put-off for most guys, but not for me. I'd razz her while making sure mine were ahead of hers. As you may have noticed, I'm sort of competitive."

"Na-a-ah." Drew laughed and sent the pebble skipping across the water. He picked up a rock and juggled it with yet another. "I still don't see a problem. Why don't you call her? I assume she's in college. Where's she in school?"

"Her school's only eight miles from mine. And yes, there's a problem."

A deathly silence followed. Cameron again wrapped his arms around his knees, drawing them close to his chest as he related details about the party three years earlier on the weekend before graduation. "Justin lied about my date's name." Cameron clenched his lips and related the whole miserable mess. He pressed his forehead against his knees. "I can still see her smile as she climbed into the backseat of Justin's car. She was so vulnerable. What he did was wrong, but I made it worse." Cameron released his legs and slid down from the rock. He strode out to Drew. Without taking the time to find a flat stone, he grabbed one, wrapped his finger around it, and hurled it across the water. It bounced for an eternity.

"Ow-w-w-w." Drew snickered and whipped a pebble across the water. "I'm impressed."

"Damn! How could I be so *stupid?*" He hurled another stone and another. "I didn't want a girlfriend, so what did I do?" Another stone skipped into the distance. "I ignored her. No, I wasn't ignoring her, I was hiding—not from her, but from me." He threw several more pebbles; each skipped across the ripples.

Finally, he went on, "All I had to do was talk to her, but instead ... Justin handed me a beer, and I took it ... and another." He paused, staring at the water, and flicked another stone across it. "She trusted me." He watched the line of circles spread out. "I should have protected her." Dismay contorted his face. "If I'd only talked to her." He hurled five stones in rapid succession. Each skittered far out across the surface. The circles left by the stones widened and faded.

"But that wasn't the worst of it." He described hearing Justin banging on the door and waking him up, the arrival of the police, and the scene of the accident. "I liked Mrs. Duncan. She was very nice." He juggled a stone. "By then, talking to Lydia was pointless."

Drew stopped skipping stones and turned to Cameron. "I'm sorry."

The lingering silence, though, had caught Stan's attention. "Is that the end?" His question sounded sympathetic yet detached—but he wanted to hear the whole story.

"I wish it was ... but I don't want to bore you."

"I'm not bored," Drew declared and sent a stone, low and perfect, skipping into the distance.

"Go ahead," Stan laughed. "We're into boredom."

Cameron glanced at Stan. The ancient half of the truth had rushed out like bats fleeing a cave at sunset. The more recent half would not tumble out so easily. In the ominous hush of the high mountains, Cameron described the previous year. "I've done a lot of really dumb things." He flung a stone across the water, unconcerned that it skipped only four times. "After Mrs. Duncan died, Dad refused to go to my graduation, and we started arguing. Constantly. Strangely, it made me want Lydia all the more—I missed her friendship. It also reminded me why I couldn't call her."

He picked up a stone and juggled it. "I dated other girls but ended up comparing them to Lydia. They all flunked. By last Thanksgiving, it'd been two years since I last saw her. The relationship I had with Addie, who I'd been ... um ... dating—it wasn't working. Surprise! She wasn't Lydia. So"—he stared at the round, smooth stone— "I decided to prove that Lydia wasn't perfect. With that astute thought, I invited her to Paul's New Year's Eve party. I had everything figured out until she opened the door and smiled ... at me." He described the party and how afterward he'd gone to Justin's and needed to be dropped off at Uncle Nathan's house. The last stone slipped from his limp fingers. A few feet away, ripples washed across the glassy pearls beneath a cloud-strewn sky. "I shouldn't have left her alone. I didn't need to talk. I could have listened. And asked questions."

"You didn't, did you?" Sympathy echoed through Drew's soft voice.

Cameron shuffled the pebbles with his foot. "No." He turned and walked back to the boulder where Stan now sat, holding his hat in his hand. With a sigh, Cameron turned to face the mountain as if the encompassing ridge held a line of benches with a judge atop each. All stared silently down at him. Soon the image faded, and only Lydia's eyes—the moment before she closed the door—met his. A weight, heavier than the boulder he'd sat on earlier, fell on his chest. "I thought about calling her, but I ... I can't."

Drew climbed up on the rock. "Why can't you?"

"Why?" A sardonic smile escaped. He shook his head as it faded. "Because when I was close to her, it was like being slammed with a defibrillator. I couldn't breathe. Everything about her was exciting—her voice, her smile, her body, everything." He drank the mountain air. "I can smell her perfume even up here."

"I had no idea. You cover it well." Drew shrugged his shoulders.

Stan slid down his rock. "Yes, he does." He pulled out a bridle. "We need to get going."

Cameron glanced at Drew, who followed Stan but turned to Cameron. "So, why aren't you gonna call her?" Drew slid the bit into Obed's mouth.

Cameron slid the bridle over Azariah's ears, "Because if the roles were reversed, and it was your girlfriend, not mine, none of this would have happened."

Drew laughed, "I could only wish!"

"It's true. You're courageous." He tightened the straps on the bridle and checked the cinch. "I'm not." He mounted Azariah and turned the horse to face the stony cathedral and the crystal lake. If only he never had to leave this place.

Drew pulled up beside him as Stan continued down the trail. He nodded toward Stan. "Don't worry about him. We'll catch up." When he turned to Cameron, his face wrinkled with thoughts that Cameron read to mean: *You idiot* and *How can you be so unromantic?* But all he said was "And—?"

"I won't compare my dad to your mom, but ...." Cameron watched his fingers play with the reins. "When he heard that I'd asked Lydia out, he went ballistic. He knows nothing about her, but it's as if he doesn't like anything that I like .... She's just another reason for him to get on my case." Of course, there was also his father's problem with Addie and every other girl Cameron slept with, the last part being the most offensive.

Drew was nice and civil, but he wasn't inexperienced or naive. He knew about substance abuse. He also had to know what Cameron did with the women he dated. Plenty of men would call Cameron's problem good fortune, but neither sex nor alcohol had led to love. "You know I'm not a saint. When Addie called an hour before I was supposed to pick up Lydia for Paul's party, she was sobbing drunk. I didn't want Lydia to see me like that. Staying sober that night was my last shred of dignity."

As Drew predicted, Stan now waited far down the mountainside for them to catch up with him. "Dad didn't send me out here. It was Uncle Nathan. He knew Stan, but he had no idea that I'd make friends with a guy who could turn me around. And you did." He laughed and nudged Azariah to join Stan. "It's a good thing that Uncle Nathan doesn't gloat—he warned me about this place. He said it might change me. —I want to believe that I left a lot of bad things back there, atop this mountain." He nodded to Drew. "Thanks for helping."

Now close to Stan, Cameron saw his eyebrow twitch before he turned and urged his horse toward home.

"Hey, Stan," Cameron called. "This is where your story picks up. Right?"

"You tell me."

"If I'd gone home, instead of going to Uncle Nathan's, I'd be in Chapel Hill, not here. Right?"

Stan only shrugged.

Cameron turned to Drew. "After Grandpa died, Uncle Nathan did for me what your dad did for you. He didn't give up on me."

Drew smiled and nodded, seeming to agree.

The downhill ride took far less time than Cameron expected. Perhaps if time stalled or slowed he could absorb more of the peace that now enveloped him. Maybe then he could carry some of it home with him.

After dinner, Stan stretched his legs out and leaned back against his pack. With a sly smile, he winked at both Cameron and Drew. "Just before Nate called, I had talked to Pete about this summer. I didn't think Drew needed to come back, but after I described my conversation with Nate, Pete suggested that you two might be able to help each other in ways no one else could."

Cameron and Drew exchanged glances, and then Cameron turned to Stan. "What made you think it'd work?"

Stan grinned. "Golf." A hearty laugh followed. "Early on, I saw Drew rooting around for his clubs. So I hid them." He tipped the brim of his hat toward Cameron. "After Nate said you'd play golf on dry dirt if you had a club and a ball." Stan laughed. "The only question after that was when."

"What did Uncle Nathan say about Dad?"

"He said you two have problems. Said you both talk past each other, and neither listens. So Drew's right. Take him as he is—even if he never returns the compliment."

"But what about Lydia?" Drew blurted. "Stan, tell him to call her." Despite Stan's cheerful but dismissive laughter, Drew persisted. "You have to."

Stan ignored him and crawled into his tent. "Good night."

"What if I brought her here?" Cameron mused aloud. He turned to Drew. "Do you think she'd forgive me?"

"The only thing I know is that you can't grab your bootstraps and pull yourself together. I've been too close to Hell to think anyone can walk out of there on their own." The gladiator had returned, but with helmet in hand, his breastplate unlatched, and sword sheathed. "Jesus picked me up and put me on solid ground. Stan was hinting loudly that Providence, not your uncle, brought you here. And maybe God is using Lydia to help you the way Stan helped me."

"That's theology. And I can't go there." Cameron arched a brow, caving to Drew's kindness. "You see, in the South, everybody is saved, and they think it's their job to save everybody else. That's Dad. They're hypocrites. Christianity isn't for me."

"You don't want to know where Jesus found me." Drew spread his sleeping bag in the tent he and Cameron shared. "So tell me, if everyone in the South is saved and they're all hypocrites, does that include Lydia? What does she believe?"

"She loved working at the Diner. What does that say?" Cameron opened his sleeping bag.

"That the real problem between you two isn't the past." Drew pulled off his boots and slid into the bag. "It's the future."

Odd.

Drew slid into his sleeping bag. "If someone like Lydia liked me, I'd do anything to get her back." He turned away from Cameron. "Have you ever wondered whether she worked in the kitchen because *you* were there? Good night."

"Who thought that one up? Stan or you?"

Drew glanced over his shoulder with a self-assured smile. "It was mine. All mine."

19

In the blue light of dawn, several days after returning from the mountains, Stan tossed Cameron's duffle bags into the back of the truck while Cameron said goodbye to Hannah and Leo. He exchanged a punch-hug with Drew and then walked to the fence, where Azariah waited. Seeming to recognize that Cameron was leaving, the horse nuzzled his friend and let him stroke his velvety nose. "Sorry, bud. I wish you could come with me." A knot rose into Cameron's throat. "Who would have guessed that I'd rather stay than leave? Maybe I'll be back."

Cameron glanced at the mountains and let the moment linger. Then, with a sigh, he climbed into the truck. Oh, how wrong he had been three months earlier, and how grateful he felt for having spent the summer in the Wyoming boonies. As Stan turned the truck around, Drew called out to him, "And tell Lydia hello for me." His grin widened. "I want a report."

Cameron nodded, "Sure." As the ranch, Shell Valley, and the Bighorns slipped behind them in the brightening morning light, the rolling landscape looked very different from the barren waste he had seen in May. Where he'd seen lifeless brown hills, now he saw a green irrigated valley dotted with cottonwood trees and blanketed with corn and alfalfa. Beyond the fields, colorful Cloverly Foundation bluffs presided over dusty rangeland. —All now lay in the shadow of the Bighorn Mountains that hid the rising sun. Both men rode in silence until they passed through Greybull. A sign pointing to Basin stirred cheerful recollections that soon petered out as the arid Bighorn Basin reached out and surrounded them. With the mountains now far behind them and the Absaroka Range and Cody drawing closer, Cameron stared out the side window, drinking in every detail of the flat grasslands: the dry creeks, rocks, sagebrush, and scattered antelope that dotted an expanse stretching away to distant mountains shrouded in haze.

At the appearance of farms east of Cody, Stan broke the long silence. "You may or may not want it, but I'm going to give you a piece of advice. The moment we think we know what we want is when we discover that we most desire something we never thought we would like."

Puzzled, Cameron glanced at him and shrugged. "Yes, sir."

"Did you finish *Crime and Punishment?*" Stan asked.

"No, but almost."

"So what do you think about Raskolnikov now?"

"He was a lucky failure." Cameron noted the increasing number of houses.

"Why do you say that?"

"He did terrible things, obsessed about punishment, but ultimately dodged the consequence of his behavior, namely death." Why, Cameron wondered, was Stan starting a book discussion as they entered the outskirts of Cody?

"Interesting. Did Raskolnikov think he was lucky?"

"No," Cameron laughed. *Where is he going with this?*

"Cameron, it's been a pleasure having you with us this summer. You've been every bit as interesting, challenging, and smart as Nate said you'd be. So I have a gift for you, a challenge of sorts. *Crime and Punishment* has been in publication for more than a century and a half *because* Dostoevsky uses a murder mystery to project a thesis. If you uncover it—his thesis, you might learn to accept your father not as you want him to be but as he is."

Cameron lifted his eyebrows as Stan continued. "Here's a hint. Self-interest led Raskolnikov to murder both women. Righteous indignation led to the first murder while fear led to the second. When I was your age, it was well known that Dostoevsky used the plot to warn his readers about an increasingly popular social philosophy that nullified—destroyed—the individual. His reasoning is less well known. Dostoevsky saw societies as masses of unique individuals who share a common humanity. All of us share qualities that he embedded in two of the primary characters. Though flawed, Sonya represented our potential for goodness. Raskolnikov, who was gravely flawed, represented the power of self-interest, or more bluntly, self-preservation.

"This summer you and Drew became friends by validating goodness and learning to manage self-interest. You arrived with a penchant for self-interest, which hurt rather than helped you. Drew arrived with lingering trust issues. By being yourself, he learned to trust you, but also to trust himself. You probably didn't see the change in him, but Hannah and I did. You gave him hope. Without hope, living becomes an endurance race, a struggle that we *cannot* win. Without hope, we give up, like Svidrigaïlov.

"Nate called in January because he was afraid you were close to giving up, perhaps buying into the self-defeating belief that 'this is as good as it gets.' Whether it's true or not, he thinks Lydia is both a link to a happier time in your past and to your better self, your aspirational self. He sent you here, hoping you'd learn to dream again. We need dreams as much as we need bread."

Stan had not made leaving Wyoming any easier, yet he continued as he turned onto the airport road. "You might find that Dostoevsky's theme is the key to understanding your heart's desire, whether that's medical school, peace with your father, or Lydia. Never accept that 'this is as good as it gets.' It can be much more." Stan pulled into a parking place then reached behind his seat and pulled out a package. "Here."

Inside, Cameron found a copy of *Crime and Punishment*. Looking only at the cover, he whispered, "I know you want me to love God, but I can't."

Stan smiled and opened the door. "Hannah wanted me to give you a blank journal book to record your thoughts, but I ignored her. Listen, Cameron. Listen to your heart."

Cameron opened the door, grabbed his duffle bag and backpack, and followed Stan to the terminal. After checking in, he turned to Stan. "Thanks for everything, sir." He smiled and extended his hand.

"My pleasure." Stan shook his hand. "By the way, Drew was right. Give Lydia a holler. If she's the woman you described, she'll probably give you one more chance, but be wise."

"Nothing like making a hard task harder." Cameron grinned, still gripping Stan's hand.

After passing through security, he walked to the window overlooking the runway and sloping foothills of the Absaroka Range, a wasteland teeming with life. Nothing had been as he expected, and that was a good thing. Later, as his plane rose above the jagged mountain range south of Cody, he read the multicolored layers of earth, cloven by deep valleys, mottled with forests and rocky peaks. Nothing seemed strange, yet both home and Stan's ranch seemed a galaxy away.

In Salt Lake City, he boarded the flight back across the continent to Atlanta. Hours later, his pulse quickened as the plane descended over the forests, houses, ribbons of roads, and brick-red fields of North Carolina. Seeing the tall buildings of downtown Charlotte through the sepia haze of the setting sun, his heart soared. He was home. He smiled at every passerby as he strode toward the main terminal. At the top of the steps leading to the luggage pickup carousels, he furtively scanned the assembled crowd that awaited arriving planes. Some had small, expectant smiles. Others fixed hopeful eyes on the escalators. A few notably detached souls held white cards displaying the names of strangers. Suddenly the crowd parted, and a woman with arms flung wide and a brilliant smile on her face ran toward him. She was not a stranger. She was his mother.

"Hi, sweetheart. I'm so glad you're home." A knot tightened Cameron's throat as he trotted down the moving steps. Then her arms wrapped around his neck, and he wrapped his around her waist. The sweet sound of her voice and the delicious smell of her perfume penetrated the deep corners of his heart. Nothing had changed. A second later, she released her embrace, stepped back, still beaming, and surveyed him. "You look wonderful. Randy. Aren't you glad to see him?"

What a surprise, though a dubious one at that if his father's expression hinted at his thoughts. He looked rather like Cameron had felt at age five when his mother dragged him along to buy shoes for his sister. His mother had a talent for towing her intransigent family along—with oblivious cheer and always with their best interests in mind, or rather her assumption of what might be their best interest, while the cobbled soul thought the experience couldn't end fast enough. Thus she had succeeded again. Perhaps his father was disappointed that Cameron hadn't staggered off the plane, an empty mini bottle in each pocket. The truth was that Cameron hadn't even thought about ordering a drink until that very minute, even though he was now of legal age.

At least his father had come. Cameron extended his hand. "Hi, Dad. Good to see you."

"Hello, son. Welcome home." His father grasped Cameron's hand with a quick, firm shake and stepped away.

"Cameron, look," a high voice called, grabbing his attention. The familiar but unexpected voice quickened Cameron's pulse almost as much as had the sight of his mother.

In the days and weeks before he left for Wyoming, he had not thought about his sister or remembered that she and Shaun had been expecting a baby. How had he been so insensitive about someone he loved so much? "Andrea, I can't believe you came all this way."

"It's not that far from Linville. Of course I came. Besides, I have bragging rights. Look. You're an uncle. This is Jacob." Shaun held up the baby carrier for Cameron to see inside.

"Hey, buddy." Cameron grinned at the tiny baby, who stared back wide-eyed and then smiled. Cameron turned to Shaun and laughed. "He looks just like his old man. Bald! Shaun, I can't believe you came too."

"Andrea wasn't going to miss meeting you at the airport, and I didn't want her to drive down alone with the baby." The scruffy young man shook Cameron's hand and then half smiled. Once upon a time, Cameron had wondered about Shaun's fatherly instincts. A salesclerk by trade and potter by avocation, Shaun seemed very comfortable with his new role.

Shaun's grin widened. "Besides, Trent sent me on a mission." He handed the baby carrier to Andrea and stepped back, eyeing Cameron with his cell phone in hand. "Turn around. Trent wanted a picture to see if you came back bowlegged."

"Now, that sounds like Trent." Cameron laughed as he spun around for his brother-in-law. "I'm not bowlegged, but—" He held up his cowboy hat and grinned. He dusted the brim with a flick of his hand, though little dust remained, and set it on his head, pushing it forward until it tipped down over his forehead. His smile widened. "What do you think?" Shaun tapped the phone.

"Boys!" His mother rolled her eyes as she wound her arm around Cameron's. "I'm just glad he's finally home. I want to hear every detail."

"Here." Andrea stood in front of him, smiling and holding the baby, minus the carrier. "Hold him. He likes you."

Cameron took the tiny, awkward bundle that kept staring at him. He glanced at his sister, desperate for instructions about what to do next, but she and his mother had seen someone that they knew and were busy talking with animated cheer. His father scanned the luggage carrousel while Shaun talked to a stranger about building a larger crib—artists make their own; they don't buy them. None seemed to remember either Cameron or the baby. Chuckling, he looked down at Jacob. "Such is life, bud. You'd better get used to it." The happy child stared at him and gurgled.

After spending a few days with his parents—enough to satisfy his mother—Cameron joined Paul and several other friends for barbecue and a friendly game of ultimate frisbee. Finally, he made his obligatory pilgrimage to Justin's basement. Three months earlier, he had hated the macabre stuffed heads that lined the walls of Mr. Sloane's trophy room. Now, having seen mule deer by the dozen around the ranch and a moose wandering the meadows of the Bighorns, he felt sad. The stuffed pronghorn antelope gave no hint of the stunning animal's ability to spring from docile grazing to full speed in a second—or to lounge in the shade on a golf course. Having earned his freedom, Cameron no longer saw himself as the fish pinned to Mr. Sloane's wall, forever leaping toward the unknown. Instead, he remembered the camaraderie of the various fishermen who rented Stan's camp.

"Here." Justin handed Cameron a beer.

Cameron smiled. "No, thanks, but I'll place bets on a game of 8-Ball." Justin's friends smirked, but whether they laughed at his declining the offer or at his bet, they should be more judicious about their opinions. "So Justin," he asked, "are you going back to Chapel Hill?"

"Sure, why not? There's nothing to do around here."

"Are you going back to school or the body shop?"

"UNC? You've got to be kidding. Howard, my boss, lets me come and go as I like 'cause he knows he can't find somebody who's as reliable as me."

"Reliable? You?" A noisy chorus arose from the group, but Cameron didn't join in, despite wondering who might be less reliable than Justin.

"I'll take his bet if you won't," one friend ventured.

"I'll take it." Justin glared over his shoulder at Cameron. "How much?"

After setting the wager and racking the balls, Cameron offered to let Justin break the rack, but Justin insisted that Cameron go first. "Are you sure?" Cameron asked.

"Yeah. Take it. It's all you'll have."

For a second Cameron wondered if he should warn Justin. Then, with a half-smile, he decided against it. He aimed his cue and shot. Balls scattered across the table and bounced against the rails; the three dropped in a side pocket. He made a call, gesturing with his cue: "Five in the side pocket." Call after call followed as ball after ball dropped, until only Justin's stripes and the eight-ball remained. Cameron walked around the table studying the lay of Justin's balls, then called, aimed, and shot. The eight ball fell, followed by a loud whoop from everyone except Justin.

Cameron smiled and slapped his old friend's back. "You should have asked how we spent our evenings. They could get long on the ranch." He dropped the cue stick into the wall bracket. "Todd may have been obnoxious, but he could play pool. For me, it was improve or die." He laughed and flopped into the padded side chair. "That wasn't fair. So tell you what. I'll let the bet go, and you can start next time." The others snickered, but Justin's glare confirmed Cameron's progress: he no longer needed Justin's friendship. Still, Justin was due some pity because he just didn't get it. Not one little bit.

The following morning Cameron awoke late, thought about calling Lydia, but turned over and pulled the covers up. Since arriving home, Drew's voice had badgered him, but not enough to make him act. When his mother sent him on an errand that took him near Lydia's street, he thought about calling but didn't. Finally, shortly before returning to Chapel Hill, he resolved to call her. He even turned onto the street, but his nerves frayed when he didn't see her in the yard, so he passed without stopping. Relief and disappointment conspired to assure him that if he did, he'd mess up again. Instead, he resolved to call after he settled into the house in Chapel Hill.

The next morning, he bounded into the kitchen, where he found his father. "Hey, Dad, I'm on my way to hit some balls at the country club. Want to join me for a round?"

"You know I hate golf."

Cameron tried again. "What about going out to Uncle Nathan's? We can take the horses out."

"Go ahead without me."

Cameron offered another suggestion, but after his father rejected that as well, Cameron drove out to Uncle Nathan's farm. He joined his uncle in the barn and described every conceivable detail of the summer before broaching the questions that needed answers. "Thanks for sending me out to Stan's. I hated you at first ... well, for the first half of the summer, but I'm glad I went. You'd be proud of me. A couple of nights ago, I went to Justin's house to kick back. We played pool, but I didn't drink. It was cool." A comfortable smile caught a corner of his mouth. "Whatever you intended, I think it worked."

"That's good," his uncle smiled. "But take it easy when you go back to UNC."

"I know. Stan and Drew both warned me, but I feel more than pride. I feel better, stronger."

"Good." For the rest of the afternoon, they talked about horses, cattle, the ranch, and the range. Cameron reached for the door of his SUV and then paused. "I have a question. Stan gave me a copy of *Crime and Punishment* and told me to find Dostoevsky's thesis. Have you read the book?"

"No." Uncle Nathan laughed. "Literature was Stan's passion." His cheek hinted that he might smile. "His obsession! But not mine. Sorry."

"Oh, okay."

"Tell you what. I'll read it, and next time you're here, we can discuss it."

"Sounds good."

20

Lois set the mail on the narrow walnut sideboard that stood in the entrance hall of her century-old bungalow on Beaufort Street. An assortment of framed photographs covered the wall above the makeshift mail room. As she often did, she leaned close and examined each portrait. One photo, taken two years earlier when her eldest grandson earned a master's in economics, drew a smile. She kissed her index finger and pressed it against each of the faces, including her elder son Marshall, his wife Anne, and their children: Luke, in his graduation robe, Tristan, and Lydia. Lois turned to the picture beside it, kissed her finger, and pressed it against the faces of Luke, still wearing his graduation robe, her younger son Steve, her daughter Marrah, Marrah's husband Jake, and their son David.

Her gaze lingered on Steve. It'd been almost a year since his death, but she remembered his smile as if she'd seen it yesterday. She turned to the oldest photo on the wall. In it, Steve, age two, sat on her lap while Marrah and Marshall stood beside her. Her late husband Tom stood behind her. A flood of memories washed over her, too many for any to gain dominance, yet she smiled. Tom had been a good man, a loving father, and a generously kind husband.

With groceries in hand, she continued to the kitchen just as the phone rang. "Hello … Jake. How are you, dear?"

After the most basic of pleasantries, Jake's deep baritone voice lowered and became somber. "It's time … I found her pills."

"Are you sure you're ready?" A silent breath emptied Lois's chest. *Poor Jake.* He had endured so much that Lois had been helpless to prevent.

"Yeah. There were prescriptions from four different doctors"—each word seemed to catch in his throat—"and an antidepressant. I tried to confront her, but she's in denial ... I'm sorry."

"You've done all you can."

"But I couldn't do anything ... not until I had proof." In the heavy silence, Lois searched for words of comfort but found none. Jake sighed. "I feel like I've cheated on her."

"No!" Lois insisted. "You haven't."

"It looks like I don't trust her. I didn't tell you, but a few weeks ago, I found her on the floor of her closet. At first, I panicked. I thought she'd passed out. I've been tearing the house apart ever since, looking for those pills. How'd she get so many prescriptions?"

"Where there's a will, there's a way." Lois wound the ancient phone cord around her finger. "Are they all Norco?"

"There are some others, but they're marked with the same precautions. It looks like she's taking between six and eight a day."

Lois's mouth clenched. Rather than panicking, she switched to the portable phone and walked to the window overlooking her garden, trying to calm her pulse. "That's too much." After Steve's death, Lois saw ominous, worrisome hints about Marrah's state of mind. Now there was only one way forward.

"I'll talk to her about it—"

"No!" Lois interrupted him. "Don't! Let me talk to her." He didn't need to face Marrah's wrath. "Let her aim her temper at me. I'm used to it."

Silence lingered before he spoke. "It's the same as last time, isn't it?"

"Maybe not." Perhaps now it would end differently.

"I thought it was behind her."

No. Far from it. Lois sank into a chair at the breakfast room table and picked up the glass pepper shaker. So much history; so much waiting. She tipped the shaker to one side and mourned for Jake. "It's been a long time coming." She stared at the shaker, willing the future to be different, wanting the end to be near. "I wondered if Steve's death would be the catalyst. It seems I was right."

"Should I call a psychologist?"

"No, not yet. It may come to that, but let's wait." Lois rocked the pepper shaker back and forth.

"Are you sure?"

"No, but"—Lois set the pepper down— "I can hope. So we'll go ahead as planned. How's David?"

"Not good."

"I'm so sorry. Where is she right now?"

"In the kitchen cleaning up after dinner."

"Okay. I'll come right over. Have you called Nathan and Becky?"

"I'll call from the car. I know they can help me with David. Oh, and, I put the pill bottles next to the tea jar. I'll call the pharmacies from Nate's."

"Good." All was going according to plan. "I'll be at your house in about ten minutes."

As she lowered the phone, his voice, tired and worried, touched her ear. "Lois, if you're right and she's still grieving her father's death, when will she stop? It's been more than thirty years."

"Losing a parent when you're sixteen is hard enough, but seeing him die ... I doubt she even knows what she's running from. Pray for her." She held her breath and then whispered, "And pray for me. Ask God to give me patience. And pray that our long wait has come to an end."

"I'll pray for all of us."

Cameron checked his list: computer, clothes, sheets, laundry stuff, posters, and various other gear he would need when he returned to school the next morning. As he pushed a set of folded bed sheets into a duffle bag, he congratulated himself on his visit to Justin's house. One test down. He fist-pumped the air. Best of all, though warmth had not characterized his interactions with his father, not a single terse word had been exchanged—another milestone. As Drew warned, the effort had not been entirely easy, but he had persevered. Hope had returned. He placed a rolled-up T-shirt in a duffle bag and resolved to call Professor Krasotkin within a few days.

"Cameron."

He looked up, and his smile widened. "Yo, Dad. What can I do for you?" He reached for the next sweatshirt and rolled it up.

"We need to talk."

Never in Cameron's life had those words preceded a pleasant conversation. Still, he smiled. "What about?"

"Before you leave, I thought we should talk about your drinking problem."

"Dad, I don't have a problem." Cameron cocked a friendly smile even as blood rushed to his cheeks. He rolled another sweatshirt.

"You just think you don't have a problem."

A cold wind blew through the air vents. "No, I don't." Cameron calculated the degree of his father's temper. Uh-oh. Approaching minus-seventy. Not good. He picked up a T-shirt and rolled it up. "Yeah. I've hung with my friends—even Justin. They got drunk while I drank a Pepsi. I wasn't even tempted. I'm doing fine. Thank you."

"You don't seriously think that's true, do you?" The irritating growl that often heralded an argument appeared.

Cameron grabbed a T-shirt and refused to cower. "Why shouldn't I?" He stuffed the shirt into the duffle bag.

"Problems like yours don't go away that easily."

"Why not?" Cameron snapped but then reined in his temper and rolled up another T-shirt. He recalled Drew's admonishment: *Honor your father.* And he had. Cameron pushed the not-so-neatly-rolled shirt into the duffle bag and heaved a deep sigh. "All right." He stood and turned to his father. "Both Stan and Uncle Nathan warned me about going back, that it'll be hard. So yes. I'm *going* to make it work."

"Well, I'm glad you're so sure of yourself." Without relinquishing his air of superiority, his father walked over to Cameron's desk, laid a folder down, and opened it. Cameron leaned close enough to scan it. It was an application, with his information filled in, to the MBA program. Only the signature was needed. What was his father thinking?

His father turned and walked toward the door, then stopped. "I talked to a friend in the business school. He assured me that if you keep your grades up, you'll be accepted for next year. You're lucky. Not every kid who parties the way you do has a father who can bail him out. You should be damned glad that I own a business, a very successful one, because—"

"Dad!" Cameron interrupted him. "What were you thinking?" He struggled to keep from shouting. "I've already applied to several medical schools. I did it before I left."

"I know. And I'm not wasting any more money on that fool's errand." His father's eyes narrowed. "What school will accept you? Do you have even one reference letter? You're not med school material." He snorted. "Be realistic. And take my help."

"Help!" Cameron threw the next shirt into the bag unfolded. "This is not helpful."

"Son, this is what I'm talking about. If you can't control your temper, how will you ever control your drinking?" His father tapped the application. "You need to sign these."

Waves of anger swept over Cameron, flushing his cheeks. For a split second, he remembered Drew's admonishment, then it vanished. "I have the grades. I'm going to medical school." Cameron stared down his father's cold frown. "I'll prove you wrong."

His father didn't flinch but spoke slowly and evenly. "Son, I hope I *am* wrong, but you're just like my father. All talk. All talk."

Cameron's pulse stopped. "Dad!" He dropped his voice to a controlled monotone. "Leave Grandpa out of this!"

"I'm not naïve," his father continued with the chilling precision that Cameron hated. "I know what kind of man he was. He ruined everything he touched, so don't pretend he was a saint."

"He was more of a man than you'll ever be." The ancient, nauseating argument had started again. Cameron clenched his trembling muscles and looked for an escape. Turning away from his father, he jerked his arm upward, knocking over a packed box and sending books and papers across the carpet. Cameron jerked around to face his father.

"See?" A razor-thin line replaced his father's lips. "You can't control yourself."

Cameron grabbed the folder and ripped it in half. "I'm going to medical school. I'll decide what's best for me."

"Suit yourself. So what's plan B?" His eyes narrowed. "Business school."

Something between horror and fortitude nailed Cameron's feet to the floor as he watched his father turn and leave the room. Suddenly Cameron ran after him. "Don't you want to know if Uncle Nathan's *Christian* friend saved my soul?"

His father spun around. An icy smile etched his face, but no other muscle moved. "Yes. I worry about whether you'll ever make that decision. I worry about that almost as much as about your drinking, but the choice is yours. First, though, I suggest you straighten your life out."

"Oh, well good. *Sir*," Cameron punctuated his words as his father again turned away. "I'm glad to know *that's* what it takes to get into heaven because *neither* of us is going to be there. Go straighten your *own* life out."

When his father turned back, Cameron stopped, board-rigid. Every muscle in his father seemed drum-tight and rumbling in a deep, base harmonic. An instant later, his father relaxed, but his cold smile drained the last few joules of heat from the room. "Son, every day I pray that you'll turn your life around and invite Christ into your heart, but the choice is yours. I hope you do it before it's too late because that's one decision I can't make for you."

"Wow, Dad. Finally, you spoke the truth, but you'd better believe that the eternal fires of Hell will have turned to frozen ash before I make that choice, if in making it, I spend eternity with you."

Thirty-four years, Lois thought. Could the journey that began the day Marrah's father died finally be coming to an end? Was this just another skirmish, or had the final struggle for peace begun? Beyond her kitchen window, the last rays of sunlight painted the western sky a surreal pink and electric fuchsia. She closed her eyes, and with every fiber in her being, prayed that God had willed that the end was at hand. "Father. Take 'Marrah' away and give me back my dear Martha. Have mercy on me. According to your loving kindness, by your tender mercies, wipe away my sins that stand before me. Against you, and you only, have I sinned. Forgive me. Strengthen me."

Lois opened her eyes. Then taking up her keys and purse, she proceeded with the plan that she, Jake, Nathan, and Becky had devised. As she passed the photos lining the wall of the entrance hall, she stopped at the last photo taken of Marrah and Tom shortly before his death. She took the picture down from the wall and pressed it to her chest. "Please, Father, hold my Martha close to your heart." She held the picture up and kissed the images. "Have mercy on my daughter . . . and on me."

After leaving her neighborhood, Lois followed the river road and turned south toward Glenlaurel Lake. With each turn, each traffic light, her stomach knotted tighter and tighter. When she turned onto the street that ended in the cul-de-sac where Jake and Marrah lived, she stopped and prayed. If ever she needed God's strength, she needed it now. Heaving a sigh, she continued around the corner and pulled into Marrah's drive. With a practiced smile, she opened the car door and followed the flagstone walk to Marrah's lovely Tiffany-style glass front door. Focusing on her intent—an honest conversation with her daughter—she rang the doorbell.

"Mom. What a surprise." Marrah's brow furrowed. "You just missed Jake. He took David out to Barnes and Noble."

"Oh, well, I came to talk to you." Lois smiled, waiting for Marrah to invite her in, but when she didn't, Lois invited herself in. "Do you have some tea?"

"Tea?"

Undeterred, Lois smiled, as easily as breathing. "Yes, that would be nice. It's been a while since we talked."

"We never talk." Marrah lifted an eyebrow and stepped back. "Come on in. Of course, you would have anyway."

"How has your garden fared through this heat?"

"Mom, why did you come over?"

"For tea." Lois smiled and opened the cabinet door above Marrah's coffeepot. "Let's see." She picked out two cups and opened the next door. Inside, she saw two prescription bottles just as Jake had said. *Good.* With her back to Marrah, Lois picked up the jar of tea and closed the cabinet door. "How is your wrist? Does it still hurt or are you taking the Norco?"

"Yes. The other is none of your business."

"Maybe." Lois filled the cups with water and placed them in the microwave. She pressed the start button. Then she turned to Marrah. "May I see your wrist?"

"It's fine. You're nagging me again. And besides, I don't like tea at this time of night."

As the microwave hummed, Lois turned around and reopened the cabinet door. "Perhaps then we should talk about these." She picked up the pill vials and turned around.

Marrah gasped and blanched. "Mom, where did you—" She grabbed the prescription bottles. "Dr. Loring gave me those, and I still need them." She stuffed the vials into a pocket.

"Sweetheart, if your wrist still hurts that much, maybe you need to see a specialist in Charlotte."

"What do you care?" Anger twisted Marrah's mouth.

The microwave binged. "But I do." Lois took the cups of hot water and placed them on the English pine breakfast table. She then picked up the jar of tea bags. "Here. Have a seat."

"No! How did ...." Marrah's anger exploded. "You planted them, didn't you? Look. I didn't invent these. The doctors wrote the prescription."

"I'm sure they did, but you didn't tell the latter three that you already had a prescription, several prescriptions. Did you?"

"How ...?" Marrah's face contorted, became blank, and settled into a fixed stare, focused on Lois.

Lois had seen the dramatic series often enough not to be alarmed. Next, Marrah's anger would distill into a lethal concentrate of outward acquiescence and inward rebellion. Lois braced herself.

"I'm sorry," Marrah snapped. "I can't be as perfect as you, but I'm not addicted."

"Did I say you were?" Lois pulled out a chair and sat down. "Please sit with me." Marrah wasn't the only person capable of projecting sweetness and light when her insides were being yanked out. "Talk to me. Tell me what's bothering you."

Marrah's eyes narrowed into slits. She jerked a chair out and sat down across from Lois. For the next hour, she ranted through a series of excuses that Lois had heard a thousand times before: the prescription was too weak, she'd become immune to the dosage, she lost track of time, Jake didn't ... *couldn't* understand. On and on.

Meanwhile, Lois planned her response. The fall and Marrah's wrist were irrelevant. Steve's death was a good start. Then she'd work backward to Tom's death. Now, though, Marrah leaned back and glared at her mother as silence echoed through the room.

"Martha," Lois lowered her voice, "can we talk about the day Steve died?"

"I hate you," Marrah screamed and jumped to her feet. "You don't know when to quit."

Lois almost retreated, but the impulse had become too old and impotent to generate more than a flickering response. Instead, she relaxed.

"Yeah," Marrah snapped. "Let's talk about how you left Steve alone." The razor edge of her voice sliced into Lois's heart. "You left me alone. You can't just waltz in here as if *you* were so benevolent."

"You're right," Lois sighed. For longer than Lois wanted to remember, Marrah had thrust and parried with the same argument, but now it glanced off. "Martha, talk to me. Please, it's time to stop running."

"Running?" Marrah shoved her chair under the table, nearly toppling it. Lois grabbed the cups, but the jar rolled onto its side. "I'd love to run away," Marrah snapped, "but you'd hunt me down then treat me like some stupid little girl."

"Yes, I'd follow you." Lois set the cups down and righted the jar. "I love you that much."

"Love me? You don't love anyone. You didn't love Dad, and you didn't love Steve." Marrah's eyes scanned the room, jerking from the cabinet to the picture to the window, landing on nothing. "If you did"—her mouth quivered— "you wouldn't have left them." Her shoulders began to shake. "Or me. But you did."

Lois waited, unwilling to avoid discussing the root cause of Marrah's drug abuse—which lay buried deep in the past.

"Oh, wait," a cruel, cold smile filled Marrah's face. "I almost forgot. You adored Ben."

Ben was irrelevant. Lois focused on Marrah's need, not the addiction's venom. Meanwhile, Marrah pulled the Norco vial from her pocket and opened it. Seeing that it was empty, her mouth dropped open.

"Martha, this has to stop. Those pills are destroying you."

"They are not! You are." She threw the vial across the room.

Lois steeled her courage, but something had changed—peace infused the marrow in her bones. Her fears vanished. The war was over, not just this battle, but the whole war. She didn't know which word or action had ended it, but she knew it was over. Finished. "Whatever," she said then shrugged and relaxed into the chair. "Martha, you can either work with Jake and with me to beat this, or I'll have to call Dr. Loring. He'll call the pharmacies and cancel your prescriptions." No longer on either offense or defense, she shrugged. "He may take other steps, like prescribing counseling or rehab. I don't know, but first, talk to me. I want to help you."

White anger burned Marrah's face. Her lips narrowed into a thin straight line. "I want my pills."

"That was not the answer I was hoping to hear." Her calm deepened. "You can beat this. Jake and I can help you."

Marrah threw her arms up into the air, wrenching her face. The next instant, she collapsed into the chair opposite Lois and buried her face in her elbow, her arms splayed on the well-used and forgiving pine tabletop. This behavior was new.

"May I assume," Lois asked, "that you're ready to reduce the dosage?"

Marrah drew her arms in, draping one across her head and burrowing her face deeper into the elbow of the other. As a soft sob shook her shoulders, Lois reached to touch her head and gently combed her hair. They would talk about Steve and her father later, for the time had come. The end was at hand.

21

Loud music, shouting, and occasional whoops filled the rental house that Cameron shared with Neil and others, but little of it passed through the fog in his head.

"No, Cameron." Rita took his glass away. "You don't need this. You've had too many." Her voice trembled, even as he enjoyed the warmth of her breath across his face.

"Babe, I'm fine." He pulled her closer and kissed the skin just behind her ear—soft, warm skin.

"Don't do that."

"Why not? I thought you liked it."

"No. Not when you're like this."

What was her problem?

"I'm worried about you."

It was a nice sentiment, but, *who cares*. Cameron flopped against the sofa's back, causing the room to spin, which was cool. Then someone else spoke through the murk.

"I'll take care of him." Ah, Neil. Was he good with magic? Could he turn Cameron's father into a human being? Maybe he could call Lydia. Nope. To do that, he'd need to know about Lydia, and that wasn't going to happen.

"Is he going to be all right?" Rita asked. "Last spring, he could put it away, but not this much. It's like he's trying to kill himself."

An interesting idea.

"He'll be all right." Neil grabbed Cameron's arm and lifted him to his feet. "Come on, Cam. Walk with me."

"Night, Rita." Wherever she was. No matter. Cameron smiled as Neil lifted him.

"Watch your feet."

Teetering, Cameron reached for something stable but found only air. Neil grabbed him and pulled him along. Cameron's foot hit the first step. He lost his balance, but Neil's grip tightened, steadying him. Cameron closed his eyes and stumbled up the steps to the second floor.

"Okay, we made it to the top." Feeling Neil shift his weight, Cameron reached for the wall, aiding Neil who kept him from falling. "It's just a little farther. You know the way. That's good. No, no, you can't just lean against the wall all night."

Cameron stumbled over his feet as Neil dragged him down the hall. Then something hard and vertical jammed against his shoulder. The door-frame. He groped for his bed. Finding it by habit rather than by sight, he fell face down.

Neil turned him over and propped him up. "Let's get the pillow behind you."

"Thanks." Cameron's lips barely formed the word. His head rolled to one side as he stopped resisting sleep. Sometime later, music pulsing through the darkness awoke him. He sat up, which sent his head spinning. He reached to catch his balance. *Crash!*

"What?" Neil's startled voice pierced the darkness. "Oh. You're finally awake."

"I guess. What time is it?"

Neil's phone lit the room. "Three-ten. How's your stomach?"

"Terrible."

"Are you going to throw up?"

"Don't I wish." Cameron tossed the pillow aside.

"No!" Neil grabbed the pillow. "I don't want you throwing up after I go to sleep." He stuffed it under Cameron's head, neck, and back. "Now leave it there. I hate hospitals enough without having to drag your sorry ass over there because you choked."

"Pff!" Cameron drifted into a fitful sleep, bedeviled by a memory from six years earlier.

"You're sure you'll be all right?" Paul's mother asked.

"Yeah." Cameron looked up through the mist and Mrs. Rizziellio's swishing windshield wipers to the stark outline of Chalmers Memorial Hospital. "Thanks for the ride."

"Glad to do it."

Cameron climbed out of the car, wanting to run away, but knowing there was nowhere else that he wanted to be. Steeling his courage, he pressed on, passing through the oversized rotating door of the hospital. Once inside, his wet shoes squeaked against the lobby's polished floor. He snaked through a series of elevators and bright, nondescript halls that no fifteen-year-old should know so well. When he reached the double fire doors at the entrance to the ward where Grandpa had been admitted a week earlier, he paused, then forged ahead. Rather than entering his grandfather's room, he flopped against the wall. His heart pounded in his ears, but his pulse slowed.

Two voices, coming from within Grandpa's room, spoke. One voice belonged to his father. But the other? It was Reverend Patterson. *No!* Why was the preacher in Grandpa's room? Cameron wiped his suddenly sweaty hands on his pants. Only two months had passed since doctors diagnosed Grandpa with pancreatic cancer. It was too soon to need a pastor.

Cameron wanted to run, but his feet refused to move. Instead, his hands slid along the wall and pulled him into the room where he stood mute and stiff, his back pressed against the cold wall. His father had not seen him, but Grandpa smiled the moment he entered. He lifted his hand and motioned for Cameron to come closer.

"Randy," Grandpa whispered, "would you and Reverend Patterson mind leaving Cameron and me alone for a moment?"

"Sure, Dad." He glanced at Cameron. "Hi, son."

Cameron nodded to his father. Then, trembling, he lurched for his grandfather's hand. "You can't go, Grandpa." He searched his grandfather's ancient blue eyes. "I need you!" His voice quivered.

"It's all right, son. You're in good hands—better than mine. You're in God's hands." Supreme kindness softened the skin draped across Grandpa's sunken cheekbones. "Don't be afraid. This life is but a passing through ... Jesus loves you. You won't be alone." He squeezed Cameron's hand. "Hand me the Bible over there by the window." Cameron picked up the well-worn leather book, evoking a lifetime of memories, memories of curling up next to Grandpa and listening to him read aloud.

Grandpa's voice fell below a whisper. "Look in the back cover. Do you see the piece of paper? Yes, that's it. I wrote down those verses for you some time ago. Take my Bible and the paper with you; you can read it later."

Translating the implication of *later*, Cameron began to tremble. He grasped his grandfather's bony hand as his throat closed.

"Son, whenever you feel alone ... anytime you would have come looking for me ... read this." Cameron steadied himself as his grandfather's withered voice continued, calm and clear. "Jesus is calling your name. I was blessed to see it in your eyes when we took our trips up to the Blue Ridge. You belong to him. Love him ... follow him."

Tears flooded down Cameron's cheeks. "Grandpa! Don't leave me."

Grandpa's voice strengthened. "Never forget, Jesus loves you far more than I ever could, and that's an awful lot."

What? Cameron sat up, but instead of Grandpa, he saw only patterns of light cast upon the walls of his room. That long-ago night, he had slept in Grandpa's room. Two days later, he had been at school when Grandpa passed away. An involuntary tremor shook him as tears washed down his face, but only Neil's soft breathing disturbed the night. Someone shouted outside his window. Had Grandpa been right? But if Jesus knew Cameron's name, why did he seem so far away?

22

A week later, Cameron again awoke in the dark hours of Sunday morning. He propped himself up on his elbows in the ambient light from the parking area behind the house. He rubbed his temples, hoping for relief but received none. He should have stopped sooner.

He started to lie back down but was surprised by his what he saw. Only a sheet lay draped across his lap; he wore nothing beneath it. In an instant, a memory from several hours earlier yanked his attention back to his bed. Rita lay asleep next to him, wearing one of his T-shirts. *Holy crap!* Vague details returned. While she wept and pleaded, he had insisted that it wouldn't work. *Why couldn't she listen?*

Meanwhile, he had continued to drink. Now mostly sober and wide awake, he grabbed some clothes. He slipped into the hall where he paced as he dressed. What had he done? Certainly not what he had intended. He debated his choices. Staying was not an option; Rita had made that clear. But if he left, where would he go? Professor Krasotkin's house! The professor lived on a quiet street off Piney Mountain Road. He wouldn't be bothered if Cameron parked in front of his house. Nor would strange people or stray students pester him. He could sleep for an hour or so, then leave before anyone noticed him.

Cameron crept back into his room and grabbed a jacket, shoes, and his car keys. Then he left, pulling the door closed behind him. If the professor awoke early, certainly he would recognize Cameron's car. That, however, would not happen. Cameron only needed a few minutes to rest and get his head together. He'd leave before the professor awoke.

As he drove down the long grade of East Franklin Street, the empty highway—so alive and crowded during the day—caved in around him. What more could he have said to Rita? Had she heard anything he said? When he reached the professor's house, he pulled the parking brake, climbed over the console, and curled up on the rear seat, certain that the cool night air would prevent him from oversleeping. For a while, he relived telling Rita to forget him, to get on with her life, but he soon drifted into a dream.

"So, Cameron, why haven't you called Lydia," Drew asked. He picked up a pebble then sent it skipping across the waves on the lake high in the Bighorns. "You can't bring her here if you don't call her."

"But she is here." Cameron turned and took Lydia's hand. "See?"

"There's no one here."

"It's Lydia. She's right here."

"No, Cameron, she's not. And you didn't stop drinking. I said it'd be harder to stop if you ever started again. You need to call Lydia. Call her."

Knock, knock ....

Knock, knock.

Startled, Cameron sat up, his eyes darting about the car. A man stood just beyond the passenger-side window. Early morning sunlight streamed through the branches of the tall pines and scattered hardwood trees above his head. Two teenage boys stood on either side of the man who leaned closer and called to him. "Cameron?"

Professor Krasotkin! Cameron scrambled to open the rear driver's side door. "Good morning, sir." He ran his fingers through his hair, combing it into submission.

"Are you all right?"

"Yes, sir; I was ... resting. I was supposed to wake up earlier." He glanced at his cell phone, checking the time—*past eight!* A reflex almost sent his hand, cupping it, over his mouth to check his breath. Instead, he hoped it smelled only half as bad as it tasted. "I didn't mean to bother you, sir. I thought I'd leave before you woke up."

"It's Sunday, so Rod, Ivan, and I run early in the morning. These are my sons. Won't you come in and have some coffee?"

"No, sir, but thank you. I don't want to impose."

"Not at all. Besides, it's cold out here, and you're shivering."

The professor was right. Cameron was freezing, but accepting the invitation was not possible. If he went inside, he could not hide his hangover. Instead, he scrambled to find a reasonable lie. *Esther.* Yes, Dr. Krasotkin would remember that he and Esther were buddies. "Thank you, sir, but I told Esther that I'd meet her for breakfast." Again, he checked the time then exaggerated both his smile and expression of surprise. "Gosh, I'd better get going."

He nodded to Rod and Ivan, then climbed out and opened the driver's door. Before he could duck inside, the professor smiled. "Tell Esther we'll pick her up at nine ... or are you planning to take her to church this morning?"

"Um ... uh—" He'd forgotten that Esther went to church. Regularly.

"That's very good of you." The professor smiled. "She was saying just yesterday that she hates to bother us every weekend. Of course, we don't mind, but I know she would rather ride with a friend."

"Uh ... Uh. Yes, sir."

The professor stood up. "See you in a while."

"Yes, sir. Tell Mrs. Krasotkin hello, and I'm sorry for disturbing your morning."

"Will do."

Cameron grinned and ducked into the car. He waved as he turned the car on and then pulled away from the curb—slowly. Despite the cold air, sweat covered him. What had he agreed to do? Worse yet, Rita was probably still in his bed. What was he going to say now? He started to dial Esther's number but stopped. His brain was too numb to think. Instead, he focused on the road and maneuvered his way back to the center of town. When he parked his car behind the rental house, he pulled his phone out and called her.

"Cameron? Hi." He didn't need to hear caution in Esther's voice to know that she was surprised to hear his voice on Sunday morning.

When he offered to give her a ride to church, the long pause that followed was equally predictable. "Maybe you'd rather ride with Dr. Krasotkin."

"No. Um ... I'd love to ride with you."

"I'll pick you up at nine, is that right?"

"Yeah, but you don't sound too enthusiastic. Hey, what got you into this? No. On second thought, don't tell me. I don't want to know." Finally, she sounded like herself.

"It's a long story," he mumbled.

"Of that I have no doubt."

Esther's laughter was surprisingly soothing, but his new dilemma was not. What was he going to tell Rita or Neil and the others? He flopped back against the headrest. Every muscle went lifeless except the drums banging in his head. Time, though, was a-wasting. He had only thirty minutes to shower and dress before he picked up Esther. He glanced at the second story of the house. *Rita.*

Hoping to avoid her, he entered through the back door but found her seated at the kitchen table, her face stained with tears. Neil sat next to her while Patrick and Trace sat across the table. All turned toward Cameron. Seconds became eons as they stared back at him. Finally, he whispered. "I tried to tell you ... I'm sorry."

"Where've you been?" she pleaded.

"I wasn't with another girl if that's what you're wondering, but I told Esther that I'd pick her up at nine. I need to shower."

Without another word to either his closest friends or Rita, he left the kitchen.

"Cameron!" Rita jumped to her feet.

Reaching the top step, he turned and looked down into her forlorn eyes. He sighed, turned, and retreated to his room. After showering, brushing his teeth, and washing out his mouth three times, he checked his closet for a white oxford-cloth shirt, appropriate for church. As he buttoned it, he glanced out the window and saw Rita's car parked in the same spot as the night before. If facing Rita had been difficult, explaining his actions to Neil, Trace, and Patrick would be impossible. Now, though, he was out of time. He crept down the stairs, shoes in hand, and slipped out the front door.

Turning into the Granville Towers parking lot, he saw Esther standing at the entrance. He reached across the seat and opened the door for her. "Good morning. So where are we going?"

"I can't believe you're going to church. You're the last person I expect to see on a Sunday morning." She leaned close. "You're even sober."

"That's below the belt."

"Is it?" She settled back in her seat and gave him the directions to the church on the south side of town. "You're right. That wasn't fair. I don't know what you do on weekends. I hear all sorts of things when people notice we're good friends. Needless to say, they wonder if I'm being truthful."

"About what?"

"About you and me being good friends."

"We are! Aren't we?"

"Yeah, or do you just need a competent lab partner?"

"Well, that too."

Despite the silence that followed, he knew she was recording and analyzing his every move. A minute or so later, as he spun the steering wheel to make a turn, he heard a muted sigh. Typical of her forthright nature, she elaborated. "I understand why you like me. I'm not threatening."

The tone of her voice reminded him of Drew. They were both good friends and deserved better treatment from him. "What? You think I don't find you attractive? Sure I do."

"So why don't you ever ask me out? We've been friends since freshman year."

Cameron glanced at her as his smile faded. Didn't she understand that her friendship meant more to him than the girls he dated? Well, except for one, but Lydia no longer counted. Turning back to the road, he sank into the seat, as if hiding would do any good.

"Okay," Esther relented. "I know to quit while I'm ahead. That's the church. Do I need to ...?" She wobbled her hands, using them to finish her question.

"What? I've been to church. I know what to do." He lifted his chin and buttoned the top button. "Is that better?"

"No!" Esther laughed. "Unbutton it."

Happy to have appeased a small part of her disappointment, he continued.

"Listen. If he asks, tell Krasotkin that we had breakfast before we came. You did eat something, didn't you?"

"No, I never eat breakfast. I had a cup of coffee ... with lots of milk." She grinned. "What's wrong, huh? I run before church. If I eat breakfast, I get cramps."

He turned on his puppy-dog eyes. "Please."

"Okay, I'll cover for you. But I want an explanation."

At the moment, such a promise was impossible to keep, so he didn't offer it. They found the professor and his family waiting in the entrance to the education building. After a few awkward introductions—Cameron smiled and nodded throughout—he followed Esther to the sanctuary. He recognized a few classmates and greeted them with cheerful camaraderie but doubted he had fooled any of them.

Esther found seats next to several friends. Two girls leaned forward to scrutinize him, so he offered his most charming and contrite smile. They immediately blushed. Ah, yes. That was fun; then Esther rammed her elbow into his side. *Ouch.* So he affected appropriate solemnity.

Having grown up listening to long-winded sermons filled with too-good-to-be-true anecdotes about the struggles of sinless souls who decided that it was to their advantage to invite Jesus into their lives, he had an arsenal of tactics to revive him should his brainwave activity drop to imperceptible.

For an hour and a half, he sang and smiled, stood and sat, crossed and uncrossed his legs while random thoughts rambled in and out among his aching cranial lobes. Three threads unified the diverse images. First, he wondered if Lydia had gone to church. Probably. Next, he thumbed through memories of the ranch, Azariah, and the range. A few scattered thoughts about his father flicked and—thankfully—vanished. Finally, he stood for the benediction and languidly stretched each stiff muscle. He'd survived.

Once outside, and after saying goodbye to Professor Krasotkin and his wife, Esther took his elbow and smiled. "Let's have lunch."

"Uh-oh." He squelched a grin. "I thought I behaved myself."

"You did, but we need to talk."

"Eh. Those words have never brought glad tidings of great joy."

Esther laughed. "Fair enough, but I'm hungry and I can only afford someplace on campus. How about Ram's Head Market?"

"I'd have to park at the frat house and walk." *Across campus.* "Am I in trouble?"

"No. Stop worrying."

On the drive back to the frat, Esther directed the conversation, which took the pressure off him. Once or twice he mentioned the sermon (it was interesting) and the church service (where was the choir?). Though she consistently turned the conversation to various innocuous subjects, never once did he think she had forgotten his early morning phone call.

He parked behind the house, then together they crossed South Columbia Street and continued south toward the bell tower. Despite their long friendship, Cameron had rarely invited her to the fraternity house. Once he overheard her telling a friend that she wasn't that kind of girl, whatever 'that kind of girl' was. Still, Esther was a well-known and accepted part of Cameron's life. Even his various girlfriends understood that she was as important to him as Neil, Trace, and Patrick.

"Did you get back to the lab on Friday?" she asked. Following his one-syllable answer, she elaborated. "Then you missed the show. Someone's chemistry experiment failed and sent everyone running down the hall, screaming about a bromide cloud. It was easily contained which made the commotion sort of funny."

"I suppose. That is if you consider a cloud of poisonous gas to be funny."

"Overreaction is the heart of humor."

"And your point?"

"Oh. Nothing."

As they passed Wilson Library and approached the Bell Tower, a list of things he needed to do came to mind, a list that did not include being tormented. "Are you going to tell me why I'm in trouble?"

"In time." She grinned. "Besides, you're not in trouble. By the way, I have a friend who thinks Patrick is a nice guy." For a while, she described the friend, listing her major and sports interests. "She's cute, too. If he's curious, let me know."

"He's available, but I don't play matchmaker. It's all I can do to keep up with my own mistakes. Which reminds me, why am I in trouble?"

"Patience." A sultry smile appeared. "See? We're at the Market. Was that so painful?"

Yes.

After lunch, rather than taking the shortest distance to her dorm, she directed him toward Polk Place. She pointed to an open grassy spot near an old fieldstone wall in front of Wilson Library. "This looks good." She sat down cross-legged, and Cameron lay on his back next to her. Two couples lounged nearby, and a few people passed along the sidewalk that followed the fieldstone wall, but none intruded.

"Cameron, what happened in Wyoming?"

"I had a great time. Why?"

"Well, you talk about it all the time, but you came back in worse shape than before you left. That's a big disconnect. If it was that great, why are you so miserable?"

"I'm not." He grinned and rolled his R's with elongated vowels. "'Twas brillig, and the slithy toves.' Me and the borogoves are all mimsy," he said with a laugh.

"And that's why you called me this morning." She smiled. "Care to explain?"

Cameron's smile faded.

"You don't fool me." She waited, studying him. "And Neil agrees with me."

Oh. "Did either of you plan to talk to me about this?" He arched an eyebrow and pretended to count the clouds.

"He thinks it's your dad, but he was afraid to press you. I'm not—at least, not after you called this morning."

He glanced at her and snorted. His family problems were not up for discussion.

"Something's eating at you, Cameron. It's been gnawing away not just this fall but for almost a year. Yes, it's been a whole year."

A year ago? What had she noticed? A crack in his facade? Certainly not the conflict with his father; he hid that too well. Regardless, whatever she imagined needed to be ignored. He turned his attention to a contrail, inching across the sky. She'd give up soon.

"It's a girlfriend, isn't it?"

A girlfriend? Lydia? He could wish. Cameron watched the contrail grow longer.

"I knew it," she blurted. "Why do you do this? Why do you get involved with girls you don't love? If I didn't know you as well as I do, I'd listen to my friends who wonder why I keep agreeing, year after year, to be your lab partner."

That's a problem? He glanced at her but immediately turned back to the now long white line etched across the brilliant blue sky.

"You're not a totally shallow guy," she continued, "so why do you act like you are? Don't you care what people think?"

He glanced at her, half grinning and half grimacing, but as he looked away, her mouth dropped open. "You *do* like someone," she declared. "Don't you? —But she doesn't like you."

Score one for Esther.

"Who is she?" she pleaded. "She isn't here in Chapel Hill ... wait! That's it! Don't think you can ignore me. You know I'm right. So who is she?"

He met her eyes, no longer able to force a smile. Esther jumped onto her knees and leaned over him. "I knew those girls who hang on you weren't the kind of girl you'd like."

For a long cold moment, he met her stare then looked for the contrail.

She leaned close to his face. A faint grin flickered. "You know, I always imagined that I'd be jealous if you ever found someone you truly like, but I'm not. But I am dying of curiosity. Tell me about her."

How could he tell her about Lydia? His brow knitted as Esther continued to lean over his face, occasionally blocking the sunlight. Maybe he could say something, but only a little. "You have to promise not to tell." His voice sounded harsh, but it emphasized his point. "Neither Neil, Trace, nor Patrick know about her. And I want it to stay that way."

"Why? They're your best friends."

"It's my business. Not theirs."

"Do you think you're the only guy ever to get shot down? I assume that's what happened. Well, think again. My friends would have my head examined if they heard that I accepted a date with you."

His frown vanished. "Why?"

"Because they don't want me to be one of your 'girls.'"

"Ouch."

"As I said, that's what they think. Still, I can't believe that you like this girl and haven't resolved it."

"Resolved it?" he snorted. "It's not that simple."

"Well, do you care to explain why you called this morning?" She leaned an inch closer. "Oh, yeah, and why were you parked in front of Dr. Krasotkin's house?"

Cameron's jaw clenched as he watched another plane cross the sky. "We went to high school together. Her name is Lydia."

"Okay, that's nice. We're making progress. I assume she's in school someplace."

He grinned but didn't look at her. "She's a Dukie."

"No!" she gasped. Instantly, her eyes narrowed. She leaned very close. "No! You date bimbos."

"What do you mean?" He laughed as she came to within inches of his face.

"If you dated a smart girl"—cold steel glistened in her eyes— "and it wasn't me, I'd post your sorry hide on the front of Venable Hall."

For a moment he broke into laughter. Then he quickly sat up, sending her back onto her heels. He leaned close, far closer than usual. His heart raced despite his effort to look contrite and humble. "Can I ask a favor of you?" His face twisted in wordless pleading. "I'd be in your debt for life."

Esther winced as she sat down and leaned away from him. Again her eyes narrowed, examining him, but he didn't flinch. She leaned even farther back as one hand reached for the ground behind her to keep from falling over. "What kind of favor?"

She was ready to deny his request, but he persevered. "Last spring, you said there were some Robertson Scholars from Duke in your class. Right?"

"Yeah, and?"

"I've been trying to reach her, but I don't have her cell phone number—and you know I don't do social media. I have enough trouble as it is. I could ask Mom to call her mother, but that would complicate things. Could you ask one of your friends about her? Maybe they know her."

Cameron pulled out his puppy dog smile. Her indignation ebbed, but she might still refuse. As seconds ticked by, reality sank in, and his excitement waned. Though Duke was not a large school, Esther probably didn't know someone who also knew Lydia.

"Okay. I'll do it. But I can't promise anything. What do you know about her—at Duke, that is? What's her major?"

"Her last name is Carpenter. That's all I know." His cheeks flushed.

"You're kidding." She flashed a smile as delight danced across her face. "Cameron, you're pitiful. You're nuts about this girl, but you don't even know her major." She closed her eyes and shook her head. "And to think I'm going to do this for you. You don't need a friend. You need a nursemaid." She stood and reached for his hand. "Come on; a lab report awaits us. First, I've got to run over to Walmart."

Two hours later, Esther found Cameron in the lab, studying. She plopped her books down on the table next to his laptop but remained standing, smiling at him. Finally, she sat down. Pressing her shoulder against his, she whispered. "You owe me."

"Why?" Hurricane warning flags fluttered in his head.

She arched a brow. "In fact, you owe me big time."

The wind kicked up, whipping the flags as her grin widened. She laid a slip of paper, face down, in front of him and then clamped her hand over it. "What's that?" he asked.

"Hold on, and I'll tell you."

For several minutes, Esther gleefully recounted every detail of her ride to Walmart, the friends who picked her up, their conversation, and what they looked at. Since she was normally a very direct but polite person, he found her circuitous answer strange. She also seemed quite pleased with herself, which was another atypical feature. "So," she continued, "I'm standing in the checkout line, and these three girls approach. Everyone knows that the Walmart next to I-40 is the great equalizer for UNC and Duke students. We all go there. Well, guess who walks up? It was Ragini Khouri, a Duke student from my class. Petite, very pretty. Her mother was born in India, and her father is … something else. Whatever. Well, you know how guys like to bond?"

"Yeah, and?" Unable to discern the object of her discourse, he painted a patient smile on his face as he glanced between Esther and his laptop. That is, until she lowered it and turned the computer toward her.

"Okay, so guys like to smoke, drink and cuss." Her grin widened and then erupted into quiet but gleeful laughter. "Well, women like to shop, so I wasn't surprised to see that Ragini was with several friends from Duke. I naturally assumed that the girls were her close friends. Now, guess … *who* … is one of Ragini's good friends?"

"Come on." He reached for his laptop. "I don't know."

She slid the paper out of his reach. "You don't?" Suddenly, her smile vanished. "You can't guess?"

Her cheer morphed into reproach as she turned the slip of paper over. Cameron blanched as he read the name, Lydia Carpenter, and her phone number.

Stern and undaunted, Esther continued. "Cameron, I only talked to her for a few minutes, but she's very nice. If I hear that you treated her like the other girls that you date, and you know exactly what I'm referring to, I'll never speak to you again. We've got a semester of lab ahead of us, so you'd better behave."

"Yes, ma'am." Blood flooded his cheeks. Clenching his lips tightly, he ducked his head like a child accepting his punishment. "Now what do I do?"

"You're kidding." She leaned close, examined him then laughed. "You are pitiful. Pitiful! Call her. You know. Use the number."

"Yeah, but what do I say?" He searched her eyes. "Should I invite myself over?"

"Well, duh!" Esther was almost beside herself with laughter. "I can't believe that you of all people would ask that question. Ask her to do something."

"Does she know why you needed her phone number?"

"Excuse me?" Esther slapped her chest with her palm then feigned a sudden coughing spell. "I'm not that crass. She doesn't know that Ragini gave it to me. You get to explain that one to her."

"Maybe I should wait till later in the week."

"Why, so you can find an excuse not to call her? Invite her to go for a walk; then see how it goes." She turned his computer around. "Has it occurred to you that she might have a steady guy or … whatever?"

"Or what? She may not want to see me? She probably doesn't."

Again, Esther narrowed her eyes, but this time he didn't blanch.

"It seems you've already treated her like a bimbo."

"No!" He retrieved his composure, appropriate for a half-empty lab. "No, not that, but I gave her reason not to—" He reread Lydia's name and number as his heart sank through the floor. "I told Stan and Drew about what happened." His cheek twitched. "They said I should call her."

"Then call her. By the way, you know that I'm one of those Christians who *doesn't* believe in fate. Oh, and remember. There might be someone else in her life."

"There probably is ... but you don't think I should wait?"

"No, Ragini said to take her to Duke Gardens." She turned the paper over. "You can park here but meet her at the bus stop in front of the chapel." She turned off his computer and stacked his papers. "Now, on your way. This can wait." She picked up his computer. "You are a sad case. Oh, and don't forget, you owe me."

Marrah leaned against the railing of her deck, content to have a moment alone. In the distance, Jake's Flying Scot glided across the lake with their neighbor Joe manning the jib. Melanie had run to her car for something—for what, Marrah couldn't imagine—but she'd be back. A week had passed since Lois began doling out Norco pills in packaged dosages: the penalty for Marrah's sins. To say that Marrah had agreed was to apply the word only by the loosest definition. As expected, jitters had plagued her since taking the lower dosage; her brain felt as if it had been stuffed into a skull two sizes too small. On a few occasions, transient dizziness had forced her to grasp for balance, but when she reported the grinding misery to her mother, unperturbed Lois had not relented.

At four, Jake went to some meeting, probably church. Minutes after he left, Anne stopped by—not that Marrah disliked her. Instead, she wanted to be left alone.

Marrah strained an annoyed smile, and instead, opened the door for Anne while smiling through her teeth. "Won't you come in?" Part of Lois's personal brand of punishment had been to inundate Marrah with companions. "Tell Lois that I don't need a nanny."

"Oh," Anne chirped, "I was in the area."

"Yeah, right." Marrah heaved a deep sigh. "Can I get you something to drink?"

"Sure."

Marrah turned toward the kitchen. Anne had, very wisely, not chosen a career in acting—she stank at it. "Too bad," Marrah growled, "that none of y'all have figured out that the youngest kid around here—David—is in high school."

"Oh, so tell me how you *really* feel."

Marrah glared. "I have a very short fuse, and I just want a little peace."

Anne smiled, cheerful and annoying, and then picked up Marrah's notebook. "Is this for the Hope Springs Christmas program? When do you start calling the families?"

"Don't change the subject. You don't need to worry about me."

"Worry is such a strong word. I'm glad to spend time with you."

"That's what my cats are for."

The truth wrote itself in bold letters across Anne's smile: Lois had encouraged her to visit, but Anne had agreed to the suggestion. Nothing more needed to be said. Marrah would deal with her mother later. Without bothering with pleasantries, she answered Anne's question, "Yes, those are the families."

Marrah thanked Anne for her kindness by letting her stay, chatting if she wished, but then asserted, "I know you have other things to do."

"Not really." Anne smiled or rather grinned. "It's so peaceful here. And I love your garden."

Marrah reached for the phone. "I'm calling Lois. You're welcome to stay ... and listen in."

Anne checked her watch. "No. I'll pass."

After a brief goodbye, Marrah waved to Anne, closed the door, and went straight to the phone. "Mom. Why am I suddenly the center of everyone's universe?" She clipped off the words, not daring to let her mother respond. "And don't act like you don't know what I'm talking about." Her mother chuckled, though faintly. "Mom! You always laugh when I'm miserable. Don't do that. I'm deadly serious."

"Sweetheart, I'm so glad you're feeling better."

Predictable. Marrah held the receiver in front of her and scowled at it. Sarcasm had been her mother's favorite technique since before the dinosaurs. "Thanks, Mom," she snarled. "That's just what I needed." Why couldn't Lois be like other mothers? And why was everything funny? "Why did you tell everyone to check on me?"

"They volunteered."

"Great! Now everyone thinks I'm crazy."

"Nobody thinks you're crazy, but Anne, Melanie, and your close friends wanted to keep you company until you get over this bump."

"I have a headache. I'm not suicidal."

"Oh, I'm so glad to hear that." For the ten-thousandth time, Marrah considered throttling her mother. Instead, Lois continued. "You sound fine to me, but I'll send you to a psychologist if that's what you want."

"I don't need a psychologist." Marrah held the receiver in front of her, stuck her tongue out at it, and put it back to her ear. "Look, Mom, my head is killing me. My wrist feels like it's been used as a voodoo doll. My body is going haywire, so if that's better, then yeah, I'm better."

"Then good. By the way—" Lois shared a few pieces of uninteresting news and other nonsense, not that Marrah cared, but Lois would pester her if she hung up. Finally she said goodbye. Marrah wanted a Norco pill desperately. Earlier, she had called several physicians' offices and pharmacies that handled her prescriptions. The effort failed.

"I'm sorry, Mrs. Mapson," the secretary's cold voice had said. "The doctor can't renew that prescription for another month, but he wants you to keep taking the acetaminophen."

Acetaminophen! It did nothing. Marrah had called other pharmacists, only to hear the same response, each saturated with telltale signs of meddling. After taking away Marrah's credit cards, Lois had also limited access to mail order and internet service providers, which was unnecessary and rude. Marrah even resorted to taking placebos, as one nurse suggested, but nothing helped. Even when Jake cooked dinner and David pitched in to help with a few chores, Marrah had been too cranked up to make use of the extra time, and she hated wasting time.

To make matters worse, Marrah remained convinced that Jake planned to leave. He'd put off the inevitable. Out of habit, Marrah opened her scarf drawer but found nothing but scarves. *So what will Jake say when he leaves? Hey, hey, goo-ood-bye!* Perhaps. She could ask him about his plans, but she wasn't ready. Instead, she went to the kitchen, grabbed gloves, a hand-weeding hoe, and headed for the bed of New Guinea impatiens surrounding her mailbox.

"I'm glad to see you out and about," a familiar voice said as Marrah sat down next to the flowers. "Would you like some company?"

No! But the voice belonged to her next-door neighbor, Beverly Brown. Marrah groaned. "Not you, too?"

"'Me too' what?" Despite Marrah's growl, Beverly sat down. "These are beautiful. And huge."

Had Beverly been anything other than a reliable, delightfully blunt neighbor who never meddled, Marrah would have snapped her head off and dispatched her. Instead, she decided to be relatively pleasant for the time being, but only relatively.

23

"Convenience" was the dubious label that Lydia applied to cell phones. In her opinion, the device was nothing but a contemptible inconvenience that allowed others to reach her when she did not want to be found. Thus, for self-preservation, she often turned it off when she studied, such as on Sunday afternoons. Earlier, though, Ragini had asked her to keep it close so she could call about meeting for dinner. It seemed an odd request, but Lydia obliged her. So when it rang at three thirty, she assumed the call was from Ragini.

"Hello."

"Hi, Lydia. Cameron Asher here."

A silent gasp clenched her throat. She gripped the phone to keep from dropping it. "Hi." She looked at the phone and then put it back to her ear. "How are you?" She checked the sound of her voice. Calm and smooth. Good. It hadn't given her away.

"I'm fine. I was in the area ...." His blithe tone and fast pace as he went on left no room for her to speak. *Hmm.* Did he plan to just start up as if ... well, as if she shouldn't be angry with him? If so, then he needed to think otherwise. "I thought," he continued without breaking, "I'd see how you were doing. Do you have time to talk?"

"Sure." Why not talk to him? It'd prove that he had no power over her.

"I spent the summer out in Wyoming helping on a ranch," he began. "Now I'll bet you're wondering, *Why would he go to Wyoming?*"

Wondering indeed. His call had piqued her curiosity but not about his summer.

"I was really surprised," he continued with a happy lilt in his voice. "I thought it'd be dry and barren. Well, it is, but that can be mesmerizing. I know that sounds strange."

Seeming to be oblivious to her silence, he rambled on about places she was unlikely to visit and people she would never meet. Still, her pulse had returned to normal, and that was good. So as he chattered on with merry descriptions of alpine meadows and waffles made by someone named Hannah, she turned her attention back to her engineering worksheet. To be polite, she slowly tapped the keys on her laptop to muffle the sound. "Have you ever been out there?" he asked.

"Where? Oh, I'm sorry. No. I haven't." She checked the time. Ten minutes had passed. What was with the long monologue? And what was that other sound? *Is he driving?* Though puzzled, she continued to type. Again, she checked the time. Fifteen minutes! *Now it sounds like he's walking. What is he up to?*

"So, tell me ..." he asked with the same friendly candor as when they worked together at the Park Street Diner—though another ten minutes had passed, "what are you doing?"

Huh? Silence stumbled over itself. "Um ...," she stammered. "Not much. Studying."

"I mean. What are you doing right now?"

Now? Her pulse quickened. "I'm studying. Why?"

"Well, because I'm at the circle in front of Duke Chapel. Would you like to go for a walk?"

If his first question had startled her, the last question sent waves of dismay crashing against her defenses. She stared at the computer screen as her heart raced and her mouth turned into a desert. He was out front! Until that moment, eight safe miles had separated them. Suddenly, he was neither distant nor safe.

"Are you still there?" he asked.

"Uh, yeah." She had only two alternatives. She could say no, which would be cruel, and she wasn't that cruel. Of course, she'd be done with him forever. Or she could say yes. He deserved better than the first. Hence, only the second allowed her to look in a mirror an hour, a day, or even a week later. "Sure, why not?" Meanwhile, a crew of stonemasons sprang to work, fortifying the defenses around her heart, which was good since her voice did nothing to hide their activity. "Give me a minute."

"Great!" His ebullience surprised her. "I'll stand here for a minute ... or until someone sees my shirt. Oops." He laughed. "That guy saw it."

He has on a UNC T-shirt! Idiot! She could imagine the glares from her fellow Duke students. She pinched her lips, smothering a chortle. Still, who did he think he was? Did he think he could bounce back into her life? Was he really that shallow? Maybe he was.

She combed her hair and pulled it up in a ponytail. Then she glanced in the mirror. *Hmm.* It would have to do. Besides, a beautiful September afternoon was rapidly drawing to a close. Enjoying the weather was reason enough to go for a walk, even with Cameron. She locked her door and bounced down the ancient concrete-and-steel steps, grateful for God's gift of patience and a beautiful day. She pushed open the heavy oak door to Crowell Dorm and crossed the quad that spread beneath the Gothic clock tower. She strode toward the main quad, passing through the small arched portico anchoring the east end of the long, stacked-slate retaining wall that separated the grassy upper quad from the leaf canopied lower quad. Bouncing down the limestone steps, deeply cupped by thousands of footsteps, she passed other students who strolled toward her along the slate sidewalk.

In the distance, she saw Cameron, but the dappled shade of the spreading oak trees sheltered her from his view. He was dressed in his signature blue oxford-cloth shirt, tails out, over a gray UNC T-shirt and khaki shorts. He leaned against or rather sat on the top of a gray chain-and-post bollard designed to prevent cars from circling in front of the chapel. His tanned arms lay crossed on his chest while his long, trim legs, stretched in front of him, were crossed at his ankles. None the worse for being a UNC student, he appeared quite at ease—certainly with himself. Still, she had to admit, watching him was fun.

A moment later, he smiled and stood up, casually splaying his fingers on his hips. He had seen her. A breeze ruffled wisps of his blond hair, which along with his genial smile sent excitement buzzing through every cell of her body. *Did he have to make a point by being so much fun to watch?* But she reminded herself, this was Cameron Asher. His gentle masculinity would not make her forget the past. They could be friends, but that was all. Just friends.

Ragini had spent enough of the glorious Sunday afternoon sequestered in the stacks at Perkins Library. After perusing musty books and then slogging through econ calculus for over an hour, she needed a break. She had promised Lydia and Eydie that she would meet them for dinner at six, but it was only five. She watched a beam of sunlight play with the dusty air, spinning shimmering curls, and debated her choices. Similar afternoons were the bane of Duke students, but the verdict came quickly: she would waste the remaining time elsewhere.

Leaving the library behind, Ragini turned toward the chapel. her face into the breeze as it lifted her long black hair off her shoulders. She crossed in front of the chapel and continued toward Crowell Dorm, greeting a friend as she passed the archway leading to the Bryan Student Center. She passed Kilgo Quad and hopped up the limestone steps to the west portico of the tall stone-faced retaining wall that separated the lower and upper quads. As she crossed beneath the portico's covered archway, she remembered that she needed to run by Wannamaker Dorm first. She exited and turned left to cut diagonally across the quad, but the sight ahead slammed her feet to a stop. With a quick step back, she retreated to the shadows of the portico and peeked around its stony corner.

In the opposite corner of the quad, beneath a small oak tree and next to the Crowell door, she saw Lydia and a tall blond stranger. Was he the guy that Esther had mentioned? *Shame! Shame, Esther.* She had said he was nice, not that he was gorgeous. To get a closer look, Ragini returned to the lower quad and crossed to the east portico, ducking low as she passed the wide rarely-used stairway in the center of the stone wall. She waited at the base of the portico's steps and looked across the archway's slate floor.

With only her head and shoulders visible, she watched Lydia, with her arms locked across her chest, rock from side to side. She stood a safe four feet away from the young man who, with his hands jammed into his back pockets, beamed and talked. He, too, rocked, though his constant motion was more like a bounce. Intent on waiting until Lydia and the stranger parted, Ragini made herself at home by pretending to read text messages. Other students passed her, ascending and descending the steps, but her attention remained on Lydia and her friend. Several minutes passed. The stranger's smile widened. Lydia nodded slightly, seeming to agree with something he said. She unclasped her arms and stepped away from him. She said something, then turned and entered the building. With a smile that could have lit the sun, the young man turned toward Ragini.

Ragini leaped onto the walkway and climbed the portico's stairs. At the top step, she erased her smile upon seeing the blond stranger approach in long bouncing strides. His smile, posture, and gait said he liked whatever Lydia last said to him. He passed Ragini without pausing; then virtually skipped down the steps. First, though, he shared his smile with Ragini and another student walking behind her. Rather than recognition, his greeting likely reflected a fusion between good manners and unbridled happiness.

She knew better than to turn her head and watch him, but she couldn't stop herself. What about him was there not to like, for clearly, Lydia had found something. Ragini quickened her pace toward Crowell. She slid her card through the scanner, threw the door open, and raced up the half-flight of steps to the first floor. Grabbing the iron newel post, she swung around it and grabbed the thin iron handrail, ready to sail up the next flight, but stopped. Lydia stood on the terrazzo landing, sternly glaring at Ragini, arms locked across her chest. Behind her was the small Gothic window that overlooked the entrance door.

With pure "Who, me?" innocence, Ragini smiled. "Hi, are you ready for dinner?"

"What did you see?"

"See what? I just came from the library."

"No. You turned around after he passed. What did you see?"

"I saw a hot guy. Of course, I turned around."

Lydia's eyes narrowed, and her mouth pursed. Without another word, she turned and continued up the steps and down the hall to her room, shoving open one and then a second metal fire door. The contrast between Lydia's strident attitude and the stranger's glee stoked Ragini's curiosity. Ragini called,

"You ran up to that window, didn't you?" She caught up to Lydia. "How else could you have seen him pass me? So who is he?"

"Never mind."

You don't fool me; you were watching him—and me—from that window. "Come on. Who is he?"

Lydia strode into her room and dropped in front of her computer. As she called up a program, Ragini nodded to Eydie and mouthed, "He called."

Eydie mouthed back, "I saw him." She grinned and patted her heart, while also mouthing, "So hot!"

Ragini pulled a seat up next to Lydia but said nothing.

Lydia watched the screen. "Y'all need to find something to do because there's nothing to tell."

"Is he the guy from New Year's? The one who shall forever go unnamed?" If Ragini didn't want Lydia to lie, then she shouldn't lie. "Okay, I caught the last few minutes. He looks like a nice guy, except for the T-shirt. Who is he?"

When Lydia ignored the question and began to type, Ragini pressed, "I'm curious because he was so bouncy and you're so ... grim."

Eydie snickered. "She meant to say, he was white-hot fire, but you could freeze lava. What gives?"

"Not you too?" Lydia turned to her roommate, arched a brow, and then turned back to the computer. "How did he get my phone number?"

Eydie turned the question around. "Is that a problem?"

Seeing a crack in Lydia's defenses, Ragini whipped out a smile. "You can give him my number."

"You don't want him to have it."

Aha! This *was* the guy from high school. Eydie gave a thumbs-up and asked, "What did he want?"

"He asked me to go jogging with him next Saturday morning."

"And you're going? Right?"

Lydia heaved a sigh. "There's a lot of history between us."

"Maybe," Ragini agreed, "but he asked you to go jogging, not to rob a bank."

Lydia flopped against the back of her chair, looking exhausted, but Eydie pressed her. "So are you going?"

"Yes, but you don't know him."

Remembering the brilliant smile on the stranger's face, Ragini sided with him. "You're right; we don't. But he has a name. Hint, hint."

"Cameron."

"That's a nice name," Ragini said as Eydie grinned and nodded. This was indeed the same guy.

Ragini stood. "Eydie, I'm hungry." Ignoring Cameron's T-shirt and school affiliation, she added, as she walked to the door, "I guess he has extra fun wearing *dark* blue at basketball games in Cameron Indoor."

"I don't think so."

"Why not?"

"He goes to UNC." Lydia finally laughed.

"That's a good one," Eydie said and joined Ragini at the door. "A UNC fan named after Duke's basketball stadium. Ha!"

"I said the same thing, but he didn't think it was funny. It's a family name."

"Life's tough." Eydie laughed. "Come on. You can fill in the details over dinner."

24

For endless weeks, Marrah had complied—grudgingly—with Lois's dictates and reduced her Norco doses to only two pills a day. Her doctors had allowed her to continue using Ambien for sleep and the antidepressants to keep her from falling back to the opioid. Still, pressing through less-than-sunny days had been difficult. On days when soft tendrils of fog curled up from the surface of the lake and encased the woods surrounding her house, misery had been inescapable.

Regardless, she persevered. She kept her obligations, including serving as volunteer coordinator—a euphemism for unpaid servitude—for the Christmas gift charity. As she had on too many previous October days, she initiated her job—her gratis obligation—with calls to applicant families, including the first name on the present list: Ms. Jeanette Adams, mother of Sienna and Ross. After two rings, someone answered, and Marrah launched into her spiel. "Hi, my name is …. I'm calling for …. May I speak to Jeanette Adams?" Jeanette came to the phone and Marrah continued. "And you are their mother." The list stated as much. So why had Marrah bothered to ask?

"I'm their mother," Jeanette answered.

And probably a better mother than Lois. Marrah continued through the questions as the fog wafted and hung, setting her adrift in the fluid repetition of Q and A. She recalled her training class: "Trust is everything to the families." *I'm supposed to be a servant of God by serving you. Whoopee! What has anything of this got to do with trusting God? Y'all want toys, and I want my head to stop hurting.*

Lois was welcome to cling to God—to her heart's content. However, Marrah knew better. She'd been as obedient to him as anyone, maybe more than most. She'd run the Christmas ministry when no one else would.

Wisps of fog rolled through the bare branches of a maple tree just beyond her window, but Ms. Adams's voice broke through. "Ross would like a football."

Surprise! Every older boy wanted a football, a winter coat, jeans. The list went on.

A sweet voice interrupted Marrah's musing. "Oh, my dear child." Two arms wrapped around her shoulders. "I'm here. I won't let you go." The voice—her mother's—soothed her, but what was she talking about?

"Ms. Adams," Marrah heard her voice ask. "Where's your husband?" Marrah gasped. The question was totally out of bounds, but she couldn't pull it back.

"He was killed."

"Oh, I'm so sorry." Marrah winced. "I wasn't supposed to ask such questions." Suddenly her temples throbbed, and her skull almost exploded. *Dad?*

"It's been hard without him." Jeanette's answer snagged Marrah's attention. "But Jesus takes such good care of us. I can't believe how generous he's been."

God? Generous? Not that day, not when Marrah's father lay dying at her feet. Where was God when no one heard her scream? Marrah ticked through the remaining questions and ended the call, but she couldn't silence Jeanette's sweet voice and her closing words, "Thank you so much. You're such a blessing."

Blessing? In the pressing silence, Marrah's voice arose from the depths of her memories. "Dad! Say something to me! Dad! Somebody! Help me! Please!" she screamed. But no one answered.

Marrah glanced around the room filled with office supplies, shelves with books, and sundry pictures of flowers. Who was she fooling? None of it, and nothing else—not her garden or her house—had been worth even a penny since that day when she stood alone on the empty golf course next to her father's limp body. Once again, she saw the bird glide over the fairway and watched the breeze move the pin flag. Every blade of manicured grass on the tee box waited, each in its place, like so many mute sentinels. No one had answered her cries. Only silence had echoed back to her.

Without either Steve or the pills, nothing lay between Marrah and the past. Nothing.

25

Cameron smacked his alarm clock then staggered down the hall toward the bath. As he had done for more than a month, he pushed sleep aside and prepared to meet Lydia for an early morning jog. He braced his hands on the sink and leaned forward, staring into the mirror at his scruffy face. He marveled, though not admiringly, at the memory of Lydia's deft Southern hospitality—not bad for a Wisconsin native. For four weeks, with polite smiles and banter, she had turned their time together into the emotional equivalent of a museum visit: plenty to look at, but don't get too close. Each week, as they jogged along the wooded trail that circumscribed the golf course at the Washington Duke Inn, he had dropped hints that he wanted to do something— anything—with her in addition to meeting on Saturday morning, but she had ignored him.

Thus, the previous night, when Payton, a girl he'd met at a party, asked about their future together, Cameron resolved to be more assertive, to pull out his old apology, polish off the tarnish, and confess his history of blunders and inconsiderate behavior, not to Payton, but to Lydia. Perhaps then, their relationship would move forward.

Cameron returned from the bathroom and found Neil still in bed, with his head propped up on the heel of his hand. "When did Payton leave?" he asked.

"I took her back around one." Cameron pulled on a pair of running shorts.

"What's with this health kick? You already ran three times this week."

"Yeah, maybe." Cameron pulled a T-shirt over his head, then grinned at his roommate. "We each have our vices. Mine's on Saturday morning. Yours is on Sunday."

"Okay, so tell me about this Saturday morning vice."

Without answering, Cameron grabbed his socks and sat on his bed to put them on, but Neil continued. "Cam, you can't keep this up."

"What?" he laughed and threw a wet towel at Neil. "I get my morality lectures at home."

"That reminds me, your dad called last night. He left a message."

"I saw it."

"That's what I'm talking about. If your interview at the medical school went well, why are you letting your dad push you around?" Neil flopped back onto his pillow. "And yeah, it's stupid to get involved with Payton. But then I don't know what was wrong with Rita. I liked her." He frowned. "Payton is a new low for you. Have you considered getting shots?"

"Watch your mouth." Cameron grabbed his shoes. "She's a New York debutante. Maybe she has been around." He wiggled his eyebrows.

"Are you getting even with your dad?" Cameron stopped but didn't look up. "If that's it," Neil continued, "then you're gonna TKO yourself without touching him."

Cameron half-grinned as he tied one shoe. "Give me a break. I've been sober since breaking up with Rita. You should be impressed. Payton knows how things are. Period."

"Why don't you find someone you like, someone you respect?"

"I did." He tightened his shoelace.

"And you treated her worse than you treated Rita?"

Rita had been a substitute and Payton a momentary diversion. Like a moth flitting around a candle, he turned to them when the candle was pulled away. Now the candle waited to go running with him. In the past, he had feared drawing close to the candle, baring his heart, but he could no longer fear the flame. If he wanted to be with Lydia, he would need to tip his wings into the flame and apologize for the past. He stood, meeting Neil eye to eye. "Yes, I lied to Rita, letting her think I might change my mind, but I haven't lied to Payton." Nor had he been completely truthful.

"Okay. What about that acceptance letter from the business school?"

Cameron glanced at the letter on his desk; he had applied only to silence his father's nagging. Accepting their offer was not an option. He grabbed his keys and turned to leave, but Neil continued. "*And* your interview at Wake Forest's medical school?"

Cameron stopped in the doorway, his back to his roommate. Without Lydia, neither business school nor medical school mattered. He wanted her, and that required an apology.

"I assume," Neil stated rather than asked, "that you'll turn down the business school."

"I don't know." Cameron stepped into the hall. The only hopeful answer was yes.

Lydia was not the only flame around which he flitted. He wished his father would let him choose his future, but to placate him, he had considered canceling his interview at Wake Forest and accepting admission to the business school. Candles labeled medical school and family harmony burned with worthy but dangerous flames.

He climbed into his Ford Escape and turned toward Durham. If he chose business school, he might salvage his family, but he'd never be happy. If he challenged his father by attending medical school, he could destroy his family. And what about Lydia? Had she already slipped too far away? His only choice was to play with fire.

Following two days of rain, a thick blanket of fog covered Durham and the Washington Duke Golf Club. Wisps and varying shades of gray drifted between the lofty pines and scrub along the path that Lydia followed, with Cameron jogging beside her, as it meandered around the resort. Autumn had announced its arrival with brilliant colors and crisp mornings. Dew-soaked lavender asters nodded their heads while burgundy dogwoods, with droplets clinging to their leaves, intensified autumn's colors and lifted her spirits.

On previous jogs, Cameron had described every conceivable detail about his summer in Wyoming. His interesting but still safely distant descriptions had led her to wonder why he arranged and continued their weekly meetings, which lacked the personal connection so typical of the ones they shared years earlier at the Park Street Diner. She had concluded that their "relationship," if she could call it that, was nothing more than it appeared to be: exercise and fellowship—only less than before.

Also, since he avoided discussions related to either his or her social life, she assumed he shared his afternoons and evening with a significant other. He might even be engaged to the unnamed girl. But why would that matter? Cameron's preference for ... well, for party girls was well established and not something to which Lydia had ever aspired or ever would. Still, she wanted him to explain if not apologize for his past bad behavior. But after a month of missed opportunities, she decided simply to enjoy the fresh air. Thus, she jogged along, listening as he described a horse named Azariah and places like Dead Swede and Bear Rocks while praising people named Stan, Hannah, Drew, and Leo, and opining about classic novels. Classic novels? How bizarre!

Cameron had initiated the subject during their first Saturday jog when he described, with great pleasure and fascination, Stan's library. "When all you have is a pool table and a couple of guys," Cameron had said, "you quickly run out of things to do. At first, I thought it was weird. Here was this guy who could wrangle a calf in the morning and read Hugo that night."

Cameron's fascination with books that collect dust on the back shelves of libraries had whetted Lydia's competitive spirit. Thus, she had arrived at the second meeting having sped through most of *The Count of Monte Cristo*, if only to catch up with him. Fortunately, she had already read his other favored novel, *Crime and Punishment*, for a class.

After twenty minutes, and with the sound of cars whisking past on the US-15-501 bypass, just beyond a twenty-yard-wide buffer of trees and weeds, Cameron's mood changed, becoming subdued, his voice cautious. "I need your opinion. When Stan took me to the airport, he asked if I had finished *Crime and Punishment*. I hadn't, but he told me to watch for Dostoevsky's thesis. Thesis? I'm a chem major. Scientific abstracts are easy reads compared to digging for theses. Do you know what he was talking about?"

Lydia considered a few possibilities then gave the easy solution. "My professor said that Raskolnikov's egotistical behavior was the product of loneliness, which in turn alienated him from friends, family, and society. Alienation allowed him to dehumanize people and murder the pawnbroker, calling his act beneficial for the society from which he felt alienated. He called the second murder self-defense, though it wasn't. When a series of unintended consequences produced a fortuitous result—the police chief lacked enough evidence to arrest him—he should have been happy, but he wasn't.

"And so on. I don't know why the professor selected the book because it was obvious that she didn't like it. She went on and on, giving contorted explanations about why Raskolnikov should have felt relieved and instead whimpered his way through much of the rest of the book before finally confessing, which he didn't have to do. Does that help?"

"I got stuck on the idea that"—he shook his head— "he couldn't manage guilt. Ultimately, Raskolnikov's conscience won the argument, and he confessed. If that's Dostoevsky's thesis, I don't get the point. It's too easy."

Lydia laughed. "You're asking the wrong person. I gave the rote answer, not my own—which would've been different since I like the book."

Cameron continued to jog beside her, neither laughing, smiling, nor looking at her. Where was his dry humor? Not in action today. She went on, "Okay, okay. I'll be serious. Here's my opinion. Dostoevsky was a Christian writer, who opposed *du jour* pressure from French socialists whose ideas, including atheism, were gaining popularity among Russian intellectuals. To counter their influence, he pointed his spear at Russian socialists by having Raskolnikov talk about 'Superman'—Napoleon, to be specific.

"Also ... and this is my interpretation, Dostoevsky pointed ordinary Russians back to Christianity throughout the book. Shameful characters like Raskolnikov found hope in the biblical story of Lazarus, significantly, when Christ raised him from death. Also, Dostoevsky contrasted Raskolnikov against Svidrigaïlov who was despicable despite a few redeeming qualities. My professor said Svidrigaïlov was the only character who died honorably, but his solution to life's problems was suicide. The prof was wrong. Dostoevsky used Svidrigaïlov's suicide to embody hopelessness—a deed that Raskolnikov admired and contemplated but couldn't carry out.

"But there was a subtle layer that I liked—a lot. Dostoevsky wasn't just a Christian; he was a student of human nature and natural laws. His genius was in his ability to create literary tension that followed Newton's third law of motion. You know: the force of our feet pounding against the ground causes it to push back with an equally strong opposing force, which makes running fun, as opposed to running on pillows. Dostoevsky stated it in his title. 'Crime'—evil exerting itself against nature— 'and Punishment'—nature exerting an equal counterforce: consequence. But God, who lovingly created us as sentient beings, added a complication: guilt. Unlike the opposing forces of sin and consequence, guilt is a variable derived from the vast panorama of the human conscience.

"That is, by my estimation, Dostoevsky's thesis: that we respond to the crime-consequence dynamic through guilt, which we use in varying degrees to punish or absolve ourselves of sin. Svidrigaïlov absolved himself of sin and reclaimed control over his life by dismissing his sin. However, he couldn't control others, many of whom failed to see him as superior. So he pushed them away, which denied him the one thing he wanted—human love and companionship. The sum of his choices left him with one choice: suicide. Juxtaposed against Svidrigaïlov's choice, Dostoevsky used Raskolnikov's whimpering and whining to add a fourth factor: God's grace. When Raskolnikov wrestled with guilt, Sonya—pitiful Sonya—showed grace by insisting upon God's solution to the dynamic: contrition and confession. Ta-da!"

"Did you get an A?"

She smiled. "No, but I got a B+ by spouting back most of what she wanted to hear. I refused to grovel for the A-minus."

"Then I'm impressed." He laughed, but his mirth quickly vanished. "I guess that's what Stan meant when he said Dostoevsky's thesis was connected to his moral foundation."

"My professor blamed it on 'Mother Russia,' the basis of all suffering." Lydia, however, having talked enough about crimes and punishments, stopped to admire a clump of spent *Asclepias tuberosa*. "Butterfly weed. Isn't it lovely?"

She turned and continued down the path. Literary classics weren't her forte. Nor did they seem to be Cameron's. *Oh, well.*

Cameron ran beside her but said nothing despite being surrounded by a forest filled with life and no murder, guilt, or confessions to be found. Confessions? If he wanted to discuss them, then he could start by making one. That obviously wasn't on his mind. However, he seemed deeply interested in Dostoevsky's irascible protagonist, who treated the people who loved him deplorably and spent the rest of the story in whimpering attempts to vindicate himself while complaining about life's injustices. Hadn't Cameron noticed the riot of autumn colors? Wasn't he fascinated by the succession of a leaf from bud to summer's splendor, with its glorious transformation of carbon dioxide into breathable oxygen? If he wanted to talk about death, he only needed to look around as dying chloroplasts, no longer producing chlorophyll, revealed the leaf's inherent color and prepared the plant to survive winter. No. He wanted to talk about egotistical, self-righteous, vain, and vile Raskolnikov.

"Sometimes I think I'm a lot like Raskolnikov."

Why? She glanced at him, but he stared straight ahead.

"Don't worry." He smiled without looking at her. "I'm not contemplating murder."

Perhaps not, but what other depressing thoughts ran through his mind?

He lowered his voice, causing her to strain to hear him. "When I was a freshman, UNC was fun. I worked hard and played even harder. Then that spring, I went home to see some friends graduate, and something happened that was like the first time Raskolnikov went to the police station and realized that the inspector knew he'd murdered the two women. Before that, I justified what I did, but afterward, my excuses fell apart. He knew that what he did was terrible, the way I knew about myself, but regret wasn't strong enough to make him change. That day, regret stopped me from doing what I needed to do. So I hid. Hiding didn't work for Raskolnikov, and it hasn't worked for me."

Lydia nodded to two strangers who approached but barely noticed them. She looked behind her and was surprised to notice that another group had also passed, but she hadn't seen them. Strange.

Cameron, who had stepped behind her to let the runners pass, caught up with her and continued. "Like Raskolnikov, my ego blinded me. I'd hurt someone special, and I couldn't simply forget ... I sort of knew I should confess, but I don't know how. Only the thought of losing Sonya humbled him."

Had Cameron made a tangential reference to his relationship with Lydia? *No. No!* It was too oblique. She didn't dare think otherwise. Reading too much into a glancing reference was dangerous. Besides, he described a day a year *after* the weekend when Mrs. Duncan died.

Suddenly she brightened. "I know the answer to Stan's question." A smile spread from ear to ear and from brow to chin. "Dostoevsky drew a picture of original sin! That's so fantastic. Wait a minute. And you said Stan's a Christian, so he'd know." Glee lifted her feet as she danced in place. "My professor was wrong! It does matter that Dostoevsky was an avowed Christian.

That's the change the reader sees in Raskolnikov at the end." Ideas sprang to life. "Dostoevsky used murder, which is almost universally condemned, to show the nature of *ordinary* sins, which Christ condemns. 'All have sinned and fall short of the glory of God.'

"But why?" She glanced at him. "Because sin alienates us from society? No, because sin alienates us from God. That's it." She laughed and spun around in the middle of the path. "Our sinful nature allows us to think that we, myself included, are supermen and thus better than God. We condone bad behavior using the simple excuse used by Adam and Eve: I want it. Therefore I should have it. Instead, we should be like Raskolnikov when he realized that Sonya loved him. Like Sonya, God follows us into our equivalent of Siberia until one day"—she raised her hands and smiled— "particular grace! He touches our eyes, and we see what we never saw before. No longer blinded, we fall on our knees in awe." Suddenly her excitement doubled. "Oh, oh, I almost forgot. In czarist Russia, Siberia was a merciful sentence. Why? Roll the drums. Porfiry could have had Raskolnikov executed, but he talked him into confessing—the very thing that Raskolnikov fought tooth and nail against doing. Confession matters. Isn't that cool? Cameron, you're so right!"

When she looked at him, though, his face reflected neither delight nor even agreement with her analysis. Instead, he trotted beside her without smiling. "What's wrong?" she asked, her exuberance fading, but only slightly.

"Well, I understand how Raskolnikov felt while he was in exile."

And that makes sense? Nope! And why such a sad face?

"Esther, my lab partner," he continued, "says I push away the people I should embrace. Raskolnikov pushed Sonya away. It wasn't what he wanted, but he—" Cameron stopped in midsentence. "Anyway."

"But he changed." She recoiled from the chirpy tone of her enthusiasm. In contrast, Cameron seemed distinctly contrite and not the dependably affable guy that everyone loved. Her cheer evaporated. She had seen this side once before. Long ago, when they first worked together at the Park Street Diner, he had been quiet and moody. To draw him out, she had made up silly stories about the people in line. In time, the tactic had worked. His dry but warm wit had surfaced, charming her heart and kindling her silly and hopeless crush. She dared not think that it could happen again. No. Those childish emotions had died with Mrs. Duncan. Perhaps her purposes had not been God's purpose when Cameron called. His palpable pain, rather than romance, may have been the reason he renewed their friendship. Maybe he just needed a friend. Right! Since when had Cameron, an incorrigibly social creature who could make friends with anyone, needed her advice? *No! He didn't.* Rejecting her various musings, she brightened. "So, what would make life more fun?" *Fun? Ouch!* Hadn't she heard anything he said? She wanted to grab her words back, but they were gone.

His smile flickered, then dissolved. "I don't know." Then to her surprise, Cameron changed the subject and became jocular. "With all of the sororities at school, why didn't you join one?"

From what fallow field had he dug up that question? Still she answered. "I wasn't interested. They take a lot of time. Besides, Mom wasn't in one, so I followed tradition."

"Sororities and frats are fun and a good way to meet people." His cheeks quivered, became rigid, then all emotion vanished behind a stiff mask. "It's nice to have a close group of friends to hang with ... to watch out for you. My roommate Neil and my buddies Patrick and Trace keep a close eye on me." He laughed and then nudged her. "You'd like them, and they'd like you."

Uh-oh. Was that a hint? *No, no, no! See the mask? It's just "talk," Southern style.* Still, the charade dredged up memories of Justin and something Cameron had said two weeks ago. "Well," she snapped, "didn't you mention that Justin Sloane had been a member of your fraternity before he flunked out? Couldn't you do better than that?" *Snarky!* Why'd she say that? Cameron had only mentioned Justin once, weeks earlier, and he hadn't complimented him.

In the weighty silence, two joggers approached from the opposite direction and then passed. In their wake, only the sound of feet padding along the ground was heard above the hush. An ominous quiet grew and then darkened. Lydia pulled out her most contrite voice. "I'm sorry, but you should have known I wouldn't be impressed to hear about Justin or his parties." *Well, duh!* Where were caution and patience? Or kindness. "I guess we don't know each other, do we?"

In a heartbeat, her thoughtless words whirled through the breeze, rustled the pines high overhead, then boomeranged, smacking her in the head. Everything between them had changed. No, she didn't know him. Their worlds were just too different. And she'd smashed his ego—without reason. "I'm sorry," she repeated. "I shouldn't have said that. It's just that I can't see why you need friends like Justin." She glanced at Cameron, but seeing his eyes fixed on the road ahead. She, too, turned and watched the path, covered with newly fallen leaves, tossed by the wind. Rustling together, they joined the silence echoing through the woods. "Your fraternity brothers sound like great guys."

"They are."

Minutes crept by; the path fell away behind them. Silent strangers approached and passed. Why didn't he say something? What did he want? She glanced at him and started. He had never looked so sad.

She *had* to cheer him, to ameliorate the damage she'd done. "You're such a friendly guy." He glanced at her. His mouth twitched, but he looked back at the path. She leaned closer, nudging him with an elbow. "You have so much going for you besides being smart and handsome. Of course, *I* don't know of many people who would *complain* if they had all that you have, least of all me." When a minute passed in silence, she repeated herself. "*I'm sorry* .... If you don't like your life, change it." Though he still said nothing, a faint smile appeared. She grabbed the opportunity. "Sexy guys like you don't need crutches, and *don't* let the modifier go to your head." He shook his head as the faint smile grew. *What a relief.* "You're right," she added. "Friends are important. They stick with you."

When his smile again faded, she wondered about the deed he described, the one he'd committed and then regretted. Certain that it couldn't possibly stem from anything related to her, her courage grew. "Talk to me ... please." She nudged him again. "You may not know it, but over the past few weeks, we've established a contract, and you're not abiding by it. You're supposed to talk, and I listen. You're not talking."

Still somber, he turned to her. "It's not easy to get to know people, really know them. That's what I learned this summer." A ghost flickered between the dusty lines of his icy blue eyes, as if grief and fear mingled, taunting him. But why? Then suddenly she knew she had also seen something else. What else? And when? Then she remembered. *Yes! In the soup kitchen.*

One night, after the women and children had left, a few men had remained in the dining room. Lydia had started to clear the tables when one man, clean-shaven and neat, suddenly grabbed her and yanked her outside. She had screamed, but as she gasped for breath, Cameron had appeared out of nowhere, wrapped his arm around her waist, and pulled her back inside. Others had chased the man while she clutched Cameron, sobbing and shaking for the longest time. Then when she looked up, she had seen the same blend of distress and sorrow in his face, as if he had wanted to help, wanted to protect her, but had failed.

Suddenly everything about Cameron was much too confusing. No. He had not hinted. He had not been talking about her. *No!* She needed a handrail, something to keep her from stumbling back into her silly high school crush. Like Tanner, he had asked her to jog; he had not asked her to go out with him.

"I know you're tired of hearing about the ranch," Cameron said in the gentlest voice imaginable, "but being on the range was an incredible combination of safety and freedom. Nothing fake could stand out there. Either the sun bleached it, or the wind blew it away." His smile faded. "Never in my life had I felt so great, but it's gone. Instead, I do stupid things, feel terrible, hope for change, and then do the same stupid things again."

He glanced at her and then looked back to the path. When he glanced at her again, the look in his eyes grabbed her heart and stopped it cold. Had he referred to her? No. No! It was just her imagination. He'd revived their old friendship but nothing more. He loved someone else, not her. She had to believe it. She could not afford to think otherwise.

Then, despite the clamor of alarms bells, she stepped into the fire. "Most of my friends are in InterVarsity Christian fellowship. They're sort of like a fraternity, even though we're not exactly a party crew. Maybe you could meet them." Startled by her brazen statement, she equivocated. "I'm glad you and I are friends again, so I'd make it clear that we're buddies from high school. Nothing between us would change." Flames danced around her, burning her cheeks. Falling deeper, and at light speed, she backpedaled. "It's no big deal. You probably wouldn't like them."

Cameron's solemn yet warm eyes caught hers, comforting and frightening her all at once. "Actually, you'd be surprised. Drew will never be the life of a frat party, but I like him."

Lydia blushed. Had she suggested that he meet her friends? *Yes!* But he also chastised her. *Oh, yes!* And worse yet, he had not accepted her offer. Why had she opened her mouth? Where had her brain been all morning?

She half wanted to hide behind the nearest rock or to save time by sinking into a hole directly beneath her feet. *Yes. It's true. Later today, Cameron will meet his girlfriend, his beloved.* Why had she been so foolish as to invite him to meet her friends?

"I'll think about it." Cameron glanced at her and smiled. "But you probably have plans for today, so this weekend would be too soon."

She didn't have plans, but obviously, he did. Through a crack in her defenses, she chanced to look closer, causing the bud of her distress to blossom into cold fear. During the morning, he had aged, becoming more handsome than ever. *Don't go there*, she scolded herself. *Don't!*

Fifty yards ahead, the parking area appeared, dappled with shade. A minute later, they stood beside her car.

"Next Saturday?" he asked.

"Sure. What about going to one of the 'gates' off 751 for a change?"

"You'll need to give me a map, but yeah. I can do that."

"Okay. But remember our arrangement. You talk. I listen."

26

On the twenty-eighth of October—the anniversary of Steve's death, Lois entered the old cemetery south of town. She turned to Marrah, sitting in the passenger's seat, then glanced at Melanie, sitting behind her. Seeing tears rimming Marrah's eyes, Lois stopped and waited. When Marrah nodded, Lois verified her intent: "Are you sure?"

"Yeah."

She glanced at Melanie who nodded, signaling for Lois to continue along the serpentine drive. When she reached a familiar spot on the northern side of the cemetery, she pulled to the curb. Flat stones, some capped with brass urns and plaques, dotted the grassy slope. Lois climbed out, walked around, and opened the passenger door, but waited until Marrah was ready. When she stood, all three walked with slow steps to a set of markers thirty feet from the curb.

As the breeze disturbed the deep green fescue, Marrah knelt before the smaller of two white Georgia granite markers. She leaned forward and rested her hand on the bronze plaque embossed with the name: Steven Nicholas Carpenter. Lois knelt beside her as a gentle breeze whispered, reviving memories in the timeless silence.

When Marrah sat back, Lois unwrapped the first of three bundles of flowers and set it in the vase above her son's name. She, too, touched the letters, each evoking a memory—some sad but most were happy. She wrapped an arm around Marrah's rigid shoulders, kissed her temple, and turned to the engraved granite marker that lay beside her son's. Melanie handed her the second set of flowers which she placed in the bronze vase above the names Thomas E. Carpenter and her own. As she plumped them, a thousand memories flickered, drawing forth a smile and an ache in her throat. Thirty years of heat, rain, and snow had burnished the stone, but in memories as fresh as the flowers, nodding in the breeze, she still missed her husband. He had loved her when she felt sullied and unlovable. She pressed her fingertips into each carved letter as she had so many times before. Finally, she stood and stepped back. Seeing Melanie's quiet smile, she felt assured that, though full healing still lay ahead, Marrah was moving forward.

Marrah finally stood and thanked her mother and Melanie. They returned to the car and drove to a familiar place in the old section of the cemetery where a tall, ornately carved Georgia granite stone bearing the name *Asher* stood among a field of smaller headstones. Time had scarred and weathered most of them, but not the one where Melanie knelt. A long bronze plaque sat atop it, bearing two names: Sylvia M. Asher and her husband, Benjamin C. Asher. Lois handed the last bouquet to Melanie, who placed it in the plaque's bronze vase.

Melanie tilted her head slightly, reading the familiar names through soulful eyes. "About this time each year, I bring flowers to her but I was always alone." She turned to Marrah. "Thank you for being here today. Obviously, this isn't the anniversary of her death, but of the day—as I remember it—when Sylvia stepped into my life. I was seven and she was my teacher, but she became my advocate and my mother's ally, protecting both of us from my father." Her eyes drifted back to the plaque. "I was just a child in her class ... and not the only one whose life she changed. So much of her life lay ahead of her that I wonder, sometimes, how many other children she might have saved were it not for a drunk driver." A sigh whispered in the breeze. "Mom called her a gift of God's grace."

Lois had heard the story from Ben: Four decades earlier, rather than wringing her hands when children appeared in class with casts, bruises, and broken spirits, Sylvia had intervened. Ben had provided legal counsel after she compiled enough evidence to send Melanie's father to prison. *Amazing.* The fragrant scent of a nearby tea olive evoked a smile and memories of days long past and God's gracious plan.

After dropping Melanie off at her car, Lois drove to Marrah's house. She searched her daughter's eyes—that did not lie. "Are you sure you'll be okay?"

"I'm fine." Marrah stood, straight and stiff, then slumped. A sad smile appeared. "Thanks for going with me." She glanced around as Lois waited. "Okay. You're right. I could use some company. Come on in."

Lois followed her to the kitchen. "Sweetheart, I'm proud of you."

"*Pff!* I don't know why."

"The last two months have *not* been easy."

Marrah twitched a brow and snorted. "No kidding. I thought September would never end, but now it's almost Halloween." Her melancholy smile widened. "That reminds me, I have something for you."

She turned her back to Lois, opened a drawer, and then pulled something out. Returning to her mother, she extended her fist, fingers upward. Lois waited. Even as a child, Marrah had a penchant for drama. Finally, she opened her hand, displaying four pills: proof that, for four days, she had awoken, survived the day, and fell asleep without Norco.

Lois embraced her daughter, who relaxed in her arms. Yes, the end was near.

27

"Confessions matter," Lydia had said in the middle of a discussion about God, grace, and Raskolnikov. Her words had been like a bomb going off in Cameron's head, forcing him to accept the unimaginable: Lydia and his father worshiped the same God. While her faith described humanity as doomed to sin and guilt but redeemed by gracious love, his father's faith added an impossible qualifier: "but get yourself in order first." Neither were tenable, because if willingness was the necessary ticket to faith, then he would believe just to be with Lydia. Ironically, his newfound faith would be a clone of his father's shallow hypocritical faith.

He spent the following week avoiding his friends or at least prying conversations. Late Friday afternoon, while his fraternity prepared to celebrate Halloween, he settled into a sofa and considered his future and a luckless twist of faith: Lydia was attracted to strong Christian men. Hence, she would never love him.

As the party cranked up—and fearing a confrontation with exotic-but-tedious Payton, he called Esther. "Hey, do you have plans for tonight?"

"Yeah, me and the dust bunnies are having a blowout party."

"Then you need to let me buy you a pizza."

The next morning Cameron tumbled out of bed and prepared to meet Lydia. Again, he stared into the mirror and resolved to attempt another apology. He straightened his back and stoked his determination to ask her out for dinner that night, where he would apologize.

He returned to his room and found Neil with a cup of coffee. "We missed you last night," Cameron nodded and then ignored him, but Neil persisted. "What'd you do?"

"I went with Esther and some of her friends to the movies." He grabbed a sweatshirt and pulled it over his head but seeing Neil's reproachful glare as his head cleared the neck hole, he retorted. "I was with Esther. Remember her?"

"Yeah, I do."

"I slipped in the back door around ten. That's why you didn't see me."

"Payton bugged me all night. Why don't you tell—?"

"I did." Cameron leaned over and tied his shoes. "She does what she wants. Besides, I had four babes, four topnotch swimmers, all to myself."

"Four babes? Whatever."

"We had a good time, but the next time I'm out past curfew, I'll be sure to clock in." He laughed as he took the cup from Neil and emptied it. "Thanks."

As Lydia suggested, Cameron drove out to one of the "gates" in Duke Forest, the expanse of woodlands west of Durham that flanked NC-751. He pulled off the road onto the gravel shoulder in front of the one she had indicated. When her Volvo pulled in behind his SUV, he watched her reflection in his rearview mirror and reviewed his plan: he'd invite her to a quiet restaurant and worry about religious differences later. After he greeted her, they stretched and started down the gravel roadbed that led into the pine, oak, and hickory-filled woods.

"So you make great pizzas," he said, bolstering his courage. *So far, so good.* "Maybe you can teach me how to make one."

"Sure." She described her technique but neither asked for nor offered a time or date to demonstrate the lesson.

He persevered. "Have you been to Manzetti's out at South Point?"

"No. It's too expensive. By the way, I was wondering. Did the ranch come with the name G-Double-T?"

"No. Stan named it. Said it's from a Bible verse." *Yes!* An opening, something biblical, something he could handle. "Stan wanted me to guess which verse. I think he enjoyed watching me squirm. Do you have any ideas?" He almost said, *Don't worry about the cost; I'll pay. What about tonight?* But the words didn't materialize.

"It's a Bible verse?" she laughed. "Hmm. Did he give any hints?"

"None, and believe me, I tried, but he wouldn't budge." For the next hour, excitement and discouragement tumbled together as he dropped hints and watched her ponytail bounce and swing from side to side. However, she ignored his oblique inquiries about her plans for the evening, which made a forthright invitation to dinner sound forced, contrived, or impulsive and even less likely to happen. Still, he tried again. "Earlier this week, I did something really stupid, but I couldn't stop myself."

"What did you do?"

"I went to the internet and looked up the Bighorn Mountains. It was like, if I could see it, then a small part of me would be there."

"Really?"

"Yeah. There's a real-time cam set on a boundary fence. It gives the temperature—around forty, not bad for midday. It'll drop tonight."

"Had it snowed?"

"Yeah, a few days ago. There were patches of snow around the fence."

"And that's where you'd rather be?" Lydia laughed. "You're crazy. You know that, don't you? Here we are on an absolutely beautiful, picture-perfect fall day. The sun is bright. The sky is blue. It's going to get hot, but where do you want to be? On a frozen mountain."

Mildly chagrined, Cameron laughed. It was an absurd idea.

Lydia flashed a smile. "See? I am listening. And since you seem to want my opinion, I'll give it. I know people like Drew at Duke. Okay, so their addiction is 'academic success'—or rather excess." Lydia laughed. "But I'm sure they're at UNC too. You just haven't met them."

The irony of her observation wounded his ego. Neil and Patrick were great friends, but male bonding was not his problem. "So what is your suggestion?"

"I don't know, but you'll never convince me that you can't meet new people. I've known you too long."

Good opening. "Maybe I'm just particular."

"Could be, but you're always talking about Shell and not Chapel Hill."

"Oh." His smile twitched. He could talk about Durham since "particular" applied to her.

"I was thinking," she continued. "Since your ranch friends sound a lot like some of my friends." Hope climbed atop a ladder and beamed. She babbled on, "The distance between Duke and UNC hasn't stopped us from getting together. I could introduce you to the group I hang out with—that is, if you're interested." His pulse quickened. Grab the moment! Invite her somewhere. But she spoke first. "Of course I'd make it clear that we're just friends."

No! He didn't want to be just friends. His knees weakened.

"Okay, you don't like that idea."

He didn't say that. But joining a group of her friends beat out not seeing her, though he preferred something one-on-one, personal and romantic.

She continued, "Maybe we should talk about something else." She nudged him. "Something non-threatening but exciting, like politics or gum disease. Hey, we could always talk about how much better my basketball team is than yours."

Normally, he would have defended his team, but he was stuck on the words *just friends*.

Again, she chirped, "Do you watch the Barrett-Jackson auction?"

So she knew about the famed auto auction. "It's a ritual at Uncle Nathan's house. How do you know about it?"

"I have a father and two older brothers." Her eyebrows bounced. "What's your favorite car?"

"A 'seventy-eight Porsche 930."

"Oh." Followed by silence.

Too expensive? But not anymore. Nothing he said was right. Nothing was going right, and they had reached the end of the path. His opportunity had passed.

"I'm sure," she said, "that you have plans for tonight."

Why couldn't he say, *No, I don't?*

"I'll probably go out for dinner with friends," she continued, "stream a movie. We might even sit out under the stars and watch Orion rising. It probably sounds dull, but we have a good time."

It sounded good to him, except that it didn't include an invitation. *So invite her to dinner.* "It sounds fine." *Fine? What's that!* "But then again, I've seen Duke's Crazies, and there are plenty of people at Duke who'll be partying tonight." *That was even worse!*

"Of course! And your point?"

"Well, I thought maybe ...." What was the use? A mirthless laugh slipped out. "It's nothing."

"By the way," she added with an "I dare you" grin. "Did you avoid saying Cameron Indoor, Mr. Heels fan? I've wanted to ask that question for so long." Lydia added a quick jig that drew a laugh, but disappointment dissolved his smile.

She wiggled her shoulders. "I'm sorry. I shouldn't make fun of your name."

"That's okay." Maybe it wasn't too late. "I *cannot* cheer for Duke, but otherwise, your plans sound like fun." He waited, hoping she picked up the hint, a strong hint, but she didn't. All morning, the moth had flitted about the irresistible fire. He examined his tattered wings. "Want to meet next Saturday?" he asked.

"Sure."

Once again, the moth would return to the flame.

28

By Saturday evening following Halloween, only one family still needed to be called for the Hope Springs Christmas program. Marrah dialed the number. The phone rang twice, then a third time.

"Hello?" a child's voice asked.

"Hi, my name is ...." Marrah recited. "May I speak to Danielle Johnson?"

"She's not here."

"Alexi. Who's that on the phone?" a woman's voice called in the background.

"It's somebody from some hope somethin'."

"Don't let them go, child. I've been expecting that call." The sound of other children and footsteps echoed through the earpiece.

"Hello? This is Danielle. Please excuse my grand-nephew. May I help you?"

Marrah repeated her introduction and listed Alexi, Ryan, and Mindy.

"Oh, yes. Lord, yes. I wasn't sure what I was gonna do for Christmas. Hearin' about this program. Well, I'm thrilled with what they done for Mindy, and now somethin' for Alexi and Ryan. My, my ...." The words poured from Danielle as if she feared Marrah would hang up before she finished.

"It's my pleasure." Marrah repeated her scripted questions while the children chimed in, listing desired toys.

Without moving the phone from her lips, Danielle scolded them. "Ryan, you need to wait. I can't think that fast. Ma'am, I'm sorry, but you know how kids get when they hear the word *Christmas*."

They sounded like normal kids, which wasn't bad.

"Mindy has made such progress through the ministries. Precious people! At first, the doctors said she might not make it. But she did. I just prayed and prayed for that child. Everyone prayed, all the neighbors and our church prayed. We had special services just for her, and Jesus—praise the Lord—he answered our prayers."

Marrah rolled her eyes. *Every* family thanked Jesus for her call. So what else was new? But Danielle had mentioned Mindy's health. Marrah scanned the information sheet: Mindy, aged eight years; Alexi, aged seven years; Ryan, aged five years. The background noise implied that Alexi and Ryan were healthy, precocious children, but Mindy sounded no older than two.

"Yes, Jesus answered our prayers," Danielle continued with unflagging enthusiasm. "Not just when he saved her life, but again when he brought us you wonderful people. I know I don't deserve it but look at Mindy now. Y'all've been so good to her. Mindy, come over here, honeybun, and say hello to a lady from your school." Marrah cringed at the false assumption but listened as Danielle's voice, sweet as molasses, called to Mindy. "There we go, baby. You can do it .... You're so smart .... Look at that smile .... Take my hand. Oh, yes." Marrah imagined a child, who was of an age to be riding a bicycle, walking step by precarious step toward Danielle. "One more, honeybun. She's been this way for so long it's hard to imagine her any other way, but Jesus healed my bitterness. My daughter's ex says she fell off the bed, but the doctors, they didn't believe him, and neither did I. Humph! You'd think he'd make up a better excuse." Marrah's fingers twitched as grisly images howled in her head. Danielle lowered her voice and continued, "I shoulda never left her with them—both of 'em, 'cause I knew he didn't like her fussing. At least my daughter knew enough to take Mindy to the hospital when she blacked out."

Marrah gulped down her horror as soft cooing reached her ears. "Hello, Mindy," she said, mimicking Danielle. "My name is Marrah. How are you?"

Mindy gurgled into the receiver, and then Danielle returned to the phone. "Baby, that was great." Danielle heaved a sigh as the sound of children retreated. "I do appreciate what y'all do. When we learned about what would be Mindy's future, my daughter flipped out, and now she's in on drug charges. And I got the kids. And I'm not even fifty—"

Wholly inadequate words stumbled out of Marrah's mouth. "I know, you've been ... wonderful. I ... I need to ask a few questions ...."

Danielle answered the last question, but Marrah's mind wandered. Why couldn't she say more, something comforting? Danielle believed that God had spared her and the children. Why? How? Soon, long-forgotten voices from calls made to the families over the years whispered, then grew louder, becoming a cacophony of misery.

"He was standing outside yelling. He had a gun just like the last time ...."

"I thought I'd taught Tracy to be a good girl, but along came these kids of hers. She was too doped up to take care of them, so I did ...."

"I'm so sorry Miss. He thought you was a bill collector ...."

"I worry that these kids will end up in prison just like their mama ...."

Slowly, the tenor changed, becoming less coarse.

"If the Hope Springs program hadn't taken Marcus in, he'd be in prison right now ...,"

"For a toy? They like games, but I want something educational. Maybe a book or ...."

The voices began to harmonize.

"He'd love a new Bible. His was a hand-me-down from ...."

"We prayed that Jason would listen ...."

"Sometimes, it takes my breath away to think that Jesus loves even me ...."

"I don't know how people who don't believe can manage when ...."

"I was the biggest cynic. I hooted when people said, 'Jesus loves you.' But then ...."

The voices merged into a choir.

"I couldn't live without his help ...."

"And to think that Jesus cares about folks like me ...."

Despite knowing every alley and street in the old mill district and similar areas around the county, Marrah added Danielle's directions to her notes. They were all too familiar: a small house with blue shutters, tan vinyl siding, and a trashed car next to the drive. Marrah's description would have been quite different: flaking paint, missing shingles, a small, century-old mill house or a faded trailer home like ten others on a street that better resembled an alley: houses set back by a hard pack dirt yard—only three feet deep. The description, though, didn't match her feelings about the houses or the families who filled them. Rather, many of the tattered exteriors hid tidy, comfortable interiors that confounded her definition of poverty.

She set her earbuds aside, trying to erase the veritable cesspool of human misery described by a hundred nameless voices. She clamped her eyes shut and turned on the radio. Anything distracting. But everything failed. A much-too-ingrained habit carried her to her dressing room. She opened the drawer with the neatly folded scarves and reached inside. She jerked her hand back. *No ... no!* Reversing the impulse, she pulled two blankets down from the shelf in her closet, grabbed a pillow, and tiptoed downstairs. After slipping past Jake and David, who were watching explosions on the television—*men!* —she opened the door to the deck and descended the steps to the dock.

Ambient light from the city lit the night sky as she unlocked the storage box and retrieved a folding recliner. She carried it to the wider side of the dock next to Jake's boat that rested on a hydraulic lift. Wrapping herself in the blankets to ward off the chill, she nestled into the lounger. Indifferent to any neighbor who might think they saw a cocoon, she nestled into the warm blankets and listened to the gentle slosh of the water against the floats.

Soon a song, borne by the water, joined the harmony of the creaking dock. It sang with the voice of rustling leaves clinging to the branches overhead and waves lapping against the shore. The lyrics described the wealth of the Hope Springs families and the poverty of her soul. She listened with a degree of brutal honesty that, a day or an hour earlier, she would not have allowed. Her breathing grew measured, and her jaw clenched not against the cold but against the truth: Her tangled web of calculating insensitivity, denials, and falsehoods was the product of her own choices.

Minutes disappeared while the gentle roll of the dock masked time's passing. Finally, her heart accepted the truth. For years, she had lied more times and in more ways than she wanted to imagine. She had created diffuse, cruel, and insidious lies against, to, and about Lois but also to and about Jake. Marrah had hurt those who loved her while expecting forgiveness without owning her deeds. She had railed against God, demanding his protection while withholding gratitude for his mercy. While basking in Jake's and Lois's love, she had felt alone and abandoned.

Other voices arose … "but for Jesus's love." The words reverberated in the silent breeze. While her work added nothing to her days, she had inflicted pain upon her mother, to the point of wanting to destroy her. She gripped the blanket, pulling it close around her shoulders. Why had she wanted to ruin Lois? A cold breeze lifted off the water and blew away the curtain of her deceit, revealing her soul—black as soot, and her heart—lonely and worthless. Christ had not doled his love according to the merit of her work but out of the depth of his love.

An old memory materialized, a fleeting image of the day her father died. She sat bolt upright, her eyes wide, seeing into the darkness. What happened that day? She couldn't remember. She honestly could not remember.

Casting off her cocoon, Marrah jumped to her feet, grabbed the blanket and pillow, and then abandoned the lounger. She raced up the steps, tiptoed into the kitchen, and grabbed her keys—and left her phone. Jake would wonder where she had gone, but she would only be away for a moment.

29

A week earlier, after watching Lydia's Volvo disappear around a bend on NC-751, Cameron had returned to the rental house, picked up some books, his computer, and his clubs, and then drove out to UNC's Finley Golf Course. He hit a few practice balls, then joined a threesome of strangers for eighteen holes. Hitting his par required focused attention, which left time for little else. Afterward, he dragged his wounded ego to the library for the rest of the day and returned to the house that night.

When he entered, he found Payton in the kitchen talking to Trace. Seeing Cameron, Trace jumped to his feet. "Yo! Glad to see ya, man. I gotta run."

He scrambled out the door as Payton sauntered up to Cameron. She draped one arm over his shoulder while her other hand slid across his chest. "So where have you been?"

"Studying, but Esther's expecting me." Oh, how quickly that lie had appeared. "Um … I've got to run up to my room. I'll be back." He brushed past her and dashed to his room. Closing the door behind him, he dialed Esther's number. "Yo. Have you had dinner?"

"Cameron. Why are you following me?"

Ah, her soothing sarcasm. "Because you're beautiful and great company."

"You lie so well," she said with a sigh. "I'm heading over to the Ram's Head for pizza stuff. And yes. You can join us."

To avoid confronting Payton, Cameron slipped out the front door. As he strode toward Franklin Street and Granville Towers, Lydia's words haunted him. "I'll make it clear," she had said, "that we're friends." Just friends.

On Sunday afternoon and for the next several days, Cameron found relief in the lab, the library, or—as he ended up on Tuesday afternoon—at the driving range. He set himself, lifted the club, and let it fly. *Ping*. Great connect. The ball lofted out across the range exactly as he had intended. Not too shabby.

That evening, Esther found him in the stacks of the library. "I've never seen you like this," she said, shifting her backpack, but without putting it down. "You spend the weekend with me and then hide in here." She leaned over his shoulder and waited. He looked up long enough to meet her stare and looked back at the computer screen. "Something is wrong." She pulled out the chair next to him and sat down. "There's a pattern in this. It's the girl at Duke, isn't it?" He flinched and hunkered closer to his computer. "It is!" she exclaimed in a sharp whisper. "You didn't try to get her in bed, did you?"

He jerked his head up. "No! That's *not* the only thing I think about."

"I'm sorry. That wasn't fair." The edge in her voice softened. "I'm sorry it didn't work out."

Yeah, so was he. "I'll be all right."

"Are you sure?" Typical of Esther, she sounded more cautious than sympathetic. "I heard you canceled the interview at Wake Forest. You didn't also cancel your interview at UNC's med school, did you?"

"No. It was in early October."

"That's what I thought, but why'd you cancel Wake before you heard from UNC? I don't doubt you'll get in, but don't you want to see it in writing?"

"I have it in writing, but I sent an acceptance letter to the business school."

"Tell me you didn't." She pulled away and tilted her head, clearly puzzled by his decision. It made no difference; his mind was set. Esther leaned closer. "All you've talked about is medical school." Her voice was more kind than cautious. "What's going on?"

"You don't understand."

"Try me."

"It's done."

"This isn't ...." Esther's skepticism dimmed and then disappeared. She sat down and opened her backpack, pulled out books and a notebook, and set each one on the table. He glanced at her again and returned to his work, satisfied that she had dropped the subject.

The following morning, he found an invitation to interview at the University of Virginia School of Medicine in his mailbox. The letter tickled his desire to attend medical school. Perhaps his father would relent, maybe even help pay Cameron's tuition. It was worth a try. He dialed his father.

"Dad, UVa's medical school sent an invitation to interview. I want to go."

"I called the business school." Irritation crackled his father's voice. "They said that you should have received their letter of acceptance. Did you?"

"Yeah. I sent my acceptance, but that doesn't mean I can't look at Virginia. It's an honor to get an interview."

"That's not an acceptance letter."

Cameron tightened his jaw, determined to be civil. "I know. It's the first step. And—"

"Son, I want to be proud of you, and I'm trying to help. I got to where I am no thanks to your grandfather."

Frost blasted into the deepest reaches of Cameron's lungs, suffocating him. "Please leave Grandpa out of this."

"Why should I?" his father snapped. "He was a worthless father. Besides, when Trent flew off the handle, he hurt your mother. I don't need ...."

Yeah. Blame everything on Grandpa. And now Trent, too? Cameron's chest fell.

"Your grandfather ruined everything he touched."

"Dad, Grandpa was—"

"Don't lecture me!" His father's wrath sent Cameron reeling backward. "If your grandfather had been a better—"

Cameron had heard it all before. "Dad, please—"

"Someday I'll tell you the truth. Then you won't think ...."

Cameron stared at the floor, listened a little longer, and then spoke just above a whisper, interrupting his father. "Look, I've got to go. Can you put some cash in my account? UVa scheduled—"

"No!" his father snorted. "Use the money your grandfather left to you."

His father donated to every Christian charity imaginable, but he refused to pay for gas and a hotel in Charlottesville. Perhaps it all came down to Grandpa. Judge Benjamin C. Asher, whose memory the city honored by naming a wing of the courthouse after him. Everyone loved Grandpa, everyone except his son. Cameron's voice trailed away. "I've gotta go."

30

Cameron looked up from his computer and started. Lacy whorls of frost appeared across an expanse of windows in front of him, climbing upward across the glass, partially hiding the trees beyond it. Fingers of ice grasped the stark white walls that flanked the window, each moving toward the ceiling. Before him sat a white office desk and two white acrylic chairs. Two file holders, both empty, sat on the desk next to an empty calendar. A set of empty white shelves stood against the wall. When he looked again at the window, everything outside, the trees and sky, had disappeared behind the cold, white filigree. Suddenly, he realized the walls had moved. They were closer, closing in on him.

As his heart raced, a door opened, and his father appeared. He wore a black suit, white shirt, and scarlet tie. With measured steps, he approached Cameron; then he dropped a massive pile of folders on the desk. "Here. Take care of these." He turned to leave. Flecks of ice churned in his wake. Wind, blowing from nowhere, lifted the cover of the top folder, fluttering its edge. By the time his father reached the door, the wind had exploded into a gale. It battered the walls and flung folders and papers everywhere, slapping Cameron's face. He lifted his arms to protect his head as folders rained down on him, darkening the room. Through the flying debris, Cameron saw his father's satisfied "See, I was right" smile before he left and closed the door.

"Stop," Cameron cried, but his mouth didn't move. He struggled to stand, but his legs refused to obey. He struggled harder and then leaped to his feet.

Startled and breathless, Cameron found himself sitting bolt upright in bed, staring wide-eyed into darkness. Only Neil's soft snoring and his racing pulse filled his ears. He checked the time. Four in the morning. What day was it? Friday. Yeah, everything was okay. He lay back down, but a memory, not the dream, haunted him.

Several days before Christmas—four months after Grandpa died and a month after Trent stormed out of the house—Cameron had returned home from Paul's house and entered through the garage. As he opened the door, he heard his father's raised voice from the kitchen. Stepping closer, he looked around the door frame into the room.

"Randy," his mother pleaded. "Please call Trent. Ask him to come home for Christmas. Don't let this go on. He's your son. He's my son." A miserable silence followed. Then his mother whispered, "Please."

"I will *not* have him marrying that girl." His fiery voice scorched each word.

"Why not? Emily's darling, and she loves him."

His father turned and left the room. Fearing his father's anger, Cameron waited a moment before tiptoeing into the kitchen, where he found his mother at the breakfast table, weeping. "It's okay, Mom."

She gasped and sat up. "Oh, honey, I'm sorry." She wiped her cheeks with the back of her hand and smiled, but her fingers quivered. "I thought you were at Paul's house." She stood and wrapped her arms around him, holding him tightly.

"Why doesn't Dad like Emily?"

"Please forgive him. He doesn't mean the things he says."

"I most certainly do!" his father declared.

Jerking his head up, Cameron saw his father standing in the doorway, stiff and erect. He had never been a violent man, but after Grandpa's death, his temper had erupted almost daily.

"But Randy," his mother pleaded. "Trent said he wouldn't come home again. Please call him and apologize. If he wants to marry Emily, let him."

"Valerie, he *will* get over her. He'll come home, and he'll marry someone else." His father turned to leave but spun back around. He stepped closer, cold rage seething from every pore. "Furthermore, I've heard enough about my father."

His mother grasped Cameron's shoulders, but he pulled away, clinched his fists and jumped between his parents. "No! Dad."

"Randy, please." She grasped Cameron, putting herself between her child and her husband. "Not now. Let the child grieve."

Cameron intensified his glare, meeting his father toe-to-toe and eye-to-eye, for he had grown tall enough to do so.

"Oh, I'm sorry. I forgot." Sarcasm laced his father's voice. "So you still want to defend the great Judge Asher. Son, someday you'll learn the truth, and you'll see that he put one over on you."

"What has this got to do with Emily?" his mother asked.

"Everything! Just take my word for it, Valerie." He turned on Cameron. "Want to know about Emily's grandmother?"

"Dad! Stop!" Cameron shouted. "I don't care!"

"Oh, but you will."

Shadows dappled the ceiling of Cameron's darkened room. His heart pounded until his ears rang. Long ago, Grandpa had promised to reveal the cause of the enmity between himself and Cameron's father, but that day had not come. After Grandpa's death, Cameron had asked his mother, but she only said that it began before Cameron's birth and for reasons that lay too far in the past to cause so much pain in the present. With every prospect of reconciliation having vaporized, Cameron decided that it was his father, not his grandfather, who feared the truth. Furthermore, after willfully driving Trent away—the son he loved, his father would not hesitate to alienate Cameron whom he loved far less.

In the dim light, Cameron rolled onto his back and thought about his mother and the ugly tentacles of ancient and irrelevant hatred. On every Christmas, birthday, and holiday since Trent left, his mother had disappeared into her room and closed the door. Each time, she had emerged with red and swollen eyes and a too-perfect smile. Once, Cameron had held his ear to the door, listening to her weep, knowing she wept for Trent, but also for him.

Cameron sat up in bed, leaning on his elbows and watched the shadowy lines of the empty branches outside the window. Though his chest ached for himself and Trent, he steeled his determination to protect his mother. Thus, his dream of attending medical school had become yet another levy exacted by a conflict that should have died long ago. A tear trickled down his cheek as the certainty of his future coalesced. Both Lydia and his dream of becoming a doctor had slipped beyond his reach.

Shortly after nine on Friday morning, then at ten and again at eleven, Neil leaned over Cameron's bed and shook his shoulder. "Hey, bud, shouldn't you be in class?"

"Get lost!"

Neil recoiled from the sharp epithets that followed. Trace reported to Neil that he, too, had tried without success to awaken Cameron. Finally, at eleven thirty, Neil called Esther. "I don't know what's bothering him," Neil shrugged. "I was hoping you knew what was wrong."

"I do, but I can't help him." Esther sounded cocky, but then she hesitated. "Is he really still in bed?"

"Yeah. Can't you come over and talk to him?"

When she growled, he knew she'd agreed but needed an important detail about Cameron's vile temperament. "I think it's about his father."

"All right. But don't be so sure that it's just his father."

When she arrived, she pulled them into the kitchen and added details that helped Neil better understand Cameron's recent behavior—with emphasis on a girl named Lydia. Esther frowned, and her eyes narrowed, not in anger but in clear disbelief. "Y'all don't know a thing about her, do you?"

"I suspected." Neil waffled and ducked his head. "Well, he mentioned that he liked someone, but the only girl he's been with lately was Payton, and—well. What can I say?"

"Didn't you wonder where he went every Saturday morning?" Sure, Neil had wondered, but he'd kept the eleventh commandment: thou shalt not meddle.

"Obviously, you didn't." She snorted. "I've met Lydia, and she seems very nice. Look, I know you hate to hear this, but Cameron really does know how to make women feel good. Why he hasn't gotten her attention, I don't know. So on my way over, I called Ragini, a friend at Duke, to see if Lydia is in a relationship. Ragini said she isn't. I was afraid to ask if Lydia had ever mentioned Cameron, but Ragini volunteered. She said that they've been meeting together every Saturday to go running."

"What?" Or rather *Oops!* Esther rolled her eyes and shook her head. Apparently, the commandment was backward. It should have read, "Thou shalt meddle." Why, not how, Neil wondered, had his roommate been so secretive?

Esther lowered her voice and glared at Neil. "Now, before I say anything else, I need to tell you one important fact about Lydia. She attends InterVarsity."

"What's that got to do with me?" Neil grimaced, glancing at Trace. Then he turned back to Esther. "Look. Cameron and I've been good friends all these years *because* I don't talk about Jesus. I mean, don't ask me why he's so sensitive about stuff like that."

"Men!" Esther huffed. "Well, Ragini said that Lydia has also been totally closemouthed about Cameron, but she thinks Lydia likes him. The strange part is that *Cameron* doesn't think she likes him. And Lydia is normally an open book, according to Ragini. Now, look. You guys can be weird. What's going on?"

Nothing good, Neil thought. Meeting Trace's agreeing look, he charged up the steps with Trace on his heels. When he reached their room, Cameron was gone.

The voice pricked Cameron's ears. He lifted his head from the pillow and listened.

"So right after you called me," a girl's voice said.

Esther? Yes, he was right. He *had* heard Esther's voice from downstairs through his door, which stood ajar.

"I called my friend at Duke," Esther continued, "to see if Lydia is in a relationship ...."

Holy crap! Esther had told someone, probably Neil, about Lydia. Cameron yanked a sweatshirt over his head, grabbed his shoes, computer, and book bag, and dashed—without showering or brushing his teeth—out the fire escape. He attended his one o'clock class and then found a deserted corner of the chem library where Esther wouldn't think to look. At six he picked up a hamburger; then he drove down to the ABC store in Carrboro. He waited in front of the shop for a moment, ready to blow sobriety right out of the water, but he also remembered Drew's admonishment that Lydia was likely the key to his ability to stop drinking. Drew had been half right: he had stayed sober since reconnecting with her, but his hopes now lay in ashes. *What the hell!* He threw open the door, walked into the store, and bought a bottle of Jack Daniel's. Once back at the house, he slipped past everyone and went to his room but hid the whiskey. Sometime later Neil entered. Trace and Patrick followed. All had tried to get him to stop drinking, but Cameron ignored them.

Later, Neil returned and shuffled through his stuff. "Hey, come on down. You're missing a good time."

"No doubt."

Neil said something more, but after he left, Cameron turned off all the lights except the desk lamp. He sat down at his desk, stared at the bottle of Jack Daniel's, and then poured a shot—and then another. He pulled out the tattered photo of Lydia from his high school yearbook and drank the whiskey. He took another shot and reread two letters—an invitation to interview at Duke's medical school and his acceptance letter from the UNC School of Medicine. Such was the irony of space. Were he to attend either Duke or UNC, he would be physically close to Lydia, yet effectively at the other end of the universe.

At ten, a shadow appeared in the doorway. "Why so glum?" Payton slurred the question. Her hips swayed as she sauntered up to him and sat down on his lap. With her back to him, she swayed to a rhythmic rumba that thumped the floorboards.

"Not tonight." Dispassion flattened his voice.

"Why not?" She stood and turned to him. With one hand resting on his shoulder, she floated her other hand through the air, tracing the movement of her hips.

He studied her with detached pleasure. "No reason." He almost looked away, but her eyes, hidden behind long draping eyelashes, caught his attention. He'd never noticed the jet-black streaks that radiated through gray irises. Half smiling, he stood, forcing her to stand. "You have beautiful eyes." He teetered for a second, grabbing his desk. Straightening his back, he wrapped one arm around her waist and kissed her throat. He found the empty glass, dropped into the chair, and then half-filled it with whiskey.

He lifted the glass to his lips, but Payton took it from him. "I've never seen you drunk, but you've had more than enough."

"Oh, how little you know." He took the glass from her and emptied it. "But that's not what you want, is it?"

"What do you mean?" She sat down facing him, straddling his lap.

"Do you believe in God?" It was a simple question.

"You *have* had too much to drink. But not enough of something else." She leaned closer and kissed his neck, mouth, and temples.

"No, I'm serious. Did you grow up in a church?" His hand waggled the glass.

"No! I'm from New York. Remember?" She pulled her sweater over her head, revealing a delicate tank top. She tossed the sweater aside. "If anything, we're Catholic, not Baptist." She tossed her head back, stretching the tendons, then lowered her head and smiled at him. "For what it's worth, no one believes that crap anymore."

She slipped her hands beneath his T-shirt and ran them across his skin. "I was four when my parents divorced. And no, they don't go to church. Dad's cool. Mom's a harpy." She pulled his T-shirt up, exposing his muscles. "Wouldn't you know it," she said, kissing his neck, "Mom left him for a girlfriend. Imagine what the people in Pittsboro would say!" She tilted her head and ran a finger from his collarbone to his navel. "This I know, going to church doesn't make you good."

She was right about that. "Have you ever been to Pittsboro?" He half-filled the glass with whiskey but left it sitting on the desk.

"No, why should I?" She nuzzled his neck, evoking a faint tingle, but it faded. "It just sounds like a holier-than-thou place where everybody speaks in tongues, you know. Snakes. Pits. That crazy stuff. Does it even exist?"

"The town? Yeah. It's just south of here. You shouldn't judge people you haven't met." He picked up the glass and turned it, watching the amber liquid coat the inside. "It's a nice place. I drove through it once. It's like Chalmers, only smaller." Payton nuzzled his neck as he downed the whiskey. "Don't you feel guilty?"

"For what?" she asked. "Certainly not about this." She interlocked her fingers behind her head and swayed to the music rising through the floor. "You don't fool me. You're no more religious than I am, especially considering your father, that self-righteous prig." Cameron reached behind her for the bottle. "If this is about your dad"—she took the glass— "forget him. He's just playing with your head. He doesn't believe that stuff. Besides, if my dad was like yours, I know what I'd say. Sucks to be you." She set the glass out of his reach and pulled his T-shirt over his head. "But isn't this more fun?" She leaned forward and draped her arms over his shoulders.

"Nothing bothers you, does it?" He brushed her hair back from her face and lifted her chin to see into her eyes.

"Why should it?" Payton stood. Then as a smile curled the corners of her mouth, she slowly undressed—lacing each sway, tilt, and pause with desire. Then she slipped between the sheets. Still, he felt no desire to accept her tacit offer. Instead, he poured another drink. Finally, she took his hand and pulled him toward her. "Lighten up," she purred. "Besides, why *should* I be bothered?"

He stood, grabbing the desk to brace himself. "Because I love someone else."

"Love? Give me a break."

"Well, I do." He reeled backward but kept himself from falling. "She's not like you and me. She believes in Jesus. And trusts him."

"Then she's a bigger fool than I thought."

"But what if you and I are wrong? What if she and my dad are right?"

Payton grabbed the loops of his jeans and pulled him toward her. "Why are you even worried?" she whispered low and breathy. "It's not like something bad could happen. Prudes like her are bent on making us as miserable as they are."

He was miserable, but not for the reasons Payton described. "I don't want to do this."

"Why not? We've always had fun in the past." She undid his jeans.

"Yeah, because I pretended you were Lydia. Doesn't that bother you?"

"I don't care. Everybody fantasizes. Why should you be any different?"

"Because it's dishonest."

"By whose standards?" She slid his jeans and everything else down over his hips.

His head whirled, tangling his thoughts. Still, he answered. "Mine."

Cameron downed the glass as Payton pulled him off balance. Finding himself in bed next to her, he dropped the glass, slid under the sheets, and enjoyed the warmth of her skin. He closed his eyes and kissed her, sliding his hand along her hip. But she wasn't who he wanted. When he opened his eyes, he saw only Payton. Only Payton had kissed him. He flung the sheet aside and staggered to his feet. Reeling backward, he grasped the desk and stared at her. His heart raced, nearly jumping out of his chest. *No!* He lurched for his clothes, grabbing something of each.

"What's wrong with you?"

"I have to see Lydia." He pulled his clothes on. After fumbling with his shoes, he managed to pull them on, grabbed his keys, and ran out the door, banging into the frame as he went.

"Cameron!" she screamed. "Who's Lydia?" Payton, wrapped in his sheet, shouted to him as she leaned over the handrail. "Cameron!"

"Patrick!" Trace hollered and then bent over, his chest heaving as he braced his hands on his knees. He gasped for breath. "Get Neil! Run!"

"Why?"

"Don't ask. Just run!"

"I'm right here." Neil opened the screen door. "What's the problem?"

"Cam just took off in his car. He is *really* smashed. I tried to talk him out of driving, but he wouldn't listen. I ran after him, but he wouldn't stop. He's going to kill himself."

Neil checked his watch. Twelve twenty in the morning.

"Earlier, I tried to get him to come down, but he wouldn't. When Payton went up, I stopped. I thought he'd be with her all night."

"Did he say where he was going?"

"No. Payton was screaming something at him about Lydia."

"Who's she?" Patrick asked.

Neil dashed back into the house. "I'll tell you about her later." He grabbed his keys and ran to his car. Trace hopped in the front seat and Patrick in the back.

"He can't drive to Durham at this time of night, can he?" Trace asked as Neil turned onto East Franklin Street. "He's too blitzed to make it."

"Durham?" Patrick asked.

"You're right," Neil answered. "Say a prayer."

Neil hoped the worst did not lie ahead of him. After passing the planetarium and stately homes east of town, the road descended the long grade toward Durham. *So far, so good*, he thought as he surveyed the empty street.

"Look!" Trace yelled. "Isn't that his car?"

"It is!" Patrick shouted. "Turn left."

Neil slowed then turned into a gravel parking lot. In the middle of the lot and about fifty feet from the road sat a Ford Escape that bore Cameron's UNC decal and parking sticker. In the front seat, Cameron sat with his head against the steering wheel; his face turned away from them. Neil blew air from his lungs while the other two jumped from the car.

"Cam!" Trace yelled as he pulled on the handle of the front door. "Open the door!"

Patrick went to the passenger side and pounded his fist first on the window, then on the windshield, slapping it with his hands. "Cam. Wake up."

Neil joined them and peered in at the driver's door. Cameron raised his head and turned tear-stained eyes toward him. How, Neil wondered, had his friend reached such a pitiful state of mind? Cameron opened the door and fell sideways, but Neil and Trace caught him. Neil looped Cameron's arm over his shoulder and, with Trace lifting Cameron's other arm, led him back to his car.

"I've got to see Lydia," Cameron whimpered.

"She's fine." Neil settled him into the front passenger seat. "You'll see her tomorrow."

With Patrick in the backseat and Trace following in Cameron's car, Neil drove back toward the center of Chapel Hill. In the lonely silence, Neil realized that he had misjudged his roommate.

31

Cameron awoke before his alarm sounded. In a little over an hour, he would again meet Lydia for their run. He remembered getting into bed with Payton and then taking off after Lydia. *That was dumb!* Seeing him drunk would not have made her happy. He groaned and rubbed his aching temples and then curled up under the blankets, half wishing his friends had left him outside in the cold to die. Since they had not, he mulled the inevitable course of time and his inability to alter the future.

When his alarm sounded, he fell out of bed and stumbled to the bathroom. Leaning over the sink, he stared at his bedraggled reflection. The moth still craved the candle. He brushed his teeth twice to erase some of the foul taste in his mouth and filled his water bottle. He'd need lots of it to cut through the muck in his mouth. When he returned to his room, he found Neil sitting not on his bed but on Cameron's bed and holding Cameron's sweats.

"Where are you going?" Neil asked.

Without looking at him, Cameron snatched the pants from Neil and put them on. When Neil still didn't move, Cameron grabbed his jogging shoes from under the bed and sat down on Neil's bed to put them on.

"Come on Cam, talk to me. You could've killed yourself last night."

Too bad he hadn't succeeded. Cameron threw on a T-shirt and sweatshirt and dashed out the door. Halfway down the steps, Neil grabbed his arm and stopped him. Ticked, Cameron spun around ready to yank his arm out of his roommate's grasp but stopped. Locking eyes with Neil, his indignation collapsed. "I'm sorry. Thanks for last night ... but I've *got* to go."

"Why?"

A dozen answers taunted him, none of which he cared to share. "Because I have to."

"What are you going to tell Lydia?"

How much had Esther said? Too much! He ripped his arm away and charged down the steps.

Neil grabbed him again. "Aren't you curious about what I know?" Cameron glared and pulled away, but Neil's grasp held firm. "Cam! Ask."

Too much! Again, Cameron tried to break free.

"What's wrong with you, man?" Neil snapped. Cameron recoiled. "You don't believe she likes you. That's your problem, isn't it?"

"Who turned you into an expert?"

"Esther!" Neil's face contorted. "Man. Think for a minute." His fierce glare vanished, replaced by a half smile, but his grip on Cameron's arm remained strong. "This is crazy! You're so used to hookups hopping into bed with you that you don't know what to do when a girl expects you to pursue her."

Neil was wrong. Cameron could have chased Lydia to the end of the world, but it wouldn't have changed anything. Again, he yanked his arm away, this time succeeding.

"Cam. Get a grip," Neil called as Cameron ran down several steps. "Lydia's friend told Esther that she likes you."

Cameron stopped then turned toward him. Blood flushed his cheeks. "It's not that simple."

"You're right," Neil shot back as Cameron continued down the steps. "Faith. That's the problem. Lydia has faith in something greater than herself, just like I do."

Cameron spun around. "Don't go there!"

Neil came down several steps. "Yesterday, Esther came by while you were weirding out. She said that I'd let you down because I've been afraid to talk to you about Jesus. Maybe, but I let God down. Being pleasant and nonconfrontational was cowardly and wrong. Our friendship should have meant more to me, so yes, I *did* let you down. I'm sorry."

He descended to the last step, staring at Cameron. When he stopped, a mirthless half smile appeared. "You shouldn't keep Lydia waiting. From what I hear, she's worth fighting for." The smile vanished. "Cam, I need a Savior. Esther needs a Savior, and it seems that Lydia does too. What makes you so much stronger or wiser than any of us?"

Neil stepped back, turned, and went up the stairs while Cameron watched. At the landing, Neil glanced over his shoulder. "I thought you said you were late." He shrugged and lifted one brow. "Well, get going!"

Cameron hesitated and then spun around and dashed out to his car. For fifteen minutes he drained his mind of thought until he pulled off NC-751 onto the gravel shoulder in front a Duke gate. His head ached and his breath tasted worse but those feeble miseries mattered little. Instead, he thought about Lydia. He didn't want to jog. He wanted to hold her in his arms and hear her whisper in his ear, saying that she loved him and that everything was going to be all right.

A moment later, the sound of tires rolling over gravel caught his attention. He jerked his eyes up and saw Lydia's Volvo in the rearview mirror. He cranked the winch in his cheeks until the appropriate smile appeared. In the span of a week, his world had fallen apart, but there she was, cheerful and more beautiful than ever. When she climbed out and waved at him, he smiled. The moth had returned to the exquisite flame.

Since seeing Cameron a week earlier, Lydia had wondered—often and a lot—about their relationship, about her feelings for him, and about what she wanted from life. On Thursday, however, those musings and the status quo became problematic after Ragini described meeting Esther, a friend of Cameron's, who claimed that Cameron liked Lydia—very much—but was Esther right? She looked at Cameron's car, drew a deep breath, and climbed out. It was time to do or die.

"Good morning," she chirped as she bounced up to him. "Wow. It's brisk this morning but smell that air. Isn't it wonderful? D'you like my sweatshirt?" She grinned and pulled on the front of a gray sweatshirt that displayed, in large letters, Duke University. "I picked it out for the State game later today, but I knew you'd be wearing your uniform, and you did. See?" She tugged at his sweatshirt displaying U-N-C. She wiggled her eyebrows and laughed. "Now, when people pass us on the trail, they'll know that you're my guest and that you're not trespassing. Ready?"

"Trespassing?" He cocked an eyebrow but smiled. "I thought the gates were open to the public."

"They are." She smiled as she rocked back on her heels, her toes pointed up, stretching her calves. "But"—her grin widened as she rocked in a wider arc to draw his attention— "the word *public* may be a bit broad when you're wearing a UNC sweatshirt while running on Duke property. You think I don't pay much attention, but I'm a detail hawk. Hence, I noticed that you always wear *that* UNC sweatshirt or its matching T-shirt." Her thin-lipped grin spread from ear to ear. "Now we match. Well, in reverse."

After stretching a minute longer, she jogged back to the chain strung between two iron posts that, plus a heavy chain, constituted the gate to keep cars from continuing down the road. Once there, she gave him a gotcha smile. "I almost forgot. My friends dragged me down to the Duke store this week and bought these for me." She wiggled her hip. "They're called stadium pants. They made me promise I'd wear them for you." She laughed and blushed. "I would never have bought them on my own—they're pink! But friends are friends, and promises are promises." She turned her back to him and lifted the hem of her gray sweatshirt to her hip. "Can you see it?" She glanced down at her leg. A blush warmed her cheeks as she read aloud the block letters, "D-U-K-E U-N-I-V-E-R-S-I-T-Y," that marched down her left leg. His instantaneous smile assured her that he liked them. She lowered the sweatshirt and turned to him. "Shall we go?" Soon he trotted beside her down the gravel road. "How was your week?"

"All right."

"Anything worth mentioning?"

"UNC's medical school sent a letter, offering me a place next year."

"Wow! That's fantastic," she raved, but also noticed his lack of enthusiasm. "Aren't you excited?"

"Yeah, I ... just ... I'm sorry. I was out with ... my roommate and two housemates rather late last night. I guess I'm just tired."

"Oh." For a second, his solemnity became contagious, but she stoked her cheer. "By the way," she bubbled, "I thought some more about Stan's comment about *Crime and Punishment*."

"Which one?" He perked up, but only slightly.

"Stan's comment that a person's understanding of Raskolnikov's alienation depends on their moral perspective. Remember?"

"Yeah, and?"

"I read *The Brothers Karamazov* … I know. You have a weird effect on me, but Stan's challenge to find Dostoevsky's thesis, reminded me that the professor who discussed *Crime and Punishment* alluded to the 'Grand Inquisitor' in *Brothers*. There Dostoevsky made a cogent argument against God by describing the mirror image of biblical Christianity and used it to tell his readers about God and the Christian faith. He left the door open for the reader to decide: Those who don't believe in God see a good story about the human struggle to find wholeness in a broken world, to find love among the ruins." Lydia glanced at Cameron who seemed distracted. Maybe Esther was wrong. "I'm boring you, aren't I?"

"No, I'm listening."

"Have I said anything that helps?" His smile flickered then disappeared. She waited for a response, but when none came, she propped-up her enthusiasm and continued. "I love Dostoevsky's characters. They're like us. We're fallen and broken, but God loves me, and he loves you." She waited, hoping he would speak. Oh, how she missed his lighthearted chatter. Something was wrong, but having no clue what it might be, she continued. "Dostoevsky understood that nonbelievers think God doesn't care or that he meddles. We are free to make mistakes and form misconceptions . . . Thankfully, God mercifully shows us what existed all along. Take Raskolnikov. Only the depths of despair silenced his ego. In that silence, he finally heard that he was loved. Then the absence of despair prevented him from ending his life." Lydia looked around. "Cameron?"

Spinning around, she saw him standing in the middle of the road about seventy feet back. Utter patience, or rather disdain or boredom, stretched tightly from his face to his toes. Maybe so, but if talking about faith bored or offended him, she needed to know it. Better to break her heart now than later. She painted a smile on her face and jogged back to him. "I'm sorry."

"What does this have to do with Stan's question?"

His terse question stung, but she refused to flinch. "It's about the way we see life." She propped up her sagging cheer with a smile. "It's about what gets us out of bed in the morning. When you were in Wyoming, something wonderful happened, and it changed the way you look at your life." She ran a few steps, waiting for an answer. When none came, she answered for herself, not him. "There's no reason you can't find it here." To her distress, he seemed even sadder than before. Disappointed? "Let's go."

Lydia ran down the path and turned around, but Cameron had neither moved nor altered his mask. "Sometimes," she said while running in place. "I feel God's hand leading me, but not always." Cameron's face said he didn't like what he was hearing. "Come on, let's go." She ran up the road but saw over her shoulder that he hadn't taken a step. As she turned back to face him, every doubt and fear about Cameron and their relationship taunted her. But if Ragini was right—if their friendship was to continue, then he had to know this side of her. She turned and jogged back to him, her heart breaking with every step.

She considered changing the subject, but since she had nothing to lose, she persevered. "Look at it another way. A lot of Christians talk as if God only loves believers, but I disagree. I believe that it isn't inconsistent to say both that God has a plan that can't be thwarted and that every human will, whether a believer and nonbeliever, is utterly free. Therefore, God blessings anyone who, when troubles surround them, hopes for something better. He does this for the sole reason that his nature is to do what is impossible for us to do. It's who he is. Cameron, God loves you." She continued to run in place. "Is it possible that, when you were in the Bighorns, you were alone with God?" She forced a smile, spreading it across her face. "And awash with his love and his hope?"

Seeing shadows in his eyes, Lydia realized she had said too much. Ragini and Esther had been wrong. Ignoring the ache in her chest, Lydia painted a smile on her mouth. "Come on. It's a beautiful day, and I have sun-brain." Sporting a bright smile, she motioned for him to follow, but when he didn't, she trotted back to him, smiling and bouncing in place, but subdued. "I told you I'm a detail hawk. I've been collecting pieces from the things you described. Come on." Again, she ran backward and motioned for him to follow. "It's like a puzzle."

"A puzzle?"

His grumpy tone singed her ears and her heart, but she widened her smile. "Sure! You've talked about all sorts of stuff and about people I don't know, so I've been putting the pieces together, to learn more about you."

Finally, he started to trot and soon caught up with her. "Why do you want to know about me?"

"Because I find you interesting."

He shrugged, and half smiled. "I'm sorry. I had a bad night last night. It's not your fault, and I shouldn't take it out on you."

"You know what the real problem is, don't you?" *Of course, the real problem is that Esther was wrong, and something has gone wrong with his girlfriend, wherever she lives. Hence his moodiness.*

"What's my problem?"

"You forgot our contract." She smiled, which had become more difficult by the minute. "Remember? You talk. I listen."

"You know"—kindness colored his voice, which hurt more than his retorts— "most girls don't listen, much less remember what I say. And I am sorry."

"You're forgiven." She nudged him with her elbow, "So tell me more."

For the rest of the hour, Cameron talked, but with little enthusiasm and lots of silence. And nothing about Wyoming. Meanwhile, Lydia closed the door that she had opened in hopes he would walk through it. Nothing made sense. She had no idea why he continued to meet her each Saturday. This was probably the last. Her face ached as she pulled up the corners of her mouth. Friends? Perhaps they weren't even friends.

A few yards short of the end of the path, Cameron again stopped. His mouth twitched as he studied her face. "Want to meet again next Saturday?"

She hesitated. *Whatever for?* But though her heart lay in a thousand pieces across the gravel path, she agreed. "Sure." *Why not?*

Long after leaving Lydia, the nasty taste in Cameron's mouth reminded him that their morning run had been a disaster. Rather than facing his friends and their chastisement, he walked to McCorkle Place and sat down on the lawn in front of Person Hall. He leaned against an ancient oak tree easily two feet across, as his energy drained away. An occasional sip of water from a half-filled Nalgene bottle cut the muck in his mouth, though only slightly. Mostly he stared into space, numbed by a strong dose of reality. He'd screwed up, again, because she went where he could not go. He remembered watching her wiggle her sweatpants with Duke written down the leg. He could have at least said that they were hot, which they were—and she was.

"If only ...." A sigh emptied his chest as a pair of squirrels dashed across the crabgrass and up a tree. In the distance, traffic whisked along Franklin Street, but he mulled through memories of running with Lydia, fixating on her discussions about the Bible. Her interest and depth of knowledge tied knots in his stomach. Believing wasn't that simple.

One truth was simple: his future had been cast and without his consent. In the following weeks, he would meet Lydia again and again until she called it quits, which she would. Afterward, he'd go to business school, join his father's company, find a desk in a corner, do what was asked of him, and forever remember that at least Grandpa had believed in him. Locked into that dreadful future, he would wake, eat, work, sleep, and maybe marry but never complain. In so doing, he would spare his mother and preserve the last remnant of his family. He leaned back and studied the lattice of empty branches high overhead. He would see Lydia again the following Saturday, allowing the moth to flutter around the flame.

At one, Cameron wandered over to Finley Golf Course for the respite of playing eighteen holes; then he studied before returning to the house. When Neil asked about Lydia, Cameron immediately retreated to his room. Content in his solitude, he pulled out his chemistry book and turned on his computer.

Ten minutes later Neil poked his head into the room. "You are not spending another night up here getting plastered."

"I won't," Cameron mumbled without looking away from the screen. Beneath his feet, music and noise vibrated the floorboards. "I'm not going to get drunk."

"Okay. So." Neil pulled up a chair next to him and sat down. He waited as Cameron studied the formula displayed on the screen and then asked the question that Cameron had avoided throughout the day. "What happened this morning? Didn't it go well?"

"No."

"Why not?"

"It's nothing." In the grim silence that followed, Cameron typed and clicked, but Neil refused to leave. Finally, Cameron turned to his roommate. "I'm sorry. I'm not like you. If deciding to be a Christian was all it took, I'd do it, if only to be with her. But she wouldn't be happy with me." He sighed and smiled. "She'd want someone like you. You'd know what to say. But me?" Hope seeped out, emptying his chest. "I felt like a brick." He turned back to the screen and wondered if his heart had ever felt lonelier. "I've got work to do—and no plans to get drunk."

"Why can't you be a Christian? What about Dr. Krasotkin?"

Cameron snorted. "Yeah, right." He admired the professor who lived his faith, but he could never be like him. "Go on, have some fun." Neil ignored him. "Look. I threw the rest away, so I can't get drunk." He lifted an empty Jack Daniel's bottle from the trash can. "Okay?" Neil leaned back, relaxing with his hands behind his head, and waited ... and waited. Finally, Cameron sighed. "All right."

Once downstairs, Payton quickly found him and berated him for skipping out on her the previous night. Though her justifiable tirade improved his mood, the boisterous crowd only intensified his loneliness, so he returned upstairs and went to sleep.

Before anyone in the house awoke, he retreated to the library lest anyone ask about Lydia, including Esther, the person he talked to when all else failed. Around four, as he pulled a book from his backpack, a slip of paper floated to the floor. Picking it up, he smiled. It was the note Dr. Krasotkin had handed to him at the Blue Feather Café at the end of the spring semester.

"'Twas brillig, and the slithy toves / Did gyre and gimble in the wabe."

Since returning from Wyoming, Cameron had rarely used the humorous verse. He rolled and unrolled a corner of the worn scrap of paper, wondering whether he should call the professor. The effort seemed pointless, but he tapped the professor's cell phone number anyway.

"Hello, Dr. Krasotkin. Cameron Asher here. —Yes, sir. It's been a good semester. Yeah, Dr. Edelmann's a cool guy. I was wondering about the note you gave me last spring. You said you'd explain it to me. Maybe if you have some time this week ... Now? No, sir. I don't— Yes, sir. Thank you."

Fifteen minutes later, he arrived at the office just as the professor unlocked the door. "Good to see you, Cameron. Would you like some coffee?" Dr. Krasotkin fixed a pot and inquired about Cameron's research work and grades.

"He's great, and I like the project." Cameron described the results of his work. Finally he broached the question of the note.

Dr. Krasotkin tipped the reclining desk chair back. "The first time I heard you use it, I was intrigued and wondered if you knew its origins."

"It's by Lewis Carroll. I like how it sounds." Cameron sat down in a small lounge chair.

"It rolls off the tongue. Doesn't it? '"Twas brillig ...." The professor rolled the *Rs* and laughed. "When I first read 'Jabberwocky,' I assumed Mr. Carroll had created the toothy beast, but like many British kids of his time, he had recited it as a child. Interesting, no? A lot of people say the book was just a wild mushroom trip or at best a political satire. Maybe so. I'm no expert on either Mr. Carroll or his book. I'm a humble chemistry professor, but I found it very interesting, which is also the reason I wrote it in the note after asking you to give up your summer for a higher cause."

"Higher cause?"

"Yes. Bear with me. In the book, Alice steps through the mirror and finds herself in a world that looks like but is completely backward from the world she left. Inside the mirror, flowers talk and hay revives kings, which is particularly odd since humans can't digest hay. One of my favorite tidbits of sanity within the 'looking glass' occurs when the White Queen declares, 'Speak when you're spoken to!' To which Alice replies, 'But if everybody obeyed that rule, and if you only spoke when you were spoken to, and the other person always waited for *you* to begin,' so nothing is ever said. The Queen promptly proclaims Alice's logic to be ridiculous! Backward logic? Of course, because 'why?' is a logical question. And you and I are men of logic." He smiled and rocked his chair. "Alice encounters the poem about the Jabberwock in the first chapter, which I think is important, and finds that she must use a mirror to read it. Why?"

"It's written backward."

"Correct. I brought this from home." Professor Krasotkin smiled as he held up a copy of *Through the Looking-Glass.* He opened it and read, "'And if I hold it up to a glass, the words will all go the right way again.' That was no accident. The reflection of the backward printed text does indeed turn it around, and the unintelligible becomes intelligible."

Professor Krasotkin stood and poured a cup of coffee. "When my daughter, who is left-handed, was three, I found her standing in front of a mirror craning her head to one side as she looked, not into the wall mirror, but into a hand mirror. I asked what she was doing, and she answered. 'I want to see how other people see me.'" He handed both the cup and book to Cameron then leaned against the edge of his desk. "She simply wanted to see the image of herself as you and I see her. So what did Alice find about the Jabberwock?"

Cameron flipped to the page opposite a pen-and-ink drawing of a clawing dragon. "The first and last verses are the same. "Twas brillig, and the slithy toves ....'" He grinned. "But the four stanzas between tell a story. Some of the words sound silly, so I suppose it's ironic that the hero is led to believe that the Jabberwock is dangerous."

"Hero? I suppose the boy holding a sword in the illustration could be a hero. And yes, the Jabberwock is dangerous, but what happened to it?"

"It was slain, and everybody was happy. 'Callooh, callay.'"

"Correct. Now, why would anyone use words that have no meaning?"

Cameron hesitated, puzzled by the question, and then gave what seemed the only logical answer. "To confuse?"

"Seems logical." Dr. Krasotkin returned to his chair and leaned back. "Yet according to Mr. Carroll's published comments, the part that you quoted made sense to the Anglo-Saxons who recited it a thousand years ago. He was kind enough to translate the ancient poem and explain the strange words and apparent idiosyncrasies, thus making sense out of nonsense. But as I said, I'm not a Carroll scholar. So tell me something. You're a good student, one of my best, in part because you work hard, but why?"

Cameron sighed and pushed himself into the cushions of his seat, the same cushions in which he had happily lounged a year earlier. "I wanted to get into med school."

"Ah. I heard you were accepted."

Cameron pushed himself deeper into the folds of the chair. "Yes, sir, but I decided to go to business school."

"Why? To please your father?"

"No, sir. I can't please him." Cameron slid his fingers into the crease between the arms and seat of the chair. He touched something grainy and hard. Crumbs ... bits of snacks left over from days gone by when he listened as the professor talked about molecules, formulas, and the eclectic clutter that filled the room.

"I know part of the story," the professor said with a faint smile, "but why would you turn away from your dreams?"

"It's what's best." Sinking deeper into the chair, Cameron imagined that the crumbs had become giant puffs of yellow foam behind which he could hide.

"Why?"

From the shelter of the yellow puffs, Cameron summarized the six-year estrangement between his father and brother Trent, the arguments that led to Trent's departure, hearing his mother weep, and knowing that she simply wanted her family to get along. "It won't bother Dad if he and I never speak again, but it would tear Mom apart. I can't do that to her."

The professor rocked in his chair and studied Cameron. "If you destroy your dreams, you'll break your mother's heart as surely as if you moved a thousand miles away. When I encouraged you to obey your father and go to Wyoming, it was for a summer, not a lifetime. If you've been accepted here at UNC, then you should go."

"But—" Cameron had no other choice. *None!* He sprang from the chair and stood in front of the window. With his back turned to the professor, he locked his arms and set his jaw. "I can't!" Protecting his mother was the last and only noble choice left to him.

The professor gently rocked his chair. "You think you've lost control of your life. Cameron, the 'Jabberwocky' was a forward-facing poem in a backward world. Not the other way around. We live inside the looking-glass. Adam and Eve dragged us through it, and ever since, we've been like Alice, looking back through the glass and wanting to go home. Does this make sense?"

"No." Cameron walked back to his chair. Sinking into it, he gazed across a neat stack of papers and journals. "But even if it did ...."

Dr. Krasotkin smiled and leaned back, entwining his fingers behind his head to form a headrest. "You know, it's great to be paid to do something you enjoy, but as knowledge about the energy and interactions of photons increases, I realize how little we know. There's much we can't explain, but that doesn't bother me. Instead, it drives me. That's why I asked if you know why you study so hard. What do you live for? What puts air into your lungs and pulls you out of bed in the morning? There's so much more out there than simply this." He spread his hands and then leaned forward, bracing his elbows on the desk. "Which leads me back to Mr. Carroll's poem. There's a world beyond this looking-glass life, but we can't see it. Instead, we see this, a reverse reflection of the unimaginable, and we fear the Jabberwock."

Cameron threw his head back. "You want me to say that the Bible is the hand mirror, that it turns this world around. Professor, I know the spiel. Dad has shoved it down my throat all my life. But I'm not like you."

"Tell me about the people who slew the Jabberwock— 'Callooh, callay!'"

"I don't care about them. I just want—" What did he want? He wanted his brother to come for Christmas dinner, and he wanted Lydia at the table too. Was that so much to ask? And med school? It was no longer worth the fight.

"So," the professor mused, "you think that the fierce Jabberwock will destroy you."

"Maybe. But it's not that easy." Cameron sank into the chair.

The professor's tone changed, becoming gentle and warm. "Not everyone stuffed their beliefs down your throat. You knew someone who lived an abiding faith."

"Who?" No name came to mind as Cameron crossed his arms and stuck his hands into his armpits.

"Your grandfather."

A spasm twisted Cameron's insides. "How do you know about him?"

"Your uncle told me. He was quite a man of God." Indeed he was. If only Cameron could hide in that past. "Listen to your heart," the professor said with a smile. "I was once like you. I dug my heels in, but my heart, like Alice, longed to go home. Cameron, God isn't weak. He isn't standing behind a closed door waiting for you to peel back the ivy and bang on it." Why had the professor used the same words Cameron's father threw at him? "The door is open." Professor Krasotkin's voice softened. "He seeks you."

Cameron's throat closed so tightly that it ached. "But I don't feel …." He jammed his hands deeper into his armpits.

"I know."

Cameron bolted to his feet and turned away from the professor. "No, you

274

don't. I never want to be like my father." He turned, focusing his defiance into a laser beam aimed at his mentor, but the professor remained calm, unflappable. Cameron turned his back on the professor, facing the window and buildings beyond it. "What do I live for?" A knot lodged in his throat. "Except for Mom, everyone I've ever loved, every dream I've ever had, is gone. Grandpa and Trent are gone. The girl I love, medical school—they're all gone. Unless I go to business school, my family is as good as gone .... I have nothing."

"No, you're not alone." The professor's voice sounded as unassuming as ever.

Cameron spun around. "But they're gone!" Embarrassed by his brazen outburst, he lowered his eyes and wiped them with the back of his hand. Dr. Krasotkin had been a mentor, not an adversary. "I'm sorry." Cameron's legs crumpled beneath him, dropping him into the chair.

"Cameron, do you believe that it was an accident that you found that note today?"

"What do you mean?"

"There's a great line in Genesis where Joseph talks to his brothers after they discover that he isn't dead. He says to them, 'As for you, you meant evil against me, but God meant it for good.' There are both real and illusionary aspects of your losses."

"But they're gone!" Cameron threw his head against the stuffed back of the chair. "And it hurts! I miss Grandpa so much. That's not perception. It's as real as anything gets."

Professor Krasotkin stood and reached for a box of tissues. Then he scanned the bookshelf and pulled out a small volume. "Here." He handed Cameron the tissue box. "I believe that Providence brought you here today. Providence led your uncle to call me and ask for my help. He is very proud and fond of you, but he also explained why he wanted you to spend the summer out west."

"But you said you talked to Dad," Cameron interrupted.

"I did, but it was your uncle who told me about Stan Boehmer. Last spring, I thought I should explain my reasoning to you, so I bought a book for you. Providence didn't provide an opportunity for me to give it to you until now. Here."

The professor handed Cameron a new English Standard Version of the

Bible and returned to his padded desk chair. Cameron thumbed the feathery pages. To his surprise the soft flutter breathed life into a long-ago day when he reached for the Communion plate as it passed in front of him. Grandpa had stopped him. "Wait," he had said; "take these elements when you understand why you need them." He had not taken communion since Grandpa died.

Looking down at the Bible and speaking barely above a whisper, he confessed. "Grandpa gave me his Bible a few days before he died. I can't even pick it up. I didn't go back to church until the day I went with Esther." A tremor shook his shoulders, and his chest heaved. "Why does it hurt so much?"

"Sometimes it just does." The professor leaned forward, again resting his arms on the desk. "Until we realize that we can't fix ourselves." He laughed, but Cameron didn't share his amusement. "As long as air fills our lungs, our hearts can break. That's the way it is in this backward world." The professor became notably solemn. "But there's hope for broken hearts. Once I thought as you do now. The pain was so bad that I wanted my heart to stop beating just to ease it, but God ignored my plea." Cameron stared at the ceiling, wishing his heart would stop beating.

Dr. Krasotkin continued, "My dad was a preacher, so our family moved a lot. I hated constantly having to make new friends; so I blamed Dad for my misery. During college and afterward, I stopped going to church and refused to speak to him; then God compelled me to return home. What might compel a son to reconcile with his father?"

Not a single reason came to Cameron's mind, but then the miscellaneous decorations cluttering the walls and shelves caught his attention. "Weren't your parents missionaries in Africa?"

"Yes. In Uganda."

A chill spread over Cameron and erased every thought about his miserable state. "Your mother died before you reconciled with your father."

"Yes." Without smiling, the professor again rocked in his chair. "When my parents moved to Africa, I was working outside Washington. Mom pretended that only the Atlantic Ocean separated my father and me, but she knew better. I also knew she loved serving God, but I wanted her to be with me. Cameron, do you know where I'm going?" Cameron shook his head. "It's perspective. This," he waved his hands, indicating the room, "is our reality, but Mom imagined Christ's reality, not because she was a mystic or thought of herself as brilliant, but she looked at this world as a reflection of God. She trusted him in everything. Everything." A faint smile appeared, but only in his eyes. "I resented God because she loved him that much. After she died at fifty of a disease that could have been cured had she lived in the States, I went to the area where they lived and met the people she served." He stood and picked up a smiling, round-headed wire figure riding a bicycle with a passenger holding a bundle of bananas and riding sidesaddle above the rear wheel. "They are wonderful, resilient people." He turned to Cameron. "Today, Dad is my closest friend, and I know beyond a shadow of a doubt that Mom lives."

Feeling smaller than a neutron, Cameron didn't deserve even a minute more of the professor's time. He stood, lowered his head. "I'm sorry."

"Don't be." Professor Krasotkin walked to the window with its view of other bland research buildings. "There's a great deal that we don't understand." He turned to Cameron as a smile lit his face. "But enough of my problems. We've solved a few things such as the question about med school: you'll go, but what about this girl?"

"Lydia?" Cameron flushed. He packed away his tattered ego and, to the obvious delight of Dr. Krasotkin, gave an overview, omitting a few embarrassing details, of his relationship with Lydia.

The professor asked, "When do you move beyond weekly jogs?"

"It's too late."

"Let me see if I have this straight. You two have met *every* weekend for the past two months, including the expectation of seeing her on Saturday. She even bought a sexy little pair of sweatpants just for you, but you haven't even taken her to lunch. Do I have that right?"

"Yes, sir."

"And you think she doesn't like you." Dr. Krasotkin burst into laughter. "Son, you do *not* understand women."

32

"You're sure you don't want to come?" Jake asked. "It's a great day for sailing. No boats, great wind. It'll be fun."

Marrah glanced between David and Jake. Both wore shorts and jackets zipped up to their chins. Soon they'd don life jackets and truly be a sight, two walking oxymorons. "Y'all are nuts."

"Maybe next time." He kissed her cheek.

Marrah watched until they'd pushed the sailboat away from the dock and set sail; then she returned to the house. Between the morning services, members of her church had taken half of the tags from the Hope Springs Christmas tree. Now their names needed to be typed into her spreadsheet. The task invited a headache, but she ignored it—or tried to. When the effort failed, old habits carried her to the drawer filled with scarves, though it now only held scarves.

Rather than panicking, she walked out onto the deck to look for Jake's sailboat. When she stepped outside, the strong breeze engulfed her, but its strength was minimal compared to the wind that clipped the tops off waves across the lake. If Jake had set out hoping for a challenging wind, he had picked the perfect day. But the wind had not deterred him. Nor, for that matter, did it worry Marrah. She'd grown used to her husband's romance with the lake and boats. She crossed her arms and leaned against the handrail, enjoying the breeze and watching for his boat which, earlier, had sailed west—out of sight, hidden by the point of land that jutted eastward into the lake. In time, he would reappear. Of that, she had no doubt.

As she waited—and avoided her obligation to the Christmas gift program, her thoughts wandered back to the night when memories had called her away from the safety of her blanket cocoon and Jake's dock. That night, memory had not carried her to the leafy neighborhood surrounding the Montebello Country Club. Instead, she had made a pilgrimage to the old Sedgefield textile mill village south of town with its small, weathered century-old saltbox houses and families whose indomitable love for each other had vanquished her haughty sense of superiority. Money, she had learned, could be a blessing, a bane, or utterly useless.

The journey had fortified her desire to be a better person, but her demons had not gone away. She still heard their taunts, which had chased her since high school. Marijuana had silenced their voices during college. Valium had carried her through a depression following David's birth. Norco and antidepressants had patched her together after Steve's death and through her surgeries, each an on-again, off-again suffocating cloak of dependence. All the while, Jake had set a steady course for her to follow. She couldn't lose him.

A strong gust of wind, scrambling through the tops of the trees overhead, startled her. After tossing the upper branches, it departed, dancing as it crossed the lake, whipping up whitecaps beyond the point. Around Jake's dock, though, only small ripples ruffed the water. Marrah had seen the phenomenon a hundred times before but gave it little thought. Now, though, it tantalized her imagination. The point of land had protected the cove and Jake's dock from the ferocity of the wind that wrenched and twisted the upper branches of the trees along the point.

Then she saw a white sail skipping across the waves in the center of the lake. It was Jake, sailing straight and true toward the opposite shore. As she watched, the sail luffed. He pointed the boat into the wind and turned it toward her, caught the wind again, and came across the waves with the boat listing no more than twenty-degrees off true. He had been and was in control of the boat, though not the wind. She looked again at the placid water below her dock. Had God been the point of land protecting her from her fears? Had he given her Jake, who sailed straight and true, to tame the winds in her life and set a firm and steady course for her? How different they were each from the other. And yet he had neither dominated her nor left.

"But God shows his love for us," she whispered words she had memorized years earlier. "But God ...." Since her father's death, God and his love had seemed so far away. Where was he when she stood alone on the sixteenth tee box, with her father lying lifeless at her feet? She couldn't remember. Her pulse increased. She needed a Norco. *No. No!* She refused its lure. The tremor passed, and peace followed, revealing ugly thoughts. *I wanted to hurt Mom, so I lied ... I've pushed Jake away, hurting him before he could hurt me. I don't deserve a husband like him ....* The next confession found her voice. "God, why did you take Dad? You're supposed to be good. Why didn't you save him?"

A fresh gust of wind tousled the trees on the point. In the distance, a gust tipped Jake's boat sideways, but it quickly righted. *Jake let out the sail.* He knew the ways of the wind as well as she knew the roads through the Sedgefield mill district. Her legs weakened. *I saw you, Lord, in Danielle's strength, but I refused to see your hand.* Jake drew close and let the sail luff as he turned the bow into the wind; David released the jib and switched sides. The boat picked up speed and cut across the choppy water—sail taut, course straight.

How can Jake be so sure? She pushed herself away from the railing and straightened her back. Jake and Lois had long navigated wind-tossed seas, knowing that God had appointed a spur of land, a barrier to protect them when they sought shelter. Marrah's heart eclipsed the urge to run away. Instead, she grabbed her keys and left, not knowing how long she would be gone.

Fifteen minutes later, she turned into the neighborhood surrounding the Montebello Country Club. She followed the serpentine road until she reached the stone and rail fence that marked the entrance to the club. Instead of entering the property, she turned left and followed the fence alongside the tennis courts. Just past the courts, the road dipped into a deep ravine and then climbed a steep hill to parallel the fourteenth fairway, a par five. At the top of the hill, the road forked. To the left, it turned away from the golf course. To the right, it became a service road that circled behind a hedge at the fourteenth pin.

At the fork, Marrah pulled to a stop beside the rail fence that marked the club's property. She turned the engine off but did not get out. A good golfer could hit a drive that reached the center of the dogleg fairway in front of her, beyond the fence, without overshooting the curve.

The fairway, though, had not called to her. Instead, she looked across toward a stand of tall oak trees sheltering the approach to the sixteenth tee. Without opening the window, she smelled the faint odor of closely mown grass. When a group of golfers passed, she smiled.

Some time later, she opened the door and walked up to the fence, stopping next to a tree to protect herself from wayward balls. She leaned against the top rail and gazed across the well-manicured grassy slope. When a threesome of golfers approached, she straightened her back and again smiled. She watched as each took his approach shot. One gripped his club too hard to release it in time. The ball veered left. The other two shot well. One ball landed close to the green. Nice.

After they passed, she turned her attention back to the distant trees. She heaved a sigh and ripped off the bandage, saturated with tears and soaked with blood, that had for too long covered the gaping hole in her heart. A tear trickled down her cheek, unattended by the tissues in her pocket. Instead, ancient sepia-colored boxes opened in her imagination. Technicolor pictures emerged and gained new life, images from a time when she answered to a different name, the only name her father had called her by.

"Martha," her father said as he stopped the golf cart next to the sixteenth fairway tee boxes. "That was a great drive, but your putt for birdie ... that was a beauty." He rubbed his left arm and smiled. "You'll do well in the upcoming tournament."

Tournament? It was enough to see her father's smile. "I'll give it a try." She hopped out and walked to the red tee markers. She glanced back at him. His face looked strained. "Dad? Are you okay?"

His smile widened. "Oh, I'm fine. Those spicy corn muffins are paying me back." He lifted his chest and tried to take a deep breath, then winced.

"We can go back if you want."

"No, no. I'm fine." He climbed out of the cart, waving for her to continue. She checked the location of the pin on the long up-sloping par-three hole, positioned her body and her five wood, timed her breath, and swung, making excellent contact. She watched the ball loft and then drop onto the green. *Great!*

"Did you see that, Dad?" She spun around to her father. But where was he? Then she saw him, lying on the ground behind the cart. "Dad?" She rushed to him, "Dad!" She shook his shoulders, but he did not respond. "Dad! What's wrong?" She leaned forward and looked into his open but sightless eyes. "Dad! Stand up! Dad!" She screamed. "Help! Somebody! Help me!" She screamed until her throat ached, "Please! Somebody help me!"

But no one had come. The ancient hole in her chest gaped open, but instead of panic, Marrah felt resigned. Then an arm reached around her shoulder, startling her, even though she knew without looking that her mother had found her. A tear trickled down her cheek. "I thought if I came, I would remember." Marrah looked across the fairway. "He said nothing was wrong."

"I know," Lois whispered.

"I couldn't help him." A single sob convulsed Marrah's chest. "Did you know he was sick?"

"No. I had no idea." Lois dabbed Marrah's cheek and sighed. "I would have taken him straight to the hospital if I had known. He never said a word."

"But I screamed. Nobody came." Her throat ached as it had that day. She turned to her mother, no longer afraid of the kindness that filled her gentle smile. "Oh, Mom, last year, when Steve died, the memories of the day Dad died came back." She heaved a sob. "I wanted to die with him."

"I'm glad you didn't."

More sobs followed, shaking Marrah's shoulders, but her mother's arms pulled her close. Marrah buried her face in her mother's shoulder as her body heaved and quaked.

Some time later, her tears abated, becoming sniffles. She had drained her eyes dry, yet guilt tickled her memory. "I'm so sorry I lied. I do remember the night Steve died. His breathing had become labored, so you stepped into the hall to call a nurse. I was so scared." Something other than her strength lifted her chin. She met her mother's patient gaze. "But you came back and sang to him .... When death came, you were singing to him—lullabies. I don't know how you did it .... He loved to hear you sing." A soft sigh slipped out. "I'm so sorry. How can you ever forgive me?"

Lois brushed Marrah's cheek. "Easily. Because I love you."

Marrah closed her eyes and leaned her head against her mother's warm and peaceful body. Tenderness trickled over the rim of the abyss into which Marrah had fallen so long ago. Sunlight joined it, pouring over the edge, filling her heart. Finally, she asked the question that had driven her to the fence on the fourteenth fairway. "I still don't understand why no one came. I screamed and screamed. Someone should have heard me."

"I heard you." Lois cradled Marrah's cheek in her hand. "You were a very good golfer, and Tom was so proud of you. He wanted to show you off to his old friend Parker Randolph." She looked across the fairway and continued. "Parker and I had gone back for my pitching wedge at the fifteenth hole. When we returned and rounded the corner down by the woods, I saw Tom lying on the ground."

Lois stared into the distance before turning to Marrah. "There wasn't anything we could do. The doctor said Tom was dead when he fell. When you saw me, you fainted. Parker drove you to the clubhouse while I stayed with Tom." Time waited while Lois wiped Marrah's cheeks. "Later, I set you up with a counselor, hoping that she would help you, but it didn't work."

"I hated her."

"That was obvious, and the why no longer matters."

Musty anger churned in Marrah's chest. "She said that God had taken Dad away— 'home,' she said—and that I should be happy. How could I love God after that?"

"I was afraid that had happened." Lois's mouth twitched, perhaps with sympathy. "You wouldn't talk about it."

"But why did it take thirty years?"

"That's how much time you needed." Her kindness caressed Marrah's broken heart, but the answer wasn't enough. Lois lifted a strand of Marrah's hair and tucked it behind her ear. "After Tom died, I often dreamed that he was alive, that we talked and laughed, and then I'd wake up and realize that he was gone. The darkness swallowed me. I felt utterly alone. I hated the dreams;

it was as if Tom died over and over again. I cried, asking God to make the dreams go away."

"Did he?"

"In time, God spoke through someone else who had suffered from dreams like mine, someone with great guilt mingled with his loss. He said to read Psalms."

"Did it work?"

"In time, yes." Lois brushed Marrah's cheek with the back of her fingers. "In time."

"Jake knows, doesn't he?"

"Yes." Her mother's smile surprised her. "He has known for a long time." Lois took Marrah's hand. "The weekend when he came home with you during college ... if I remember right, you were classmates—more acquaintances than friends, until that day. As he listened to your tender heart, talking to Steve"— Lois's smile turned melancholy— "Jake Mapson fell for you. A couple of months later he called, frustrated by the two people that he saw in you—one part sassy, sarcastic, and funny, which he liked, but he *loved* the other side, the one you shared with Steve and David. After hearing about your father's death, he decided to wait—before I could suggest it." Her mother squeezed her hand. "Jake still wants that side of you."

Marrah's knees collapsed. She grasped the fence rail to keep from falling. "Mom, I want Jake more than anything, but there's something else." One tear after another escaped down her cheeks, though her legs gained strength. She tried to speak, but a laugh came out, a sort of slobbering chuckle; she pulled a tissue from her pocket. "I'm sorry. Look at what a mess I've made of myself. And look at you! Here, have one." She handed a tissue to Lois.

"This afternoon, I learned something phenomenal." She described the wind-whipped waves and seeing Jake's sailboat skipping across the lake. "As I drove here, I remembered hearing you say that you met Jesus on the highway after dropping me off at Georgia Tech my freshman year. I thought it was phenomenally dumb, and I hated you and God for it." She lowered her head. "I remember seeing Dad working on his Sunday school lessons, but you weren't like him."

"Sweetheart, I was worse than you think."

"You'll never convince me of that," Marrah laughed. "You're a flaming do-gooder—"

"Flaming, eh?"

"Yeah. Sometimes you are much too perfect. And you're psychic. You knew to come here."

"No. Carol Bradley lives right there." She pointed to a brick Tudor-style house. "She saw you and called." Lois smiled, but Marrah laughed until she cried, which didn't take much.

She looked into her mother's marvelous gray-green eyes and uttered a long-overdue confession. "Mom, I want to be called Martha, the name *you* gave me." Her mouth made a squirrelly smile. "'Marrah' was a camouflaged cross between Martha and Mara, from the book of Ruth ... but I like Martha."

"Then it's yours."

"What do I tell Jake?"

"Tell him you love him. Men don't need long explanations. A kiss and a hug will go a long way." Lois embraced her daughter. "Welcome home, Martha."

Long after leaving Dr. Krasotkin's office, Cameron considered and reconsidered the professor's claim that God wasn't waiting for him to make a decision but was instead standing in an open doorway, saying, "Child of mine, come home." He also wondered about the professor's analysis of *Jabberwocky* that contradicted every other expert. Still, he left these heavy-duty thoughts for another day and followed his other admonitions. On Monday, he sent a letter to UNC's School of Medicine, accepting their offer, but waited to send a letter to the business school. He assumed they didn't compare responses.

On Tuesday, he emailed Stan, Drew, and Uncle Nathan. "Okay, I'm trying hard not to think that God enjoys occasionally spiking me, but I'm glad that he isn't wringing his hands, waiting for me to 'decide.' I still think God expects me to do or to feel something, but I haven't worked that part out. It raises too many questions, but here I am."

Their encouraging replies improved his mood, but Friday evening arrived without his having called Lydia. *Groan.* The moth stretched out his wings and examined them. *Hmm.* Not good. Holes and black singe marks testified to his longing for the flame. However, even as he stoked his courage by remembering Neil's and Esther's declaration that Lydia liked him, he decided against calling her. An up-front and personal "no, thank you" with good eye contact would erase any doubts. So he joined Neil and Patrick for a video battle with pirates.

"What?" Neil snorted. "You haven't called her?"

Cameron grinned and pushed a button that sent mortar rounds flying.

"Ignorance is bliss. Why do now what can be put off? And give me a break! It took me all week to decide whether to talk while jogging or over coffee afterward."

"So which did you decide?"

"I haven't."

"You're pathetic!" Neil smacked him with a mangy throw pillow. Cameron grabbed the pillow and hurled it at Patrick, who blocked it with his video controller.

"Hey!" Patrick grabbed the pillow and smacked Neil. "It's not my fault that you have to put up with Neil's sorry company instead of cozying up to Lydia."

The ensuing free-for-all proved fatal for the pillow.

In the morning, Cameron awoke to the sound of rain drizzling outside his window. Providence, as Professor Krasotkin used the word, had made Cameron's decision for him. But what if Lydia called to say that she didn't want to run in the rain? Panicked, Cameron dashed into the shower, dressed, and ran to his car, wanting to be at the gate before she could call to cancel. What if she didn't show up? But if she did, he needed to be prepared. He circled back to Rosemary Street to scout out the Blue Feather Café. *Good.* It was open for breakfast. He arrived at the gate ten minutes earlier than usual. His pulse pounded loud enough to drown out the patter of rain. Despite the chilly weather, sweat soaked his palms. How had he not recognized the difference between "having the hots" and being in love? He'd had the hots for plenty of other girls, which were easy, fun relationships. Love was scary.

Finally, the sound of tires rolling over gravel caught his attention. The sight of Lydia's Volvo in his rearview mirror tingled his fingertips. Before she opened the door of her car, he jumped out and trotted up to her window. "You know, we don't have to run. We could do something else."

A light gust of wind sent heavy droplets of water across her lap. "It is wet, isn't it?"

"They serve breakfast at a café on Rosemary Street. It's really good. Want to join me?"

"Sure. Do they have hot chocolate?" she asked. "I got cold walking out to my car. It's a long way from Crowell to the Blue Zone lot."

"Hot chocolate? On a day like today, you'd think so. I know they have a woodstove. So maybe if it's lit, we can sit nearby. You can follow me."

Throughout the ten-minute ride from the gate to downtown Chapel Hill, Cameron's heart raced as he glanced between the traffic on Erwin Road and Lydia's Volvo in his rearview mirror. He parked and again wiped his sweaty palms on his pants. Calculating a chemistry exam with a slide rule could not be more fearsome than "discussing the future." With chemistry, he'd have a fighting chance of getting it right.

A wide porch, filled with ornate cast aluminum chairs and tables with closed umbrellas, wrapped the shingle-clad bungalow that housed the café. Outside, the rich scent of burning oak greeted them. Inside, the aroma of fresh bread and coffee filled the air. To Cameron's delight, the dismal weather had limited the number of patrons. Those who braved the rain huddled in small, scattered groups. He chose a table near the woodstove and pulled a chair out for Lydia.

"This is nice." She surveyed the room. "What is it about rainy fall days that make cozy and warm so comforting?" She laughed while Cameron steeled his nerves.

After the waitress brought their order of hot chocolate for Lydia, coffee for him, and bagels for both, Cameron asked a few safe questions about her classes. Remembering Professor Krasotkin's description of prayer, Cameron also said one, though it felt awkward. Regardless, he was grateful for the help, even from Providence. Some time later, he noticed that his coffee had turned cold. An hour had passed. He needed to state his intention before she decided to leave.

"So congratulations on getting into UNC's med school," she commented. "Did you accept?"

"Yes, I did." He took it to be the springboard he needed. "Everything just fell into place." His fork slipped between his sweaty fingers. "Sometimes things work out ...." *Don't stop now!* "It's like the rain. I didn't want to run. I wanted to talk to you." He swallowed hard and jumped in—*Heaven forbid*, as his mother would say. "I never told you, but I should have, that I enjoyed working with you at the Park Street Diner. My grandfather had died a month earlier ... and I was in bad shape. You made it easier."

"I did?"

"Yes." Cameron fidgeted with his fork, remembering the horror and pleasure of those early days. "Grandpa had asked me to go, but I thought the people were disgusting. You showed me that they were interesting—weird and toothless but valuable." To his relief, his palms were dry, but then his eyes met hers. She looked kind but also something else. Sad? Perspiration drenched his hands. He double-clutched up a gear, stoking his courage. "Those first weeks, I was running away from a lot of things."

"Where did you run?" Patience and sorrow mingled in her voice.

He eased into fourth gear. "Well, think of it like driving down the road, and an eighteen-wheeler comes over the hill heading toward you. He's in his lane, and you're in yours, but you think, *What would happen if I turned into his path?* Well, it'd be over for you. When you think those kinds of thoughts, and I did, you don't want to think. Instead, you do whatever it takes not to think and hope the pain will go away."

He wrapped his hands around his cold coffee cup, wishing it was her hand. "When I was with you, I didn't have those thoughts." He gulped noiselessly and pressed on. "I liked being with you. I still do." More than anything he wanted to touch her, to take her hand. "Last Sunday, I was in another dark place, but Providence—that's what Dr. Krasotkin called it—reminded me to call him. He was my thermo prof last spring, but he's also a good friend. He was the good part of the reason I went to Wyoming. Uncle Nathan arranged for me to go, but Dr. Krasotkin talked me into it. I hate to admit it, but Uncle Nathan sent me. Can you believe it? I didn't want to go." He paused. Something about her smile had changed. Had it faded? "Being on the ranch changed how I viewed many things, but most importantly, I stopped running away."

He almost reached for her hand but instead twitched and gripped the cup more firmly. "I started running toward something, but I kept looking back. So I'd run, then stop, then run again. But I have reason never to run away again." He paused but then pressed ahead with the most fearful words of all. "And you're central to those reasons. Med school is important, but so are you." Lydia's smile vanished, and she leaned back. What had he said wrong? Panic slipped his courage out of gear. "I must have said something you don't like."

"No, that's a great compliment, but you give me too much credit."

Something *was* wrong, very wrong. Her cheek twitched, and she glanced away. Finally, she whispered, causing him to lean closer. "Your version of those first weeks at the Diner are funny. I thought you were snobby. Mom told me to be nice because she knew you'd lost your grandfather. I followed orders, but I didn't feel sorry for you." She shrugged and played with her mug. "She scolded me, calling my behavior a pity-party because at least you knew your grandfather. Mom's dad died when I was two and Dad's father died years earlier. To be nice, I made up those stories about the people." She tipped the mug to one side, watching it, "to keep from envying you."

Cameron had never imagined that someone would envy the pain he felt. But the confession hadn't caused her gloomy mood. "What's wrong?"

Lydia dropped her hands to her lap and glanced around the room. Anywhere but at him. "I've enjoyed our weekly runs, but ... maybe it's time to go our separate ways."

"No!" he blurted. Then he softened his tone. "I mean, why?" If only he could wrap his arms around her, he'd tell the world that she was the most wonderful girl he'd ever known.

"You have ...." She stammered, still looking away. "I mean—"

He interrupted her, fear igniting every nerve. "If it's because of that date in high school, please let me finish. One of the reasons I wanted to talk was to apologize for the stupid things I've done." He looked for her hands, but they remained out of reach. "I should've said something a long time ago." When she turned to him, he saw into the icy green depths of her eyes and knew she was gone. Adrenaline exploded into words. "Wait! I know I hurt you then and last winter. Call me anything you want, but please accept my apology. I'm sorry about Mrs. Duncan. I should've kept Justin off the road that night. Lydia, I've been a jerk. Please, let me make up for it."

"That's not the problem but thank you." Her lips tightened into a thin line, not in anger but incredible sadness. "Aimee has been after me for years to forgive you. And I do."

"Please believe me, with all my heart; I'm sorry for everything."

Her eyes searched his as she repeated, "That's not the problem."

"Then what is it? Why do you always hold back?"

Her eyes widened. "What do you mean?"

Not wanting to frighten or overwhelm her, he imagined the ocean's breeze, blowing across the wet sand at sunrise. "I called you in September to spend time with you. I wanted to rebuild your trust." He reached into her lap and gently took her hand, lifting it onto the table. "I'm glad for the rain, for Providence, so we could talk ... and rebuild our friendship." Emotions ruffled across her face. He cradled her hand with both of his and waited.

"I'm sorry," she whispered. Her eyes watered, but her voice said she was far away, too far.

"You shouldn't be sorry. I'm the one whose brain drops reception and has zero bars."

She glanced back at him and half-smiled. "You're funny, but that's not what I'm talking about." The gloom that covered her smile grew darker.

His heart leaped into his throat, but he spoke softly. "Tell me what I can do to make things right between us."

"Nothing," she whispered.

His heart tumbled into an abyss, but determination feasted on his fears. "Are you sure?"

"I *have* had fun this fall." She blinked hard and looked away. A moment later, she turned to him with quiet determination, matching his. "You can't change ... at least not for me."

"Then tell me what to do."

"It's not that easy." To his surprise, she had seen the depths of his heart. Panic flickered, but he didn't flinch. "You're right. I have held back. When you called in September, I was still angry with you, because I didn't want to get hurt. I got over that. Now I see that we're too different in a way that neither of us can change."

"I promise. I won't hurt you ... and whatever it is, give me a chance to change."

The gloom in her eyes faded to weariness, not as one feels at the end of a long road, but emotional exhaustion. A similar unfathomable gloom had embraced him when he first saw the lake nestled beneath the glistening Wyoming peaks. If he could take her there, she'd understand. She wouldn't hold back.

"It's not that easy," she said, looking away, "because we travel different roads." When she turned back to him and smiled, small and slight, his heart leaped. *Yes! She likes me.*

"You never noticed during those nights at the Diner?" she asked. "I fell for you long ago." The gloom returned, shrouding her smile. She turned to the rain-spattered window. "If you knew me better, you wouldn't feel this way."

A glimmer of hope! "Why not? What wouldn't I like? You're kind and thoughtful. You're smart, and I think you're very funny ... and beautiful."

Lydia turned to him and blushed, but it faded as did her smile. "It's my faith in Christ. I take it very seriously."

"I'm a Christian," he blurted. "A Baptist, to be specific. Why is that a problem?"

She grinned. "For one thing, Bible drills."

"Bible drills? They were a mainstay of my childhood." He grinned. "And I was good."

"Why am I not surprised. And I'm *still* lousy at verse memory." Lydia laughed and then looked at his hands, cradling hers. A half smile appeared, "I truly believe that God pitied me so much that he didn't ordain my birth until someone wrote software with a concordance ... just for me."

He stifled his laughter. "I'm trying to be serious. What can I do?"

"It isn't about doing." Her smile dimmed. "Look at our lives. Tonight, you'll be at a frat party while I'll do something with my InterVarsity friends. I can't believe you haven't met a beautiful, kind, smart, and ... What else did you say?"

"'Funny.' I suppose you want me to believe that forgetting that word was a Freudian slip in reverse." His smile, set free by a thin ray of hope, relaxed into a playful grin. "And no, I haven't. And don't ask if I've looked. You know I have."

Seeing the waitress stop at their table, Lydia flushed—the exact response he hoped for. His smile widened as the young girl asked if they needed anything. After she left, Lydia snapped, "You timed that! You rascal."

"Not really." He laughed, "It was Providence."

Lydia scowled at him, sending relief washing over him. Plus, she did not pull her hand away as she repeated her now-teetering stand. "It isn't that easy. I can be very boring."

"Then bore me." He laughed. "It's my due after talking nonstop about Wyoming. —Lydia, I want to take you there." *Aha. Her ears perked and her eyes widened. I got her attention. Wow.* She was good at concealing her emotions. But that was all right. She'd eased her guard.

"I'm serious," she insisted. "You only *think* you can live with our differences."

"Lydia, you're anything but boring." He smiled and squeezed her hand. "So teach me."

"You made my point. It can't be taught. When a person professes faith in Christ to please someone else, it verges on being a sham. The day will come when, out of anger or simply boredom, you'll deny your testimony and say you did it only for me. I never want to hear those words."

Cameron suffocated an ebullient smile as he watched Lydia twist a corner of her napkin with one hand while her other hand clung to his, relaxed and soft. "Just give me a chance," he whispered.

An eternity of silence followed as Lydia looked anywhere but at him. Finally, she turned to him, but thinking sadness had again darkened her heart, his heart stopped. "Okay," she said. The corners of her mouth lifted.

Fireworks rocketed into flight and jets roared overhead. Cameron leaned forward and matched her faint smile. In response, her weary mask took on a wry calm. Had he been so inclined, he could have kissed her. Instead, he lingered, inches from her, then leaned against the chair's back. With a flick of his brows, the playful smile that greeted her nearly every night at the Park Street Diner returned; he lowered his voice. "When do we start?"

Lydia squeezed his fingers hard, and her eyes narrowed. "Ouch!" he exclaimed.

One eyebrow arched. "Liking you is very easy. The thought of getting close and then losing you because of my faith—that I can't do."

"I understand." He smiled as his thumb brushed the back of her hand.

Her smile flickered, and she withdrew her hand.

Yes! She likes me. More than ever he wanted to kiss her, but not now. He could wait. A rakish smile caught one corner of his mouth. "You're tantalizing me. Aren't you?"

"No." She sat back in her chair with a chuckle. "I'm measuring you."

"Not for a coffin, I presume." The worst was over.

"No. Tell you what." Lydia tilted her head, appraising him. "Next weekend Duke Chapel holds a sing-along of Handel's *Messiah*. The main performances open the week after Thanksgiving, but they're packed. The sing-along is easier to get into and no less beautiful. Afterward, my friends are planning a pizza party—it's fix-your-own. It's my idea of fun. As I said, I like boring things."

Surprised by her invitation, he paused, studying her.

"See what you're up against?" she insisted without flinching.

"Give me a chance to catch my breath. It isn't every day that a stunning brunette invites me to dinner." He took her hands and pressed them together, palm to palm, between his. "Please don't expect me to sing. And I *am* familiar with *Messiah*—I'm not a total cultural dork." He turned her hands over. "I'll say yes, but only if after we're full of pizza, you will come with me to the house. My friends want to meet the mysterious woman I steal away to see each Saturday morning."

He released her left hand and turned the other palm up. With his eyes fixed on hers, he lifted it to his lips and kissed it. Her eyes widened, and her cheeks flushed bright red. "Of course," he continued, his voice barely louder than a whisper, "you could say no." He blew a warm breath across her palm. "But then I'd have to flirt with your friends until you agreed to go, just to get me out of there."

Her mouth popped open. "You'd do it, too, just to see them faint over your Tar Heel eyes." She laughed but didn't pull her hand away. "Okay, it's a deal."

"I also thought that tonight we could go out to dinner, and then afterward, we could find a movie, sit in the back, and ...." He raised his eyebrows and wiggled them.

34

Lois had long believed she was too old to be surprised, but the glee and excitement that she'd heard in Martha's voice ten minutes earlier, inviting her for afternoon tea of all things, had proved her wrong. She turned onto the cul-de-sac that led to her daughter's house. As she rounded the corner, she saw Martha standing on the front porch, appearing to bounce, just barely. *Bounce?* Her smile could be seen a mile away. As she pulled to a stop, Martha opened her door. Lois thanked her and climbed out, happy that she was not too old to be surprised.

"Hi, Mom."

"Hi, dear." Lois smiled.

Martha stepped up to the porch, and Lois followed her inside. "I found your favorite tea, and I made the best cinnamon-nut scones. But first, there's something we must do." She took her mother's hand and led her to the powder room. There, with a great flourish, Martha held out her left hand, the hand she had hidden from sight since opening Lois's door. In it was a vial of Norco. "Please observe." She opened the vial, held it over the toilet, and emptied it. She swirled her hand above the toilet and flushed. "There you have it. The last of the Norco."

Finally, she grew a little serious. "I haven't had a pill since a week before we met at Montebello. And I know I never will again. I can't, ever again. And yes, I'll go to the physical therapist—regularly."

"That's wonderful." The two embraced. Then Lois held Martha at arm's length, trying not to laugh. "When can I tell you that you're not supposed to flush pills into the sewer system because they will end up in the river?"

"Not so!" Martha beamed. "We're on septic. If I see some pretzel-knot worms, we'll know what caused it."

Lois joined her in the best of all laughs.

Shortly before four, Cameron bounded up the steps of the rental house and flung the door open. As expected, an audience greeted him, but the small group did not include Neil, Patrick, or Trace.

"Man, what's with the grin?" one of the guys asked. "Neil's upstairs."

"Thanks." Cameron raced up the steps, taking them two at a time. When he reached his room, he again flung the door open, but the room was empty. Hearing Patrick laugh, he strode down the hall. Since the door was wide open, he stomped his foot as he stepped inside. "Ta-da!"

His friends looked up from the cannons and mortars that blasted across Patrick's television. "Woo-hoo," Neil said with a laugh. "Are you trying to cough up a canary or a hairball?"

"Neither."

"Have you been with Lydia all this time?" Patrick asked.

"Yeah, isn't it great?"

"She's coming over here tonight," Trace asked. "Right?"

"No, but I did invite her."

Patrick and Neil exchanged quizzical glances. "So why isn't she coming?"

"She'd already promised to celebrate some guy's birthday."

"Obviously, that doesn't bother you," Neil noted.

"Not at all. I have something almost as good." He wiggled his eyebrows. "She gave me her email address."

"Explain how that's better."

"Well, I suppose it isn't," Cameron answered with unbridled delight, "but you'll get to meet her next weekend."

"I have to wait a whole week."

"Yeah, I know." Cameron laughed. "Life's tough."

"No kidding!" Patrick shot back, then grabbed his pillow and jumped on top of Cameron. Neil joined in as the pile of flying arms, legs, and pillows tumbled to the floor. Patrick rolled off the top and landed on his back, laughing. "Oh, man! Cam has it bad."

Cameron was going to be fine. Nathan smiled and closed the email from his nephew, but he needed a cup of coffee. When he entered the kitchen, he found Becky on the phone.

"I hope you're right," Becky said to the caller and frowned.

Nathan ignored her. No telling who was on the phone. His wife didn't look happy, so he poured a cup of coffee and turned, ready to return to the computer. Becky, though, stamped the floor and frowned. When he turned, she motioned with a finger, pointing at the phone, and mouthed, "Don't leave!"

He did anyway.

"Bye," Becky said to the caller and ended the call. "Not so fast."

Nathan stopped and turned.

"That was Valerie."

"What did she want?" No telling.

Becky clamped her hands over her eyes. "I thought I could handle this on my own, but I can't. It's going to be a disaster." Becky dropped her hands as her face took on a scowl followed by a sickly smile. "You know I love my sister-in-law." Becky drummed her fingers against the counter and glanced around the kitchen. "We aren't best buddies, but we like each other. And I know she thinks Tricia Sloane is her best friend."

"Am I supposed to know who that is?"

Becky's face contorted. "She's Justin's mom. Remember Justin?"

"Okay. And ..."

"And I don't want to tell Valerie what to do, but ..."

Nathan arched his brow upward, warning her to get to the point.

"Yesterday," she continued, "I stopped by Ashmore Methodist Church to pick up a book that a friend had left for me. I went to the receptionist's window, but she was on the phone and signaled for me to wait. So I did. I should have picked up the book and left, but that would've been rude. So I waited. I didn't eavesdrop."

Nathan nodded, urging her to get on with it.

"Well, the receptionist hung up the phone and was so upset about the call that she started venting, at me. The call was from a church member named Charring Appleton. According to the secretary, Ms. Appleton had asked to change not only her address but the address of another member, a married man, to the same address."

Nathan chuckled and pulled out a chair at the breakfast room table. This was not going to be quick. He sat down and leaned back.

"Don't laugh. The receptionist said she felt humiliated because she had to call the man—I'll get to his name—for verification. She then told me more than I wanted to know. And I would have forgotten the whole thing except that I know the man." She nodded, ready for Nathan's questions, but he had none yet. "It was Alan Sloane. None other than Tricia's husband.

"The receptionist had known about his affair with Charring for two years. The Sloanes and Appletons were in the same Sunday school class. She was appalled because Charring has small children and doesn't want custody of them. What kind of mother leaves her children?

"Now here's the worst part. When I got home, Valerie called, wanting to know if we minded if she invited a friend and her family to Thanksgiving dinner. Supposedly, they were having marital problems, and Valerie wanted to help. Well, guess whose marriage she wanted to save."

Nathan grinned. "Tricia and Alan's, I suppose."

"Yep. According to Valerie, since Randy and Alan are friends and attend the same Sunday school class, she thought Randy could talk to Alan, maybe change his mind. I love my brother, but that's crazy."

"So what are you going to do?"

"You're not worried?"

"About what?"

"Thanksgiving. Valerie has a good heart, but she invited *all* of the Sloanes. That means she invited Justin. Is this beginning to add up?"

"What do you want me to do? Call Randy and tell him that we won't come because Valerie invited the Sloanes? Look, if Alan has already moved in with this woman, Charring, then I doubt he'll want to spend Thanksgiving with Tricia—much less the Asher clan."

"But what about Cameron?"

"He's a big boy, and from the email that I just read, he'll be fine."

"What'd he say?"

"Not much, but he's happy." Nathan smiled. "He has a date with Lydia Carpenter next weekend."

"Then I'm happy for him. But back to Thanksgiving. If Cameron is seeing Lydia, will that present problems if Justin comes?"

"Relax. Valerie picks up stray cats from parking lots, gets them their shots, and finds homes for them. You're not going to change her." He stood and enjoyed a good laugh.

"Nathan! Tricia and Alan are unpredictable, and I intend to protect Cameron."

Seeing Becky cross her arms and tap her forefinger while scowling at him, Nathan regained an appropriate degree of solemnity. Alan might be a notorious womanizer, but he wasn't a fool. "If you're that irritated, ask her to take back the invitation."

"I can't do that," Becky snapped. "I already tried to reason with her, but it went right over her little head. She said, 'I prayed about it.' *She prayed about it.* Excuse me! God may yet answer her prayer, but will she be happy with his answer?"

Nathan tried very hard not to laugh. "Probably not."

Becky dropped into a chair next to him. "Oh, Lord," she moaned.

"I'll pray for you"—he managed not to laugh— "because you can't stop it."

Becky looked up, her face drawn. "I know."

"Feel better now?" he said, allowing himself a chuckle.

"No."

The week passed too slowly for Cameron. He emailed Lydia several times—keeping his comments light and brief—but his cool demeanor remained in cyberspace. He drove his friends nuts, but other students and hardened strangers returned his smile as he strolled across campus.

On Saturday morning, he met Lydia for their weekly jog but tempered his zeal. Finally, shortly after one-thirty that afternoon he parked in the deck behind Duke Chapel, crossed a sunlit road, and ascended the path leading to the rear of the church. He passed several students with backpacks and stern faces who strode along the slate sidewalk that ran beneath a canopy of pines and hardwoods. Other people, including some who appeared to be visitors, ascended the slate walkway toward the church, which dominated the surrounding campus. He flashed a casual smile, but his heart danced. Had he been asked, even as recently as six months earlier, if he, a dyed-in-the-wool UNC fan, would ever feel comfortable walking around Duke, he would have howled. Strange as it seemed, though, he enjoyed walking through the compact, stone-encrusted campus of his school's archrival.

After passing beneath one of two loggias that flanked the church, Cameron crossed a wide slate-covered walkway that marked off several large grassy rectangles on a wide terrace fronting the church. He stopped at the top step of several limestone steps, all of which stretched from one side of the quadrangle to the other. Before him, beyond the base of the steps, spread a grassy mall and even more Gothic buildings. Everywhere he looked, people strolled along the stone sidewalks, waited for buses, admired the chapel, or simply talked and laughed. Still amazed that he liked the view, he briefly looked up at the chapel's spires that soared into a glorious blue sky. It was, indeed, a magnificent building. Prepared to wait, he sat down on one of the limestone steps and rolled up the sleeves of his blue oxford shirt. With his back braced by his elbows and his elbows on the uppermost step, he stretched his legs across the lower steps. He nodded to several passerby then closed his eyes and turned his face to the midday sun.

"Are you ready?" asked the voice that laughed and sparkled in his dreams. "I hope we didn't keep you waiting too long."

"No." He smiled and hopped to his feet. With a slight bow, he smiled as Lydia introduced her friends, Ragini and Eydie. Both smiled, polite and restrained, but their eyes said they approved of him. With a gentleman's deft hand to Lydia, he followed them to the base of the steps in front of the dark oaken doors of the chapel. A larger group of friends soon joined them. As he shook hands and nodded, he found curious pleasure when Lydia mentioned only their high school friendship and failed to mention his UNC affiliation. No explanation was needed.

Lydia turned to him. "I know we're early; we hope to get seats near the front."

Happy to be with her, he smiled. Whatever. When the doors opened, cool, musky air spilled from the dimly lit narthex. Low voices and the soft shuffling of feet echoed noisily off the stone interior. Cameron picked up a brochure and followed Lydia down the long center aisle of the nave while cataloging every detail of the cruciform structure: brilliant stained-glass windows, the slate floor underfoot, the hint of musk, and oaken pews, darkened by age to the hue of Grandpa's antiques. High overhead, the vaulted stone ceiling surmounted massive limestone columns.

Lydia leaned close, her voice low and somber. "This music and the chapel are magical."

"This isn't a chapel," he whispered. "It's a cathedral."

Smiling, Lydia followed her friends into a pew flanked by one of the fluted columns. Others in the gathering crowd stood among the chairs and pews, quietly talking. An arching set of risers, each deep enough to hold a chair *and* standing room, sat in front of the ornate chancel and between the transepts. Music stands and chairs filled the floor in front of the risers. Choir members and musicians wandered about. Some stood at their appointed seats; others mingled, speaking in muted tones. Finally, the musicians and singers took their places, and a hush spread through the building.

The conductor, followed by the soloists, entered and took their places in front of the choir and the orchestra. After a brief welcome and instruction for the audience, the Sinfonia began, followed by the first soloist, a tenor.

"*Comfort ye,*" he sang. "*Comfort ye, my people, says your God, says your God.*" Hearing the muted volume of his voice, Cameron wondered if people sitting at the rear of the chapel could hear him. As the music progressed, the soloists' voices grew louder. During the arias and recitatives, Cameron worked to focus his attention so as not to drift off and give Lydia the idea that he wasn't listening. The cramped seating, which caused his shoulder to press against hers, was delightful enough to keep him wide awake.

At each choral section, Lydia and the assembled crowd stood and joined the choir. Cameron stood but didn't sing. "*His yoke is easy, and His burden is light, His burden is light.*"

His eyes widened. *I know that one: Matthew 11:30.*

"Are you enjoying yourself?" Lydia asked during the first intermission.

"Absolutely." An amazing equivocation. He liked the building and music, and enjoyed her company, but he was most happy about being able to stand and stretch.

The second section began, progressing at the same burdensome pace as the first. A yawn almost loosened Cameron's jaw, but he clamped his mouth shut and remembered that a third part awaited him. As the piece droned on, his head nodded then snapped upward. He also stifled another yawn.

"*The kings of the earth rise up, and the rulers take counsel together.*" The strong bass voice demanded his attention. "*Against the Lord, and against His Anointed.*" Cameron glanced at the program, happy to see that the end was near. A few minutes later, he stood with the assembled crowd, who sang the "Hallelujah" chorus. Relief at last! While Lydia sang, Cameron employed isometrics to stretch his stiff back, arms, and legs.

As the last chord resounded down the nave, Lydia whispered. "The third part is my favorite. It's full of hope."

Cameron gathered every joule of energy in his body and smiled. "So what do you like about it?"

Lydia's eyes sparkled. "It's about Christ's resurrection and our salvation. I know you're bored. The "Hallelujah" chorus is the best known, but for me, the best is yet to come. It isn't long—well, other than the amen. I'm an alto, so I listen rather than trying to sing through the endless amens. It's impossible for me."

With full-throated volume and confidence, the soprano opened the third section. *"I know that my Redeemer liveth, and that He shall stand at the latter day upon the earth."*

To Cameron's surprise, the lyrics sounded familiar. More surprisingly, though, the song conjured memories of clear, crisp mountain mornings, and feelings buried deep in the past. The choir and audience followed, in a solemn recitation. *"Since by man came death, by Man came also the resurrection of the dead."* All around him, voices sang, *"Even so in Christ shall all be made alive."* A solemn choral dirge followed: *"For as in Adam all die."* The voices around him touched the depths of his heart, quickening, awakening his soul with perplexing but familiar lyrics as they exulted, *"Even so shall all be made alive!"* He rechecked the program as the bass soloist sang, *"Behold I tell you a mystery. We shall all be changed, in a moment, in the twinkling of an eye."*

A blast of trumpets shook the buttressed building until even the stone floor seemed to resonate. For years Cameron had avoided discussions about faith, yet something in the music grasped him—something strong, yet as gentle as the rope halter he'd placed on Azariah to bend the horse to his will. Cameron, too, had willingly given up some of his freedom, and he didn't care.

A trumpet joined the bass soloist, echoing through the nave, but the musty memory of Grandpa's words, spoken a few nights before he died, returned and overwhelmed the bass. "I was blessed to know that Christ is calling your name." Cameron stiffened, startled by the memory echoing from the past. "Son, Jesus loves you .... He knows your name."

The soloist proclaimed, *"The trumpet shall sound, and the dead shall be raised, be raised incorruptible, and we shall be changed."* Cameron turned his ear to the bass soloist. *"For this corruptible must put on incorruption, and this mortal must put on immortality."* The alto and tenor sang, *"Death, O death, where is thy sting?"* What had Grandpa meant? Could he be dead and yet alive? *"O grave, where is thy victory?"* Victory? Over death? How was that possible in a world structured on atoms and cells, on Newtonian physics and quantum mechanics?

When Grandpa died, Cameron had not looked into the casket for fear of losing the memory of Grandpa's smile. He was gone, and only the cold shell of his body remained. There was no victory over death.

Cameron closed his eyes, wanting a different thought, a happy memory, but instead remembered lying in the cleft of the W four months earlier. Though he felt broken and alone, the breeze had cajoled a memory of Grandpa reading to Cameron from the Bible as a ray of sunlight caught Cameron's imagination.

Bored after the hour-long drive but happy to be with Grandpa, Cameron climbed out of the car and kicked aside pebbles that lay scattered among clumps of mowed grass and weeds just past the edge of the parking lot. On the opposite side of the parkway, three sightseers stood admiring the vista of a wide valley crisscrossed with a patchwork of fields lying far below. Grandpa, though, strolled up a sequestered path leading into the forest. Cameron followed him to a small waterfall that spilled over huge lichen-encrusted boulders protruding from the mountainside. Having visited it before with Grandpa, Cameron easily found a perch and crouched beside the stream. Beyond the leafy canopy, cars sped past, but none slowed down, increasing the solitude of the small stream.

"When I first happened upon this stream," Grandpa noted with a smile, "I stopped to enjoy the overlook, but when I returned to my car, something in the air, a cool breeze, slipped out from the woods. Curious, I walked to this side of the parking lot and heard gurgling beneath the leaves. I followed the sound to this spot." Grandpa sat on a small bolder, opened his Bible, and read aloud as Cameron tossed pebbles into the water.

Ready to toss another stone, he stopped to watch a flickering light beam that pierced the canopy and danced atop the ripples of the swift stream. He cupped his hand and scooped up as much water as his hand would hold, though most of it ran between his fingers. "Grandpa. Look." Cameron laughed at his open palm. "See? I caught the light."

Grandpa smiled and continued reading, "When the perishable puts on the imperishable, and the mortal puts on immortality, then shall come to pass ...." To Cameron's surprise, something odd happened. The light ceased to flicker and instead grew brighter and warmed him, but not his hand. It warmed his chest. Curiously, a prism of colors sparkled in his hand where there had been only the brilliant white light of the midday sun. Grandpa read on, "was ... shall come to pass the saying that is written, 'Death is swallowed up in victory. O death, where is your victory? O death, where is your sting?" Grandpa's eyes twinkled. "Cameron, I have a riddle for you. There's a water in life that will make your bones ache and yet refresh you to the core. It is the water of life."

A faceless voice echoed in his ears, "The words your grandfather speaks are true."

Too surprised and perplexed to respond either to Grandpa or the strange urging, he jumped from his perch and splashed in the cool, oddly refreshing water.

Cameron again heard Grandpa speaking to the sky, "Lift up your heads, O gates! And be lifted up, O ancient doors, that the King of glory may come in." Cameron's lungs stopped. The choir had sung those very words. He flipped his bulletin open and scanned the lyrics, finding them in the second section. *Yes!* Ignoring Lydia, who watched him, Cameron whispered, or rather recited: "The Lord of Hosts, He is the King of Glory." Once again, he felt the cold mountain water washing over his feet. Was this the water that solved Grandpa's riddle? His skin tingled. The water he spoke about wasn't a stream or waterfall. It was God, washing Cameron's heart, breaking and healing him all at the same time.

"If God be for us, who can be against us?" The soprano's measured voice repeated the question. *"Who can be against us?"*

Cameron's lungs responded, filling themselves with air as cool and de-licious as the sage-filled breeze across the Bighorns and as comforting as clouds cloaking the Blue Ridge on an October morning. The aria enveloped him and returned him to Grandpa's hospital room. "Son, whenever you feel alone, and you think of me—read these verses." The final piece of the puzzling memory slipped into place. After leaving his grandfather's room, Cameron had found, tucked into Grandpa's Bible, the same verses that the soprano now sang. "Who shall lay anything to the charge of God's elect? It is God that justifieth, who is he that condemneth?" A thought zigzagged through Cameron's memories, gathering fragments and linking them together. "It is Christ that died, yea, rather that is risen again, who is at the right hand of God, who makes intercession for us."

Whether on the expansive range or among the imposing peaks of Wyoming, or along the busy parkway or the bustle of studies and socializing, in each day of Cameron's life God had been calling to him. He had been at his side, comforting and leading him, but when Grandpa died, Cameron had stopped listening. In the weeks and months following Grandpa's death, he had recited the passages, memorizing the easy part: "Lift up your heads, O ye gates, and be ye lift up, ye everlasting doors, and the King of Glory shall come in." Sorrow had prevented him from hearing the quiet voice of Christ claiming him, redeeming him.

Memories of a thousand sins flipped through his thoughts on fluttering pages, some writ bold. He'd cursed his father and disrespected his mother, used his friends—both the good ones like Paul and the dismal ... Justin. His girlfriends had been free tickets, used then tossed aside. The refreshing joy of revelation faded, shredding his pride as he remembered Drew and Lydia. They had received as much of Cameron's haughty abuse as anyone, yet both had forgiven him.

The verses of Grandpa's final gift repeated themselves:

Who shall bring any charge against God's elect? It is God who justifies. Who is to condemn? Christ Jesus is the one who died—more than that, who was raised—who is at the right hand of God, who indeed is interceding for us. Who shall separate us from the love of Christ? Shall tribulation, or distress, or persecution, or famine, or nakedness, or danger, or sword? As it is written,

"For your sake we are being killed all the day long; we are regarded as sheep to be slaughtered."

No, in all these things we are more than conquerors through him who loved us. For I am sure that neither death nor life, nor angels nor rulers, nor things present nor things to come, nor powers, nor height nor depth, nor anything else in all creation, will be able to separate us from the love of God in Christ Jesus our Lord.

Throughout each solo, Cameron had looked around, seeing nothing. Now, he saw, carved into the upper portion of the ornate fretwork in the rear wall of the chancel, a cross, plucked from the shadows of the dark wood by a beam of light even though, high above the choir, night had darkened the stained-glass windows.

Cameron smiled as the voice of the choir thundered, "*Worthy is the Lamb that was slain,*" filling every crevice and corner of the gray stones lining the nave. "*And hath redeemed us to God by his blood to receive power, and riches, and wisdom, and strength, and honor, and glory, and blessing.*" Every stone, from the vaults overhead to the foundation of the sanctuary, answered. "*Blessing and honor, glory and power be unto Him.*" Though he didn't know the tune, Cameron whispered rather than sang, "*be unto Him that sitteth upon the throne and unto the Lamb—for ever and ever.*"

The last chorus, the one Lydia had said would be long, passed in a flash. While the audience applauded, Cameron turned to her and smiled. "That was impressive." As strangers and friends stirred from their seats, he saw only Lydia. Her curious expression told him that she had watched him, but he didn't mind. Rather than trying to describe the indescribable, he put his hand on her waist as they exited together.

Eydie leaned close to Lydia and whispered, "When Cameron talks to us, his eyes are on you."

Were Lydia to smile, her friend might get the wrong impression. Nothing could be easier than falling for Cameron, and nothing could be more dangerous.

After the *Messiah* concert, she and Cameron joined the group for pizza in two neighboring apartments in Duke's student housing at 300 Swift Avenue. Ever the Southerner, Cameron introduced himself and chatted with her friends, the guys as well, but always returned to her side. Several pizza slices and perhaps an hour later, his smile indicated that he was ready to leave. Lydia thanked her hostesses, and Cameron extended his hand. With a beguiling smile, the rascal turned her friends—a chem major and an engineer—into giggling Jell-O. Yes, falling under his spell was too easy.

To her surprise, as they followed the taillights of other cars swarming along US-15-501 and headed for Chapel Hill, Cameron retreated into pensive silence. When they entered Chapel Hill, he turned to Lydia and momentarily let his eyes linger. "I'm sorry, I'm not ignoring you. It's just that ..."

Again, he retreated into silence, but Lydia remembered Eydie's comment and decided not to assume the worst—perhaps because sitting next to him felt as natural as breathing. As they crept through the traffic lights on Franklin Street, waiting for him to speak was disquieting but easy.

On the long grade leading up to the old town, Cameron broke the silence. "Thank you." He glanced at her then back at the road. "The lyrics were amazing." Whether by habit or instinct, Lydia's defenses sprang to attention despite his kind smile and attentive manner. "I was surprised to recognize verses in the earlier section. Then one in the last section carried me back to Grandpa and driving up to the parkway. We visited different parts, but the one he liked best looked to everyone else like a parking lot with picnic tables. Nothing special."

Cameron heaved a sigh. "The last time we went, I didn't know he was sick, but he must have known. A few days later Mom told me he had cancer." Lydia buttressed her defenses, though for what reason she wasn't sure since he finished the thought and said nothing more. Instead, he watched the road as they entered the uphill grade of Franklin Street.

"Well," Cameron stammered as they passed the shops across from the main campus, "there are ... ideas I need to sort through." He gave no other hint about the ideas and said nothing more until he turned into the driveway behind a brightly lit white Colonial building. His fraternity, she assumed. He stopped the car but didn't move, speak, or smile. His hands dropped to his lap. She knew enough, though, to wait.

"You know," Cameron said with his eyes fixed on the house, "not until this very moment did I wonder whether you would like my friends." His cheek twitched. He turned to her as sorrow hung from his shoulders. "You worried that I might not like yours—and I do—but I never thought about this." He sighed. "We live in two different worlds, don't we?"

"It's okay." She opened the door, knowing what he meant. "I know I'll like your friends. Besides, I've been to Duke frat parties. There's little left to surprise me."

He watched her a moment longer, and then one corner of his mouth lifted. "I suppose not."

As they walked up to the back door, he placed his hand on her back, sending sparkles racing up her spine. Once inside, he took her hand as gusty hellos greeted them. Cameron returned them, but while the sparkles reached her toes, a mildly discomforting thought startled her. She had known him since the ninth grade, but the fraternity was his domain, a realm she had never entered. Cameron worked his way through the kitchen and into a large room at the front of the building.

"Cam, my man!" A man of medium height and slim-but-muscular build called and motioned for Cameron to join him in a slightly less crowded corner. A petite brunette stood next to him, while a lanky, redheaded guy made room for them.

"Lydia, this is my dorky roommate, Neil." Cameron thumped the side of the shorter man's head. "He's the one who keeps me awake with his snoring, and this is Catherine, a woman much too kind and special for him."

"Hey, what about me?" The redheaded guy with a happy smile squeezed past Neil, took Lydia's hand, and kissed it. "Hi, Lydia. I'm Patrick, your humble servant. Will you marry me?"

"Not so fast." Cameron grinned as he reached around Lydia's shoulder. "Pay him no attention."

Patrick winked at Cameron. "You sly dog, sneaking out all those Saturdays and not inviting us along. What kind of friend keeps such a beautiful secret?" A sincere smile replaced Patrick's jocularity as he turned to Lydia with perfect Southern grace. "It's a pleasure to meet you—finally."

The quick arching of Neil's eyebrow and his terse grin caught Lydia's attention, but the signal was aimed at Cameron. "Yeah, Lydia, it's nice that sponge-brain here brought you by. We've wondered if he planned to keep you only to himself."

"Lydia, just ignore them." Catherine elbowed Neil. "I've been hoping Cameron would find someone like you."

As Catherine Kilpatrick introduced herself, Neil pulled Cameron aside and whispered into his ear. Cameron turned his back to Lydia but held her hand.

"How was the concert?" Catherine asked.

"It was beautiful …," Lydia answered, but Neil's voice distracted her.

"An hour ago, Trace took Justin back to his apartment, but …."

Justin? She concentrated on Catherine and hoped Neil was talking about someone other than Justin Sloane. Cameron's grip on her hand tightened. Earlier, as Cameron parked, Lydia had seen inside the house and thought she saw someone who looked like Justin. Now she hoped she had been wrong.

Catherine motioned to a tall, dark-haired man with an easy smile. "I call Trace, along with Neil and Patrick, Cameron's musketeers." She nodded to a strikingly lovely girl with a shy smile. "And this is Tina, Trace's date for quite some time now. He's a lucky guy."

A bashful smile appeared as Tina extended her hand. "Hi."

Clearly, Cameron's close friends were more than that. They were good friends—and some seemed intent on keeping him out of trouble.

As Catherine continued, Neil's voice broke through, speaking to Cameron, and no one else. "Justin knows her?"

Her who? Oh, he means me.

"Yeah." Venom laced Cameron's voice.

Justin—one and the same. Lydia masked her fears behind a polite smile as Catherine introduced several other people, but a fragment of Patrick's comments caught her ear. "Justin was smashed, but he asked about Lydia. What's with him?"

Again, the noise drowned Cameron's response. Lydia waited a second, her ears alert, and then heard his voice. "Don't let him anywhere near her."

A chill slid down her spine. Neil added something, and Cameron's grip on her hand loosened. The next moment Neil and Patrick left. Cameron turned to her and smiled. "Yo, Trace. Hi, Tina." He released Lydia's hand, but—rather than leaving—wrapped his arm around her shoulder and spoke into her ear. "I'm sorry. I had a small issue to take care of."

Several minutes later, Neil returned and signaled a thumbs-up. Cameron responded with a nod which, from the return of his easy smile, led her to believe that Justin was no longer in the house. "Can I get you something to drink?"

"A Sprite would be fine."

Cameron turned to Patrick. "Do I dare leave her with you for a minute?"

"My proposal still stands," Patrick answered gleefully, "so be quick."

"Right!" Cameron left and soon returned with her Sprite. For the rest of the evening, he drank Pepsi and either held her hand, wrapped his arm around her waist, or draped it over her shoulder as he chatted and laughed, but he never left her side. Meanwhile, Lydia said little, listened a lot, and enjoyed the warmth of standing so close to him while the sound of his voice and the sparkle in his smile sent her heart pounding. Such intimacy with him had been a foolish, impossible high school dream. Now, it seemed, God had answered her inconsequential prayer, at least for an evening.

Later in the evening—and several times—Cameron leaned his cheek against her head. Each time, her knees melted, and only steely determination propped up her guard. She needed to remember that, like the royal coach-and-four that turned into a pumpkin and mice at the stroke of midnight, everything could change.

36

Late Tuesday afternoon, Cameron finished packing for Thanksgiving break. Then he aimed his SUV onto southbound I-85 and headed home. As the miles fell behind him, he reminisced. Saturday had been fantastic—being a part of Lydia's world and she a part of his. Thankfully, his good friends had dispatched Justin, leaving Cameron to imagine that he might one day be able to whisk her away and have her only to himself. In the meantime, she had agreed to meet on Friday morning at Chalmers's equivalent of a private place— the abandoned railroad bed, now re-purposed as a jogging and bike trail, that ran west through two neighboring towns. She also agreed to go out with him Friday night, though he needed Paul's advice about where to take her.

On Wednesday morning, he drove to Uncle Nathan's farm, where he regaled his uncle and cousin with every detail from the *Messiah* concert, the dinner, and the frat party. He also asked a boatload of questions about Grandpa's faith.

"Your grandfather," Uncle Nathan said, nodding pensively, "was one of the godliest men I've had the honor of knowing because he fixed his eyes on the holiness of God."

Whatever that meant, Cameron wasn't sure, but he knew it to be a compliment. Also, and happily, Uncle Nathan avoided asking about Lydia. Instead, he saddled his horse Amos and handed Cameron the reins. "There's a gate at the end of the field. Go easy on Amos. He's old like me."

"Will do." With a nod and a smile, Cameron turned Amos toward the field. A gusty November wind roared through the empty treetops, swirling the dry leaves around Amos's hooves. He was glad to be home. In the future, he'd feel doubt and face disappointments and sorrow, but they would not defeat him. Lydia, Stan, and Drew had all been right: It felt good to be alone with God.

On Thanksgiving morning, Cameron slept late and awoke to the delicious aroma of his mother's cooking. He showered and dressed then went to the kitchen, but instead of finding her leaning over the stove, he found both of his parents in the dining room adding a leaf to the table.

"Who else is coming?" he asked.

"Tricia Sloane just called and accepted your mother's invitation to dinner." His father snorted as he shoved the table leaves together. "I keep hoping your mother gets tired of Tricia."

Cameron gulped hard then asked as adrenaline roared through every vein, "Justin isn't coming, is he?"

"But of course." His mother forced a bright smile. "I couldn't invite his parents without also inviting Justin and his brother Ned, not for Thanksgiving."

Ned, too? Suddenly the sky turned black, hail beat against the windows, and coyotes howled—or so it seemed. Why would his mother ruin a week that had been as close to perfect as Cameron could imagine?

"Valerie," his father turned to his mother, "I thought Tricia said she'd help you."

"She will." With a thorough knowledge of the subtle turns in the roadmap of his mother's voice, Cameron recognized irritation in her terse tone and a stiff smile. "I may have said eleven," she continued with a hint of self-defense. "You know Tricia. I don't expect to see her before two. Don't worry. I'm fine."

"Can I help?" Cameron asked. He doubted Mrs. Sloane would show up before four.

"No. You and your father can go upstairs and watch the game."

Despite her stiff smile, Cameron decided to oblige her, at least for a while. Besides, the absence of Mrs. Sloane dimly suggested that the entire Sloane family might beg out.

At three, Cameron went downstairs for a Sprite and found his mother no longer smiling as she dashed between stirring a pot on the stove, washing another one, and reading a recipe. That she was still alone might have perturbed her, but it relieved him. He pulled a wooden spoon from a bubbling red mixture. Cranberry sauce. "I can stir this."

"Sweetheart, I *really* am fine. Everything is almost ready. But thank you anyway. Go on back upstairs."

Cameron was now certain that his mother was far from fine. Calling upon experience gained at the Park Street Diner, he quietly cleaned a few dirty pots, stirred things on the stove that bubbled, and pulled things that looked brown out of the oven while his mother continued to insist that he go upstairs and relax. At 3:40—twenty minutes before the guests were supposed to arrive—Cameron consented to his mother's admonishments and climbed the steps, believing that the likelihood of an enjoyable dinner had decidedly improved.

After Cameron returned upstairs, Valerie set out eight tomatoes that needed to be sliced in half, topped with cheese, and grilled. How many hours, she wondered, had she spent, over the life of their friendship, waiting for Tricia Sloane? Too many. She lined up the tomatoes on a baking sheet, but other unpleasant aspects of Tricia's friendship jeered at her for attempting to please her self-absorbed friend.

Yes, that's right, my dear, the shadows sneered as she sliced a tomato in half. *Of course you're the one who does all the work, which is why Tricia is always late.* Valerie leveled the blade on top of another tomato. *You're so disgustingly dependable .... Tricia waits a while and then shows up with her other friends—her real friends—and has all the fun. But of course, she's your best friend.* Valerie jabbed the knife into the soft vegetable. "Ouch!" Her finger shot into her mouth. She checked the cut and then stuck the wounded digit under the faucet to stanch the bleeding. After wrapping a paper towel around it, she continued. The cut wasn't deep, so the bleeding would soon stop.

Valerie, sweetie, the shadows taunted, *why does she always have to help Mary Hayes "take care of her mother," even though Mary Hayes rarely visits her mother? You're such a delightful sucker!* Valerie placed the tomato halves in a line on a baking sheet and then brushed each with olive oil, but the shadows refused to relent. *You may not think Becky is a very good cook, but her plain-Jane apple pie will be here on time, and it'll taste good. Ha! You wouldn't know a good friend if your life depended upon it.* Valerie grated the cheese and pressed past the echoes in her head, but still they chided her. *You should pick your friends more wisely. After all, you may need them. Silly, silly woman!*

At five minutes until four, neither Tricia nor any of the Sloane family had appeared. Valerie rubbed her temples to loosen the tension. Five minutes later, at the exact time she expected her guests—and exactly when everything was ready—Tricia, stylish as ever in black ankle slacks, sequined stilettos and a tight knitted top, appeared at the door.

"Oh, Valerie," she gushed, "I am so sorry I'm late. Oh"—she leaned close and whispered— "you might want to go put on some lipstick." She glanced in the direction of the dining room and instantly threw her hands up. "Look at the table! It is just gorgeous, and the house smells divine! Oh, I almost forgot." With pomp and pride, she handed Valerie a grocery bag. "I felt so bad about being late," she said, smiling through hooded eyes, "that I brought you a dessert. I knew Becky's pie would be pretty sad, so I decided to rescue you from the embarrassment of having to serve it."

Valerie forced a "thank you" as she opened the bag—and then froze. Had she, at that moment, been able to send telepathic waves, then anyone within a ten-mile radius who had ever bitten through their tongue in silent agony would have turned their heads in the direction of her lamenting cry, for within the bag sat a pumpkin pie, still frozen, and a no-name tub of imitation whipped cream, also frozen hard. "That was sweet of you." Valerie's smile congealed, and her stomach soured. She set the pie and whipped topping on the countertop.

"Well," Tricia chirped, "I'm at your disposal. Just tell me what to do." A hundred horrible suggestions popped into Valerie's head, including "Please leave," but Tricia paused only long enough to take a breath. "I'm surprised Becky isn't here already," she continued mercilessly. "She's usually so punctual."

And you're punctual? Valerie corralled her indignation, took a deep breath, and recharged her smile. "Becky called. They're almost here. Also, Andrea and Shaun called. They're only a few minutes away. Where are the boys and Alan?"

Before Tricia could answer, the back door flew open and banged against the chest that stood behind it. "You better not have invited my father," Justin hollered. "After what he just did, he can go to hell ...." He staggered backward, "He needs to go play in the street—a busy one."

"Justin, stop it!" Tricia screamed back.

"Isn't that what Dad tells me ... go play in the street?"

Valerie stifled a gasp and stepped back.

"What are you talking about?" Tricia snapped.

"You know exactly what I'm talking about. Thanks to you, he disinherited me."

"You can't blame me for that!"

Valerie turned as Randy, with Cameron on his heels, bounded down the steps from the media room.

"Yeah, I can!" Justin sneered as he mimicked words Valerie had heard from Tricia's lips: "I didn't do anything to deserve this." He went on, mocking his mother with effeminate sarcasm, "I love your father." His lip curled, and his eyes squinted. "You don't fool me! Dad has pictures of you. Or didn't you know?"

"Justin!" Randy commanded. His low but icy voice pierced the air and pushed Valerie back against the cabinet. "You will not speak or behave like that in my house. Apologize to your mother. Now!"

"You're not my father." His snide, foul mood contorted his features, deforming what might otherwise have been a handsome face. "I don't have to listen to you." Justin lowered the volume while raising the level of his insubordination. "And Cam, you can count the days till Lydia tosses you aside for a Wall Street Dukie."

"Young man," Randy commanded, "unless you apologize to everyone here—especially my wife—and improve your attitude, then you need to leave. Immediately."

"Well spoken, Randy." A slow, acerbic baritone voice caught everyone's attention. "I didn't know you had it in you."

Valerie turned to see Alan Sloane—slender and stylishly dressed in a trim Italian suit, and standing in the doorway to the front hall. Horror closed her throat upon seeing Charring Appleton standing behind him. If Alan's sharp eyes and outsized presence had long intimidated Valerie—though she stood an inch taller—she judiciously avoided Charring, a slim, raven-haired beauty who, with bloodred lipstick and hooded eyes, could with a glance make wolves quiver.

Charring's presence, however, seemed to increase Randy's determination, but Alan still commanded the room. He turned to his son, "Hey, boy. You need to listen to him."

Justin had long been a walking trove of bad behavior, but Alan's attack had been heartless and unwarranted. Randy—who stood between father and son, may have reached the same conclusion for now fire flashed in his eyes and his icy voice barked. "Enough! Alan, not another word. You and Charring need to leave. Now! Cameron, take Justin to the car. You and I will drive him over to his Uncle Brent's house. Tricia—" He scanned the hall and kitchen. "Tricia?"

"I think she's in our bedroom." Valerie's voice shivered.

Just then Justin yelled. "I said you can't talk to me like that!" His mouth gaped open, but nothing more came out. He slumped onto the last step just in front of Cameron.

"Cameron," Randy kept his eyes fixed on Alan, "get him into the backseat of the car and stay with him. Alan, I don't know what you're waiting for."

Seeing Cameron reach under Justin's armpits, Valerie wanted to help, but her feet wouldn't move. She turned back to see Alan smirk at her husband, a noxious, cruel smile.

"Come on, honey," Alan said with silver-tongued sweetness. "We know when we're not welcome."

With Alan and Charring out the door, Randy helped Cameron walk Justin to the car. Valerie followed but stood several yards back. Justin slumped into the backseat, still muttering in maudlin tones about his parents' failures. Randy turned to Cameron. "I should go with you, but I need to take care of Tricia." The thought of Cameron driving alone with a very intoxicated Justin awakened Valerie's deepest fears, but what could she do? At least it wasn't dark yet.

"Dad"—she strained to hear Cameron's voice— "I've taken Justin home in this condition lots of times." She shuddered yet craned her head to see Justin. Perhaps his belligerence had dissipated. She certainly prayed that it had. "I'll be all right." Cameron turned to his mother. "I'll be careful."

Valerie tamped down her fear and watched her son back out of the drive. She continued to watch until he disappeared down the street. Then she went back to the kitchen and collapsed into a chair. Why hadn't she listened to Becky and others who tried to dissuade her from the folly of helping Tricia?

"Valerie." Randy rested a hand on her shoulder. "Are you all right?"

She couldn't answer but instead lifted her chin and composed herself. "We need to check on Tricia."

She had guessed correctly. Tricia had run to the master bedroom and lay sprawled, face down, across the bed, sobbing. "Tricia." Randy pulled her arm up and attempted to turn her over. "It's time to go home."

"I can't," she wailed, then pulled her arms under her chest where he could not reach them.

As he tried again, Valerie heard voices coming from the kitchen. "Shaun, Andrea," she called, "is that you? We're in the bedroom. Your father needs Shaun's help."

When her daughter and son-in-law entered the bedroom, Valerie almost cried, but both tears and explanations needed to wait. Shaun and Randy struggled to lift Tricia, then carried as much as coaxed her to the car. After they left, Valerie stood, watching the empty driveway, until Andrea, with her son asleep on her shoulder, took Valerie's elbow.

"Mom, why don't you sit down in the sunroom? You can hold Jacob for me."

Valerie turned and sighed as she brushed her grandson's head. How had she managed to raise such a kind and loving daughter? "No. You take care of him. I need to lie down for a few minutes."

She returned to her bedroom and dropped into a lounge chair. Her chest collapsed. For a while, she simply stared into space. Nothing had gone as she had hoped.

Perhaps ten minutes later, she rose and walked toward the kitchen. Her heel caught the carpet, tripping her halfway down the hall. She caught her balance then leaned against the wall and hung her head. From the moment Justin slammed the back door against the chest, to the sight of Randy dragging Tricia out of her bedroom, no more than ten minutes had elapsed, but it felt like a lifetime. She clutched her collar to her throat. Why had she let such terrible people destroy her family's celebration? "Imprudent folly" came the answer, which she accepted. Instead of arguing, she heaved a sigh and continued toward the kitchen where she found Andrea busily filling a dish with potatoes. "Is Jacob asleep?" she asked.

"Yes, he's in the crib. Here, why don't you sit and talk to me."

Valerie glanced around the kitchen where Andrea had been hard at work while Valerie rested. "Thank you." She embraced her daughter and then held her at arm's length. "I'm so sorry."

"It's going to be fine." Andrea took her mother's hands and smiled. "You always said that God uses our mistakes for his good. —Oh! That's the doorbell. Wait here."

Andrea disappeared around the corner and returned a moment later with Nathan, Becky, and Matt. "Look what Aunt Becky brought." Andrea held out a steaming apple pie, replete with a woven crust.

"I'm sorry we're late, but the pie took too long." Becky shrugged. "Then we had to go back for the phone."

The cause of their delay didn't matter; Valerie was too happy to see them to care. She started to explain the absence of everyone else. "Um ... Randy is—"

Andrea stepped forward with perfect charm. "Dad, Shaun, and Cameron should be back any minute. Uncle Nathan, if you and Matt will take the leaf out of the table, I'll reset it. Aunt Becky, you can help Mom fill the serving dishes. Mom's cooking always smells so good, doesn't it?"

Not surprisingly, Becky and Nathan pitched in and helped without asking questions. Though lacking both energy and enthusiasm, Valerie pulled the au gratin potatoes from the oven, relieved to find that Andrea had reheated them. Soon Becky and Andrea had restored order to her meal and assembled a table filled with elegance and love.

"Hey, Mom, this looks great." Cameron wrapped his arms around her shoulders; she had not seen him come in. She braved a smile as he whispered in her ear. "You're the greatest. We all love you."

Valerie fought back her tears. Since they would have been from self-pity, she turned and hugged her son. "I love you too. What would I do without you?"

When Randy and Shaun returned, her energy revived. For the next several minutes, bustling laugher and chatter filled the house as her family dashed between the kitchen and the dining room. The grotesque consequences of her arrogance—yes, as much as her folly—had not ruined the entire day. And her family seemed to have forgiven her. Trent called from Richmond, closing the circle of her family.

Later, the dinner dishes were removed, and Valerie sliced Becky's apple pie while Matt chided his cousin. "Hey, Cameron. Does Andrea know about your new love life?"

Valerie brightened but then felt her heart sink. A new girlfriend? How had she missed such an important part of Cameron's life? However, curiosity trounced shame. "Is she a *real* girlfriend?"

"Yes, Aunt Valerie. Cameron's in love." Matt laughed. "He told us all about her yesterday. You couldn't shut him up."

Valerie looked at Cameron, who had turned bright red. "You didn't tell me!" She laughed. "Shame on you."

"It's not serious. That's why I hadn't said anything."

"Don't believe him," Matt chimed in with a wide grin and an elbow in Cameron's side. "It's Lydia Carpenter."

"Double shame on you!" Valerie turned to Cameron. "Lydia's a delightful young lady."

Cheer soon eclipsed any lingering hints of chaos as the last piece of the pie landed on Matt's plate and quickly disappeared. Valerie turned to Becky. "That was the best apple pie I've had in a very long time." And she meant every word. She turned to Randy, but the look in his eyes startled her. She saw kindness and—perhaps? Yes—forgiveness and a smile she had not seen in many years. Her embarrassment and weariness faded behind the joyous reminder of why and how much she loved him.

37

At five-thirty on Friday evening, Lydia picked out a skirt and then stood in front of a mirror. She turned sideways. With an hour and a half remaining before her date with Cameron, she put on the skirt and cinched the waistband. That didn't look good, so she pushed it down on her hips, but that made her waist look thick. Out it went.

She changed into a pair of pants. Still dissatisfied, she replaced the pants with a trim pencil skirt that sat just below her waist. She then tried on three sweaters, two necklaces, and five earrings sets before deciding that nothing looked good, but no other choice remained, let alone anything better. Sighing, she picked an outfit and then joined her mother in the kitchen.

"I can't believe this," she exclaimed. "I haven't been this nervous since high school."

"You look very nice."

Slightly irritated, Lydia stared at her mother, who laughed but also said it was "cute" that Cameron had asked her out. Great! Just what Lydia needed, a sassy mother, though, her mother was also sympathetic. She knew everything about Cameron, which sometimes seemed to be more than Lydia knew. Lydia readied a good retort, but the doorbell rang. She closed her eyes. The moment she had longed for and feared had come.

Her mother gave her a quick hug. "Have fun." Then she turned her toward the front door. Lydia paused with her hand on the knob, took a deep breath, and finally opened it.

"Ready?" Cameron asked with a disarming smile.

"Yeah." When he took her hand, she felt as warm as on a hot August day. *Relax!* Nothing good would follow if he thought she was nervous.

Cameron had made reservations at the Milestone Restaurant, an upscale establishment located in a renovated nineteenth-century carriage factory one block from Main Street. She had not expected him to choose such a sophisticated establishment, "an urbane dining experience," as one magazine described it. Inside, ancient exposed beams and sleek decor surrounded guests while waiters and waitresses clad in white business shirts, dark blue jeans, and indigo denim waist aprons hurried among the tables. An occasional clatter from the partially exposed kitchen increased the casual but refined atmosphere.

The hostess seated them at a table on the upper level overlooking the pastry chef, who drizzled icing and dusted sugar over scrumptious desserts. The activity, though, held little of Lydia's attention. Cameron owned the rest, because, as she reminded herself, both the night and her relationship with him might be fleeting. "Have you been here before?" she asked.

"No. I asked Paul, but he was clueless. Trent suggested it after a friend said that I should take you here if I intended to impress you."

"I am impressed." As her heart lifted, sadness flickered in his eyes when he mentioned his brother. She hesitated and then asked about his sibling. After all, he had said he liked her candor.

"It's a long story." Cameron described a family history that made her heart ache for him and his family. "I'm used to it now," he said, smiling through a shrug. "Trent and I keep in touch. His wife Jacqueline is cool." He pointed to the menu. "The veal scallopini sounds good."

"It does, but I'll have the lobster ravioli. By the way, I heard that your Aunt Becky made an apple pie for your family's Thanksgiving. Was it good?"

"Excellent. How'd you know? Oh ... yeah." He laughed. "Mom said she saw your grandmother in the grocery store. I don't think Mom has ever met a stranger."

The waitress arrived to take their order. When she left, he reached across the small table and took Lydia's hand. While he described visiting his uncle's farm, his fingers, playing with hers, held most of her attention. "It was fun to ride alone even if Amos—"

"Now isn't this cute," someone snarled in a loud voice. "Hey, Cam, I hear you've turned into a teetotaling prig."

Lydia looked up into the trademark sneer of Justin Sloane. Anger surged, but not a single nerve twitched. Julia Gielzecki, a former classmate of Lydia's, stood behind him. The two—he in sloppy jeans and Julia in an off-the-shoulder sweater and skinny jeans—were the last two people Lydia wanted to see, especially now. Cameron squeezed her hand, catching her eye. He released her hand, wrinkled his brow, and turned to Justin.

Justin hunkered down, looking more weasel-like than ever. Julia wore her perpetual ennui. Some things hadn't changed. "Aren't you going to invite us to sit down?" Justin pulled a chair away from another table and sat down, straddling the chair's back, at their table.

"Hi, Cameron." Julia shrugged, adjusting the wide strap of an oversized bag that hung from her shoulder. Turning to Lydia, she grunted, "Hi," and then tugged on Justin's jacket. "Come on. The hostess has a table for us, and the rest are already there. You don't need to bother Cameron."

"No. I'm going to sit here," Justin glared at Cameron.

Lydia's eyes darted between the intruders. Go *away!*

"Pull up a chair," Justin aimed his retort at Julia without the decency of looking at her. "I've got things to discuss with my *best* friend. Right, Cam?"

Julia continued grinding a piece of chewing gum and shrugged. "Suit yourself." She turned and followed the hostess.

"So Cam," Justin said loudly, slurring his words, "what'd your dad think about yesterday?" He glanced at Lydia. She allowed a faint smile but wanted to recoil from Justin and anything near him. He turned back to Cameron. "Did ya see Dad's face? What a jerk!" He leaned close to Cameron. "You know you'll pay for what you did."

Cameron sat stone still with his eyes fixed on Justin, who swayed. Startled, Lydia leaned away to avoid his alcohol-drenched breath. "You betrayed me, Cam, taking me back to Uncle Brent's house." Justin glanced at Lydia, sneered, and then fixed a curdling glare on Cameron. "I hate you, man!"

As Justin's truculent monologue continued, Lydia noticed his face wasn't as ugly as she remembered. His cleft chin and deep-set hazel eyes, buried beneath a thick brow and a stock of chocolate-brown hair, gave him an air of mystery, but his perpetual pinched scowl, puckering the bridge of his nose, emanated from his dark and miserable heart.

Cameron looked at Lydia, catching her attention. A relaxed strength echoed from his fierce eyes and set mouth, assuring her that he, not Justin, was in charge. *Be patient*, he seemed to convey. Lydia nodded, leaned back, and dropped her hands into her lap.

"That twit Charring isn't worth hating," Justin snarled, causing the couple at the next table to turn around and stare. "But it doesn't touch how much I hate Uncle Brent. He's nothing but ...." A torrent of profanity followed. "He's always preaching at me." Justin continued his rant, but his volume dropped, and his vocabulary dwindled until it was little more than slurred incomprehensible sounds. Cameron motioned to a waiter, who came quickly and leaned close. Cameron whispered to him. Meanwhile, Justin revived a degree of dignity and turned to Lydia. "I see Cam got you back."

She recoiled, but a shadow in his eyes quickened an unsettling feeling of sympathy. Until that moment, he had been merely an obnoxious drunk who crossed every line and ignored every warning. He tilted toward her, banishing that impression, but Cameron, almost jumping from his chair, came to her defense.

"That's enough!" he commanded Justin without raising his voice. His taut cheeks and mouth exuded calm and acute attention. When he nodded his head to her, maturity enveloped him, assuring her that Justin would not touch her. "I hate to do this, but I have to take him home." Her heart seized as she watched him turn to Justin. He measured each move. Like a police officer with his gun pointed at a dangerous criminal, his eyes telegraphed his intention: Justin would not harm another family.

A day or a year earlier, Lydia had found nothing in Justin to like, but as she watched him, she wondered how he had caused her to conjure such opposing feelings as disdain and sympathy. The thought was neither pleasant nor avoidable since Justin had, yet again, ruined everything between herself and Cameron. A slim chance existed that her assessment was premature, but caution led her to think otherwise.

Cameron stood. "Come on, Justin." He reached under Justin's upper arm and whispered something in his ear. Justin stiffened, but Cameron stood and smiled. "Let's go outside and have a cigarette."

"You don't smoke!"

"Doesn't matter. Come on."

The waiter reached under Justin's other arm, but Justin jerked away. "Don't touch me!"

"Give it a break." Cameron lifted him. "He's got the cigarettes."

"You want to get yourself fired?" Justin spit at the waiter.

Cameron nodded to the waiter and again whispered to Justin, who looked more puzzled than angry. As the other two led him out of the restaurant, a few patrons turned to look but mostly ignored them. Still, as Justin drooled and stumbled over his own feet, Lydia wished with all her heart that he would disappear. Once outside, Cameron handed Lydia his keys and seated Justin on a low brick wall. As she walked to his car, she prayed again that Justin would vanish and leave her alone with Cameron.

When she returned with the car, Justin appeared docile and somber. Cameron helped him into the backseat and Lydia climbed out, leaving the door open for Cameron. As she walked around to the passenger's seat; she never took her eyes off Justin. Cameron slid behind the wheel, locked the doors, and spoke to Justin. "Behave, or I'll take you to your uncle's."

"Really?" Lydia asked. Why not go straight to his uncle's?

Cameron lowered his voice and spoke to Lydia. "If I left him at the restaurant, he'd be back on the road. I'm sorry."

His eyes, his shoulders, and even his hands said he had no other choice. Lydia, though, begged God to let them return later. With every passing streetlight and with Justin muttering in the backseat, Lydia's hope that God might yet grant her petition slipped further away.

Several minutes later, Cameron stopped in front of a compact, brick, ranch-style house. "Damn it! You said you'd take me to my brother's," Justin yelled, but Cameron ignored him. When Cameron opened the car door, Justin lurched from the car and threw a punch but lost his balance. As he fell to the ground, an older man ran from the house with a young man close behind. The two, neither of whom looked disturbed by Justin's behavior, lugged him into the house. Cameron took Lydia's hand and followed.

Inside, the neat displays of local pottery, country antiques, and an interesting variety of decorative roosters and chickens spoke of a home more used to gracious welcomes and quiet discussion than the noisy cursing that emanated from a rear bedroom. Lydia tightened her grip on Cameron's hand. A woman's voice, gentle and calm, wove in and out through the melee.

A minute later, the older man returned. "Won't you stay for a while?" He glanced at Lydia. "Forgive me. I didn't introduce myself. I'm Justin's uncle. Please call me Brent."

Cameron opened his mouth, ready to introduce Lydia but she extended her hand. "I'm Lydia Carpenter." Although he had addressed Justin's uncle as "sir," "Brent" seemed appropriate since it disinherited him from his surname and the foul people attached to it. She nodded politely but wanted only to leave. Now.

Instead, Brent motioned to two wingback chairs covered with a Williamsburg blue, diamond-and-dot fabric. "My wife will join us in a minute. Please. Have a seat."

"Thanks, but we can't stay." Cameron reached for the doorknob.

"Wait. I need your help." Behind his calm and polite veneer, panic etched lines across Brent's brow and tense cheeks. "Please. Won't you sit?"

"My help?" Cameron released the doorknob but did not move toward the chairs.

"Yes. If Justin doesn't get treatment, he'll end up in prison or dead."

Prison wasn't a bad alternative in Lydia's opinion; after all, Justin's father had bailed him out of the legal consequences of Mrs. Duncan's death. Despite the testimony of an independent witness to the 3:00 A.M. accident, Justin's father had miraculously cleared him of a manslaughter charge. Nor had clemency altered his behavior.

"Last week," Brent spoke at a brisk paced despite his deep Southern drawl, "a judge gave him one last chance before sending him to prison. It surprised me because this time, Alan wasn't involved. The treatment program, which is in Raleigh, is strict and effective, or so I've heard. I can make arrangements with my sister, who lives outside Pittsboro. She can pick Justin up at your fraternity house and take him to Raleigh. Everything is ready if I can get him there. I need to stay here; our daughter Cecilia is scheduled for surgery on Monday."

As he stumbled over these words, Lydia noticed two frightened eyes, staring at her from the hallway door. Out the corner of her eye, Lydia saw

Brent turn to her. "It was a godsend when Cameron brought Justin here on Thanksgiving—a godsend."

Brent turned to Cameron and continued, "I'm wondering if you might be able to take him back with you." He glanced between Cameron and Lydia. "Alan has a long, sordid story and only himself to blame." His mouth pursed as his eyes scanned the ceiling. He shook his head and turned to Cameron. "Alan cut Justin off ... from everything. He's done that for years—hiding money in accounts without Tricia's knowledge. Neither she nor her lawyer will ever find it." His lips formed a thin, down-turned line. "I'm doing this for Justin. I can't leave him thinking that he's all alone."

Cameron's mouth tightened, but a visible calm crept over him. Lydia had seen the same infectious, authentic, and reliable peace in her father but not in men her age. "I'll do it, but on one condition." His grip tightened on her hand. "Justin has to be sober, totally sober when I pick him up."

Lydia's stomach pitted. Meanwhile, Brent thanked Cameron and promised to keep Justin sober for the next thirty-six hours.

"I'll pick him up around eight Sunday morning." Cameron opened the door. "I want to beat the traffic."

Since moving to Chalmers, Lydia's family had plied I-85 on the Sunday after Thanksgiving to visit her mother's sister, Aunt Deborah. Too often, fender benders had snarled traffic along the highway, even along the eight-lane stretch between Greensboro and Durham. The vast strip of asphalt shared by Interstates 85 and 40 was trouble enough, but Justin could make it worse.

After they said goodbye to Brent, silence followed Lydia and Cameron to his car. He closed her door and climbed into the driver's seat, but sorrow spoke to her. "I guess I should take you home."

No! The night was still young. Her jaw clenched, and silence took up residence. She was ashamed that, while he thought of others all along, she had thought only about herself. She wondered what it was that bound Cameron to Justin, in whom goodness seemed such a remote possibility. But something did. Her responsibility was to let go and trust not just God but Cameron. "I guess so."

Cameron pulled away from the curb and into the circle of a streetlight. "Cecilia, Mr. Sloane's daughter—the girl we saw in the hall—she's Justin's half-sister from one of Mr. Sloane's girlfriends. He, Justin's father, wanted the woman to get an abortion, but she wanted to keep the baby. According to Mom, it wasn't the first time, but his brother, Brent Sloane, decided to make it the last. He threatened to expose his brother's other shady dealings if he didn't help Brent and his wife adopt the baby.

"Cecilia has a good relationship with her birth mom. Even though she hasn't married or had other children, she doesn't seem to mind that her daughter calls the Sloanes mom and dad. That took a lot of courage on the birth mother's part." He shrugged. "Maybe someday she'll marry, and Cecilia will have lots of family. That's what her birth mother wanted for her child—a family with siblings, including my cousin Ethen who you saw. There was talk that Justin's dad threatened her, but who knows. Regardless, agreeing to Brent's terms was probably the only good thing he ever did." Darkness returned and retreated as streetlights illuminated the car and then faded, one after another.

"Want to know something really strange?" he asked, sounding parched and tired. "I have a weak sense of smell. It's like being nearsighted; only instead of being unable to see well, I miss subtle odors." He half laughed. "It made living in a frat house easy, though I can smell day-old spilled beer. Now that's gross, but mild odors go right past me."

"Is that bad?"

Cameron grinned and then laughed, a hearty laugh that dispelled the gloom. "Obviously you haven't spent that much time around fraternities. Sunday, I won't be able to smell Justin's breath. I'll have to *read* his behavior."

"Oh ... so his breath didn't knock you over when he sat down?"

"No." He laughed, a delightful, infectious laugh.

"I thought it could wilt steel. So what can you smell?"

"Lots of things, but they have to be strong. I can smell Mom's cooking and sweaty socks left out too long, but don't get upset if I miss a subtle perfume you're wearing."

"Then you didn't smell my sweat when we were running?"

"Not once. But you have a scent I can't forget."

At last, the lighthearted mood that marked the early evening returned, but it was too late. Cameron had stopped in front of her house. It wasn't even nine, yet the evening had ended. As they walked to the front door, Cameron again took her hand, but with each step, his somber mood darkened. A gust of wind picked up a few stray leaves and scattered them ahead of her. Maybe Justin's intrusion had been God's way of protecting her, of cautioning her not to become too attached to Cameron. Maybe. Lydia put her key into the front door as Cameron stood close.

"I'm sorry Justin messed things up." His shoulders slumped. "I wanted to start the evening over, but I couldn't get past the thought of driving him to Chapel Hill."

"Then why did you agree to do it?"

"I had to." Lydia looked into his eyes and started. The peace she had seen earlier remained, but now a film of sorrow covered it. "You've been very patient with me." He brushed a strand of hair away from her face, but Lydia wanted to grab his hand, confess that she'd been anything but patient, and beg him not to leave. He took her hand. "We could try again tomorrow night, if you don't have plans."

"I'd like that." Speak of an understatement! If only he wouldn't leave, but he'd made up his mind. She put the key in the lock then turned it.

"Same time?" he asked.

"Yes." A smile escaped. "Good night." She paused as an impulse grabbed her and sent her up on tiptoe. She kissed his mouth—his mouth! Then in the space of a heartbeat, she released his hand and opened the door to slip inside.

"Wait!" Cameron grabbed her wrist. In a step as smooth as if he'd practiced it a thousand times, he slid one arm around her waist and the other around her back, pulling her to his chest. He pressed his lips against hers, moving, lingering, pausing only long enough for his breath to warm her face; then he kissed her again. Entwined in his arms, she felt his heart beating, pounding along with hers. Finally, he loosened his embrace enough to smile. Then he kissed her once more before releasing her.

Blood rushed to her cheeks and tingled her toes as she stepped inside. "Good night."

"Good night." When he smiled, her heart almost stopped.

38

For Lydia, shopping on Saturday after Thanksgiving capped a list of things that gave her hives. Cameron's kiss, however, had left just enough giddy intoxication to keep her from saying no to her mother and Aunt Martha when they asked her to join them. As she wandered between flickering Christmas lights and glittering displays of gift boxes, massive bows, and fluted ornaments, all artfully staged to attract her attention; she revisited the dramatic changes she had seen in Cameron during the previous two weeks—but only two weeks. Of the many roads that lay ahead—potentially divergent roads for Cameron and herself, Lydia feared most the avoidable danger of allowing her heart to convince her head to believe a lie. Thus, with no evidence to the contrary, she wisely remembered that a relationship with him was not likely to last. That said, for the moment, she could rest assured that his warm kiss had not been an illusion.

At seven the doorbell rang. When she opened the door, the most enigmatic smile greeted her, as if two Camerons stood before her. One bowed his head, apologizing for having cut the previous night short, while the other, a sly little devil, visibly relished the memory of wrapping her in a passionate kiss.

"Shall we try again?" he asked with a mischievous glint lighting his eye. "Do you like sushi? If so, we could go to Bistro Izakaya." The devil winked. "It's casual but classy. And since Justin hates sushi, he won't interrupt us."

"Sounds good. And I do like sushi."

The waitress seated them in a corner of the smaller of two rooms that decades ago had housed a gas station. Lydia slipped onto one of the long bench seats that lined two walls. Tables and pairs of accompanying chairs followed the bench around the room. To Lydia's delight, Cameron slid next to her rather than taking the chair facing her. He cradled her hand in his as he described helping his mother prepare dinner on Thanksgiving. "I tried to be helpful by adding sugar to her cranberry sauce, but Mom said it wasn't sweet enough." He grimaced, mimicking her reaction to the sour taste. "That's what she did, then added another cup of sugar. But I suppose you're wondering about the recurring theme—the thorn named Justin."

"Sort of." This should be interesting.

"I can remember a time"—peace settled over him— "before high school when he was one of the best people you'd ever want to know. He was funny, generous, and smart." She listened as Cameron regaled her with descriptions that bore no resemblance to the Justin she knew—descriptions of humorous and occasionally stupid antics that he and Justin once shared. "Justin's grandfather had a farm in a valley west of Chalmers. Once, when we were about eleven, his mom took us out to burn off some excess energy. Well, for a couple of years, Justin had watched his grandfather blow up stumps and beaver dams that blocked two creeks that crossed his field. To Justin that was about as cool as it got, so he decided that using a few sticks would be a good way to make a swimming hole—that's what his grandfather called it—in the big creek. If the beavers could build a small pond, he could build one big enough to swim in. Don't ask if we knew how to build a dam. We were kids, so we didn't think that far into the future. Justin thought that, if it took one stick to blow up a stump and two to blast a beaver dam, then we'd need a lot more to make a hole big enough to swim in.

"So we took a bunch of sticks from his grandfather's shed, and off we went. We dug a hole in one wall of the creek bed and stuffed it full of dynamite. Now you have to realize that Justin hadn't paid attention to the length of the fuse. So he stuffed in a fuse and then guessed at how long it should be. He lit the fuse, and then, like his grandfather, we casually walked away." Cameron's smile grew broad before he broke into laughter.

"So what happened?"

"Well, it was the biggest explosion that area of the county had heard outside of blasting for road work. When it went off, it knocked us flat to the ground. I mean face-in-the-dirt, arms-spread flat out. When we got up, we were covered with mud. His grandfather came running down the field and gave us a whipping and a lecture like I'd never had. We'd scared the pants off him. He thought we'd killed ourselves." Cameron leaned back, laughing.

Idiots! Lydia imagined the appalling sight of two mud-slathered boys. "Did you succeed?"

"Not really, but the hole's still there, and thanks to the beavers, there's also a shallow pond. I suppose it's still there." Again, he broke into laughter.

"I would like that Justin." Though humbled, it was still hard to imagine associating anything humorous with Justin. "When did he change?"

Cameron looked around the room, seeing something other than the restaurant. When he spoke, a soothing rhythm paced his words. "I don't think you know what a mess I made of my life before last summer. Maybe if I had talked to Uncle Nathan sooner," he half smiled. "Dr. Krasotkin would call that Providence." A half grin lit the shadow that covered his eyes. "Sill, maybe I wouldn't have made so many mistakes."

She nudged him. "Someone once equated Providence to a bungee cord jump. We 'will' ourselves into leaping off bridges for the adrenalin rush, but Providence—like the bungee cord, keeps us from slamming head-first into the rocks below. I don't know what that says about free will and consequences, but what would I know about Wyoming, cattle"—she grinned— "or beaver dams if you had been a paragon of wisdom?"

"So true." He laughed and shook his head. "And we helped the beavers."

Seeing his smile fade, Lydia smothered hers, not an easy feat with his shoulder pressed against hers.

"Justin was right. I told you the 'happy ending' to Thanksgiving ... but he came close to ruining the day. This morning, I talked to Uncle Nathan about what happened, and he said much the same thing that you just said. God had a purpose, and I should look for it. But when it comes to Justin, finding something good is difficult."

For the next few minutes, she listened, aghast, as Cameron related the events of Thanksgiving. "I did find something good. If Justin had screwed up Thanksgiving dinner a year ago, I would've been mortified. I would have taken him home and stayed there ... and gotten drunk." Cameron dropped his head, erasing any semblance of mirth. "I'm ashamed to admit it, but that's where I was a year ago when I called you." He lifted his head but didn't smile. "This year, it was like being a medic who comes in after a disaster and does whatever is necessary to help." His fingers played with hers. "Last night, for the first time in forever, I felt sorry for him." A faint smile caught the corner of his mouth. "And I understand why."

Lydia clicked a mental picture of Cameron's eyes, filled with innocent wonder and aged wisdom. Only the waiter, setting their order on the table, distracted her and then only for a moment.

"Looks good." Cameron picked up his chopsticks and gave them a try. "The sad side of having a weak sense of smell is that it affects my taste buds. I can taste spicy!" He rambled for a while, leaving her wondering about the day, years earlier, that changed Justin.

Then he stopped, leaving his meal half eaten, and took her hand. "The *Messiah* concert dredged up a lot of old memories." His eyes scanned the room, but his thumb rubbing the back of her hand said he wasn't distracted but instead had revisited some long-ago day. "I still wish it hadn't happened. It started as one of those bright September days with a crisp, cool morning that—under a brilliant blue sky—later warms into the low eighties. I was thirteen, and Justin had turned fourteen a week earlier. After school let out, we had planned to go to the apartment where Justin's older brother, Ned, lived with his girlfriend."

He shook his head. "That fact didn't go over well with Mom. She didn't like Ned and would've been happy to hear that, because Justin forgot his key, we went to his parents' house instead—which we did, thinking we'd find it empty. It was far from empty. We walked in and found Justin's mom, half dressed, and a notably undressed man. Clothes were thrown everywhere." With his right hand holding Lydia's hand, he reached out with his other hand and spun his water glass, tipping it on the edge of its base and rolling it around, making it behave like a wayward toy top—a precarious trick that left her momentarily fearing for the glass almost as much as for Cameron. "It was embarrassing." He released her hand to spin the wobbling, teetering glass between both hands.

"Justin recognized the man as a supervisor at the bank where his mother worked. Then, just when it seemed like the situation couldn't get worse, it did." He rolled the glass in wider, more erratic circles. "The man tried to buy our silence. He offered us a lot of money. I wouldn't take it, but Justin did. Meanwhile, his mom cried and begged Justin to forgive her, saying it wasn't her fault."

His voice dropped to a quiet monotone while the glass settled into a rhythmic spin. "After we left, Justin swore he'd never forgive her. I don't have the details, but afterward he secretly followed her and promised to make her pay if he ever caught her with another man. He *claimed* he'd caught her a couple of times, but nothing was said. He also claimed that the men had too much to lose if they were indiscreet. Who knows? I only saw the first guy." Cameron set the glass on the table, stared at it for a moment, and then looked around the room. "Later, when someone caught the man in an affair with another bank employee, the bank transferred him out of town. Nothing was said about Mrs. Sloane, though, and she kept her job. I heard that the guy's wife stayed with him. I still feel sorry for Justin's mom. I've never heard rumors that she cheated on his dad. But look what he did to her at our house."

Relieved that he no longer bedeviled the glass, she hoped instead that it carried the weight of his burden. Cameron lowered his head and took her hand, cupping it between his hands. "That day ate at Justin and slowly destroyed him."

"It wasn't your fault. Why did you blame yourself?"

His mouth twitched. "Because we should have gone to my house. I was mad at Mom. She had punished me for doing something stupid, so I didn't want to go home."

"What did your parents say when you told them?"

Cameron leaned his head back and examined the ceiling. "I didn't. Dad would've flipped out. He would've charged off, and—well, it was already bad enough, or at least it seemed that way." He sighed. "I couldn't tell Mom. It would have devastated her. For reasons I can't imagine, Mom always looked up to Mrs. Sloane—as if she thought that woman had it all." A sad smile etched his face. "Mom works hard to find the best in people. She has lots of friends who adore her. Even strangers admire her." He smiled at Lydia. "Mom doesn't think Ned's a dork or that Mr. Sloane is a crook. She doesn't think like that. I guess that's why she encouraged my friendship with Justin. If I had dropped Justin as a friend after that day—which was my initial reaction; I wanted out in the worst way—she wouldn't have believed me. So I turned to Grandpa, Dad's father. Mom's family lives in Birmingham, but Grandpa was great."

Every bit of Cameron, from his fallen chest to downcast eyes, begged for comfort. Lydia looked at her half-eaten meal, then slipped her hand from his grasp and wrapped it around his elbow, evoking a smile. "What was his advice?"

"At first, he said I should tell my parents, but I couldn't. So he listened and told nobody. I could always go to him when things got bad. It wasn't just that he listened; he trusted me. When he died, my life came apart." He smiled at Lydia, a kind and gentle smile that sent her head spinning and set off warning alarms. "These past two weeks have been great. I've thought about Grandpa so much." Cameron kissed her temple.

The waiter arrived and asked if they were finished. Cameron nodded, asked for the bill, and then pressed his shoulder against hers. "During the *Messiah* concert, I almost imagined that Grandpa was with me. I know he wasn't, but the whole thing—the music, the chapel—acted like a magnet, pulling the pieces back together, making me whole again. I remembered Grandpa's incredible faith ... and discovered mine."

Fear and joy leap in her chest: joy for what he said and fear, knowing the likelihood that they would grow apart.

"Esther believes," he continued, "that God takes care of us long before we profess our faith. I think Grandpa would agree, and maybe I should, too. I've played with a lot of matches, but as bad as things were, they could have been worse."

Cameron signed the receipt, thanked the waitress, then as they left, his hand guided her to the door. Once outside—as the restaurant door closed behind them, he leaned closer. His breath warmed her cheek as he wrapped his arm around her shoulder. Seeing a couple approach on the sidewalk, he paused. When they passed, he continued. "Two weeks ago, I thought I'd lost my family, my dreams—and worst of all, I thought I'd lost you."

He touched his temple to her head, igniting alarm. No. She couldn't afford to believe that he meant what he said.

"Last night," he continued with a voice like velvet, "when Justin went crazy, I knew what to do. Saying yes wasn't about pity or some heroic duty. I *had* to say yes. Saying no would have been a gut punch."

He took her hand and lifted it to his lips, touching without kissing it, which she loved but tried to ignore. Fear bubbled and boiled deep within her. *We're too young. It won't last.*

A casual half-smile, which was far from frivolous, caught the corners of his mouth. "By chance .... It's an interesting thought—chance. Uncle Nathan said that nothing happens by chance. Dr. Krasotkin agreed. He said this world doesn't just seem backward. It *is* backward. Last night, I saw Justin from the opposite side of the looking-glass, and from that perspective, the only answer was yes."

"But you're not ... but—" She faltered, seeing that they had reached his car. "Do you think you're supposed to save Justin?"

"No, not at all." He leaned against the passenger door and pulled her against his chest, wrapping both arms around her. She smelled his delicious breath and felt his muscles, taut and warm. "I have to give him a ride. That's all. What can be so hard about that? Well, let me rephrase that. If he's sober, what can be so hard about that?"

"But ... what if he's not?" The words stumbled out of her mouth.

He kissed her forehead, lighting glittering sparklers that filled the air. "I spent the past nine years running from the sight of Mrs. Sloane and that man and everything since, but last night I remembered those two stupid kids, Justin and me, both covered with mud, kids who'd played with dynamite to make a pond. Lydia, don't you see? I'm just like Justin, but I've got great parents. Look at what Justin has."

Despite, or maybe because of Cameron's overwhelming serenity and intimacy, Lydia's fear redoubled. She clenched her jaw and listened, ready to refute any positive statement about Justin. "God is in this," he whispered. Confidence and determination colored his voice. "It's going to be all right."

Her mouth quivered. No, she did not, could not agree.

Cameron lowered his voice. "You're worried."

Of course! "It's a long drive."

"If Justin isn't stone sober, I won't take him. I won't take any chances. I promise."

Every rebuttal turned to mush. Hadn't she insisted that he listen to Jesus? How could she tell him to ignore God's leading just because she didn't like where it might take him? Hadn't she said that God was sufficient in all things? Yes, but she wished she had not.

Cameron whispered in her ear. "I'll call you when I pick him up and let you know whether or not he's sober. Will that help?"

"A little." She tried without success to ignore the electricity in his embrace, the warmth of his breath flowing over her. A corner of her mouth twitched. Fear spread its mighty wings. "You think my faith is strong, but I've never had to lean on God." Cameron again kissed her temple, causing her to stammer. "Please, it ... it's not your job to save Justin."

"I know. It's going to be okay."

Lydia looked around at the half-empty parking lot and composed herself, but the effort deflated. "I wish I was more like my grandmother. Nana's been a widow for more than thirty-five years. After my uncle died last year, I know she's been lonely at times, but she lives in God's hands." Lydia's chest collapsed. "I'm not like her. If Justin does something stupid—"

He released her and stepped out enough to open her door. "Nothing will happen." When she sat down, he asked, "So what shall we do now?"

A cold breeze rustled his hair. He leaned down and kissed her. As fear screamed in her ears, a suggestion popped into her head, a provocative suggestion that would test his sincerity. She watched him walk around the car. Immediately upon sitting behind the wheel, he leaned over and kissed her again. This time he lingered, raised an eyebrow and smiled.

She returned a demure, calculating smile. "We could do something really exciting and sexy."

"And what would that be?"

Her idea was perfect since Cameron knew her mother from working at the Park Street Diner. He had even met her father on a few occasions. "We could go to my house and watch TV with my parents."

His smile widened. "Sounds sexy to me, but are you sure you want me to meet your parents?"

His instantaneous response sent her heart into her throat. "Yeah. You know Mom." From the Diner!

"I remember." Ten minutes later Cameron parked in front of her house but took her hand before opening his door. "Are you sure you want to do this?" she asked. "Your palm is clammy."

"I'm sure."

He leaned toward her and cupped her cheek in his hand, electrifying her all over. He pulled her toward him until his lips touched hers. He lightly brushed her lips as his hand slipped over her ear and his fingers combed into her hair. He knew exactly what to do to turn everything inside of her into pudding. "See?" He brushed his lips across hers. "I'm sure."

As panic and euphoria washed over her, Lydia smiled and watched him open his door and walk around to hers. Alarms clanged, metal against metal. Her future with him was much too uncertain. It was just a kiss! They were too young. She drew her jacket around her and tugged it shut as he opened her door. When they reached the front door, he again kissed the side of her head as she fumbled for the key. He again combed his fingers through her hair and kissed her. Without a doubt, he drew upon years of experience, but she didn't care. He tasted wonderful. Finally, she turned the key in the lock. Once inside, he followed a pace behind her. As they approached the family room, noise from the television greeted them. Seeing them enter, her mother hopped to her feet.

"Hi." Lydia grinned as her surprised family turned to her, smiling. "Mom and Dad, you remember Cameron. And this is my brother Luke and his fiancée, Stephanie."

Her mother offered her hand. "It's nice to see you again. Won't you sit down?" With a flick of her other hand, she motioned to her husband to make space on the sofa. "Marshall, sit over here so they can sit together."

Her father stood and pulled a chair in from the breakfast room then sat down close to Cameron, who had taken a seat at the end of the sofa. Lydia sat in the middle, keeping a polite distance between her and Cameron, who smiled sheepishly as he surveyed the room and her family but said nothing.

"What are you watching?" Lydia asked, hoping to redirect her family's attention away from him.

"A chick flick." Luke rolled his eyes. Regardless, Lydia's ruse had succeeded, that is, with everyone except her father. He watched Cameron's every move with unmasked skepticism.

Ignoring the movie and its noise, her mother turned to Cameron. "Lydia tells us that you've been accepted at UNC's School of Medicine."

"Yes, ma'am." Cameron's hands lay clasped together in his lap.

"I know your parents are very proud of you."

"Yes, ma'am."

"How is your mother?"

"She's fine, thank you."

Lydia glanced between Cameron and her parents. Happily, though, and despite his brief answers, Cameron appeared relaxed. The film finished shortly before eleven, and everyone stood. Cameron nodded to Stephanie and shook Luke's hand, saying he was glad to have met them. As they left, Cameron turned to Lydia. "I need to go too."

Her mother interrupted him. "No need to. Marshall and I are tired. We're going upstairs. You're welcome to stay for a while." She took Lydia's father's hand. "It was nice to see you again. Marshall, tell them good night."

"Good night." Her father kissed Lydia's cheek, but his eyes never left Cameron.

Her mother smiled at them both, took her husband's elbow, and called over her shoulder, "Tell your mom hello." Then she dragged her husband out of the room. As soon as she heard her parents' feet on the stairs, Cameron smiled and took her hand. He sat down on the sofa and pulled her down next to him, turning her around until she comfortably faced him. Again, he knew *exactly* what to do.

"Now." His breath brushed her cheek. "Where were we?"

She ran her fingers across his forehead. Why rush, she thought as she combed his hair back from his forehead. How many nights had she wished to have him all to herself? Too many—foolish thoughts for a friendship confined to the soup kitchen. Now, though, she savored the moment, for it was momentary. On some dreary future day they'd part, and she'd patch her life back together. It wouldn't be much fun, but she'd done it before. She could do it again. Meanwhile, Cameron slipped his hands around her back, paused, and then pulled her close, brushing his lips against hers. Finally she let him kiss her, a warm embracing kiss, both soft and confident, tender and reassuring.

When he loosened his embrace—and instead of letting her go, he pulled her head down on his shoulder, tucking her forehead against his neck. He wrapped one arm around her shoulder in a warm, comforting way that made her feel safe. Through the fabric of his shirt, she listened to his soft breathing and felt the pulse of his heart. Fear retreated for this ephemeral pleasure.

"The year after I graduated from Chalmers High," he said, his breath tickling her ear, "Paul and I went back for the graduation ceremony. I watched the most beautiful woman I'd ever seen walk across the stage. I'd seen her a thousand times but never saw her. She was stunning. After the ceremony, I looked for her, but when I found her, I couldn't even talk to her."

Her insides knotted. Was he talking about her? *No! No! Don't think that!*

He kissed the side of her head. "That day I wanted the whole world to disappear. I wanted to take you in my arms, to hold you like this, but I couldn't even say hello. Instead, I turned around and left."

Panic ripped apart every other emotion, stopping Lydia's heart. She almost sat up but didn't. "I thought I saw you ... turning to leave." She had hoped he had come to see her.

He held her closer, "You may have. I wanted to ... I was close enough. But every mistake I'd made stood like a wall between us." He rested his cheek on her head. "All I wanted was to be like this. To be with you." He pulled her closer, warming her. He kissed her temple and then whispered, "I love you."

What? Had he said that precious phrase? What should she say? She sat up. Terrified, she looked into his eyes, trying to calculate the depth and truth of his words. Did he love her, or had the moment gotten the best of him? *Speak*, she commanded herself. "I love you, too." The words tumbled out of her mouth.

"I'm glad." He smiled and lifted a lock of hair that had fallen across her brow. As he did, his face changed. Though still smiling, he seemed less happy. He kissed her again, a long, warm, tender kiss but less passionate than before. Again, he embraced her, holding her head to his shoulder, but this too felt different, less intense, more fraternal. "I guess I'd better get going." His voice lacked enthusiasm.

What was wrong? She'd said she loved him. What else did he expect? He stood and then took her hand and drew her to her feet. "I told Mr. Sloane that I'd pick Justin up early." As they walked to the front door, he held her hand, but—what was *wrong*? Why did he seem to hurt? How could everything suddenly change? He opened the door and stepped out. "I'll call you in the morning." He then kissed her one last time and pulled the door closed.

Something was wrong, terribly wrong. She looked through the sidelight and watched him walk away, his head down, shoulders slumped, perhaps against the cold. Then she realized her mistake. She flung the door open. "Cameron, wait." As he turned, she ran up to him but stopped a foot short. "I'm sorry. I'm so sorry." His smile became quizzical.

"You were right," she blurted. "I've been pushing you away. Like an idiot, I've thought of myself as Sonya in *Crime and Punishment,* and you were Raskolnikov. I thought I was the patient but unloved and maybe neglected girl whose duty it was to forgive you, but I was wrong, very wrong. I've been Raskolnikov. I've been so egotistical. I didn't mean to punish you ... I never imagined that you could love me." Her eyes searched his. "Yet you have. I want you to love me. And I do love you." She stepped closer and touched her fingertips to his lips. "From the very bottom of my heart, I love you."

He smiled, and before she could blink, he wrapped his arms around her, moving them across her back while her arms slipped over his shoulders in a kiss more passionate than her vivid imagination had ever conjured. Holding him close, she felt her heart pounding along with his. Yes, he did love her.

39

During the night, the wind picked up, rattling the branches outside Cameron's window, brushing them against the glass. At daybreak, the sun broke through, turning the sky iridescent blue, heralding a clear, cold day, but Cameron had been up for a while. He zipped his duffle bag shut and remembered Lydia's arms around his neck and the taste of her lips. Delicious. He called Mr. Sloane, who assured him that Justin was sober. Then he bounded down the steps and into the kitchen, where his mother and a breakfast of scrambled eggs and grits awaited him.

"Mom, thanks." He kissed her cheek then sat down at the table. His father, seated across from him, did not look up from the newspaper that covered half of the table.

"How is Lydia?" his mother asked. His father, if he showed any interest, appeared less than pleased, perhaps even uncomfortable with the question. Having seen similar reactions before, Cameron brushed it off. Soon his father would meet her, and she would charm even him. At 7:45, he threw his bag into the back of his SUV.

"Are you sure Justin can't find another ride?" his mother asked.

"Yes, Mom."

"You're sure?" she asked again, and he nodded again. "Will I see you before Christmas break?"

"Probably not."

"I still wish he wasn't riding with you."

"I'll be fine. Besides, after I pick up Trace outside Rocky Mount, it's mostly back roads. Traffic shouldn't be a problem, but I'll call you when I get to the house. Okay?" She nodded. He kissed her goodbye and smiled. "I'll be careful."

Fifteen minutes later, he was relieved to find Justin subdued, sober, and glowering. While Mr. Sloane loaded Justin's bags into his car, Cameron stepped aside and called Lydia.

Lydia poured a cup of tea and then pulled out a chair and joined her mother in the breakfast nook.

Mona Lisa, not her mother, looked up and smiled. "Well, last night must have gone very well."

"Yes! I had a great time." Lydia flashed a smile, daring Mona-mom to ask more.

"Good." Mona returned to her book, ignoring the invitation.

"Oh, Mom. He said he loves me!" Her mother closed the book and listened as Lydia recounted the entire evening. Halfway through, Lydia's cell phone rang. Seeing Cameron's number, she grinned as Mona smiled. "Hi."

"Good morning, Beautiful." His voice sent tingles all over her. "You can rest easy. Justin is his normal sour self."

"Okay." But she still wished Justin wasn't riding with him. "Call me when you get to Chapel Hill."

"I promise, but I was also wondering if I could come by tonight, say about seven?"

"That's fine."

"Good." Cameron paused for a second. "I want to ask you something."

Oh. Lydia hesitated. What couldn't wait until Friday, when they had made arrangements to meet. "Are you offering any hints?"

"No. I've said enough," he said with a laugh.

"Oh, I almost forgot," Lydia interjected. "I have to pick up a friend at the airport at six. I'll be back by seven. But call when you get to the house."

"I will."

"Okay. Bye." Now her worries could begin in earnest.

Cameron ended the call and climbed into the car. Justin, whose face resembled a perturbed bulldog, sat hunched over, leaning against the door. After riding in silence for ten minutes, Justin took his earbuds out and turned the phone to blast level. Cameron pulled over, took Justin's phone, and then put it in the trunk. Justin snorted and cursed but hunched into the seat.

To lighten the fetid silence that followed, Cameron turned the radio on, but they couldn't agree on a station. He turned it off and recalled various childhood antics that they had shared. The tactic worked but only for a while. As they passed High Point, Justin grew restless and dredged up nettlesome memories. Gritting his teeth, Cameron turned the radio back on, but Justin complained about everything, so Cameron turned it off.

Justin snorted. "So tell me. If God is so good and he's everywhere, why is there evil?"

"I don't know," Cameron retorted.

"Yeah, but you must have some idea."

No, he didn't.

"Come on, Cam. Explain my dad. He's gone to church his whole life, but what good did it do? Want to know what he said when I asked?"

"What?" *This should be interesting.*

"He doesn't believe in good or evil—or heaven or hell for that matter. Sweet." Some cruel thought twisted his frown. "It's all a front. He and Charring are a perfect match." Justin tossed a wadded-up paper towel at Cameron. It dropped to the floor without reaching the console. "They hooked up during church. And of course nobody said anything, but he complains about people who mind his business." Justin turned to stare out the window, grumbling unintelligibly. At least he wasn't ranting. Then he turned and snapped, "You didn't answer me. If God's so good, why does Dad get a pass and I don't?"

"I don't know."

"Really? Well, God is neither powerful nor loving," he mumbled, then blurted, "because Dad always floats to the top . . . Scum!" Justin grabbed his stomach and laughed or rather howled.

Having no interest in discussing theology with Justin, he said nothing. They passed Greensboro while Justin spewed obnoxious proclamations and asked irrelevant questions. When they reached Burlington, Justin dropped the pretense of civility. "Hey, remember when I fixed you up with Lydia? It was really fun watching you make a fool of yourself."

Cameron contemplated the possibility of simply stopping the car and dumping Justin on the shoulder. Instead, he ignored the attacks and kept driving.

"So. Is she as frigid as everyone says?"

Cameron shot a glance at Justin. "Drop it, Justin."

"Ooh. Touchy, touchy. I heard Lydia's the talk of the fraternity, and you know how guys talk." Justin punched Cameron's arm to make sure he'd heard him, but Cameron focused on the traffic, which had increased in size and lowered its speed. Justin's bile turned ugly. "Yo, dude. What'd she say when she found out about Rita and Addie?" Justin howled with laughter. "Or doesn't she know that you lived with both of them? Sweet! Can I tell her?"

Cameron's anger reached a boil, but he calmed himself by imagining Justin tied to the hood of his SUV like a dead buck. It'd look cruel, except to passing drivers who had to listen to him flapping his foul mouth. They'd smile in sympathy for Cameron, not Justin.

Justin's churlish glee intensified. "Does Rita know that you dumped her for Lydia? I mean, Rita's hot! And when she's mad, mm-mm! Honey on hot toast!"

"Give it up!" Cameron snapped. Though Justin was unlikely to give it up, Cameron discovered that his jabs no longer drew blood. He eased his grip on the wheel. Surprisingly, Justin also quieted down. When he turned north at the first exit past Burlington, he caught a glimpse of Justin's icy glare. At least he was quiet.

Ten minutes later Cameron pulled into the driveway that led to the farm owned by Trace's parents. "Wait here." He climbed out of the car. "I'll be right back."

Justin rolled down his window and watched Cameron cross the gravel drive. As his old friend approached Trace's house, a cold wind blew through Justin's heart, and it felt good. Just who did Cameron think he was anyway?

"I overslept," Trace called out. "My parents can drive me in later."

"No problem," Cameron answered. "Take your time."

Losers! Justin watched Cameron disappear into Trace's house. Alone at last, he fidgeted and grumbled for a minute then realized the advantage of his situation. Both the distance to the house—at least a hundred yards, maybe two hundred—and a dense screen of bare branches sheltered him from prying eyes. He reached into the backseat, retrieved his bag, and withdrew the small bottle of rum that a friend had snuck into his uncle's house. Uncle Brent had checked Justin's duffle bag once but didn't recheck it. *Fool!*

Justin unscrewed the cap and grabbed a can of Pepsi from the backseat. After emptying half of the can onto the grass outside his door, he filled it with rum. He leaned back in the seat and drank the entire can. Several minutes later, he repeated the process with another can of Pepsi. Finally relaxed, Justin turned around and leaned his back against the dashboard. With a foot stuck through the open window, he watched the front door of Trace's house and poured another drink—this time minus the cola.

"Cam, you're such a drag," he mumbled. "You're no better than me. Uncle Brent," he shouted, "you can take your piety and stuff it."

He then poured another drink.

After saying goodbye to Trace's parents, Cameron tossed Trace's duffle bags into the backseat and climbed in. Trace climbed in behind Justin. Several miles down the road Cameron noticed that, except for several rants, Justin's mood had improved. Nice, he thought. Attributing the change to Trace's presence, he fell into a light conversation with Trace about their respective holidays.

When Cameron described the brighter part of his Thanksgiving dinner, Justin interrupted him. "Hey, Trace. Cameron's telling only half the story. That's like his new girlfriend. Everything's sweetness and light. Come on Cam, tell him what happened, or should I do the honors?"

"Justin, just shut up. We were doing fine without you."

"Wo-oo," he said in a loopy tone; "sensitive, are we?"

The retort caught Cameron's attention. Justin was no longer sober. Glancing to his right, he also noticed that Justin had unbuckled his seat belt.

346

However, stopping to make him put it back on didn't seem wise. It might supply an opportunity for him to make the situation worse.

"Yeah, Cam," Justin hollered, "tell him about how my old man brought his pathetic honey to dinner at your house. That's right. Cam's mom doesn't know my father very well. It wouldn't have been so bad except Mom was there. Of course, that's why Dad went. They don't care about anybody besides themselves."

Rather than further antagonizing Justin, Cameron motioned to Trace, silencing him.

"Hey, Trace," Justin shouted without turning from Cameron. "Ask Cam how Lydia is in bed. Addie was so hot! Bible Girl looks like she'd be cold as ice, but I bet she's hot as a volcano, all oozy. You know you weren't the first. Cam, don't you want to brag about how good she was? Or wouldn't she let your grubby hands touch her?"

Cameron gripped the wheel and stared ahead, relieved to have chosen the shortcut that took him west of Hillsborough and through a remnant of the ancient Uwharrie Mountain range. Though the grade of the road rose and descended through turns that clung to the hillside, it was safer than the interstate, which Trace's app described as jammed with traffic.

With each mile, Justin's malice seemed to increase. "Cam, ya want to know what the guys said they'd like to do with Lydia? Trace. Tell him what you told me."

"Cam, he's lying! Don't listen to him."

"I know."

"I don't have to lie!" Justin cried out; then he muttered, "Why'd you take this road anyway? It's making me sick ... I gotta piss."

"Put your head back and relax."

"You can't boss me around," Justin hissed. "I get that from everybody else. I don't need it from a loser like you."

Trace suggested swapping seats with Justin, but Cameron said it would only worsen his condition. Meanwhile, Justin moaned and held his stomach. Then as Cameron entered a sharp downward turn in the road, Justin roared to life. "Damn it! Can't you make this thing go straight?"

Suddenly he lunged toward Cameron. He grabbed the steering wheel and pulled it toward him. The SUV swung hard and careened toward the parched roadcut rising beside them. Cameron saw Trace's hand grab Justin's collar and yank him backward, releasing Justin's hands from the steering wheel. Cameron turned the wheel to the left and pressed hard, but not sharply, on the brake. For an instant, he regained control but had veered into the oncoming lane.

A hundred or so feet ahead, the pavement curved to the right around a steep cut in the old mountain. Suddenly a car appeared, coming toward him. In the same lane! Cameron slammed on the brake. Fearing that swerving to the right would send him into the hillside, he yanked the wheel hard to the left, hoping the shoulder was wide enough to avoid a collision. His front wheel left the pavement. *Thump!* The car jerked hard to the left, ripping the steering wheel from his hands. A hole! The embankment! The car plunged over the edge, crashing through branches. Glass shattered.

The car rolled over and then slammed to a stop. A fierce wave of nausea washed over him. He tried to inhale.

After leaving the early service at their church north of Chapel Hill, Albert Greene and his wife Sarah decided to have lunch and spend the afternoon in historic Hillsborough. To avoid Thanksgiving traffic along Interstate 40, Albert decided to take the back roads. Shortly before noon, he rounded a curve and saw a small, silver SUV hurtling at him in his lane.

"Albert!" Sarah screamed as he slammed his foot on the brake. As suddenly as he had seen it, the SUV swerved to his right. He jerked his car to the left. "Oh, my no!" Sarah screamed as the SUV rolled on its side and disappeared over the embankment. "Stop! Stop!"

Albert pulled onto the right-hand shoulder. Then he jumped out and ran to the edge. About seventy feet below, among a tangle of vines, brambles, and trees, he saw the SUV lying on top of a large boulder. A double-trunk tree held the rear portion, but the boulder appeared to have crushed the driver's door. At the sound of a van rounding the bend to his left, Albert glanced over his shoulder and saw Sarah rushing toward it, frantically waving her arms over her head. Albert waited long enough to see the van stop; then he climbed down the embankment toward the SUV.

"A car rolled off the road!" he heard Sarah yell.

"Have you called 911?" the driver asked.

"No ...." Her voice faded as he descended the slope. Two young men, probably from the van, appeared at the top of the slope and joined him as he descended the hill.

"Dad! Dad!" one of the younger men called. "Someone landed over here!"

Albert looked up the hill and saw an older man lean next to the lad, who was pointing to a tangle of kudzu vines. "I'll help him," the older man said. "You go on down the hill."

"Man, does he stink!" the youth said when he caught up with Albert. "He threw up all over himself."

"Is he choking?" Albert hollered.

"No, he's breathing fine," the man called back. "He's okay."

When Albert reached the car, he looked up to see another man and a woman appear at the top of the embankment. The man descended into the brambles. Turning back to the car, Albert tested it and found that it was firmly wedged against the tree and boulder. Satisfied that it would not move, he climbed up onto the door and peered in. A duffle bag moved, and then a hand appeared. "There's one here in the backseat," he called to the lad. "Can you climb around and see into the driver's seat?"

"Yes, sir."

Albert reached in and grabbed a duffle bag, threw it out, and hauled another through the window. Finally, he saw a lanky dark-haired young man. "Don't move," he cautioned him. A large duffle bag hid the driver.

"Ou-wah— What?"

Albert heard the distant whine of sirens. "Take it easy."

The young man, ignoring Albert's admonishment, heaved himself up enough to look between the two front seats. "Where's Justin?" he asked. "Cam ... Cam!"

"Who's Cam?"

"He's my friend." The young man pushed the bag aside and then pulled on the driver's limp arm. "Cameron!"

40

"Is this the residence of Benjamin Asher?"

Hearing the woman's bureaucratic voice asking for Cameron, using his first rather than his middle name, perked Valerie's caution. "Yes, it is. May I ask who's calling?"

"Ma'am, I'm calling from the North Carolina Highway Patrol in Orange County. Are you related to Mr. Asher?"

Valerie's knees nearly collapsed. She grabbed the counter as blood drained from her head, and the room swirled. "Yes, I'm his mother."

"Your son is en route to the emergency room at Duke Hospital in Durham."

"What happened?" No longer steady, Valerie leaned against a barstool. "Is he going to be okay?"

"Ma'am, I can't answer that. The air transport should arrive at the hospital soon. I have some ...."

Helicopter? Nausea swept over Valerie, but she managed not to drop the phone. Helicopters only transported gravely ill patients. The woman continued with a list of information and numbers, but horrific thoughts zigzagged around the voice in her ear. What had happened to Cameron?

She jerked her attention back to the dispatcher. What had she said? Was he conscious? *Pay attention!* Valerie straightened her back. She couldn't help Cameron in such a state. She grabbed a pen and her message book and with mechanical precision started writing phone numbers and instructions.

Finally she thanked the dispatcher and hung up. She drummed the pen against the countertop. Whom should she call? Her mind went blank, but then adrenaline reminded her to call Randy's cell phone. When he didn't answer, she thought about her sister, which was crazy since she lived in Atlanta. Next, she called Becky, but Nathan answered.

"I need your help." The words flew from her mouth. "Cameron's been in an accident. They're taking him to Duke Hospital, but I can't get ahold of Randy. I think he's fishing. The dispatcher said Cameron was on a helicopter."

"Do you know ...?" Nathan started to ask, and then his voice changed. "I'll call Jake Mapson." Unflappable kindness replaced alarm, a trait Valerie admired and now desperately needed. "He lives on the lake, and no one knows it better than him. If Randy's anywhere near the lake, Jake will find him. Becky just came in. I'll let you talk to her."

Valerie listened as Nathan related the details. "It would be helpful," he spoke as much to Valerie as to Becky, "if someone who lives nearby could go to the hospital."

"I can't think of anyone." Becky's voice drew closer. "Hi, Valerie." She spoke into the phone. "Dear, I'm so sorry!" Kindness softened the air. "Can you think of anyone?"

"No. No one." Valerie's voice cracked, and tears burned her eyes, but she stuffed them away. There'd be time for tears later.

"I'll try to think of someone, but in the meantime, I'll call Andrea." Becky's voice eased Valerie's fears. "Andrea knows your friends and what to do. She'll know what bills to pay and handle things here. Pack what you need. I'll be at your house in thirty minutes. If Nathan hasn't found Randy by then, I'll drive you to Durham. Is that okay?"

"Yes." After Becky said goodbye, silence echoed through the house as the walls seemed to do what Valerie could not: breathe. Finally, she followed Becky's instructions. Thirty minutes later, exactly as she had said, Becky appeared at the door. Over her shoulder, Valerie saw Randy jump out of his car and race toward her.

He grasped her shoulders, his eyes wild. "We have to leave right away." He yanked Valerie to his chest, wrapped his arms around her. *Good heavens! He's trembling.*

When he stepped back, Valerie reached up and cradled his cheek in her

palm. "I've already packed, and the suitcases are by the back door …. He's going to be all right." Valerie no more believed her own words than she believed
she could beam herself to Durham, but Randy needed her assurance. Becky
and Nathan arranged cars and drivers. Then, while a phone call occupied
Randy's attention, Valerie took Becky aside. "Since Cameron is seeing Lydia,
shouldn't we call her mother?"

Becky's face went blank, "Absolutely, yes. I'm glad you thought about
Anne."

Valerie was loath to admit that Anne Carpenter's name had jumped
into her mind when the police suggested calling people who might know of
someone living near Durham. Anne had grown up in Durham. For many
years before Becky's and Randy's father Ben "went home," an appropriate term
for his death, Valerie, Becky, Nathan, and the Carpenter family had deftly
shielded the decades-long friendship between Ben Asher and Lois Carpenter
by hiding its existence from Randy. For reasons that Valerie deemed to be
too old and irrelevant to impact the present, Randy had been too willing to
voice his disapproval of the December romance, about which he knew so little
and which warmed Valerie's heart. Both Ben and Lois had been widowed
for several years before the friendship developed. Life goes on, or at least it
should. Thus, she deemed Randy's opposition to be selfish and immature.
Ben, though, had asked that all knowledge about the relationship be withheld
from his grandchildren, as he said, to keep the acrimony between himself and
Randy and not let it boil over and hurt the children. Valerie had agreed, but
only because she loved Ben and thought him to be wise.

No similar attempt had been made to hide the friendship from Marshall's
and Anne's children, though Lois continued to cloak Ben's identity in mystery. Among those in the broader community who knew and loved the older
couple, the charming romance had long been counted as one of the worst
kept secrets in town. After Ben's death, the town had been abuzz with kind
condolences for Lois, which irked Randy. When he blew up at Trent, effectively ending Trent's engagement to Emily Wilson, he also let loose his wrath
on Lois, which seemed cruel and misguided, since Lois neither knew Emily
nor was related to her. Valerie had voiced her opinion by happily honoring
Ben's final request that she and Anne take Cameron and Lydia to work at
the Park Street Diner. "Then leave them alone," he had said, "and see what

they find while helping society's forgotten souls." So Anne's name had been on Valerie's mind long before receiving the call.

"Becky, pray for Randy," Valerie said with a sigh, "that he'll see how much he loves his son. I've lost Trent. I can't lose Cameron."

"Do you want to talk?"

"No. I can't go there." She looked toward the kitchen where she saw Randy pouring ice into a small cooler. "You heard Cameron on Thursday. You should have seen him this morning. He's in love." She shook her head and smiled. "They're in love." Tears rimmed her eyes. "Lois needs to know."

"I'll call Anne. She can call Lois. But we need to get on the road."

"You're right. And tell Lois I love her." Valerie embraced Becky. Nothing justified Randy's hostility toward Cameron. Nothing. If only he would forgive his father, then everyone could come together and pray for Cameron.

She walked up to her husband. "I'm ready."

Randy stuffed something into his back pocket, but his flushed cheeks and red eyes lifted Valerie's heart. *He does love his son.* She flung her arms around him, and for a moment they wept.

For the next two hours, Valerie leaned back, deploying the headrest in the backseat of Randy's car and staring out the window. Randy rode in the front passenger seat after Nathan insisted upon driving. Beyond the window, trees, fields, and sundry buildings whizzed past as they sped northward. Occasionally, Valerie checked on Randy, but mostly she pleaded in prayers, asking God to spare her child.

When they passed Salisbury, Becky texted. "Talked to Anne. You won't believe our luck. Her sister Deborah lives in Hillsborough. She'll go to Duke H and call when she hears something. I'll text you."

Valerie replied her thanks. Now though she needed a plausible reason to explain why Anne's sister would meet them at the hospital without souring Randy's mood. As they passed Greensboro, Becky texted again. "Justin Sloane was thrown from the car. Unharmed and discharged from the hospital. The other boy is being kept for observation."

Valerie texted, "And Cameron?"

"Nothing yet." Becky listed medical terms that Valerie had no stomach to web search but knew Randy had heard the beeps and typing. "That was Becky. She found someone in Durham who went by the hospital." She repeated the disconcerting information then leaned back. Again, she watched the landscape rush past, and waited, and prayed.

Anne looked into the mirror on the back of the visor above the steering wheel. She had tried to hold back tears but had been only somewhat successful. Her eyes looked a bit puffy but weren't red. She pushed the door open and walked up to the front porch of Lois's bungalow, rehearsing the words she would say. At the oaken door, she straightened her shoulders and turned the knob on the ancient buzzer. Steel slats slapped noisily against iron cogs, and then she heard Lois's feet approaching.

"What a pleasant surprise." Lois's eyes turned quizzical. "Are you all right? Please come in."

She opened the door wider as Anne gathered her courage and kept tears at bay. She swallowed the lump in her throat as Lois closed the door and led the way to the small sofa in her living room. Once seated, Anne took Lois's hand and delivered her message. "Becky Stedman called a few minutes ago. Cameron was in an accident on the way back to Chapel Hill this morning." Lois blanched, and Anne steadied her. "I called my sister Deborah. She's at the hospital now, trying to learn what she can. The boys who were riding with him are okay, but we don't know how Cameron is doing. Valerie, Randy, and the Stedmans are on their way up." Seeing Lois's brow knit, she paused.

"Does Lydia know?"

"No. I haven't called her. I want to wait until I know more about his injuries." Anne described Lydia's date with Cameron the previous night and watched as Lois smiled. "They are so much in love. Ben knew this would happen, didn't he?"

"Maybe." A wry smile lifted Lois's cheek. "Maybe it was just wishful thinking." She sighed. "He was a rascal. It'd be just like him to play matchmaker from heaven." Her smile vanished. "Do you have time to drive up to Durham?"

Anne nodded. "Yes. And if anyone asks why I went up, remind them that I'm from Durham, and my sister lives in Hillsborough. Leave the details to chance and their imaginations. News gets around, especially in Chalmers. So, given that Lydia is at Duke, Randy shouldn't be surprised that my sister will already be at the hospital. Besides, Becky thinks Randy is too worried about Cameron to be angry at anyone."

"Are you driving up alone?"

"I want to ask Martha to go with me. She was ... she never made the connection between Ben and Cameron and isn't likely to now, at least not today. Besides, she adores Lydia and would be hurt if I didn't take her with me."

After absorbing the initial shock, Lois seemed to have sorted the information according to the various relationships and estimated the unintended consequences. "You're right. Martha should go with you." Lois led Anne to the door. "Give Valerie my love." She paused and sighed. "Keep an eye on her. She's stronger than she appears, but she's not invincible. And call me. Please."

"I will."

Five hours later, an hour longer than usual due to traffic on Interstate 85, Anne reached the entrance. Tall letters—Duke University Hospital—marched across the top of a structure that reminded her of the Guggenheim Museum. After parking, she and Martha followed signs through the underground walkway that connected the parking deck to the hospital. After making several wrong turns, they finally found the emergency room waiting area.

As Anne passed through the security screening booth, she saw Deborah jump to her feet. Tall and attractive with streaks of light gray highlighting her natural blond hair, she made it hard for strangers to imagine that she had a short, fair-skinned, brunette sister. As always, Deborah wore her simple khaki pants—this time with a plum pullover, with casual ease. She looked perfect. She also looked worried and slightly aghast.

Anne turned to Martha, with her back to Deborah. "Something's wrong. She doesn't look happy." Anne turned back to her sister, whose eyes revealed something less than panic but more than worry.

Deborah took Anne's elbow and pulled her to one side of the wide room. "It isn't good." She turned to Martha with a smile that said she knew a lot more about Martha than Martha knew about her—which was true. "Hi, I'm Deborah." She turned to Anne. "When the car hit the rock, Cameron was thrown against it. It could have been worse. They said that somehow his left arm protected his head—sort of—as the car tumbled. He broke that arm and clavicle, injured his pelvis, and maybe his knee when the rock rammed into his door. They said he came to and tried to talk but then slipped into a coma."

Deborah turned to Martha, nodding her head to make her feel included. "The worst part is that he tore his esophagus and fractured an upper vertebra. I don't know what that means, but the nurse said the tear is rare in guys his age." She glanced between them. "It can be fatal because of massive bleeding, but by God's grace, the medic recognized his symptoms from a class he had just completed and knew how to treat it, on the spot. Otherwise, Cameron might have died right there." Deborah's caution returned. "He didn't completely protect his head. He also has a concussion. Supposedly it's not quite as bad—that's their opinion, not mine—because he's listed as critical."

"Critical? With a head and neck injury?" Martha blurted.

Anne put her hand on Martha's back to calm her. "The outcome was a blessing. Maybe there'll be more blessings." What, though, would she tell Lydia?

Deborah's voice dropped to a whisper. "But there's more."

More?

"One of the boys who rode with Cameron," Deborah continued, "someone named Justin, was still here when Cameron's parents arrived. He needed a ride to the frat house, where his aunt was supposed to pick him up. When Randy heard that Justin's drinking caused the accident, he almost ripped the kid's throat out. Security had to restrain him. Nathan calmed him down, but then he went ballistic on Valerie." Deborah hesitated. Her mouth, though tightly pursed, twitched as she glanced between Anne and Martha. "He started screaming at her. He said something about ruining Thanksgiving. He blamed everything on her and then demanded a divorce."

"What?" Martha gasped. "But why?"

"I don't know, but I've never seen anyone turn so quickly from a loving husband and father into a ... a monster."

"Where *is* Valerie?" Anne asked, leaning forward, eager to find her. "And Randy?"

"Randy and Nathan took Justin to Cameron's fraternity house. Nathan wanted Randy to stay here, but Randy insisted on meeting Justin's aunt.

Heaven knows what more he planned to say, but Nathan seemed able to rein him in. Personally, I'm glad he's not here."

"So where's Valerie?" Anne asked, ready to leap when Deborah finished.

"She's with her sister-in-law—Becky. Am I right?" She glanced at Martha then back to Anne, hiding the fact that she knew Becky and Valerie far better than Martha might expect—which was true. "Becky wanted to find some place quiet, and the chapel was the only option."

Anne's eyes widened, "And where is it?"

"It's right across there," she said, pointing to an interior wall. "It's not far, but there's no easy way to get there. You can stay inside but you'll take several turns and walk nearly twice as far as the other way—which takes you outside and back inside."

Anne scanned the large, fluorescent-lit waiting room lined with rows of metal and Naugahyde chairs filled with half-awake people. Some listened to the announcements; some watched incessantly blaring video screens; others stared into space. The scene remaindered her of nearly every airport terminal she had visited, making the dismal room at once forgettable and impossible to forget—and no place for solitude and rest.

Deborah shook her head. "Neither way is great, but Becky was right to take her there. I'd go outside. You cross in front of an ambulance bay then enter through a set of entrance doors just beyond it. The chapel will be right ahead of you." She stepped back. "I'll wait here."

"Then outside it is," Martha chimed in.

Deborah smiled at Martha. "I'm glad we finally met. I'll see you after a while. Maybe I'll have some good news."

Anne followed Deborah's loose directions, with help from strangers, before stumbling upon the chapel. Inside, they found Valerie lying with her eyes closed and stretched across several padded seats that, only in a pinch, might suffice as a bed. Becky sat next to her head with her hand resting on Valerie's shoulder. Anne dropped to her knees and took Valerie's hand. "Valerie, dear." Anne stroked her hair. "Randy doesn't know what he's saying. He doesn't want a divorce. He's afraid."

Valerie sat up and dried her cheeks with her fingers. "I know," she sighed. "I know." She glanced at Martha and squeezed out a faint smile. "Hi, Martha. We met once or twice. I think you know Cameron's Aunt Becky."

"A little. Our husbands race sailboats together, but I ...." Martha's brow knitted as her eyes turned a furtive glance at Anne. "I'm looking forward to going to some of the regattas next spring."

"Nathen is honored to be one of Jake's mates. I look forward to seeing you there." Becky smiled but quickly turned to Anne. "You're right. Randy is reliving our mother's death." She turned back to Martha. "He was in the car with her in an auto accident. He survived; she didn't. I wasn't in the car—and I'm three years older, so it wasn't the same. We look back and see through different eyes."

Anne patted Martha's shoulder. "If you sense that you can relate to Randy, that's not a bad thing. Losing a parent when you're a preteen or teen is never easy."

Valerie, struggling to smile, if not out of general kindness then perhaps in sympathy for all that Martha had been through, details of which Valerie knew quite well. With a voice as gentle as a sigh, she began. "I'm so glad you came." Sincerity swathed each word with kindness even as weariness wrapped its miserable shroud around her. "I'm afraid you walked into the second half of a very old and sad story. You see, Randy, my husband, thinks he hates his father, and anything related to him. We—that is, Becky, her husband Nathan, Anne, and your mother Lois—thought he would give it up after his and Becky's father died, but his anger increased."

"My mother?" A curious frown wrinkled Martha's brow. "Are you talking about Ben, Mom's friend from church? He was your father ... and Randy's father? Randy is angry at Ben? How could anyone be mad at Ben?"

Melancholy tinged Valerie's answer. "When Randy was twelve, he and his mother Sylvia had just bought ice cream when a drunk driver crossed the centerline and hit them head-on. Sylvia always put him in the backseat because she thought it was safer. He was bumped around but not hurt. Sylvia's seat belt lacked a shoulder strap; it only crossed her lap."

Valerie's chest caved, and her head dropped. "It crushed her pelvis. Shards of it punctured her bowel. The doctors couldn't stop the infection. A month later, the bacteria won. For reasons I don't understand, Randy blamed and still blames his father. Ben had absolutely nothing to do with the accident, but sometimes grief clogs our thinking."

Martha grimaced. "I'm so sorry. That could've been me."

"But it wasn't you," Anne insisted. "God spared you from that grief."

"Martha, we all make mistakes." Velvet kindness cloaked Valerie's voice as if she remembered committing a thousand transgressions and now felt the joy of having been forgiven. "When Becky first told me about her mother's death, Cameron was five and a little blond version of Ben. They were so close and adored each other. It drove Randy nuts, and he made things worse."

Martha's eyes darted to Anne. Hoping to calm her, Anne again patted her shoulder.

Valerie continued. "When my son Trent announced his engagement to sweet, darling Emily, Randy turned against him. And I almost walked out. I stayed for Cameron and because I loved Ben. He was so patient. Randy had no right to interfere between Trent and Emily, but he did. After Trent moved away, Randy turned on Cameron." A shroud seemed to engulf her, as if—long ago, sorrow had taken up residence and refused to leave. "So, I had to stay."

Kindness, though, lit her eyes, "Martha, Lois loves you so much. I prayed with her for you. You've come so far. And I'm thrilled you're here. Lydia loves you so much. She'll need you—today. And she'll need you until we hear better news." She looked from Becky to Anne and then to Martha. "None of us gets it right, not really." Her chest heaved a sigh. "I hope Trent loves Jacqueline. I sometimes think he married her to spite Randy, but she's perfect for him. And she adores him." A smile crept into her hollow eyes. "Someday he'll see how lucky he is, but not yet." She heaved a deep breath. "This, too, will work out. It has to." Tears rose in her eyes. She looked at Anne and Becky and then lifted her chin. "Enough of this. Shall we find my wayward husband?"

As the others returned to the waiting room, Martha tapped Anne, urging her to wait. "I had no idea. Why didn't someone say something? ... Oh." Her cheeks dropped. "You couldn't, could you?"

Seeing tears wet Martha's eyes, Anne embraced her. "Valerie was right. We all make mistakes. But your mother is so proud of you and excited that, shall we say, you've come home."

Shortly after five o'clock, Lydia stopped in front of the baggage claim area at the Raleigh-Durham airport to pick up her roommate.

"Thanks so much," Eydie said as she lifted her carry-on tote into the trunk of Lydia's Volvo.

"I don't mind. It makes the time go faster."

"That raises a question," Eydie said as she climbed into the passenger seat: "Why would time be going slowly?"

"It's nothing." Acid burned Lydia's stomach as she checked her watch yet again. Cameron should have arrived four hours earlier. Why hadn't he called to tell her he was safe?

Listening to Valerie had reminded Martha that, though she had exiled the Norco walrus that nearly had her for dinner, much as Lewis Carroll's chatty walrus ate the foolish oysters—"every one"—even so, many sensory triggers, thorns, and buttons remained, surrounding her, taunting her. Thus, while sitting among the chairs and magazines of Duke's emergency waiting room, she needed Anne's and Valerie's patience as they waited for news from the doctors.

An hour earlier, Deborah had left for home, fifteen minutes after Randy and Nathan returned from dropping off the kid named Justin. Rather than sitting with his wife and Becky, Randy had picked a seat at the opposite end of the room, which was rude since he owed Valerie an apology or at least an explanation for his earlier tirade.

Anne disagreed. "Sometimes, the less said, the better."

Still, Martha wished Randy would talk to Valerie. Just talk—about anything kind and gentle. Martha was, though, the odd man out—an intruder into the Asher family's grief, a tagalong companion for Anne. So she waited.

Shortly before six, a nurse invited the family and friends to follow her to the third-floor waiting room, which stretched along a bank of windows outside the surgical suite. A foreboding gloom, too similar to the nights Martha and her mother had spent in Steve's hospital room, followed the family. She hoped, though, that this wait would come to a better end. Once settled in the room's somewhat more comfortable chairs, Martha whispered to Anne. "Shouldn't we call Lydia?"

"No. Not yet."

"But you know she's worried."

"I know." Anne squeezed Martha's hand. "I know."

The surgical waiting room was everything and nothing like Valerie's expectations. The long, brightly lit room overlooked a grassy plaza encircled by small, twiggy trees. On some future day, perhaps in spring, it might be inviting, but not today. Instead, winter had painted the Bermuda grass lawn the same dull tan as the honeycomb shades covering frameless windows. Beige walls encased the room. Bureaucratic chairs—adorned only with dark blue cushions and chrome-plated arms—lined the walls. Two couples, seemingly related, sat near the reception desk while a large family, who perhaps lived nearby since they spanned multiple generations, huddled near a rangy, potted palm that stood in one corner. One woman lifted her head, glancing at Valerie, but no one else moved.

Anne selected two sets of chairs that, with a square side table, formed a corner. Randy chose a similar set of seats at the opposite end of the room. Nathan joined him. After a while, Nathan caught Valerie's eye; then he stood, inviting her to take a walk.

Kindness, reflected in his eyes and gentle pace, joined them as they strolled down the empty hall, lined with a bank of tall windows. "Justin's aunt picked him up and promised she would take him directly to the center. She was devastated when she heard about the accident." Valerie nodded and half listened. At the end of the hall, they turned and entered a bright, glass-enclosed elevated crosswalk. Halfway across, Valerie stopped. For a long moment, she stared out the window while Nathan waited and said nothing. Finally, she looked up into his face. His thoughts echoed hers. Neither of them had the power to grant her prayer for Randy. Neither she nor Nathan could change Randy's intransigent mind.

She returned to the waiting room and joined Martha, Becky, and Anne. Time dragged as the others talked. Valerie heard little of what was said and remembered even less. Once in a while, she glanced toward Randy. *How had they fallen so far apart?* Occasionally a nurse appeared, called a family name, and then disappeared. Each time, Valerie's heart raced, but the nurse never asked for the Asher family.

At seven thirty, after watching Martha, grim-faced and with her fingers pressed tip-to-tip and rapidly tapping, each against another, Valerie asked, "You're worried about Lydia, aren't you?"

"Yes," Martha answered, though, barely a muscle moved.

Valerie patted her arm. Waiting wasn't easy for anybody.

At seven, Ragini stepped into the hall of Crowell dorm, closed the door to Lydia's room, and then called Ester. Speaking softly, she asked, "Have you heard anything?"

Esther conveyed information passed on from Cameron's roommate, who had seen Justin arrive at the frat house and then leave with his aunt. "No, nothing more, but thanks for calling. If you have a text thread with her mother, please add me to it. I'll pass on whatever I hear. I still can't believe Neil's description of Cameron's dad. He usually gets steely mad, not livid. Neil also said that it was a good thing that Justin's aunt took him away because *he* would've torn him apart."

Ragini sighed. "Lydia's doing just the opposite. She's pretending to study but hasn't turned a page in an hour. She's pitiful. I'll add your name, but also text if I hear something."

"Thanks. I'll do the same."

Ragini ended the call and then bounced the phone in her palm. Someplace down the hall music played, and people laughed. She poked her head into Lydia's room. Lydia startled, shooting a furtive glance at the door, and then wilted. Ragini dragged Eydie's desk chair over and set it down next to Lydia, who watched her every move.

"Something terrible happened," Lydia whispered. "I just know it."

Ragini hoped she was wrong.

In the surgical waiting room, Valerie waited as minutes trickled along, falling—drop by drop, into the past. Never ceasing. Never changing. And without hearing a nurse call the Asher name. Occasionally she watched Randy, who sat with his back to her. Mostly, though, she stared into space and waited.

Finally, a nurse appeared. "Mr. and Mrs. Asher." Valerie stifled a gasp and stood. Ignoring a surge of adrenaline that made her head spin, she read every detail of the woman—her uniform, her face, and even her walk—looking for clues that might offer information about Cameron's condition, but the woman revealed nothing.

The nurse opened the door to a small office near the waiting room. It was little more than a spacious cubicle with the same bureaucratic chairs and decorations as in the waiting room. But what did she expect? "Dr. Callaway will be with you in a moment." The nurse patted a chair for Valerie to use. "Can I bring you anything?"

Valerie shook her head and turned to Randy, who sat down, clasped his hands together, and then stared at them. If only he would wrap his arms around her. Finally, the doctor entered and sat, facing them. When his list of medical terms threatened to overwhelm her, she listened all the more intently: lacerated esophagus, splintered clavicle, et cetera. The major problems—hemothorax, a concussion, and a cracked vertebra—echoed in dire tones through her head.

"We'll monitor his neurological activity." Dr. Callaway's words sent a chill over her. "Your son must have a guardian angel watching over him." He then described the timely diagnosis of the lacerated esophagus. "The EMT's diagnosis and proper treatment saved his life. So far, we see no bleeding in the brain, which is good, but we induced a coma." The doctor paused, causing Valerie to grip the chair's arms to steady herself. He then detailed Cameron's prognosis: he was not out of danger. He then concluded the meeting by asking if they had questions.

"Is he going to be okay?" Valerie asked, hoping to negate the doctor's implication that more bad news might still lie ahead.

Dr. Callaway shook his head. "I can't say, but your son's in the hands of the finest people here."

His answer was neither as definitive nor as positive as Valerie had hoped. But it could have been worse.

The doctor left, and the nurse returned with a packet of information about the procedures, the hospital, and the region. "I'm sure you'll want to make some reservations ...."

As the nurse described arcane treatments, schedules, procedures, and local traveler's information, Valerie's thoughts retreated to memories. The little boy she'd once rocked to sleep in her arms was in critical condition.

"Your son is a fighter," the nurse said then smiled and turned to Valerie. "My name is Ellice. I'm the pastoral care associate that you requested. I'll be your liaison with the doctors and staff. If you need anything, call me." She handed Valerie and Randy flat square pagers reminiscent of the ones used by restaurant maître d's. "Keep them with you when you're in the hospital so we can reach you." She added a few obvious notes and precautions. "I have your cell phone numbers, but here is mine. When your son is settled, I'll take you to the sixth floor to see him."

"I can see him?" A cold shiver ran down her spine followed by a flush of heat.

"Yes," Ellice answered with the kindest of smiles. "And I'll stay if you need me."

Her kindness salved Valerie's fears, but she could not grant Valerie's greatest wish: she could not turn time back and prevent the accident. Nor could she change Randy's heart or ask him to hold her and say he loved her.

41

Having heard Valerie describe Cameron's prognosis, Anne turned to Martha. "It's time." She turned to Becky. "We'll see you tomorrow."

Neither woman spoke as they drove west, following Erwin Road to Duke's west campus. Martha turned off the radio, leaving only the groan of the engine and hum of the tires to fill the silence. *How much*, Anne wondered, *does Lydia need to know?*

Anne turned onto Towerview Drive, passed the crosswalk connecting the Gothic dorms to the university's sports facilities, rounded the traffic circle, and pulled to the curb just past the crosswalk to Crowell Quad. She pushed Lydia's number.

"Hi, sweetheart." Her voice was all casual cheer and sincerity. "I'm behind the dorms ... yes, by the tennis courts. We'll talk in a minute."

Martha switched to the back seat. Minutes later, Lydia appeared from beneath the double archway that led to the quads, jogged up to the car, and opened the door. She seemed too blithe and young to hear the news that Anne was about to deliver.

"Mom, why are you here?" Fear darkened her greeting.

Anne mustered a smile. "Let's talk at the Bryan Center."

Lydia climbed in. "What's wrong? What happened?"

Anne drove toward the parking deck behind Duke Chapel. "Aren't you going to greet your aunt?"

"Hi, Aunt Martha." Lydia then scolded her mother, "Mom, whatever it is, you're making it worse. Please, tell me."

Anne remained silent as she passed a large wood, filled with tall oak and hickory trees and thick with undergrowth, and turned right onto Science Drive. She glanced at Lydia. "Honey, Cameron was in an accident on his way to school this morning."

In the ambient light, Anne saw Lydia blanch. Looking in her rearview mirror, she saw Martha pinch her lips. A moment later, Lydia's eyes—wide with panic, relaxed, but she set her jaw and pulled her lips into a razor thin line. When Anne pulled into a parking space, Lydia slumped forward; her arms crossed her chest and grasped the opposite shoulder. "For you to be here, it can't be good," she whispered.

"Honey, let's go inside." Anne patted Lydia's shoulder. "You'll get cold out here."

Lydia didn't move, but Martha opened her door, stepped out, and opened Lydia's door. As they walked toward the main entrance, Lydia's vacant eyes looked straight ahead. Once inside, Anne led them to a set of cushy, over-stuffed sofas and chairs in a quiet corner near a concrete wall that overlooked a three-story-tall atrium that fronted an equally tall wall of windows. Dining areas and student services filled each floor that stacked downward to the base of the window—two floors below. More terraces and shadowy woods stretched beyond it. Every surface, including the coffered ceiling, had been built of concrete. The carpet and something else, perhaps the coffered ceiling, muffled the voices and sounds that rose from the dining area and drifted over the concrete half-wall.

Anne sat down next to her daughter and wrapped her arms around her. Martha sat opposite them and said nothing. Sometime later, Lydia's breathing slowed. "When Cameron didn't call this afternoon, I knew something was wrong. Was Justin at fault?"

"Yes," Anne said softly.

"No-o-o-o," Lydia wailed barely above a whisper. "I knew Justin couldn't be trusted …." Determination cut a razor edge between her thin lips. She spun to face her mother and her aunt. "He's going to be okay," she pronounced. "God is in this. I can feel him."

"Honey," Anne said, stroking Lydia's hand, "he's in critical condition."

Lydia repeated herself, emphasizing each word. "I *know*. I can feel it here." Lydia grasped her heart. "I saw such a difference in him on Friday. He said that even before he agreed, he knew he had but one choice, to say yes. He doesn't like Justin and didn't want to bring him here. But he'd made up his mind. He needed time to get used to the idea—not to change his mind."

She turned to Martha. Her shoulders dropped, and peace enveloped her. "There're no words that describe how much I dislike Justin, but Cameron feels a connection, not a friendship. Instead, he understands him." She slumped into the soft cushions. Embraced by the sofa, she described both nights and then sat upright, her back rigid. "Don't you see? God is in this. Cameron believed that God would protect him, and now I must too. God will bring him through."

Martha's eyes said she wanted to repudiate Lydia's interpretation, but Lydia's mind could not be swayed. Finding herself sitting between images of faith and frightened doubt, Anne sympathized with both.

Out of the silence, Lydia's eyes flashed. "Cameron said Justin was sober when he picked him up. And I believe him. Somehow Justin got drunk when Cameron wasn't looking. But God was watching." She turned to Martha. "Cameron wasn't careless."

Anne watched Martha's hands, motionless with fingertips pressed together, and waited.

Lydia heaved a soul-wrenching sigh, "Mom, my faith isn't strong—or at least it wasn't. I'm leaning on Cameron's faith. He knew Justin could be unpredictable." She took her mother's hand. "Justin may have meant harm, but God can use it for good. I can't let Cameron down."

"Honey." Anne modulated her voice, imagining the undaunted flight of a hawk, high in the sky, with only air below him. "Sometimes the things that show God's glory don't end the way we hoped."

"I know what you're saying." Lydia's temper flashed, but then patience returned. "Cameron is in God's hands. I know he's going to be okay."

She turned to Martha and squeezed her hand. "Last summer, when you weren't yourself, Mom gave me a set of verses from Isaiah 43. I used them to pray for you. God created you. He says, 'Fear not, for I have redeemed you; I have called you by name, you are mine.' We are his. Cameron is his. Aunt Martha, you came through because God willed it." She squeezed Martha's hand. "Praying for you gave me hope when I felt hopeless. Cameron needs our prayers."

Martha's eyes widened. "Aren't you frightened?"

"I'm scared to death. That's why I need your prayers." Lydia turned to Anne. Tears glazed her eyes. "Can I see him?"

"Maybe sometime later." Anne held her daughter closer. Lydia clung to her, burying her face in Anne's shoulder. Anne rocked her as she softly sobbed.

Later that night, after returning Lydia to her dorm and settling into a room at the Holiday Inn Express near Chapel Hill, Anne, sitting on her bed, closed her book and watched Martha. In the space of a few weeks, Martha's life had reversed course, but change is never easy. "Care to talk?" she asked.

"I wasted so much time." Sorrow filled Martha's soft voice. "I could have loved Mom." She flexed her misshapen wrist. "What is Providence?"

"It can be many things for many people, but Lydia nailed it: before God created you in Lois's womb, he knew your name. Fear is what Satan wants us to feel. God called you by name. You are his because he loves you." She paused to let the thought sink in. "Grace brought you through in the way he chose, to make you an instrument of his love." Anne stood and squeezed Martha's hand. "And you are. Your love plunges into depths of God's mercy because of what you endured. For that, Lydia needs you, and they both need our prayers."

"I still don't understand."

"You don't have to."

42

Throughout the night Lydia tossed in a futile attempt to find rest, but sleep came in brief moments. Monday dragged. Friends asked about Cameron and offered prayers, but her mother didn't call or give an update on his status. At six, Eydie dragged her to the West Union and forced her to eat. At seven, she called her mother. "Has anything changed?"

"Some. The surgery went well, and he's in recovery."

Surgery? Again? For what? She heaved a sigh. "How is Mrs. Asher?"

"She's holding up."

"Can I see him?"

"Probably not, but I told Valerie the things you said about Cameron's decision to give Justin a ride. She would be happy if you shared those reasons with Cameron's father. She believes you can help him. Do you have time?"

"Yeah"—though she wasn't sure how helpful she would be, but if she could give his father hope, then she'd try. Thirty minutes later, Lydia followed her mother through the hospital's maze of halls and elevators.

"How do you feel?" her mother asked.

"I still believe he's going to be fine, but it's harder today."

"That's okay." Her mother looped her arm around Lydia's as they exited the elevator. The signs pointing to the surgical waiting room flushed her cheeks. "I want to see him."

"We can discuss that later." Inside the waiting room, Aunt Martha, Mrs. Asher, and another woman turned, smiled, and then stood. Mrs. Asher extended her hand. "Lydia, you've grown into a lovely young lady since I last saw you."

"Thank you." Lydia shook her hand while her eyes caught every detail in Mrs. Asher's appearance, her demeanor, and the lonely room.

"Please, sit here," Mrs. Asher offered the seat next to her. Then she introduced Lydia to the fourth woman, Becky Stedman, Cameron's aunt.

"It's nice to meet the young lady who has my favorite nephew over the moon. And please, call me Becky. Mom was profoundly Southern, but also taught me to stand on principle first, and protocol second."

Mrs. Stedman ... *Becky* had quick eyes and a quiet demeanor, making her very approachable, so it was easy to do as asked and call her Becky. On another day and in another place, Mrs. Asher, dressed simply in khaki slacks and a ruby sweater, could have intimidated Lydia, but in the antiseptic-scented room, she was tender, gracious, and elegant. Aunt Martha, though, seemed fretful.

After asking a few questions, Mrs. Asher became somber. "Please, tell us what Cameron told you."

Lydia left many details out and focused on one point. "He believed that he owed Justin for their friendship but also because he said he felt blessed to have wonderful parents. Justin doesn't. For that reason, he felt that God had called him to step forward. When he picked up Justin, he called and said Justin was sober. His uncle had kept his promise. There's a lot more to say, but this is the important point. He wasn't careless."

Mrs. Asher listened, seeming to absorb every word, though she wilted as Lydia finished. "Thank you. I pray your message will help." Her eyes narrowed as if she was weighing a thought; then she described the tragic death of Cameron's grandmother. "I worry that my husband conflates the two accidents and thinks history is repeating itself. I want to erase that fear." Her eyes softened, and her body relaxed. "I know this is asking a lot from you."

Yes, it was. And before she spoke to Cameron's father, Lydia needed a specific answer, "Do you believe that Cameron was trusting God?"

Mrs. Asher squeezed Lydia's hand. "Yes, I do."

Lydia studied her eyes and relented—a response that must have written itself across her face, for Mrs. Asher sighed, emptying her chest.

"Becky will introduce you to his father."

A furtive glance at her mother drew an assuring nod that boosted Lydia's courage. Still, her insides knotted, relaxed, and then knotted again as she followed Cameron's aunt. When they reached Mr. Asher and Cameron's uncle, Becky introduced both men. Then she motioned for her to sit next to Mr. Stedman and across from Mr. Asher. Becky took the seat next to her brother. Since Cameron had talked often and fondly about his uncle, Lydia focused her heart on his kind face while speaking to Cameron's father.

After a brief introduction, Becky encouraged her brother. "I think you'll like what she has to say."

Mr. Asher's eyes scrutinized rather than welcomed Lydia. Seeing his forthright distrust, she steeled herself. She had rehashed Cameron's assurances a thousand times in her head, so she began. "He didn't want to take Justin with him." Mr. Asher's eyebrows arched, and his eyes narrowed as she related her message. When she finished, Becky nodded her approval. "So," she concluded, "I believe Cameron was cautious. Justin wasn't drunk when Cameron picked him up."

"So I've heard." Mr. Asher's frightening scorn in no way resembled any emotion she had seen in Cameron.

"Yes." She set her jaw. "He took every precaution, but Justin hid the alcohol from his uncle. Cameron wasn't negligent."

"Well, he should have refused to take him."

Lydia held her ground. "I trust Cameron."

"I'm sure you do."

Becky stood, a bit abruptly by Lydia's assessment, but spoke kindly to her brother. "Thank you, Randy, for listening."

Lydia also stood and wondered how such a vile man had raised a son as fine as Cameron. When she returned to her seat, she took her mother's hand and nearly squeezed the blood out of it, releasing it only when she saw her mother wincing in pain.

Mrs. Asher patted Lydia's arm and smiled kindly. "Thank you. Please, don't let his gruffness hurt you. You were more helpful than is obvious. — Would you like to see Cameron?" Lydia's heart stopped. "Your mother and I talked. Now it won't be easy, but I'll be with you."

Lydia's head lightened. She turned to her mother, searching her eyes. "Do you think I should?"

"It'll be hard," she said, patting Lydia's arm, "but I know how much it means to you." She paused. "You won't recognize him."

"I know."

Lydia's mother nodded to Mrs. Asher, who left and returned with a nurse. Lydia washed her hands and entered the intensive care unit. Inside, intermittent beeps and the odor of antiseptic and polypropylene blended and assaulted her. When she reached the sliding doors at the entrance to Cameron's pod, she stopped, taken aback by what lay before her. Tubes, machines, gauges, and wires were everywhere; casts and bandages, some ugly and discolored, seemed to cover every inch of his body. For a second, she doubted that Mrs. Asher had taken her to the right room, but turning around, she saw his mother's eyes, rimmed in tears, and knew she was at the right place. This was Cameron.

She stepped to the foot of his bed. His face was too swollen and discolored to be recognizable. Nausea rushed to her throat at the memory of Aimee, weeping as she combed her mother's hair. But this wasn't Mrs. Duncan. She stepped closer. Dark purplish patches covered his cheeks and eyelids. Air wheezed from a small slit in the tape that held a tube and plastic device over his mouth. Gone were Cameron's easy smile and the wonderful humor that brightened her life. A tear trickled down her cheek as she brushed his brow.

"The Lord is my Shepherd," she whispered, then recited the comforting psalm. When she finished, she repeated a verse. "'Even though I walk through the valley of the shadow of death, I will fear no evil.' Yes, my love. He is with you. Do not fear." She leaned forward, kissed her fingertips, and pressed them against his cheek. It felt warm, too warm.

When she reached the hallway, she collapsed, but Mrs. Asher caught her. As quiet sobs convulsed her shoulders, Cameron's mother cradled her, weeping softly with her.

43

The following morning Valerie rode with Anne and Martha to the hospital and then said goodbye. "Thank you for coming. I'll call if anything changes. And I'll watch over Lydia."

"Call anytime," Anne insisted and then hugged Valerie to her chest.

Dredging the silt that filled her soul, Valerie retrieved an ounce of bravery. "I will."

After Nathan returned home Monday morning, Martha's and Anne's departure on Tuesday morning made Durham even lonelier and sadder. Having bundled the dangling shreds of her heart, Valerie returned to the waiting area, choosing a seat in an isolated corner which formed a sort of niche with a large window where she could look out at winter's gray sky—and be ignored.

When the receptionist greeted her, she led her directly—with clipped steps—to a small cubicle where Randy waited. "Dr. Zander will be with you shortly," a nurse assured her with a demeanor that piqued Valerie's fear. When he arrived, Dr. Zander's reticence and description of Cameron's progress undermined her fortitude. The concussion was still a concern—the medication inducing the coma would continue, but he frowned while describing Cameron's hemothorax and dissolved her courage. Perhaps she merely misunderstood his vocabulary. Since prayer had always been a more fruitful endeavor than worry, particularly as she prepared for an extended stay in Durham, she nodded to him, lifted her chin, and then returned to the waiting room.

To her surprise, she found only Becky. "Where'd Randy go?"

"He's on the phone with his office, making arrangements to handle it from here, at least until Cameron is out of danger." Becky, though, seemed none too happy with his behavior.

"Oh ...." *Why isn't she happy that he decided to stay?* "Well ...." At least he planned to stay, but where did he plan to stay? Specifically, "Did he say where he's staying tonight?"

"No."

That answer didn't bode well. After his outburst on Sunday, he had demanded that Valerie share Becky's room—which she did both Sunday and Monday nights. Maybe he just needed space. Randy often needed time to be alone, but he never moved out. Valerie forced a smile. "I'm glad he wants to stay."

"He doesn't mean to hurt you."

"I know." In the wake of Ben's death, words had been said that should have been withheld—and Randy had not been the only offender. Valerie had defended her ego by doing too little good, and thus failed to ameliorate the damage done by Randy's ill moods. For now, those regrets were irrelevant— much needed to be done.

"I can stay with you again tonight," Becky offered. "Andrea offered to help by staying at the house for a few days; she can check the mail, pass on the bills, and relay messages. And you'll need a ride back. Will you ride back with me?"

Poor Becky. She loved both Valerie and Randy, and she loved well, for which Valerie was grateful. "Yes. I'd like that."

After arriving in Chalmers early Wednesday afternoon Valerie packed a larger wardrobe and transferred the family's financial information to her laptop computer and tablet, and arranged with Andrea and Becky to coordinate miscellaneous matters that arose in her absence. Everything else could be handled using her hotspot since she refused to use the hotel's internet when paying bills.

She met Anne, Martha, and Becky for an early dinner. "I'll take good care of Lydia," she assured Anne and then patted Martha's hand. "I promise." Turning to Becky, her heart ached. Becky was the best sister-in-law a woman could want, but her loyalties were to her brother, Randy, and not entirely to Valerie.

"Nathan and I love you," Becky said. And she meant it.

Anne reminded her to call Deborah. "She's just minutes away."

Then sad, pitiable Martha, who said more with her eyes than words could ever express, added her salve. "You're not alone."

Holding back tears, Valerie embraced each of them. Then she climbed into her car, ready for the long, lonely drive to Durham. And the lonelier wait for Cameron's recovery.

In Durham, disappointment and sorrow greeted her on every corner. Whether in her single occupant hotel room with its king-sized bed or sitting alone at the far end of the waiting room, she tried to remember that Jesus was with her. It helped but only a little. The nurses offered encouragement when possible, but only time would heal Cameron and dispel her fears. When allowed to see him, she stroked his cheek, wishing, hoping for a miracle or at least for grace. She returned to the waiting room and a book on prayer, given to her by a friend.

A woman's voice startled her. "Hello, Mrs. Asher." Guarded, Valerie looked up into the almond eyes and oval face of an Asian woman. "Hi, my name is Fujiko and I'm a pastoral layman at Deborah Schaeffer's church."

"Deborah? Is her sister Anne Carpenter?" On the assumption she had made the right connection, Valerie smiled, relieved that her face remembered how to do so.

"Yes. May I join you?"

"Yes, please." For the next hour, Fujiko asked questions about Valerie, Cameron, and the rest of her family, but mostly she listened. She offered to run errands and show Valerie around town. Valerie assured her that she was familiar with the area but accepted her offer to return the following day. After Fujiko left, several friends called, and time moved more quickly.

The next day, Lydia visited. "God is wrapping him with his love," she assured Valerie—several times. The child's strength amazed Valerie, but her optimism was only slightly infectious. Later that night, when Valerie huddled beneath the blankets in the empty hotel room, the walls collapsed around her. During the day, God's love, seen in many helpful faces and kind words, had lifted and embraced her, but in the darkened room sleep seemed elusive and hope equally so. She laid her Bible on the bed next to her and tried to sleep. On Friday morning, she returned to the hospital. "May I go on back?" she asked the receptionist.

"Ellice wants to speak to you first."

For a second, Valerie's pulse stopped, but she decided to remain calm. If Cameron's condition had worsened, someone would have called, but no one had. She sat down, but within minutes, the receptionist approached her. "Mrs. Asher," she said very softly, "would you and Mr. Asher please follow me." The woman's severe manner sent blood rushing to Valerie's cheeks. The receptionist led them to the same small cubicle as before. She took a seat next to Randy, and they waited, side by side, frozen and silent. When Ellice entered, she handed Randy a set of papers. "Dr. Evans would like for you to read these. He should be here in a minute."

Valerie leaned closer to Randy, trying to read the title. Though it made no sense to her, Randy seemed to understand. He blanched, and his brow knotted.

"What's wrong?" she asked.

Randy leaped to his feet, threw the papers onto a side table, and bolted from the room. Valerie jumped up and followed close behind as he strode toward the elevators.

"Damn!" he shouted. "Damn! This can't be happening!"

"What?"

He spun around and faced her. "He's dying, Valerie."

Valerie's heart stopped. "What? But why?"

"Remember when the doctors said that he had a small rupture in his esophagus?"

"Yes, but they fixed it."

"No. It didn't work. Either the hole got bigger, or they closed it but it didn't stay closed. Either way, he's dying. That paper is about esophageal ruptures. They're fatal. Remember?"

Valerie didn't remember, but as he spoke, she looked past him and saw a physician approach. "Mr. and Mrs. Asher, my name is Ray Evans."

"Doctor," Valerie pleaded. "Is my husband right? Is my son dying?" He didn't answer her but instead gently took Valerie's arm and led her back to the cubicle. Randy followed, lugging his white-hot anger with him. As the door closed, Valerie's shoulders started to tremble.

"I'm sorry that I was late." Dr. Evans pulled a chair out for Valerie. "I don't want to alarm you."

"Alarm us?" Randy snapped, his temper blistering the wallpaper. "You're kidding of course."

"During the night your son's condition began to deteriorate. Early this morning, we took him back to surgery. He's in recovery now."

"Then everything is okay?" Valerie asked. "Right?"

"He's in very good hands." In a firm and measured tone, Dr. Evans described the spike in Cameron's fever that had sent him back to the OR. "Normally the rupture heals itself, but the hole didn't close. We removed the infection, and the repair looks good. He'll be on antibiotics for a while. He's in recovery. You can see him later this afternoon." The doctor's grim and controlled manner sent nausea surging into Valerie's throat.

"But the mortality rate for his condition is sixty percent," Randy barked. "That means he's worse. Right?"

"Mortality rate? What does that mean?" Valerie guessed the answer as nausea surged beyond her control. She grabbed the trash can as Dr. Evans jumped to his feet and called for a nurse. Randy grabbed Valerie's elbow. Dr. Evans steadied her as Ellice raced into the room and sent another nurse to bring a pill and a glass of water. With the bitter taste still rimming her mouth, Valerie heard Randy speaking to the doctor outside the door.

"What about the infection? I'm not a doctor, but I know insurance claims and codes. Aren't you dealing with mouth flora in his chest, most of it is resistant to antibiotics?"

Resistant? Did that mean the antibiotics wouldn't work?

"I have handled this before with success ...." Dr. Evans's voice trailed off.

Sometime later Valerie awoke, vaguely aware that someone had carried her to a small room and laid her on a bed. She sat up, waited until her head stopped spinning, and then returned to the waiting room. Shortly afterward, Ellice sat down next to her and took her hand. "Valerie, your son is a fighter." Ellice's gentle voice abated Valerie's fears. "Dr. Evans is an excellent surgeon. There is much that we can do for Cameron, things we *will* do." She patted Valerie's hand. "Can I answer any questions?"

"Is my son dying?"

"He's getting the very best care from every member of our staff."

Ellice's eyes spoke volumes. She simply didn't know, and she wouldn't lie.

At five, Lydia returned to the hospital to meet Cameron's mother in the first-floor dining hall. Even from a distance, Mrs. Asher's composure gave Lydia pause. Still, she willed her feet to walk. "Hi, Mrs. Asher," she said but did not ask about her day. What, Lydia wondered, might make her appear bent and tired—the same woman whose simple elegance had encouraged Lydia to stand a little straighter and speak more graciously? The answer was obvious and terrifying.

"It's been tiring," Mrs. Asher measured each word. "Shall we say hello to Cameron?" Lydia decided not to pry.

When they reached his cubicle, his mother stopped short of the door. A strained smile drew fine lines across her cheeks. Lydia wanted to assure her, to remind her to trust God. "He's going to be okay," she said hesitantly. "I truly believe it." Did she believe her own words? Whom was she kidding? —Only herself. She stepped next to Cameron and took his hand. *Oh!*

"Yes. He's a little warm." Sorrow radiated from his mother as she looked across the bed. "He was in surgery early this morning. The surgeon was pleased with the results."

Surgery? Again? Pleased? What did that mean? Unfortunately, Mrs. Asher's mask fit too perfectly for Lydia to read her emotions—except that clearly Mrs. Asher was very worried. He's in God's hands," Lydia said, barely hearing her voice.

She looked at Cameron. Several bandages had been removed from his face, revealing dark purple bruises around his eyes. Green and yellow splotches rimmed the bruises. The puffiness was less noticeable, but he didn't look like himself. Her fingers touched his skin as she gently ran a comb through his hair. He felt much too warm. Yes, Mrs. Asher knew far more than she was willing to tell. Still, Lydia reminded herself, God was in control. He would take care of Cameron. This too would pass. But when?

44

On Sunday morning, two weeks after Cameron's accident, Lydia joined Eydie and Ragini at Graystone Presbyterian Church but wondered with every breath whether God cared about her or Cameron. All around her, unspoken hurts, concerns, and prayers hid behind the calm veneer of small smiles and straight shoulders. Did they believe the words they spoke and the lyrics of the songs they sang? Did they doubt? If so, about what and why? Certainly, some had fears and sorrow far greater than hers. Mrs. Asher's were certainly greater than Lydia's because Cameron was her son, and he was just Lydia's friend.

An elder and his family walked to the front of the church. "We light the second candle of Advent," he said, surrounded by his smiling family. "With our hope assured by God's promises ...."

His words trailed off as Lydia's attention drifted to the neat rows of poinsettias carefully massed around the Communion table. The scarlet blossoms, brightening winter's bleak shades of gray, reminded her that only two weeks remained before Christmas, a season that had passed along the tattered selvage of her attention. Today was no different. As the sermon faded in and out, she heard a sentence and then noted a crack that etched the wall.

Reverend Mechan introduced his sermon topic, "As we move into the Advent season, we continue our study of Job." An occasional phrase synchronized with Lydia's musings. "Earlier, we looked at the question, 'Where was the God of love when Job's world disintegrated?'" *Obviously nowhere close.* "Yet,

Job didn't ask why bad things happen to good people. Instead, he asked why good things happen to bad people."

Lydia had asked that very question for two weeks. Why had God let Justin, with barely a scratch, walk away from an accident he'd caused—not once, but twice? He had endangered Cameron's life and killed Aimee's mother. He was to blame. She shoved anger aside, but memories of talking to Eliana several days earlier haunted her. Eliana had come to the hospital to sit with her, to talk about Cameron. Catching up had been a great diversion, but she had ended by asking Lydia that very question.

"Last week"—Eliana's voice dropped to a whisper— "I heard that the guy who left me under the bridge won a very prestigious, high-dollar award from the investment firm in New York where he works. He started last spring, right after graduation. The announcement listed his accomplishments." Anger knitted her brow. "And his wife. He's married. That means ...." She heaved a deep sigh and then pursed her mouth. "I mentioned the award to one of his friends who probably didn't know what he did to me. Trying to look cool and nonchalant, I said his wife should be proud, hoping he'd elaborate. And he did. That night, with me, he was engaged to her. Lydia, he got off."

"You can still report him. My friends would stand with you."

"That's not my point. And I still won't name him. I keep reminding myself of what you said last spring: I will not let him ruin my life. Since then, no one has forced himself on me. But—" The lines in her face softened, but enough remained to signal her defiance against all who might want to hurt her, even God. "What does your God do with guys like him? How does he let him not only skate but win, very big, while this happens to Cameron?"

"Oh." How could she tell Elaina, who refused to use the word *rape* and refused to let another guy steal her dignity, that the answer to her question lay in the mystical connection through which God called Cameron? "God didn't punish Cameron, nor has he let that cheating creep go free." How could she explain that God in his wisdom left the rapist to his horrible desires and washed Cameron with his healing mercy? It wouldn't make sense unless ....

She took Eliana's hand. "I don't have an answer for you. For me, Cameron's reward isn't a thing, but the person who grants it—Jesus. That guy got an award from his boss. His first boss. He'll have others. Cameron's reward is Christ, who called him. Wealth, fame, accolades—they're like cars. Old Porsches rust and burn oil. No matter what, Cameron's reward won't rust and the oil won't turn to sludge. This very moment Christ is praying directly to God the Father for Cameron, asking him to be merciful and remember his promises.

"I want Cameron to wake up. I want God to heal his wounds and make him just the way he was before this." She squeezed Eliana's hand. "I don't have an answer for you, but if you listen to your heart, you may hear a groaning—a softening of your heart, not toward him, but toward you. Today, as I did yesterday, I prayed to a God who heard me and reminds me over and over that he loves Cameron and me. He says—though I walk through the valley of the shadow of death, I am not to fear, for God, a person of infinite wisdom, goodness, and mercy, is with me. And yes, not knowing is a burden, but one he helps me bear."

"John tells us," Reverend Mechan proclaimed above the cries of Lydia's heart, "that love is the foundation of the Christian faith. Is it love? Some would say it is, and I wouldn't dispute them. But the angels didn't say, 'Fear not,' when warning the shepherds about something soft and flowery. No. Their warning was about something awesome. Something fearful. They warned about a daring, deep love that calls to deep pain." The minister's eyes seemed to be trained on Lydia and her alone. "God's love isn't soft-focus and trivial. It's mighty and fierce. It's a father's love for his child."

A pang of doubt pierced Lydia's breastbone. The fever she felt when she touched Cameron's hand had crushed every soft-focus picture of love she might have imagined. Fear had wrenched her faith. Were her fears different from Eliana's fears and doubt—Elaina who didn't believe in Jesus? Was God's love enough?

The preacher tempered his voice, "Jesus came to redeem our shredded hearts. And to renew our minds. In this Advent season, we celebrate hope and joy, knowing that when, like Job, we fall on our knees before God, saying, 'Naked I came from my mother's womb, and naked shall I return. The Lord gave, and the Lord has taken away; blessed be the name of the Lord,' God will hear us and come to us. Blessed is Jesus about whom the angels sang, 'Fear not, for behold, I bring you good news of a great joy that will be for all the people. For unto you is born this day in the city of David a Savior, who is Christ the Lord.'"

Lydia's chest collapsed. God had given her Cameron and now seemed ready to take him away. *Fear not.* It was crazy. Lydia wiped her eyes, but a tear escaped and ran down her cheek. She wiped it away as another followed. Daily, doubt had grown, ripping her apart. Why hadn't Cameron improved? Why was he still in a coma? Hadn't he helped Justin, believing that God had asked him to do so? Didn't that matter? And now the fever. The bacteria could kill him. Why wouldn't he wake up?

The day before, Mrs. Asher had looked particularly worn as she returned from Cameron's pod. "They say the fever is under control," she had said, adding, "but ...." Now Lydia joined his mother's unspoken lament, weeping as hope hung by a single gossamer thread.

Dr. Machen's voice filled the sanctuary with kindness, catching Lydia's attention. "God answered Job with a question. 'Have you entered into the springs of the sea, or walked in the recesses of the deep? Have you comprehended the expanse of the earth? Declare, if you know all this.' No? But God did, and he reached across the infinite divide. He humbled himself, becoming a baby: our Savior, Jesus Christ. And the Word became flesh and dwelt among us." Lydia's chest ached as she had never known it could as the minister spread his arms. "Rejoice!"

If Cameron never awoke, if he never again wrapped her in his arms, if she never again tasted his kiss, would God's grace suffice? Eydie squeezed Lydia's hand as the congregation began to sing the final hymn. "God hasn't forgotten you," she whispered.

"I know."

The previous night, Neil had stopped by the hospital before driving home for Christmas. "We're praying for you, too. You're the best thing that happened to him." But his eyes said that he, too, was worried.

Lydia spent Sunday afternoon in her room, listening to the quiet chatter that filled Crowell during exams. Then she walked to the hospital and

Cameron around four. When she reached the intensive care waiting room, she learned that his parents had left for the evening.

"They went out. I'm not sure where," the nurse said.

"Did they leave together?"

"I don't think so."

Poor Mrs. Asher. She, too, needed God to wrap her in his grace. Alone in Cameron's pod, Lydia read aloud from her Bible. "Deep calls to deep at the roar of your waterfalls; all your breakers and your waves have gone over me. By day the Lord commands his steadfast love, and at night his song is with me, a prayer to the God of my life. I say to God, my rock: 'Why have you forgotten me? Why are you cast down, O my soul? And why are you disquieted within me?' Hope in God ...." She had no other choice.

45

Shortly after six-thirty on Monday morning, Valerie awoke to the sound of someone banging on the door of her hotel room. "Just a minute." Then, suspecting that Randy was knocking on the door, she decided not to put in her contacts. Instead, she groped for her glasses.

Since arriving in Durham, Valerie had acquiesced to Randy's demand that they sleep in separate hotel rooms. The arrangement had seemed at once immature and expensive, but when she awoke, clinging to her pillows and wishing that Randy had changed his mind, it also felt very lonely. The Bible, lying on his pillow, had been a comfort—though only a little. Now, though, as she opened the door, weariness drowned out every other emotion. Didn't he know what time it was?

"Get ready," Randy demanded. "We've got to leave right away."

Accustomed to his abrupt manner, Valerie almost turned and ignored him, but his face stopped her. His habitual scowl, at least the one he'd worn recently, had vanished. Consternation simmered behind his grim eyes, making him appear at once limp and rabid. Valerie frowned—and then blanched. She had seen the same conflicted expression the night after his father died. "What's wrong?"

"The night nurse called. Cameron spiked a fever. They think he's septic."

"What?"

"That's the same way that Mom died. When the infection reached her blood, we ...." His jaw locked, and his cheek twitched.

Ignoring the silent gasp that sucked her stomach into her throat, Valerie grabbed his shirt and pulled him inside. "I'll only be a minute."

"Septicemia took Mom," Randy mumbled. "I've lost him."

"No. Not yet." Valerie pulled on a pair of pants and a sweater. "What did the nurse tell you?" Valerie brushed her teeth and threw a towel, soap, her hairbrush, clips, contacts, and makeup in a bag. She could fix herself up later. "Let's go. You can tell me on the way." A glance at him set her mind in motion: he looked pitiful. "I'll drive."

As she raced toward the hospital, Randy described, for the first time in their married life, his mother's accident and death. Valerie dared not mention that she knew every detail. Staring straight ahead, he mumbled, "I should have told you about Mom."

His mea culpa was welcome, but relief was not on her list of available emotions. A nurse subbing for Ellice met them at the waiting room entrance and took them to an office cubicle. "Last week," she began, "the lab report indicated that one organism was not responding to the antibiotics. That's why Cameron had a fever. Dr. Arena ordered tests on a battery of antibiotics with various combinations. This morning Cameron spiked a fever, but we also received the lab report. The organism appears to be highly sensitive to one combination."

"And that's good. Right?" Valerie asked.

"It won't work," Randy stated. Then he got up and left the room.

Valerie started to follow him but instead turned to the night nurse. Was there even an iota of extra information, perhaps something favorable, hidden behind her expression?

"This is a very grave condition, but don't give up hope yet," she insisted.

"I can't." Valerie searched her eyes. *Yes! She believed the antibiotic could, might work.* "Thank you." A surge of adrenaline sent her out the door and toward the waiting room. She found Randy in his usual corner, seated with his head buried in his hands. She sat next to him, reining in her optimism, which he'd deride. "Madeline, that's the nurse's name, said not to worry," she whispered. Randy looked up and then dropped his head again. Valerie laid her hand on his back, barely touching his shirt, counting the minutes until she could leave him to call Becky and Anne. She waited eight minutes and stepped into the hall. "I'm sorry to wake you, but—" Exuberance spewed across the line as she described the dire situation, "Anne, you were right. They ran tests on antibiotic combinations. They think one will work."

"Wonderful."

Later that afternoon, when Valerie returned to Cameron's pod, the intensity of his fever pummeled her spirits. Rather than panicking—an emotion that threatened to engulf her weary body—she picked up a washcloth, dampened it, and wiped his face, arms, and body as she had when he was a child. The new antibiotics would work. They had to work.

Martha awoke on Tuesday to a cold, drenching rain that shrouded her house and the surrounding woods in a heavy mist. A year earlier, a similarly dreary day would have confirmed her view that life was miserable, but now she looked to the rain's passing. Even in winter, sunlight would warm her garden, newly replenished by the rain, and prepare it for spring.

Lifted by the thought, she returned to her greeting cards, but the phone rang. "Hello?"

"Hi." To her surprise, it was Becky, who must have already talked Nathan's ear off and Anne's as well, leaving Becky with unrequited concern for Cameron.

"I can't believe he has septicemia. It's just like Mom."

"What's that?" Martha leaned back and watched the fog as Becky described the danger Cameron faced. "Martha, it's bad."

Oh. Martha found herself at a loss for words. Worse yet, she felt shamefully indifferent to Becky's plight—and by extension, to Lydia's plight. She pinched her mangled wrist. It hurt, but not enough to muster a smidgen of worry. Instead, she felt strangely optimistic, almost hopeful. But she must be the only person who did. *Hmm* .... And that thought came after spending thirty-plus years stuck in the miserable, worrisome past.

"Well, I should let you go." Sorrow echoed in Becky's voice.

Martha added a blandly sympathetic "I don't mind listening." Sadly, her sympathy closet was empty.

"Thanks anyway."

Martha said goodbye and, feeling quite guilty, again watched the dreary fog drift through the empty tree branches. Truth be told, worry had gnawed at her, as much for Lydia as for Cameron. The child talked a good talk, but discouragement echoed in her voice.

The fog lifted, catching her attention as sunlight brightened her study. When the mist descended again, experience coalesced into a startling realization. It was only ground fog. Above it, the sun shone. The same was true of Cameron's fever. Like the fog, it had descended over him, but God, like the steadily glowing sun, held Cameron and Lydia in his hand.

Martha dialed Jake's work number. "I have to talk to Lydia."

"Okay. Call her." Jake's trademark patience irritated her.

"You don't understand. I have to see Lydia to talk to her."

"Hold on. Hold on."

"I can't. I've got to talk to her."

"I'm sure you do. When is her last exam?"

"Tomorrow."

"Then we'll leave tomorrow."

"But what if ...?" Martha pleaded.

Calm burnished Jake's words. "We'll drive up tomorrow."

In the morning, a crystal blue sky greeted Martha, but restraint did not. Urgency simmered beneath her skin as Jake followed Interstate 85 north. Valerie met them in the hospital lobby and led them to the waiting room. All the while, Martha stuffed her buoyant smile into a grim, contrived, perhaps grotesque non-smile, to keep joy from leaking through a thousand cracks in her facade.

"Here." Valerie offered seats to Martha and Jake then sat down opposite them. "Last night Cameron's fever went down. If he continues to improve, his doctors are hopeful that he can be moved to a regular room on Friday." Martha ignored the room but listened intently as her hands mindlessly rolled and unrolled a magazine, releasing it and rolling it ever more tightly as Valerie continued. "If it isn't one thing, it's another." Discouragement choked her voice. "Dr. Evans said that they took him off the meds that induced the coma." Valerie's hands fell limp into her lap. "He implied that Cameron should have come out of it by now."

Martha's perpetual motion ceased. "Are they worried about brain damage?"

"I don't know, but I am."

Martha's heart and mouth leaped into uncharted territory then took a swan dive into absurdity. "Maybe it's not what you think." Startled by the insensitivity of her outburst, Martha pinched her mouth shut. She could no longer smother the belief that Cameron was going to be okay. "Have you talked to Lydia?"

"No. I didn't know what to say."

The simmering urgency that had propelled Martha to Durham reached a rolling boil. Lydia certainly shared Valerie's fears, but they were both wrong. Of course, Martha's idea was just a notion, lacking any basis in science or medicine. But all the same, she needed to call Lydia.

Jake intoned, as calm as ever, "Martha and I are going out for barbeque. Anne insisted we get Eastern North Carolina barbeque and listed a few places." He smiled, "She said to make sure it's served on Melamine plates with Brunswick Stew and hushpuppies. Otherwise, it's not barbeque. Oh, and taste it before you ask for more sauce. Want to join us?"

What about Lydia? Though "meek" had never been high on Martha's "must behave" list, she relented. She suffered through dinner, minding her manners while her heart and stomach churned, vying for her attention. She barely ate and half-listened while Jake and Valerie talked. As Anne suggested, she also formed a plan to meet Lydia at the Duke library. After dinner, at the exact time when Lydia was scheduled to finish her last exam, Martha dialed her number.

"Hi, Aunt Martha. Mom said you had come up."

"Yes. I thought you might need help packing." Her excuse wasn't at all clever, but it sounded legit. "How is Cameron?"

"His fever broke."

"That's good." She winced: *Sound sympathetic!* "Your uncle and I are at the library." *Marginally better.* "Can you join us?"

"Okay." No merriment or relief tinted Lydia's voice.

Great! Martha's newfound diplomatic skills had worked, no thanks to her enlightened ideas. Ten minutes later, Lydia appeared at the library entrance. "Is there a quiet corner where we can talk?" Martha asked.

"Almost anywhere, since exams are mostly over. I like the fourth floor of old Perkins. Nobody will be up there."

Jake found a magazine and a seat in the lobby while Lydia led Martha up several flights of metal steps. A notably low ceiling and long lines of gunmetal gray bookshelves set on rollers filled the center of the floor. Martha chanced to read the category of books: anthropology. Ugh. Lydia chose a set of upholstered chairs—blue cubes that some creative mind had deemed as such—and designed them to hold one person only, Martha scooted two of them closer together. By her assessment, the room screamed: "enter at your peril."

Lydia curled up in one cube. Martha sat in an identical cube facing her and leaned forward. "How was your exam?" The question was marginally better than silence.

"Not as bad as I thought." Gloom filled Lydia's soft voice.

Martha scooted closer and took her hand, cradling it. "I know you're worried. If I could grant wishes, Cameron would be here, sitting with us. I'd comment about how much he'd grown since I last saw him, but I can't. But I do have something special for *you*."

Speaking just above the quiet drone of the ventilation unit, she began, "For years, even longer than your parents have known each other, I lived on the western side of midnight. It looked good to me. I had good friends. I even attended church and did good things, like helping the Hope Springs Ministries. I read my Bible and called myself a Christian, but I was clueless."

Lydia stood, squeezed in next to Martha, and rested her head on Martha's shoulder. Martha made room for her then brushed her hair back from her brow and continued, unhurried. "As time passed, everything good felt hollow. Hope was like a wave that rises from the ocean then, as it peaks, spreads a thin film of water across the sandy beach. Quiet and reflective as it was, each hope—like the fading wave, retreated back into an ocean of hopelessness. Only a band of froth marked each passing. I could see no farther than the present moment when every hope, everything good faded—and left behind a legacy of foamy anger and disappointment. So I ruminated over the smallest slight, because in the dim light of the setting sun ... which kept retreating farther and farther west, I lost perspective. I didn't see people for who they were: I imagined that good people like Nana were bad, and bad people were good.

"But the western side of midnight grew darker with each passing hour. Even though Uncle Jake, Nana, and your parents described the eastern side of midnight, I rejected their arguments. Their descriptions didn't seem real or possible. So I assured myself that they didn't know anything more than I did. I was the captain of my fate—but I was very wrong." Feeling a damp spot on her collar, Martha paused. *Tears. Poor child.* She cradled Lydia's head. "Without the pills, living terrified me. So I raged against the dying light of that always setting sun. And I hurt the people who loved me the most.

"Then a miracle happened. As the fog created by the pills retreated, I saw someone I'd never seen before. I saw Jesus and realized that he had come to the western side of midnight. He had picked me up and carried me across the divide to a new day. He changed my heart and gave me new eyes. At one in the morning, though, it's still very dark, but it's not without light. Through the prism of his grace, I saw a light beneath my feet. I saw where to step, where to go." Martha snuggled Lydia's head against her cheek as the wet spot from her tears grew larger. "I saw that the day was growing. Soon two turned to three. The dawn was coming. The dawn is coming. Life is beginning, and everything is being made new again." Lydia nuzzled closer.

"Your doubts don't mean that you distrust God." Martha reached around Lydia's shoulder. "They mean you're trying to understand the mystery of God's grace, which isn't easy. But Jesus is light for our steps. He's lifting our load onto his shoulders." Martha wiped Lydia's cheek and whispered, "The darkness cannot hide him." A faint shudder shook Lydia's shoulders. "Jesus hasn't forgotten you, and he hasn't forgotten Cameron." Lydia's shoulders quivered. "He's holding Cameron." Martha lifted Lydia's chin and looked into her tear-stained eyes.

Tears choked Lydia's voice. "I'm afraid."

"The morning is coming. Do you want to see it?"

A sob convulsed Lydia's chest, but she nodded her head and took Martha's hand.

"Close your eyes. Up we go. We're flying east." Martha lowered her voice until it was more breath than sound. "We're going to the farthest point we can reach and still be on dry land. Look down. That's the Research Triangle and the subdivisions east of Raleigh. Oh! I almost missed Interstate 95. It's gone. Those lines are the pine forests of the sandy flatland." Lydia's grip tightened. "And there's a Carolina bay. Are those shrimp boats? They are—headed out onto the sparkling water of Pamlico Sound.

"I see our destination: Hatteras Island. Up we go into the lighthouse.

Round and round. Hear the echo of our feet on the old metal staircase? Quick. Open the door. Watch your step. The sill is high. Oh, look! The sunrise. Isn't it beautiful!" She leaned her head against Lydia's. "Just as Jesus promised, it's bright with his voice, reminding his Father of the promises he made. He says he loves you and you belong to him." She took a deep breath. "Smell the sweetness of his Spirit floating on the breeze. Reach out your hand." Martha held out hers. "Do you feel the warmth? It's the Father's love *for you*. The cirrus clouds are white with reflections of Jesus Christ." She held Lydia just a little closer, cradling Lydia as when she was a child. "He loves you so much," she whispered.

Lydia's sobs broke into unrelenting heaves. "What if Cameron doesn't wake up ... or if he wakes up, and he isn't the same?" Martha rocked Lydia back and forth. "I never knew that loving someone could hurt this much." She sat up and wiped her eyes. "What if I love him more than God?"

"Shhhh," Martha whispered. "You love both with all your heart. But right now, you're worried about Cameron. And Jesus understands."

Still, Lydia's sobs returned. "I thought this would be over by now."

As she cradled her niece, an indescribable peace embraced Martha.

"I don't know what I believe." Lydia heaved a sob. "What if I deceived Cameron? What if he decided to drive Justin, and it wasn't God's plan? What if he did it because of something I said?"

Martha cupped Lydia's cheek in her hand. "That's just the salty taste of sorrow and fear. Give your glass to Jesus and let him fill it with the water of life, the water that revives our souls. Look at me. He revived even me ... and he's holding Cameron close to his heart."

"I miss Cameron's smile," Lydia sobbed and again buried her face in Martha's shoulder.

"I know you do." Martha hugged Lydia and rocked her, as sobs shook the child's body. "I know," and her heart sang softly, "'Turn your eyes upon Jesus, look full in his wonderful face, and the things of earth will grow strangely dim, in the light of his glory and grace.'"

46

Thursday morning, December 15, Aunt Martha and Uncle Jake helped Lydia move her computer and clothing from the dorm to Aunt Deborah's and Uncle Kyle's house. Since childhood, their comfortable mid-nineteenth-century house, nestled on a wooded knoll overlooking seven acres of rolling pasture outside Hillsborough, had been one of Lydia's favorite places. Now, though, it would be her home away until ... well, until Cameron's doctors said otherwise. Each day she returned to the hospital to visit Cameron, and then retreated to a waiting room that had become increasingly tedious, not the least due to a television that droned incessantly.

Cameron's father, sullen and disagreeable, had become a mainstay who, thankfully, ignored her. In quiet moments, though, she watched Cameron's mother. How, she wondered, had Mrs. Asher remained calm when sorrow and fear most certainly lurked behind her optimistic veneer and dependable kindness? Without her courage, each of Lydia's days would have been unbearable.

The next day, Dr. Arena left orders for Cameron to be moved to a standard room to continue antibiotic infusions. The absence of excess monitors, meters, and various noisy intrusions made the room slightly more comforting, but no mention was made about the coma or his prognosis. Several days passed without note, but as she approached his room on the afternoon of the twenty-first, she paused when she heard voices coming from inside.

"So you still base your decision upon the early tests?" a woman asked.

"Yes. They showed no damage other than the hematoma. Sometimes the brain does its own thing."

Someone else spoke. "Jan, write an order for another CT scan on Tuesday."

Lydia pressed her back against the wall, as her greatest fears roared to life. The doctors doubted that Cameron would ever wake up. Barely able to breathe, much less think, she stifled a sob. Seconds later, she nodded to Dr. Arena as he and the others left. She then slipped into Cameron's room. Leaning over his bed, she brushed his hair back from his forehead. "Cameron. Please wake up." She repeated it several times, hoping for a response. None came.

Later that night, alone in her room at Aunt Deborah's house, she shook with sobs rolling over her like the wind and rain of a summer thunderstorm. She remembered seeing Cameron in September, leaning against the traffic bollard, waiting for her in front of the chapel, smiling the wonderful smile she adored. Even then she had loved him. Why had she been so stubborn? Why had she wasted so much time? As her sobs abated, exhaustion overtook her.

In the morning, as she passed the nursing station, she saw a wide gold Mylar garland braided with colored lights and a second smaller red and green tinsel garland. Numerous Christmas cards, taped to the walls, surrounded the station. A small tree decorated with happy but chintzy plastic ornaments stood atop a file cabinet. If the decorations were intended to be cheerful reminders of the season, they left her wondering whether she would ever again find joy in the holiday. Would it forever serve as a reminder of the saddest days of her life? She lifted an ornament painted with glittering swirls. She had stayed in Durham long enough. It was time to go home, to leave Cameron's parents to their private grief.

Resigned to her decision, she walked to the elevator lobby. There, leaning against the handrail, she looked up at the cloudy sky. Saying goodbye to Cameron's mother sounded too much like saying goodbye to Cameron. She wasn't ready to do that, at least not yet. She would wait until later in the afternoon. Soon enough, the day would arrive when the doctors would term Cameron's coma as perpetual or vegetative. On that day she'd say goodbye, and Jesus alone would have the strength to carry her through the days that followed. He would fill her lungs with air and make her heart beat, for more than muscles would be needed to sustain her. Then he would hold her close, so very close. *Thank you, Father,* she prayed, *for letting me hear Cameron say that he loved me.*

Lydia called Aunt Deborah and described her plans.

"Wouldn't it be better to wait until Saturday since Christmas is Sunday?" Aunt Deborah asked. "The highway will be packed tomorrow."

"Probably. Okay. I'll leave first thing Saturday morning. I can be home by noon."

At lunch on Friday, Lydia shared with Mrs. Asher her decision to return home.

"You're not an imposition. I assure you, but I know your family misses you. I have enjoyed your company. And though your mother has never complained, I know she misses you. In the meantime, come and sit with me."

Lydia spent the remainder of the day as she had so many others, sitting by Cameron, talking to him while encouraging and being encouraged by his mother. After dinner, and after Mr. Asher left for his hotel, Mrs. Asher joined Lydia, and together, they returned to Cameron's room. "You're more than welcome to stay."

"Yes, I know." Seeing Cameron's smile reflected in Mrs. Asher's smile, she wished again to see *his* smile. "Thank you for letting me stay this long." Fine lines and cracks marred his mother's gentle face, pointing to a heart far sadder and more broken than Lydia's own heart. "Mrs. Asher, how do you do it?"

Cameron's mother winced. "Do what?"

"Stay so positive."

Rather than answering, Mrs. Asher walked to Cameron's bed and took his hand. "I could say it's my excellent makeup." A melancholy laugh slipped out. "The first call from the Orange County dispatcher yanked half of my heart from my chest. I'd be a liar if I didn't admit that Randy yanked the remaining half out. I've hurt so much for so long that I've forgotten what it felt like not to hurt. Regardless, when that massive crater in my chest feels dry and empty, hope seeps in and fills the void.

"Hope is a very strange thing. It can't be conjured up. When I was too weak and frightened to hope that Cameron would get better, hope found me." Still holding Cameron's hand, Mrs. Asher reached out and took Lydia's hand. "The strength you see isn't mine. My heart aches so much, but I can't help but hope that God still has plans for Cameron. And it, *hope*, is strong." She released Cameron's hand and kissed his cheek. Turning to Lydia, she embraced her with a warm hug and then stepped away. "Thank you."

After Mrs. Asher left, Lydia stared at the empty doorway. She, too, wanted to hope, but her chest felt empty.

"Good night." Nancy smiled at Mrs. Asher, the mother of Mr. Asher, the patient in a room halfway between two nursing stations. His father had left an hour earlier. Turning back to her work, Nancy pushed up the sleeves of her smock jacket and transcribed a note into a patient's file. Once finished, she handed a printout to Gail, the medication nurse. "Is Lydia still with Mr. Asher?"

"I think so. Why?"

"I overheard his mother say that Lydia is returning home in the morning."

"I'm not surprised. Tomorrow is the twenty-fourth."

"You don't understand. Both yesterday and earlier tonight, when I took his vitals, I could have sworn he responded."

"Really? How?"

"His muscles flexed." Her evidence was strictly circumstantial. "My gut and twenty-plus years of treating patients in perpetual vegetative states says he's waking up. Besides, look at this."

Gail read the file. An eyebrow arched upward. "Hmm. Interesting. It's just a hunch."

"I know."

"Then you haven't said anything to Lydia?"

"No! That's why I need your help. I have a plan."

After Mrs. Asher left, Lydia returned to Cameron's bed. With her tear ducts having long since dried up, she could no longer weep as she studied his face. Gone were his angry bruises and swelling, leaving braces wrapping his left arm and leg as lonely reminders of his silent struggle. Even his face resembled his former self, seeming merely to be asleep.

She adjusted his blanket, kissed his cheek and then sat down and read aloud to him from Dostoevsky's *Brothers Karamazov*. It mattered little that the tome probably was not to his liking. It reminded her of happier days. A few voices echoed down the hall and then faded into the night.

At ten, she laid the book aside and stepped to Cameron's bedside. She lowered the bed and the side rail enough to sit next to him. She laid her cheek against his chest and, with the sound of his soft breathing and the beating of his heart in her ear, she whispered. "I'll love you forever."

After a while, she stood and lifted the bed and rail to their normal position. She again took his hand. "As a deer pants for flowing streams, so pants my soul for you, O God. My soul thirsts for God, for the living God. When shall I come and appear before God? My tears have been my food day and night. Why are you cast down, O my soul, and why are you in turmoil within me? Hope in God; for I shall again praise him, my salvation and my God." Lydia leaned forward and kissed Cameron's still lips. For a moment, she watched, hoping for any sign of life. When nothing changed, she gathered together her shattered heart, "Good night, my love."

Nancy checked her watch. Twenty minutes earlier, she had seen Lydia sitting next to Mr. Asher. Good. She hadn't left. She found Gail and finalized their plan. Her job was to watch his door while going about her duties. Seeing Lydia leave his room, she motioned to Gail. "Quick!"

She then scurried down the hall. "Hi, Lydia." Nancy's smile widened. "I was wondering if you could help me tomorrow night."

"I'm going home in the morning."

"Oh." Nancy faked distress. "Would you mind waiting? Maybe just one night? We have several patients whose families live quite some ways away. Well, it gets lonely and very quiet around here on Christmas Eve. We heard you reading to Mr. Asher. And well, Gail and I wondered if you could help us."

"Yes," Gail added as she joined them. "I know Mrs. Thaxton is a Christian. You know, um, she thinks the world of you and ... uh, we thought it would be nice to have a Bible reading for her and a few others." Gail smiled at Nancy, who picked up the cue and listed the details according to the plan they had devised, a plan that benefitted other patients—and also prevented Lydia from leaving Durham.

"I need to go home," Lydia insisted.

While Gail persevered and Lydia gently protested, Nancy noticed that whenever Gail emphasized the needs of the other patients rather than Mr. Asher's, Lydia waffled. That was Lydia's weakness.

"Mrs. Thaxton loves to be read to," Nancy interjected. "It'd mean a lot to her. This may be her last Christmas, what with the emphysema and all."

Earlier, Lydia seemed determined, but now? *Yes!* She was relenting.

"Okay," Lydia glanced between Nancy and Gail, "but only to help the other patients. I've imposed much too long on the Ashers."

Nancy smiled. "Thank you." Time would tell whether she read the signs correctly.

47

"Justin! No!" Cameron yelled as he ripped the steering wheel to the left. He regained control just as a car rounded the corner a few yards in front of him. He jerked the steering wheel to the left. The car jolted, whipping the steering wheel from his hands. Trace yelled. Metal crunched. Tree branches snapped as the car rolled over, slinging him about. He raised his arms as the car tumbled sideways then slammed to a stop, throwing him against the door. Pain pierced his body. He tried to breathe. Nausea washed over him. Then nothing.

A dull glow lit the black night surrounding Cameron. In the distance, voices yelled. Something hard cut into his chest. He took a breath, but the excruciating pain stopped him. The black night returned. It lifted enough for voices and a terrible clattering noise to rattle his head.

"Trace," he called, but the pain deepened, and the night, blacker than before, returned.

Silence enveloped him. Time lost its meaning. Oblivion swallowed emotion, thoughts, and feeling. A dull glimmer tempted him. A voice spoke. The night retreated but then returned and engulfed him.

Dim light intruded upon the black night .... Voices coaxed him, "You're going to feel ...."

Cameron spoke, but the black void returned. In the moonless, starless emptiness, neither numbness nor pain disturbed him .... No texture ... no touch ... no fear or urgency ... no expectation that time would or could progress. There was only the black void, but it existed. It surrounded him.

A faint glow appeared, turning the black night to starless gray. His fingertips touched something. A muffled voice spoke—a woman. His mother? Yes, it was his mother. *Mom?* Her voice faded. What had his fingers touched? A narrow board. A pallet? It was too narrow. He might fall. Panic surged. A soft voice spoke ... but the black void claimed him. Fear ceased.

Time lapsed, leaving no record, then the black night retreated before a dim light, as stars brighten the night sky. A lyrical voice spoke. "Why are you cast down, O my soul? And why are you disquieted within me?" Did it belong to Lydia? Yes, she was nearby, but the night reclaimed him.

A voice roused him. Someone was reading. He pushed against the silence. Lydia. She hadn't left. He relaxed, but now dark gray, not black, embraced him. Gentle fingers touched his face, lips ... a kiss? Lydia? *Lydia!* Only silence answered. That was fine; Lydia was nearby. He relaxed into the shadowless night.

Something warm and soft against his neck chased the night away. Pressing against his shoulder, it soothed him. Could it be Lydia? Was she so close?

"I'll love you forever," the sweet voice whispered. Something delicate brushed his cheek. *Lydia.* Something squeezed his hand. He squeezed in reply ....

Saturday morning, Lydia met Mrs. Asher just outside Cameron's room. "Nancy and Gail asked me to stay and read to Mrs. Thaxton tonight. I ... don't want to interfere, but ...." She explained why she had agreed to stay. "I'll leave first thing tomorrow morning, while the traffic is light."

"I'm glad to have you." For weeks, Mrs. Asher's grace and elegance had lifted Lydia's spirits above the unrelenting march of sad days, but Cameron · remained the same. The march of days continued. His mother stroked

Cameron's arm. "Maybe it's just my imagination, but I think he looks better. His color is better. What do you think?"

Lydia wasn't sure. Perhaps, but a sound behind her caught her attention. Turning, she saw Mr. Asher, as cool and aloof as ever. However, if he wanted her to go away, to leave Cameron, his opinion no longer mattered. Mr. Asher had his mind focused elsewhere as he picked up Cameron's charts and notes and glanced through them. Then he counted the seats—two—and the number of visitors, including himself, and then he left.

"Mrs. Asher," Lydia leaned toward her and whispered, "I'll sit in the lounge so Cameron's dad can have a seat."

"Don't let him bother you. If he wanted to stay, he would." She rolled her eyes and shrugged. "Please sit with me."

At noon, Mrs. Asher took her husband's elbow, and both went for lunch at the hospital cafeteria, leaving Lydia alone with Cameron, though not before Mr. Asher spiked her with a glare that said, *I'm not happy with this arrangement.* In the empty room, Lydia brushed Cameron's cheek with the back of her fingers. For an instant, his breathing became shallower. Surprised, she looked closer. Had she become desperate enough to imagine that he moved? No. It was but a wish. She leaned closer, looking, hoping, but he remained as still as ever. She kissed his cheek.

At seven that evening, Lydia followed Gail to Mrs. Thaxton's room where two other patients and a few family members had gathered. Cameron's mother joined them and stood near the door.

Lydia took Mrs. Thaxton's hand and dropped to her knees before the smiling octogenarian. "Merry Christmas." Lydia gently squeezed her small, frail hand.

"Merry Christmas, my dear. You're so kind to come here." Mrs. Thaxton's twinkling, electric eyes didn't miss a thing. Lydia had seen her, walking down the hall with an oxygen tank and IV pole, when the orderly brought Cameron to the ward. She had spoken to Lydia that day and often afterward, each time asking about Cameron, listening to her, and comforting her when tears refused to obey. Mrs. Thaxton had even brought her oxygen and IV pole into Cameron's room to pray for him. Sadly, Lydia knew very little about this elegant, gentle lady—except that, in a heartbeat, Lydia would do anything for her.

Gail introduced Lydia to the others who had gathered and then stood next to Mrs. Asher. She glanced around the room—so many eyes looked back at her—to her. Some sought hope, which she was helpless to give, but most silently pleaded for affection. Lydia opened her mouth, but nothing came out. Her fingers trembled until she caught sight of Mrs. Asher, who nodded, calm and assuring.

Lydia found her voice, "Merry Christmas. Thank you for trusting me. As some of you know, during the weeks since Cameron's accident"—she turned to Cameron's mother— "my faith has gone through many phases. At first, I made bold proclamations about the great things I believed God would do—so bold as to ignore my mother's warnings that my wish and God's plan might not coincide. From there I plunged to great doubt. Mom told me to trust God, but I fell farther and farther." Lydia looked around. Lonely eyes met hers. Like pictures in a tattered album set on a shelf and forgotten, the eyes traced dreams, disappointments, and fading hopes. All pleaded for the fleeting expectation that they might yet again feel joy. Hers had been pleading eyes, waiting, hoping as much for Cameron's mother as for herself.

"This bitter path has taught me, in a tiny way, to see into the breadth and depth of his love, and discovering how it feels to be wrapped in Jesus's love and mercy, has been his gift to me. My broken heart hurts more than I ever imagined possible, but tomorrow morning I will celebrate his birth—the birth of him who lives and prays for me before our heavenly Father. I cannot ask for more."

She opened her Bible and read aloud:

> Will the LORD be pleased with thousands of rams,
>> with ten thousands of rivers of oil?
> Shall I give my firstborn for my transgression,
>> the fruit of my body for the sin of my soul?
> He has told you, O man, what is good;
>> and what does the LORD require of you
> but to do justly, and to love kindness,
>> and to walk humbly with your God?

She heaved a sigh and met each set of eyes. "You know my story." She focused on Mrs. Thaxton. "You have shown me how to walk humbly with God. What is your favorite Christmas story?"

A smile folded into the lines and creases of Mrs. Thaxton's ancient face. "Once, when I was a child, my father ...," she began.

As the stories unfolded, Lydia listened and laughed, sending the ache in her heart into full retreat. With smiles shining from every face, she said good night and then walked with Mrs. Asher to Cameron's room.

His mother stopped just short of the door. "That was lovely," she whispered. For the first time since the ordeal began, Mrs. Asher's eyes brimmed with tears. "You made this time so much easier for me. Thank you." Finally, the great pain that she had long bottled up seeped out, but only a little.

Lydia wanted to comfort her, praise her, thank her, but every word sounded weak and unworthy. So she sighed. "I'm glad Nancy and Gail talked me into staying one more night."

"I am too." Mrs. Asher half-smiled and squeezed Lydia's hand. The next moment, she turned her attention to her son. She leaned over Cameron and kissed his cheek. "Good night, sweetheart. I'll see you in the morning." She turned to Lydia. "Drive carefully and call me when you get home." After a final hug, she left.

Lydia watched the empty door, hoping she would return. At length, she picked up her Bible and read, "God, you are my God; earnestly I seek you; my soul thirsts for you; my flesh faints for you, as in a dry and weary land where there is no water." She closed the Bible; then she stood and brushed Cameron's cheek. "'Because your steadfast love is better than life, my lips will praise you.' And my soul is satisfied." Lydia waited, hoping to see Cameron respond. Seeing none, she returned to her seat and *The Brothers Karamazov*, as peace crept into her heart.

Ten minutes later, the sound of a man's strong voice echoed down the hall. Approaching footsteps stopped at Cameron's door. A tall, dark-haired stranger, wearing a black felted wool overcoat, a charcoal suit, pinstripe shirt, and patterned ruby tie, stood in the doorway, commanding Lydia's attention.

"Cameron Asher?" The familiarity of his voice startled her. "This is his room, correct?"

"Yes, it is."

Though his eyes reflected the deep, blue-green hue of the ocean at twilight, they were shockingly similar to Cameron's sky-blue eyes. The stranger walked over to the bed, his brow wrinkling as he surveyed Cameron. For a second, his faint smile faded, but then he turned to her and smiled. "You must be Lydia." His smile widened. "May I commend my brother's taste in women?" He extended his hand. "I'm Trent Asher."

"Oh, I'm so sorry." She jumped to her feet. "You just missed your mother."

"We met in the lobby. She's waiting downstairs with my wife. I wanted to see Cameron." He returned to Cameron's bedside, studied his brother, and then turned to Lydia. "And to meet you. I missed you earlier. I came down the day of the accident, but I arrived late and couldn't stay long." Lydia's knees buckled as she lowered herself back into the chair. "Cameron's a really good guy." Trent pulled up a chair next to her and sat down. For a while, he related stories from his childhood, but when he finished, his mood darkened. "Mom said you were returning to Chalmers tomorrow. I want to convince you to stay."

"It's time for me to go home. I've imposed upon your family long enough."

"Trust me. You have not imposed." For a few more minutes, Trent offered reasons for her to stay, but Lydia was insistent. "If I can't change your mind, then accept my gratitude for the support you've given Mom." He glanced at his brother. "She has always wanted me to believe in Jesus, but I couldn't. She dragged me to church, but it just wasn't for me." He turned to Lydia, his gaze both piercing and kind. "Watching her faith and courage through this ... I can't say that I understand what it means, not the way you and she do, but I'm ready to listen."

Trent stood and walked back to Cameron. Looking down, he shook his head. "Cameron called me after the mess on Thanksgiving and told me about the change in him now that he was walking with Christ—those were his words."

He turned eyes on her that were at once as sharp as a hawk's and as kind as his mother's. "When Cameron told me he was driving back to Chapel Hill with Justin, I freaked out. I've known Justin too long. I told him not to do it, but he wouldn't budge. I wish I'd tried harder, but Mom ... said it was part of God's plan. It's an odd concept, isn't it?" He looked away, clearly uncomfortable with it, and turned back to her. "I can't help Cameron, but I can help Mom." He drew a deep breath. "Tomorrow I'm going to talk to Dad. We don't get along too well."

"Cameron said your father loves you."

Trent laughed, his voice dusted with cynicism, and looked at the floor. "Well ... I'm sure Cameron told the better part of the story." He shook his head, then lifting it, he met her eyes. "I realize now that I let my issues with Dad ruin my wedding day. It should have been the happiest day of my life. I didn't know it that day." He stood, studied his brother, and then patted his arm. "But you did. You saw what I couldn't. I should have listened to you." A corner of his mouth twitched. "You were right. The best day of my life was the day Jacqueline walked into it. Tomorrow, I'll make peace with Dad."

He turned again to Lydia as reminders of Cameron's affable smile peeked from beneath his piercing eyes. "I'm not doing it for Dad. I'll do it for Cameron and Jacqueline. And for Mom." Once more, Cameron, silent and motionless, claimed his attention. "Cam, I'm sorry." His smile faded as his jaw clenched, rippling his cheek. "Forgive me, bro, for taking so long."

Speaking only for herself, Lydia nodded. "I'm glad you came."

48

A faint gray light dusted Cameron's eyelids, awakening him, but he drifted back to sleep. Dreams slipped in and out. He reached to adjust his pillow, but he couldn't move. He tried to turn on his side, but his arms and legs refused to obey. He stretched, but again, nothing moved. His eyes also ignored him. He pushed harder on his lids, but they ignored him. He pushed harder, but they only fluttered. The sweet voice he heard earlier spoke again. *Lydia.* He looked toward the sound but only fog greeted his eyes.

A masculine voice spoke. "If I can't change your mind, then accept my gratitude." It sounded like Trent, but it couldn't be.

Cameron's strength waned, and the light faded into night, but not into the inky void. A timeless moment, shaded in charcoal gray, passed—and then dawn returned and grew brighter, much brighter. He told his fingers to move and his eyes to open. To his great relief, both obeyed but he saw only light, nothing distinct.

Lydia closed her book and checked her watch—ten thirty. *Sigh.* The moment of inevitability had come. It was time to say goodbye. She stood and stretched. Then she walked to Cameron's bed. She reached to stroke his cheek, but as her skin touched his, his eyelids fluttered. She gasped and jerked her hand back.

"Nancy!" she called to the open door then looked back at Cameron. His eyes fluttered again. A finger moved. She ran to the door. "Gail! Come quick. He moved!"

Gail appeared from a room as Nancy rounded the counter at the nurse's station. Lydia ran back to Cameron and leaned over him. A second later, Nancy stood beside her. "He's trying to wake up!" Lydia's heart pounded. "What should I do?"

Cameron's lips moved, though only slightly.

Gail stepped to the opposite side of the bed and leaned over Cameron. Holding his chin with one hand, she wiped ointment from his eyes. He blinked. "Hold on. Let's get this stuff off so you can see." She turned to Lydia. A smile filled her round face. "You're right. He's waking up. He's fighting me." Gail leaned back.

Cameron's eyes opened, just a sliver, as joy and fear ripped through Lydia's heart. She leaned closer and took his hand. "Hi."

He turned toward her voice but seemed unable to see her. His eyes opened wider but stopped at half-open. He moved his lips but said nothing. Lydia stroked his cheek. "Welcome back."

The corners of his mouth pulled back, forming a faint smile. Then his eyes closed, his brow relaxed, and his breathing became low and rhythmic. Lydia's heart stopped. She turned to Nancy and Gail who were all smiles.

"It's okay." Nancy patted Lydia's arm. "He's just taking a nap. He'll wake up in a while."

"He will? Are you sure?"

"Yes. I can't say when, but he will."

"What should I do?"

Gail smiled and turned to leave. "I'd relax and wait."

Nancy pulled a blanket down from the closet. "Here. Make yourself comfortable."

"Should I call his mother?"

Nancy shrugged. "Let her rest. This is good news, but if she needs one thing more than good news, she needs sleep."

"You're sure he's back?"

Nancy smiled. "Yes. Try to sleep."

Sleep? That was the last thing Lydia's adrenaline-charged mind would do.

Shortly after eleven, both Gail and Nancy returned. Nancy leaned over

Cameron and studied him. "He looks good. We're heading home. We'll see you tomorrow. Try to get some sleep."

"Thank you." Lydia wanted to believe them. Too excited to read, she wrapped herself in the blanket, nestled into the chair, and waited. A few aides and nurses shuffled along the hall as time slowly passed. She stood and checked Cameron several times. Seeing no change, she returned to the chair and blanket. Then, as sleep crept up on her, she heard something.

"Blecch." The faint sound came from Cameron.

She leaped to her feet and leaned over him. A grimace wrenched his face. He tried to spit something out, and then his eyes opened, wider than before. He looked up and turned his head, his eyes meeting hers. A faint half-smile caught the corner of his mouth. "Hi." Though more air than sound, his voice was the most beautiful sound she had ever heard.

She grasped his hand. "Hi."

"I heard you," he whispered, forming each word as if speaking a strange new language. "I knew ... you were here."

"You did?" Her throat choked shut. "Did you know how much I've missed you?"

His brow wrinkled. "Where am I?"

"Duke Hospital."

"Duke?"

"Sorry, but they were the first responders."

"Responders?" he squinted.

Take it slow. "You were driving Justin and Trace back to school, and there was an accident. Trace and Neil came by a couple of days ago." He frowned, but the doctors had predicted he would remember little if anything of the accident. Should she say more? Probably not yet. Lydia kissed his cheek. "You've been asleep, but you're doing much better." A tear escaped and trickled down her cheek.

He squeezed her hand. "What's wrong?"

"Nothing." She wiped away the tears that followed. "Nothing! I'm thrilled to see you." Joy burst the dam she had built against her fears. "Everybody has been so worried about you." For all her happy calm, words poured out. "I met Esther. She's very nice. Neil and Patrick came by, and Trace drove down or called almost every day." Between tears, smiles, and even laughter, she blathered on. "A Dr. Flinn Krasotkin also came by. I wrote the names down and your mom kept the cards. I think I met your entire fraternity and even friends from class—a girl named Sydney—but you were still in intensive care."

Hearing the last two words, his brow furrowed but she had more exciting news. "And your brother was just here."

"Trent?" Cameron's shoulders moved, and then his legs though yielding only slightest motion.

"Yes. He's very nice. You'll see him tomorrow. I'm glad you woke up before Nancy and Gail, the evening nurses, went home. *I* almost went home, but they told me to wait. I'm glad I did. They were right. You finally woke up. Your mom is going to be so happy when she sees you. Everyone is going to be thrilled." Again, he looked puzzled. "Your mom is at a hotel. She's fabulous." Lydia looked at the wall clock over his head. "Oh! It's after midnight. Cameron, it's Christmas morning. Can you believe that?"

"Christmas? How?"

"You've been in a coma since Thanksgiving." Of course, he didn't know that. "Yes, it's Christmas. Oh ... I need to let you rest."

He squeezed her hand. "Don't leave."

"I'll be right here."

Cameron's smile changed as if forgotten thoughts had awoken. A faint grin joined his hand as he patted the bed.

"I can't. You're in a hospital bed. There's no room for me."

"Yeah ... here." Again he patted the sheet.

"You're crazy." As she considered his request, his grin widened. She lowered the bed and then the bed rail. Looking down at him, she reconsidered his request. She shouldn't! A sob surged to her throat, but she strangled it.

"What's wrong?"

"Nothing. It's been so ...." The trickle of tears turned into a flood. "I've been so worried." A sob heaved her chest. "When you didn't call or come over that Sunday—I've been ...." She broke into uncontrollable sobs. "I'm sorry, I've been—"

"Sunday evening? Oh, ... I wanted to call you." Every frown, even the quizzical wrinkles and dull pall across his eyes vanished, replaced by a downright mischievous smile. He patted the bed.

"I can't." She wiped her face, but clearly he was serious. "You've got all sorts of tubes connected." An embarrassing thought! But his inviting grin didn't falter. "What will the nurses think?"

His brow furrowed as if to say, Who cares? He stretched again, but sideways, as if trying to move over. He failed.

Who *would* care? She looked toward the open door while he patted the bed. She waited, studying him and glancing at the door. For nearly a month, she had longed to see his humor. Not only had he smiled, but the little devil also wanted her to climb up and lie next to him in his hospital bed. And she was afraid of what an orderly might think?

She glanced at the door one last time and then climbed up next to him. The fit was tight, but she snuggled her head close to his cheek. "I'm not hurting you, am I?"

"No."

Lying next to Cameron, she again listened to his soft breathing and felt the pulse of his heart. Excitement tingled from her head to her toes. Then ignoring the possibility that a passing nurse or orderly might glance in and blush, she sat up, leaned over, and kissed him. His lips, soft and warm, kissed hers. Then he smiled. Lydia lifted her elbow and laid it beside his pillow. With her head propped on the heel of her hand, she enjoyed studying him. He smiled once more and then closed his eyes. She rested her hand on his chest, feeling his beating heart. Without opening his eyes, he placed his hand on hers, covering and holding it as his breathing slowed, becoming calm and even. Sleep had returned.

During the previous week, loneliness had been an unwelcome companion as she stared across the open field beyond Aunt Deborah's deck. In the dim glow of dawn, she had released hope from its bonds. Like a bird freed from its cage, it had spread its wings and took flight. In its absence, sorrow had thwarted her every attempt to imagine climbing Hatteras lighthouse. Instead, shallow waves had spread across a sandy beach and carried her dreams out to sea.

Through her doubt and fear, Jesus's love had been a silken scarf, glittering in the glow of his smile, wrapping her soul as she stood on the beach, looking east and hearing the wind speak his comforting promises. She had prayed for Mrs. Asher and Mrs. Thaxton and proclaimed her gratitude for God's sovereign wisdom, not knowing that in hours he would answer her prayers with the sweet assurance of Cameron's smile and the soft touch of his hand holding hers to his chest.

Lydia kissed his cheek and climbed down from the bed. She stretched the chair into an imitation bed. With the blanket wrapped around her, she curled up as, for the first time in a seeming eternity, sleep arrived on the wistful thought that the morning of a new day would soon dawn.

List of Characters

(significant names underlined)

Cameron Asher (Benjamin Cameron Asher, II)
Immediate Family:
<u>Ben</u> & <u>Sylvia</u> Asher (paternal grandparents, *both deceased*)
   (Ben, a.k.a. <u>Grandpa</u>, Judge Asher, nee Benjamin Cameron Asher)
<u>Randy</u> & <u>Valerie</u> Asher (parents)
Siblings & Extended Family:
<u>Aimee</u> Duncan (cousin)
<u>Andrea</u> & <u>Shaun</u> Waterton (sister and brother-in-law)
Emily Wilson (former girlfriend of Trent Asher)
<u>Matt</u> Stedman (cousin)
<u>Nathan</u> and <u>Becky</u> (Asher) Stedman (paternal aunt and uncle)
<u>Mrs. Duncan</u> (Aimee's mother and Cameron's aunt).
<u>Trent</u> and Jacqueline Asher (brother & sister-in-law)
Friends & Others:
<u>Alan</u> & <u>Tricia</u> Sloane (Justin's parents)
<u>Brent</u> Sloane (Justin's uncle, Alan Sloane's brother)
<u>Drew</u>, Todd, Sam & Mick (Wyoming, Summer ranch hands);
<u>Leo</u> (ranch employee)
<u>Esther</u> (UNC friend and lab partner)
<u>Justin</u> Sloane (Chalmers & UNC)
<u>Neil</u> (*roommate*), <u>Patrick</u>, and <u>Trace</u> (UNC fraternity brothers)
<u>Paul</u> Rizziellio (Chalmers)

Professor Krasotkin (UNC professor and mentor)
Stan & Hannah Boehmer (Wyoming, ranchers)

Lydia Carpenter
Immediate Family
Anne & Marshall Carpenter (parents)
Lois & Thomas (*deceased*) Carpenter (paternal grandparents)
Siblings & Extended Family
David Mapson (cousin)
Deborah & Kyle Schaeffer (maternal aunt and uncle)
Tristan & Luke Carpenter (brothers)
Marrah (a.k.a. Martha) & Jake Mapson (paternal aunt and uncle)
Steve Carpenter (paternal uncle, *deceased*)
Friends & Others
Aimee Duncan (Chalmers, also Cameron's cousin)
Eliana Johansson (Duke)
Marybeth (Chalmers)
Melanie Powell (close friend of Aunt Marrah)
Ragini Ramasamy and Eydie (*roommate*) You (Duke friends)
Tanner Meade (Duke)

About the Author

A native of Durham, North Carolina, Karen lives with her husband John in Greenville, South Carolina. Karen earned a bachelor's degree in biology then worked in cancer research and clinical microbiology before earning a master's in landscape architecture.

Now retired, she enjoys doting on her grandchildren.

CPSIA information can be obtained
at www.ICGtesting.com
Printed in the USA
BVHW042135021219
565466BV00017B/496/P